CHASE

BRIDGET L. ROSE

Pitstop Series
Team Names

Spark Racing

This book is dedicated to all the sunflowers who are still looking for their sun. Remember, it doesn't have to be a person, it can be anything you want it to be, as long as it helps you grow.

Content Warning

This book deals with themes of grief, loss, miscarriage, child abandonment, and mild violence. It contains explicit sex scenes as well as vulgar language.

CHASE

Part One

Prologue

Gabriel

"What happened?" my mother's voice fills my ears, only making me sob more.

"He's upset because he lost the championship," Maxime answers for me.

The Karting Championship is one of the biggest events of the year for racers my age. It has been driving me the entire season, and now that I've lost, I want to cry and cry until I can't feel this disappointment anymore. Almost everyone I love came to watch me win today, but I lost by two points. Two. Points. Mom couldn't make it because she had work, so having to explain my failure, reliving it so soon after it happened, would have been torture. I'm glad Maxime is here. He's been trying to comfort me, too, but I'm too angry with myself to listen to his advice.

"Oh, mon petit trésor," she says and flings her arms around me, pulling me against her chest. I can't help it. I weep harder than before, my mother's comfort the one thing I truly needed right now. "I'm so sorry you didn't win this time." I nuzzle my face into her side to look up at where Dad and Maxime are standing. Little Jean is holding onto our father's hand, looking more confused than anything.

"I'm sorry I disappointed all of you," I say, my voice cracking from all the crying.

"What?" My mother blurts out, frustration in her voice, and I notice my father shifting.

"Ma chérie, don't—" She cuts him off before he has a chance to finish the sentence. Instead, Mom grabs my shoulders and brings my entire attention to her.

"You did not disappoint us, Gabriel. We are so proud of you. Winning isn't always the only reward you get for trying. Experience is. Having fun this season is your reward after every race. Learning from mistakes is too. Whether you win or not, we will always *be rooting for you. I know you're upset with yourself, and it's okay to be. But don't tear yourself down when you have your whole racing life ahead of you. You may not have won the championship this year, but you'll win it next year." Mom kisses the top of my head and brings me back into the embrace where my tears slow.*

"I didn't win my first Karting Championship either," Maxime says and shrugs. When a half-smile curls the left side of my mouth, he grins and winks at me.

"Yeah, and you were crying even harder than him," Dad chimes in, and Maxime playfully punches his arm in response. "Oh, that's how you want to play it? Alright. Gabriel, hold your brother," he says before placing Jean in my lap and then raising his hands in the air.

Maxime mimics my father's stance until they are both bouncing back and forth, pretending like they're going to fight. In the end, Dad manages to get Maxime in a headlock and musses his hair. They're all laughing, and eventually, the events of today blur away as I join them in their joy.

I have no idea what I'd ever do without them, but I hope I'll never have to find out.

CHAPTER 1

Gabriel

I CLOSE THE DOOR behind me using all the strength my body has left, leaving my heart and soul with Valentina. She'll never forgive me for this. I'm choosing myself over her, but I have to. I have to do what's best for me to be everything she deserves. Since I found out Carlos Klein is my fucking grandfather, I've been the wrong man for her. Someone who drinks and wallows in pain and self-pity isn't the type of person Valentina deserves. My mess shouldn't become hers during the most important time of her life.

She's just been offered a seat in Formula One. Alfa Adrenalina saw her potential, and she'll be training the entire summer break to prepare herself for the rest of the season. The woman I love will be the first female F1 driver, but for now, she'll be the reserve driver for my team, Velocità Rossa, which is already a big responsibility. It's going to need her entire focus. I can't drag her into the dark space I've spiraled into. It's not fair. If I knew Val could be selfish, focus solely on herself, I wouldn't be leaving, but she's not that type of person. She loves me too much. And I love her more than anything or anyone else. Which is why I have to do this.

It's how I become the man she deserves again.

I straighten out my back, ignoring the tears streaming down my face as I walk down the stairs and the way my muscles try to fight against it. Every part of me is drawing me backward, back to Val, because I'm not whole without her. Half of me is her, just like half of her is me. We complete each other and walking away? It goes against my survival instinct.

"What the fuck did you just do?" *Shit.* Adrian's voice is full of anger and frustration, and I spin around to show him how horrible I look. His eyes widen at the sight of me. "Jesus, Gabriel. What happened?" he asks, and I let the tears drop down my face.

"I ripped my heart out and left it with her. That's what happened," I reply and attempt to leave again when his hand wraps around my elbow to stop me.

"Don't. Don't leave her like this, mate. You'll do more harm than good," he says gently and firmly, understanding my pain as well as trying to protect his sister from harm. If he could look inside the dark hole in my head, he'd know letting me leave is the best thing for her.

"Let me go," I say when his grip tightens around my arm.

"If you do this, there's no going back," Adrian warns me, and I know what he means. There will be no undoing the pain I've caused. Val will hate me. He will hate me. My only hope is that they loved me enough at one point to forgive me once I've put myself back together.

"If I don't do this, I will be putting Val's life in danger," I whisper-scream, ripping my arm free. This has gone on long enough. I have to get out of this house, the one that's somehow become more of a home to me than my childhood house, before Valentina hears us.

"Don't pretend you're doing this for her," Adrian replies, pissed at me now. Good. Maybe he will let me walk out the door if he's angry.

"I am. And you have to promise me you will do everything in your power to ensure she's focused when she tests the car, you hear me? Her mind needs to be in her head, not stuck on wherever I am. Do you understand me?" I ask, grabbing his shoulders as I speak to be certain he's hearing me. Nothing can happen to mon tournesol, especially not because of me.

"Val is my little sister, Gabriel, the most important person in my life. I will do whatever it takes to keep her safe," he says like I should already know this, and I do. It's one of the reasons I know I'm doing the right thing.

"So will I," I reply, leaving him standing in the middle of the entrance before walking outside and letting the hot summer sun burn my skin.

My lungs are constricting, preventing me from breathing. My heart feels like it has stopped beating, slowing my steps. My head is screaming, telling me what a horrible man I am and, at the same time, reminding me this is for the best.

God, I'm so fucked.

CHAPTER 2
Valentina

After I cry until I've run out of tears, I pull myself together and get up from the ground. My hand lifts to my chest, and I cover the area over my heart. No matter what I do, it won't stop beating unevenly. I press down in an attempt to calm it, but nothing works. Knowing it'll probably never stop reminding me of how hollow it is without Gabriel's sends a wave of panic through me. I have no idea what to do with the feeling, so I let it consume me for a little. I sink onto my bed, screwing my eyes shut and taking deep breaths. Eventually, it subsides, unlike the pain in my chest.

When I check my watch, I see it's two in the morning. I'm exhausted and lonely. I leave my room and make my way down the hall toward Adrian's. Months ago, I walked this same hallway at night because I needed my brother more than anything and anyone else.

Nothing has changed.

As it turns out, nothing will ever change, and I've never minded it less. My brother is the one constant in my life, the person I know will never leave me. Needing him isn't something I'm ever going to regret... unlike some other people in my life.

I knock on his door, and, luckily, he's still awake.

"Come in, Val," he says, and I open it. My body freezes halfway into his room, a wave of emotion crashing through me because I can read on his face he already knows why I'm here.

"He broke up with me," I inform my brother and flinch.

I didn't think I would ever have to say this unless Gabriel and I both wanted to. Anger flicks over Adrian's face before compassion is the only thing left. He lifts his blanket from the bed so I can lie down next to him. I tell him everything. Gabriel's and my whole conversation. Well, fight. It was a fight, and I have to start understanding that because I was angry in the moment. I yelled at him. I disagreed with him. It wasn't a civil conversation between two people who love each other. It was a fight that ended what should have been my forever.

"Do you think you'll forgive him?" I stare into my brother's green-blue eyes and admire how bright the brown looks with the light of the room shining into them. I wonder if mine look the same.

"I don't know. I don't understand why he has to leave me to find them. To protect me from getting distracted? It doesn't make any sense." I'm surprised by how well I'm handling this, but maybe it's because I don't feel like it's over yet. Somewhere deep inside, I am convinced he's going to come back to me, crying and begging for another chance. Maybe it's wishful thinking.

It's highly likely I'm in denial to keep the real pain at bay.

"You know, Val, I probably would do the same." My eyes go wide for a split second, but I decide to wait for his explanation. "Gabriel loves you, but he just had his whole world turned upside down. In order to turn it the right way again, he has to do it by himself. He has to focus all of his energy on this. Someone as important as you are to him can never come second, ever. He thinks you'll be able to forgive him more easily for leaving than if he didn't treat you right."

Adrian gives my chin a quick nudge with his index finger, trying to get me to pay attention to him and not get lost in his words yet.

"Not to mention, he's right about you getting distracted. It's dangerous. This is the first time you'll be in an F1 car. You're so close to getting everything you want, and he can't be the one to jeopardize it. You would hate him for it. So, yes, I understand why he did what he did, and I would probably do the same thing, as terrible as it sounds," Adrian goes on, and I swallow hard.

For someone as against romantic love and relationships as my brother, he seems to be quite the expert. Because he's making sense. It's also why my head is spinning because I'm furious. I'm beyond angry, but I want to do my best to see Gabriel's side too. Maybe that makes me naive. I can't quite bring myself to care at this very moment.

"I *am* sorry this is happening. I wish he didn't have to hurt you to figure this out, but I understand him. Please don't get mad at me," Adrian adds and lets out a short laugh.

"I'm not mad at you. I understand why he left, too, but he's hurting me. I don't know if I can forgive him." I stare off into the distance, and my brother wraps his hand around mine.

"It seems like you already have," he states, and my eyes move back to his. He's right. I've already forgiven him for hurting me. I have already accepted this is what Gabriel needs to do for himself, and I will make my peace with it. All I have to do now is move on with my life and see how things will turn out. I can't mope over him.

"Since when are you such an expert when it comes to love?" I finally ask my forthcoming brother, and he leans back in his bed, smiling brightly at the ceiling.

"I'm not an expert. I have simply paid attention to the way Gabriel has loved you for these past few years. It's been messy, and it's going to be for a while, but if I know one thing for sure, it is how he gave himself to you completely. He's loved you with everything he is. He was vulnerable, even though he was probably just as scared to have let you in as you were to let him. Yes, it may be hard to believe he loves you because he left. But you know he does. Probably more than anything."

I reach for the necklace which is still securely wrapped around my neck. Tears flow down my cheeks, and I can't help feeling a little sadder again. Not because Gabriel broke up with me, but because I miss him.

My fingers wrap tightly around the charm, and I close my eyes in response. I am on his team, and I want him to be the happiest he could possibly be. No matter what I feel, I am always going to want him to be happy, whether it is with me or without me.

Love shouldn't be this powerful.

"Gabriel came to me and showed me the necklace. He said he doesn't want me to think he gave it to you to buy you over to his side. All he wanted to achieve by giving you the necklace is to show you how much he cares about you," Adrian says with a sad smile.

"Whose side are you on?" I tease and nudge him with my shoulder. My brother chuckles and wraps his arm around mine, pressing a kiss to the top of my head.

"I will forever be on your side, but, unfortunately for me, I've grown to care about that idiot," he admits, and I let out a silent sigh.

"Yeah, me too," I say and lean into my brother's embrace, smelling his comforting, fresh scent until everything in my chest settles a bit.

"Did you know Kyle Hughes' contract was extended with Grenzenlos?" Adrian asks, and I welcome the distraction with a surprised gasp.

"Really? I thought they were planning on replacing him because he's underperforming," I reply, looking up at my brother. He's smiling down at me, a little satisfaction playing in his eyes.

"Eduardo didn't even get offered a seat yet for next season," he adds with an evil laugh, and I smack his stomach in response. "Come on, that guy's such a dick. If he doesn't return next season, good riddance." I can't help the little laugh slipping past my lips.

Contract season is often the most stressful for Adrian and James' mental well-being. This year, Cameron, Gabriel, Leonard, James, and Adrian didn't have to worry because their contracts only end in the next few years. I was the only one without one, but not anymore. I signed mine with the biggest grin on my face a few days ago.

Some other drivers got extensions, others were traded. The only unfilled seat left on the whole grid is, according to Adrian, Eduardo's. I wonder if they'll extend his contract or replace him.

"Get some sleep. Your eyes are flaming red," Adrian tells me, squeezing me one last time.

I nod, too tired to keep this conversation going. It's time I slept a little because I have a lot to do. For God's sake, I'm going to be a freaking Formula One driver. The first woman to ever reach this position. I have a lot to prove to the people in charge, which I will. I will prove I belong on the podium right beside the men who have dominated this sport for too long.

I'm ready to be the best goddamn race car driver to have ever walked this Earth.

CHAPTER 3
Valentina

MY FEET STOP ME from walking any further once I arrive at the street leading straight down to *Rush*. It's been thirty hours since Gabriel broke up with me, and it has taken me twenty-four to get to the point where I am at this very second. It's also taken a lot of battle between who I am and who I want to be, but finally, the better part of me won.

After I suck in several sharp breaths, I get my feet to start moving again. They feel like bricks attached to my legs. I'm using every single muscle in my body to try and get them to push forward. It's the beginning of August in Monaco, and the sun is burning my skin with every step I take, which certainly doesn't help. I wipe away the sweat running down my forehead with the back of my hand. The heat is ridiculous, but it's not my biggest concern at the moment.

Evangelin is.

Before I arrive at the store, my thoughts drift back to Gabriel. I wonder where he is right now. *Is he in Italy searching for his grandma? Is he in New York, visiting some cousins he never knew about?* As long as he is happy, I'm happy for him. Plus, I still have James and Adrian who will probably continue to spend most of their available time with me. James couldn't believe Gabriel broke up with me. I'm convinced his words were something along the lines of *"I always thought if anyone else would end up with you, it would be Gabriel because he knows how to love you."* My words to that were... nothing. I didn't say a thing to it.

Every time James says something like this, I realize how deeply in love he used to be with me. Recently, he's shown more affection to the mother of his baby, Annabel, and I really hope they can give each other what they need.

With a deep breath, I snap myself out of my thoughts and back to reality. I need to do this. I need to talk to Evangelin, tell her how I feel, and, most importantly, I need my friend back. I wrap my fingers around the necklace I haven't had the heart to take off yet and walk into the store I've grown to love. As soon as I step into the small boutique, Evangelin's eyes find mine from across the room. She drops the clothes she was just about to hang, surprise all over her features. My feet are cemented to the ground, and I cannot move a muscle.

It feels like we haven't seen each other in years.

"We need to talk," I tell her, speaking French for the first time in days, and she nods.

"But not here. Let's go get some coffee," Evangelin says before locking her door.

We walk down the street to the nearest café, order, and then fall into an uncomfortable silence. I watch her long, gray hair as it falls down her back. Her blue eyes seem lighter somehow, but I can only concentrate on the expression on her face. She is hurting deeply, and I don't want to be another reason why she feels this way.

"I'm really sorry your husband hurt you. I'm so sorry about what you've been going through, and I need to tell you something very important." Evangelin looks nervous then. "It's not your fault. None of what has been happening is your fault. I was mad at you for bringing this information into my life. I was so mad because, at first, I blamed you for taking Gabriel away from me, but I realize now it is more complex than that." A tear drops from the corner of her left eye, and I take her hand from across the table. "You shared something with Gabriel and Jean that has the power to make them happy, and it isn't your fault Gabriel broke up with me," I say, and her eyes go wide.

"He broke up with you?" *Fuck. I hadn't told her that, had I?* I'm such an idiot.

"Yes, he needs some time to focus on himself. He wants to find his family, and I guess he wants to find himself. If you ask me, I already know who he is, but if this is what he needs, I can't blame him either." Evangelin daps away the mascara-tear combination running down her cheek.

"Who made you this forgiving?" she asks in a gentle tone, and I smile at her. This smile feels better on my lips than any other I've smiled in the past thirty hours.

"When you lose a lot of people, you realize the ones you still have are the most important ones on the planet. I'm not giving up on anyone in my life, not even the guy who ripped my heart from my chest and took it with him." I flinch at how much I'm still hurting, and Evangelin squeezes my hand. "Don't worry, he'll come back, and when he does, I am going to take your advice. Remember when you told me nowadays relationships never work out because everyone gives up too quickly? Well, I'm not giving up. Gabriel and I worked when we were dating, and I love him. We can't be over, not when it wasn't because of differences or bottled-up feelings."

I sound completely and absolutely in denial, but it's what keeps me going. I don't want to lose Gabriel forever.

I'm definitely in denial. All of my efforts to avoid lying to myself were never successful to begin with.

"I know how that sounds," I say and let out a short laugh I don't mean.

"Only to everyone who doesn't know you are the person who knows Gabriel the best," she says and rolls her lips for a moment, thinking about something. "I would like to share a poem with you, one my friend wrote many years ago when he was going through a devastating heartbreak as well. Would you like to hear it?"

Her gaze trails over my face as she waits for me to nod, but, once I do, a small smile lifts her lips.

Evangelin sits up in her chair, straightens out her back, and stares off into the distance.

"'*Love weakens my bones,*
Love strengthens my soul,
As I share with you,
My truest joy.
The man I love,

Is my other half,
With whom I share life,
For whom I would die.'"

She stops for a brief moment, thinking about the rest of the poem as she squeezes my hand once.

"Then there are some other lines, but the most important stanza is this one:
'Through storms and rainbows,
He is the brightest light.
Even if the path is hidden,
And not easily found
Our love will carry us,
'Til we are safe and sound.'"

Evangelin lets out a slight laugh, rubbing her left arm up and down and offering me the softest smile I've ever seen on her lips. I've missed her so much.

"It wasn't the best poem to ever be written, but I like it. The point is that he and his husband went through many very difficult times, but he never lost faith in their love, even once when he left him to travel the world by himself. Like you, he always thought his love would come back, that he would realize he could travel the world forever, but nothing would ever be better than finding your home. And, you know what, he took my friend with him the next time he went, right before they adopted their first child," Evangelin explains, sending a wave of warmth through me.

I take a deep breath and let all of the information settle in my chest. It makes me feel less alone to know I'm not the only one who blindly believes in the one she loves.

"Thank you for sharing this story with me," I say, and we drink the beverages we ordered.

I play with the condensation running down my glass, and Evangelin and I fall into a casual conversation about her store. I don't ask her if she heard anything from Gabriel because I don't think I want to know. Gabriel needs some alone time, some time apart from everyone to figure himself out, and I don't want to be the kind of person who keeps tabs on him.

"There is something I've been meaning to tell you," I say. Evangelin leans back in her chair, waiting patiently. "For the next three weeks, I will be in Maranello, so I can't help you out in your store." Evangelin smiles.

"You're chasing your dream, Valentina, please stop worrying about helping me at the store," she says, waving the waiter over to ask for the bill. She pays before I can stop her, slapping my hand away when I try to reach for the receipt.

Eventually, Evangelin and I walk back to her store, and I spend the rest of the day with her. Adrian and I are flying to Maranello tomorrow for my training, and I've already packed, so I don't have to rush home.

The more time I spend in the boutique and with Evangelin, the clearer everything gets for me.

Evangelin helped me up when I was curled into a ball, figuratively. She has given me advice that has taken me far.

Forgiving someone isn't an easy task, especially when they have hurt you, but it's important to know if they did it on purpose, or if it happened because of events that were out of their control. Evangelin never meant to hurt me, she never wanted any of this. Gabriel may have chosen to leave, but I know why he did it. He didn't do it to hurt me.

He did it because he loves me enough to know when he's not right for me...

CHAPTER 4

Gabriel

"Get the fuck up," Jean says, kicking my knee.

I must have fallen asleep on the floor in front of my bed sometime last night between my sixth and twentieth drink. It was a horrible idea to try alcohol to relieve my pain because it works a little. And, right now, even a little is a fucking lot. Unfortunately, it doesn't last forever, and I feel worse when I wake up.

"Your phone has been buzzing for an hour. Answer it before it wakes up Domi. Remember? The aunt who's pregnant and needs sleep to grow a baby inside of her?" Jean adds once I've blinked so many times, the world has stopped spinning.

Someone's calling me. Oh my God. What if it's Val? I stare down at the screen, but my heart collapses in on itself when I see it's Carlos... *Shit.* Jean has to get out. I contacted the former Formula One champion, who apparently is our biological grandfather, to find out the name of the woman he had an affair with. He's been ignoring me for two days, but, finally, he's returning my calls. I can't stop my heart from racing.

"Get out," I say to Jean, trying to sober up before hitting Answer.

"Okay, God, you're acting like an asshole, do you know that?" he replies, staring at the canvas I was working on last night. I painted sunflowers all over it, the sun setting behind them. More than anything, I wish I could finish the one of Valentina, but seeing her beautiful shape, staring at it when I might have lost her forever, makes me feel like I'm dying.

"I know, but get out. I have to take this, and it's personal," I explain because I'm trying to protect him. If Carlos can't remember the name or I can't find a trail to follow, getting his hopes up would have been a cruel thing to do. I need something concrete before involving him.

"Gabriel?" Jean says right before he leaves my room. He turns in my door frame, facing me once more. I offer him half of my attention while the other half is fixated on Carlos' call going straight to voicemail. *Fuck.* "I'm here if you want to talk, you know?" I attempt a smile, but the corners of my lips don't even twitch.

"I know. And don't worry, everything will be fine. I will figure things out," I assure him, and he gives me a tight nod.

As soon as he's out the door, I run to the bathroom and sit in front of my toilet, nausea slowly building in my throat until a cold sweat breaks out across my skin. I'm not used to drinking hard liquor and neither is my body. I'm a mess. I'm such a fucking mess, it almost makes me glad I'm also lonely. I deserve to be. No one should have to deal with me in this current state. It's why I'm even avoiding Hector, my performance coach, something I'm only able to do because it's summer break.

Once I'm feeling better, I hit dial again, listening to the ringing of the phone.

One ring and my breathing hitches.

Two rings and everything starts spinning again.

Three rings and I'm standing up, incapable of sitting still anymore.

This tension in my chest makes it difficult to think straight. Then again, maybe it's the alcohol in my system. I'm not entirely sure at this point.

"Gabriel?" Carlos' husky voice comes through the speaker, sending a shock through my system, one I have no idea what to do with.

"Yeah?" I reply, hearing him inhale and exhale once.

"I found her."

CHAPTER 5
Valentina

"My ass cheeks hurt," Adrian complains as he wiggles in the passenger seat of my baby-blue Mustang. I can't help but smile a little.

"You're the one who insisted we drive down here after our flight was canceled," I remind him, but he merely lifts his hands into the air to stretch, letting out a shrill noise as he does. Laughter spills out of me before I can stop it. It feels good, too. I haven't laughed in days, but if there is one person who could get a laugh out of me under any circumstances, it would be my idiot brother.

"Well, I didn't know you'd drive like a rookie," he teases, wiping a hand down the length of his face. His eyes flutter shut, and I use the opportunity to slam my foot onto the gas pedal, shifting into the left lane to go at a faster speed. "Okay, relax," Adrian blurts out, chuckling at me.

"I'm about to be a rookie, Adrian, but I'll be the fastest rookie of all time," I reply, slowing the car again and merging onto the right lane. We don't have enough gas to go as fast as I would like.

"Damn right, you will be," he says, his attention drifting to his phone.

He's been checking it a lot more over the past several days, and I know exactly why. Adrian's worried about Gabriel, even if he tries to hide it. They've become closer this season, despite being each other's biggest rivals. Somehow, they bonded, and knowing his friend is falling apart makes him upset. I know because I feel the same way. If it were up to me, I'd have texted Gabriel already to see how he's doing. I hope better than the last time I saw him. His appearance brought pain to my joints.

"There's something I'd like to speak to you about, Val," Adrian says after a while of silence. My stomach flips at his serious tone.

"Is he okay?" I whisper, and my brother tilts his head my way. There is no chance I can meet his compassionate gaze right now. It'll bring tears to my eyes, and I told myself I wasn't going to cry over this Gabriel situation anymore. The weakness I feel in response unsettles me.

"No, he's not okay, which is exactly why we need to talk." Big Brother Mode has been activated, and there is no shutting it off until Adrian has said his piece, so I stay quiet. "For the next three weeks, I want you to forget he exists, okay? Erase him from your mind. All of your memories with him, your feelings for him, delete them for the duration of this training period. It sounds impossible, I know, but you need all your focus on learning what you've wanted for years. Do you hear me? This is your time. You can't let him taint it," Adrian says, bringing a wave of sadness to my heart and forcing my nose to burn from unshed tears.

"I know," I reply, gripping the steering wheel harder than is necessary. My knuckles turn white immediately, pressing against my skin as I breathe to try and correct the uneven beat of my heart.

"You're going to have the time of your life. I remember the first time I sat in an F1 car and raced it down the track. Best feeling in the world," he says, which sends a wave of excitement through me.

With all of the chaos going on, I haven't taken one second to check on my feelings regarding these next three weeks. I will be in a Formula One car and not just sit in it as I did in Gabriel's. I will be racing down the track I got to know so well during my time at the driver academy. Holy shit. A smile breaks out across my face at the thought of seeing my number on the car that I was told for years I wasn't good enough for.

If this isn't the biggest 'fuck you' to everyone who didn't give me a chance, I don't know what is.

Andrea's arms wrap around me the second I step into their office at the driver academy. Adrian is out with a woman he met at the restaurant we were eating at for lunch, giving me some time for myself. Unfortunately, I don't like being alone at the moment. It gives me time to overthink, and overthinking is a deadly weapon to the mind. It'll send me spiraling into thoughts about Gabriel, and I'm supposed to erase him from my head, at least for the next three weeks. Adrian's right. If I want to succeed, I can't focus on the hole in my chest or the way every breath brings me pain. Gabriel Matteo Biancheri might be the love of my life, but so is racing, and I won't jeopardize everything I've worked for because he chose a path without me.

"How are you?" Andrea asks as they pull back, a warm smile on their lips. The feeling of comfort and safety sweeps through me, just like every other time I've been in their presence.

"I'm fine, how are you?" I ask, managing to return their smile somehow. It makes me proud of myself. Maybe I can do this without being a moping mess. No. I *can* do this without being a moping mess. I know I can. For Grandpa. For Dad. For Adrian. *For myself.*

"Much better now that I'm seeing your face. Christian has been a pain in my ass all day," they say, and I can't help but cringe a little at the thought of poor Andrea still having to deal with that royal brat.

Christian may have apologized to me, but I'm far from liking him. Actually, I despise him with every fiber of my being. What keeps amazing me, however, is how sweet his brother is. Thomas Crovetto. Crown Prince of Monaco. A new acquaintance of mine. I almost smile at the thought of knowing a royal I don't want to punch in the face.

"So, how come you wanted to spend the afternoon with me?" Andrea says, pulling me back into the moment. I take a step back and toward their wall of trophies.

"I like spending time with you," I reply honestly.

Andrea raises one eyebrow, taking in my appearance more closely for the first time since I walked into their office. I know I don't look well. My eye bags reveal how little sleep I've gotten. The redness in them proves how much I've been crying. The shakiness of my hands shows how overwhelmed my body is with the loss of my first love, the one I thought would last forever. God, I feel so naive.

"Are you really okay, Valentina?" they ask and reach out to touch my arm. I let them, my eyes fluttering shut at the warmth and comfort.

"No," I admit, swallowing back the tears.

"Then, come. I have a way to cheer you up," they say and hold out their arm, waiting for me to hook mine through theirs.

This is new for us. In the past, Andrea and I kept our distance to not cross professional boundaries, but now that I'm no longer their trainee, this doesn't seem necessary anymore. This feels like a friendship I'm more than happy to have.

I link my arm through Andrea's, laughing and smiling with them as they tell me a story about Christian throwing one of his tantrums for not doing as well as the other F3 drivers in the simulator. As much as I hate the guy, it feels fantastic to make fun of him with my friend. It takes some of the weight off my shoulders as we stroll down to the garages where mechanics are working on the Formula One cars.

I can't believe I'm a Velocità Rossa reserve driver. It feels so surreal.

"What are we doing here?" I ask Andrea, who briefly places their hand over mine where it rests on their arm. It's reassuring, telling me to trust them. And I do.

Andrea falls into a conversation with one of the mechanics, letting go to allow me the freedom to walk around for a moment. Naturally, my feet bring me right in front of Gabriel's car. His number, seven, stares up at me, almost forcing my fingers to wrap around the necklace charm resting on my sternum. I love him so much, it hurts. It hurts to know he doesn't think he's right for me at the moment. It hurts that I can't change his mind. Most of all, it hurts to have had him love me like no one else, and then take it all away at once.

I squat down, feeling my breathing hitch. Some of the mechanics give me a strange look, but I play it off by pretending to inspect the car. I can't help but run my fingertips over his number, remembering he lost seven people. Seven people he loved with everything he had. His parents. His grandparents. Maxime. He lost them all in the blink of an eye. *How could I stay mad at him when he has more family out there in the world?* People who might be able to patch the hole in his chest, the same one I've been carrying with me since losing the people I loved more than life.

"Val," Andrea says, offering a hand to help me up. I try to reach for them, but sadness keeps me squatting. *Get up, Valentina.*

"Sorry," I mumble, using every ounce of strength inside of me to stand upright and straighten out my back. "They're just so beautiful up close," I say because it's not a lie, even if it isn't the truth either. I wasn't admiring the car. I was getting swallowed by grief.

"Let's go sit in your brother's," they add, and I nod, following them toward where Adrian's car is. Apparently, I will be test-driving his car this summer break, which sends relief through me.

"Already?" I ask as they hold out their hand for me.

"Yeah. They need to get the seat right for you anyway," they say, and I smile.

"They're going to mold it to fit my ass now?" I whisper, and Andrea laughs so loudly that mechanics turn in our direction. "It could take a while. Adrian's butt is significantly smaller than mine," I joke, and they clap me on the shoulder, still chuckling.

"Go sit down, Val," they say, pushing me toward the car. I go where I'm supposed to.

A minute later, I'm surrounded by three mechanics, trying to figure out what has to be adjusted in the seat to accommodate my body. I revel in the feel of sitting in an F1 car, speaking to mechanics who are acting like I'm the permanent driver, and it makes happiness bloom in my chest.

Up until I get out of the car again and spot a note slipped beside the seat. My eyebrows furrow as I lift and unfold it, spotting black ink a moment later.

Ten words.

Thirteen syllables.

One undeniable meaning.

GIVE UP YOUR SEAT. YOU DON'T BELONG IN FORMULA ONE.

My heart sinks. I have no idea who put it in here for me to find, but it doesn't matter. Knowing wouldn't change the instant surge of sadness sweeping into my heart. I push past it, placing a determined, angry scowl on my face.

Yes, I do.

CHAPTER 6
Gabriel

THIS IS IT, THIS is when I find out if it was worth losing the only girl I have ever loved for a family I don't even know exists. I've been searching for the infamous Sienna Mannello for the past two weeks, which is why I can't believe I'm standing in front of her house. I feel like I'm going to have a panic attack but swallow it down and knock on my grandmother's door. After a couple of minutes, I decide I've been a fool who has been wasting his time chasing something non-existent.

"Can I help you?" I hear a woman's voice ask in Italian from behind me and spin around.

My first instinct is to sit down. She looks like an older version of my mom. Her features, so soft and kind, are too familiar for me to keep looking at Sienna without feeling needles stab my heart. A million of them. All at once. It's one of the most painful sensations I've ever experienced, but I have to keep my eyes on the person in front of me. I can't be rude, especially because I've been looking for her since I left Valentina.

"Are you Sienna Mannello?" My Italian sounds shaky, as if I haven't been speaking it for thirteen years.

"Yes, and who are you?" She puts her bags of groceries on the ground and studies me impatiently. Then, shock covers her face as she really takes me in, scanning my features. Panic makes her breathing hitch. "Oh my God."

"I'm Gabriel Biancheri. Lilliana Leblanc was my mother." It's a good thing she put her bags down because I'm one hundred percent sure she would have dropped them now.

"My Lilli?"

Sienna puts her right hand on her chest, and I take a step closer. I feel like I should take her hand, but I also don't know this woman. I don't know how she thinks, how she acts, who she is. Taking her hand or trying to comfort her is not something I can just do. I may be her biological grandson, but I'm a stranger to her.

"Yes, your Lilli." I don't know what else to tell her, what to tell myself. Luckily, Sienna is the one who takes the first step and invites me into her home.

We talk for hours. I tell her all about my life, my career, my family, and she shares stories about hers. She has another grandson, whose father and mother both passed away when he was barely a year old. Callum lives with her and should probably be home soon. The thought of meeting my cousin excites me, just like talking to her does. She seems like a sweet woman, other than the fact that she sent my mother away, of course.

The more I study her, the more I realize she must be quite a few years younger than Carlos and Evangelin. Her hair is short and light brown, her eyes are as green as my mother's were, and her lips are thin. She's beautiful, just like Mom was.

"Gabriel, can I ask you, how—how did she die?" A tear rolls down Sienna's cheek as she asks me something no mother ever wants to ask. 'How did my child die?' Well, Mom wasn't even really her child, she was simply a decision Sienna made. Still, I know she loved my mother, I know because anyone could see it in the way Sienna's eyes sparkle with a familiar grief.

"She had a brain aneurysm. She collapsed in the grocery store. I don't remember more because those are the memories I try to forget." Sienna looks compassionately at me, and I force a smile.

"You know, when Carlos and I had our affair, he was twenty-five, I believe, and I had just turned eighteen. When I found out, I knew I couldn't ruin his life by telling him the girl he had sex with once was pregnant with his child while his wife wasn't able to have children at all. Back then, abortion wasn't an option for me, especially because my mother was very religious. So, I had the baby, and I made the difficult choice of giving her up. If I hadn't, my mother would have thrown us out onto the street. I wouldn't have been able to give her the life she deserved, the life she got from Matthieu Leblanc, your grandfather."

My grandfather...

"He was my teacher, and his wife and him were trying to have a baby for years. Matthieu was my guide, he was my counselor and friend. When he found out I was pregnant and about to give up the baby, he offered to adopt her and give her a good life. I couldn't say no. Matthieu was a wonderful man, and his wife, Manon, was the sweetest woman I'd ever met."

Sienna is very right about that. My grandparents were the most amazing people. They were always kind to everyone, and they were selfless.

"Your grandfather sent me pictures of my baby every month for the first eighteen years of her life. When she got older, he sent me a picture every four months. But then he died, and I never had the chance to find out where she lived since Matthieu still lived in Italy. He always preferred Italy over Monaco, even though he was born in Monte-Carlo, but that's beside the point. I don't even know what the point is, to be honest..." she says, and we both let out a short laugh.

I wipe away the tear that left my right eye and pretend like it never dropped from there. No part of me wants to cry in front of the woman I'd like to impress. I have to appear stronger than that, even if I have never felt weaker.

"I loved your mother very much, and I'm so sorry I never took the time to find you or her, trust me. I am so very sorry, son," she says with a sob.

Something inside of me turns upside down as she calls me *son*. I don't know if I like it or if I'm uncomfortable with it, but I do believe everything she is telling me. Since she started talking, Sienna hasn't stopped crying. Every few seconds, she wipes her eyes with the tissues she keeps taking from the box next to her on the table.

"I hope you can forgive me," she adds because I'm so speechless, I haven't said anything in a while.

The thing is, I have already forgiven her. I was never mad at her to begin with, all I wanted was to get to know her. Now that I have, I feel nothing but joy toward her. After all, Mom had an amazing life, with parents who loved her more than anything else, a husband who needed her more than anyone else, and two children who loved... *love* her fiercely.

"I understand why you gave her up. And I can tell you this, my mother had a great life. She used to tell me stories about all the good that had happened to her since she'd been able to remember. She was an incredible mother, and she was very happy," I reply, earning myself a sad smile from Sienna.

More tears fall from her eyes, and I no longer feel weird wanting to comfort her. I walk over, sit down, and put my hand on hers. My other one pulls the picture of Mom out of my pocket.

"This is the last photo I ever took of Mom. I have more copies, so you can have this one." I hand her the small image of the first person I ever loved, and Sienna takes it from me with shaking hands.

"Thank you for finding me."

I squeeze her hand and swallow the tears threatening to leave my eyes. Fuck that, fuck these emotions. I'm so sick and tired of crying, and I probably wouldn't want to do so if it wasn't for the fact that I wish Valentina would be here. She'd make everything better, but the past couple of weeks have been hell for me. The dark place I've been in is only starting to ease up now, which is why I know I've made the right choice. Even if I want nothing more than to call her and tell her I've found Sienna.

"You look exactly like Carlos when he was younger, do you know that?" I smile at her and stare into her green eyes.

"Yeah, I know, his wife showed me pictures of Carlos when he was only two years older than me. The similarities are scary." We both laugh a little, and I remove my hand from hers. "My mom had your eyes," I say, and Sienna stares at me.

"I saw them in the pictures Matthieu sent me. You know, I asked him once if I could see her, and he told me I could, but that he would appreciate it if Lilli never found out she was adopted. They loved her, but they didn't want her to start questioning everything. They made a decision not to tell her, but I couldn't bring myself to see her without telling her she's my daughter."

I can't even begin to comprehend how difficult it must have been for her to never be able to tell Mom the truth, but I also can't imagine how hard it must have been to give up that right to begin with.

"Nonna Sienna?" A male voice travels through the small house I haven't taken the time to observe yet.

Everything seems quite antique in her home, and the decorations are worn and loved. The paintings are beautiful, all of them have abstract faces with a mixture of different colors. It's the kind of art I'd put up in my own home, bringing a small smile to my face.

"What would you like to eat for dinner?" the man goes on in Italian, and then I can finally put a face to the voice. He walks into the living room, and his blue eyes go wide when he sees me. He has black, curly hair, a very muscular body, much more muscular than my own, and defined features. "Nonna, why is Gabriel Biancheri in our house?" He takes three steps closer to me, his eyes still wide.

"Callum, Gabriel is Lilliana's son." Callum looks like he's about to faint.

"No way, there is no way! Gabriel Biancheri is not my cousin!" he says with excitement before taking my hand and shaking it aggressively. "It's so nice to meet you. I've been watching you race since you started in Formula One with the Klein Racing team."

My smile gets bigger, and I shake his hand back. I love meeting fans. Knowing my cousin is one of them makes me feel like all of the pieces are falling into place. Except for the biggest, most important piece, which is drifting further and further away from me.

Mon tournesol...

Callum and I spend hours talking about my career, and, even though I try to ask him questions about his life, he rather wants to talk about me. We do, up until he tells me he will make some dinner. I don't know where Sienna went, but I walk over to the paintings I was admiring earlier. They are breathtaking. Whoever painted these is incredibly talented. One specific one catches my attention. The woman in the painting is drawn from behind, but her long, curly blonde hair moves with the wind, and she is surrounded by a field of wildflowers. She reminds me too much of Val, causing me to suck in a sharp breath.

"Nonna Sienna painted these last summer. She usually sells her paintings, but a few that are especially beautiful to her, she keeps," Callum says with a bright grin.

I finally know who I got my artsy side from. I've always been curious since no one else in my family can draw, not even Jean, but now I know. Sienna gave me my love for art, even if I didn't know it before, and Carlos gave me my love for racing. They may not have been in my life earlier, but somehow, they were.

"Do you paint?" I ask Callum, and he blows raspberries.

"Yeah, right. No, I'm useless when it comes to anything art-related, except for singing. I am a pretty decent singer." Sienna walks out of her bedroom and toward us.

"He's more than decent. Callum has been singing since the day he started to speak," she says. His cheeks turn a deep red, and I smile at him.

By the end of the night, I invite them to one of my races. Callum looks so excited, I'm convinced he would cry if I wasn't standing right in front of him. We exchange numbers, and I promise to give him a call to discuss all the details for whatever race weekend suits us both. I tell Sienna I will be back to visit her, and she gives me her number as well.

The drive back to my hotel is quiet, and it gives my thoughts time to get completely consumed by Valentina. It hurts how much I miss her. I miss her smell, her smile, her giggling, her curly hair that always needed the whole damn shampoo bottle, and I especially miss wrapping my arms around her body before we fell asleep. I miss feeling at home.

Fuck.

What have I done?

CHAPTER 7
Valentina

MY THREE WEEKS ARE up after the session today. Adrian's team and I have been making a lot of progress. I studied the data with them, spent hours in the car, and tried my best to pick up as much as possible. I'm here to test new updates for Adrian's and... Gabriel's cars. Lorenzo Mattia and I have been working closely together as well, and I've been having the best time of my life. I've set incredible times, which no one can deny. If anything, everyone has been praising me for the great job I've been doing. I've never been prouder of myself, even if I could have never achieved anything without this amazing crew behind me. They've been teaching me, supporting me, and patient, more so than any other group of people I've ever met.

Apart from the note I received weeks ago, I haven't gotten any more hateful messages. If it's anyone from Adrian's team who doesn't want me here, they seem to have understood that I'm not going anywhere. I'm here to stay, whether they like it or not.

"Alright, sweets, how are we feeling?" Scarlette Roots asks me, and I turn to my old friend.

I met my future race engineer years ago in Monaco when she went to her first-ever Grand Prix. She is one of the kindest people and one hell of a race engineer. Scarlette's been working for her husband's—Julián Alvarez's—team in Moto1 for years now. She has done an exceptional job, but her dream has always been to become a Formula One race engineer. Years ago, she was denied her opportunity, and I've been waiting, hoping one day she and I would become an unstoppable team. As soon as I heard I got the seat, I emailed her to see if she was still interested in the position.

Luckily, she was.

"I'm good," I reply, staring up at this gorgeous woman with a smile on my face.

Scarlette is stunning. Her curves are to die for, her blue eyes are crystal clear, and her pale skin is contrasted by her long, black hair, which is always tied into a high ponytail to show off her soft features. Not to mention, she's more intelligent than anyone I've ever met, apart from James, and she's hard-working and determined. We will get that championship one day, I'm sure of it.

"Good, we're ready for you," she says, and I let out a heavy breath, taking the helmet she's handing me. Scarlette is training under Adrian's race engineer, Chloe, for now, but she seems to be enjoying herself. Meanwhile, my brother is teaching me everything I need to know about being an F1 driver, too.

"Fuck, I can't believe this is really happening."

It can't be. No way!

I jump out of the car, turning to see Leonard Tick standing next to my brother, a small smirk on his face. It still sends a wave of warmth through me whenever he gives me a little smile or grin or anything. The Brit isn't known for those types of things, so when he offers me one, it feels like I accomplished something remarkable. The feeling intensifies when he opens his arms for me as an invitation to hug. This will be the second time I've hugged Leonard Tick. I never thought it'd happen.

"Hey, kiddo," he says after a friendly hug, one of his hands lifting to Adrian's shoulder. "Adrian invited Chiara and me to watch you test drive," he answers my unspoken question, and I grin up at my future business partner.

"Chiara is your girlfriend?" I ask, a bit unsure. I don't know much about Leonard's life, only that he's dating someone and has two brothers.

"Wife," Leonard corrects me, and my jaw drops to the fucking floor.

"Yeah, I can't believe she married him either," Adrian says with a teasing tone, earning himself a nudge from his friend. *Our friend.* "It should have been Chiara and me," my brother adds with a hurt sigh. Leonard scowls at him in response.

"Back off," he warns, causing Adrian to chuckle.

"Yeah, Adrian, back off before I beat you up." A woman's voice comes from behind Leonard, grabbing my full attention.

Chiara takes my breath away. She has short, brown hair, piercing green eyes, a tanned skin tone, and a curvy figure. I watch Leonard's hand slip across her shoulders before the other settles on her stomach as he presses his mouth to hers. The room starts spinning as I notice her beautiful, round belly.

"You're going to be a dad!" I tell the three-time World Champion like he wasn't involved in the making of the baby.

"Yes, but I'd appreciate it if this could stay between us," Leonard says, making Chiara smack his arm. She takes a step toward me and takes my hand in hers, squeezing tightly.

"It's nice to finally meet you. I cannot wait to see you sit in that car today." Chiara's words are followed by a soft look, and I grin at her.

"Are you all having a party without me?"

James' all-too-familiar voice fills my ears, sending tears to my eyes. I don't hesitate. I slip past everyone else and jump into his arms. Three weeks. I hadn't seen him in three weeks, barely spoke to him, and, until this very second, I hadn't processed just how deeply I missed him.

"Hi, gorgeous," he whispers in my ear as he holds me close.

"Hi," I reply, nuzzling my face into his chest as I drop onto my feet again. Tears sting my eyes, the same ones I've been doing a miraculous job suppressing.

"Missed me, love?" he asks with a little chuckle, making me melt into his embrace.

"So much," I admit, my hands gripping the front of his shirt. His hands run up and down my back, softening my tense muscles. "How's Annie?" is my first question when I step out of his arms, but his hands remain on me. His blue eyes pierce into mine with warmth, settling me.

"She's doing well, getting closer to her due date every day," he replies with his thick English accent and bright smile.

"Then what the hell are you doing here?" I scold, but he merely grabs my chin between his thumb and index finger for a moment, grinning like I'm the best thing he's ever laid eyes on.

"I'm here to watch you in an F1 car," he explains, releasing my face and stepping toward Adrian.

There's a wary expression on my brother's face as he hugs his best friend, but I choose to ignore the exchange happening between them. Knowing each other for as long as they have allows them to have whole conversations without speaking a single word. It would bother me if Scarlette didn't remind me to get back into the car because the team is waiting for me. I thank everyone—Leonard, Chiara, James, and Adrian—for being here. Then I slip on my balaclava and helmet, the one Gabriel got me for my birthday, blinking away the tears of overwhelming emotion that likes to hit me every now and then.

It was easier to ignore when I sat in the car for the first time. My dreams were coming true then. I had everything I'd ever worked for. Am I still happy to be here, to have been given this opportunity? Yes, of course. This is everything I've ever wanted, but it's also not. Because everything I've ever wanted includes Gabriel sharing this time with me, and he isn't. He's God-knows-where, doing God-knows-what. The training allowed me to ignore the ache in my chest from one of the worst heartbreaks I've ever had to endure, but not anymore.

"Hey," Adrian's muffled voice comes from next to my head, and he holds out his hand for me. I take it, my gloved fingers wrapping around his thumb. "Head in the car, Val. Take a deep breath," he says, and I do as I'm told. It comes back out shaky. "One more." Through gritted teeth, I suck it in and do my best to keep it even as I exhale. "Good. Now, focus. One last time before we go home," Adrian reminds me, placing his hand on top of my helmet.

"Thanks," I mumble, even though he probably can't hear me.

My brother steps away, leaving me feeling better and more concentrated. Racing is mine. My passion. My dream. My everything. It's come true. My number is on the front of this car. I did it. And I sure as hell won't let myself get distracted over a man who chose himself.

One last session, and then it's time to go home.

Sitting in a Formula One car is great, but racing in one? It's both hell and heaven combined. Every part of my body aches with exhaustion as I drive around this familiar track for the thirtieth time today. At the same time, I'm also beyond happy. The G-force pushing down on me is kicking my ass. It also fills my heart with joy because I get to feel it exhaust me. I'm not hearing about it from Adrian, I'm experiencing it myself, and that thought alone keeps me going. I shift gears, push the car as far as possible in the corners, and set sector times tenths faster than my brother's. I know the updates play a big role in it too, but I can't help feeling proud of myself either way.

"Okay, last lap, and then come back to the pits," Scarlette says into my radio, and I notice how badly my cheeks hurt from all the smiling I've been doing today. My arms cry in complaint as I turn the wheel again—which is a thousand times more strenuous than turning the wheel of a normal car.

By the time I slow my speed to enter the pits, I notice Leonard, Chiara, Adrian, James, Scarlette, and her husband, Julián, are all waiting for me with a bottle of celebratory champagne and a huge cake that reads 'Congratulations, Val!'. I don't even care that I burst into tears again. The gesture is too sweet, and the overwhelming amount of love they're offering me has my heart swelling in my chest.

Not everything has to be going right in life for one to appreciate moments like these. It's a lesson I've had to learn the hard way, but it's one of the most important ones life has ever taught me. Grief and sadness will always linger in some parts of your life, but without them, happiness wouldn't exist. I'm pretty damn happy right now, even with grief circling my life like a vicious vulture, waiting to prey on me when I'm at my lowest.

Lucky for me, I've never felt stronger in my life.

CHAPTER 8
Gabriel

"You found her?" Jean asks, his features brightening as I share the one thing I've kept from him until I knew for sure Sienna was out there and willing to meet him, too.

"I did. If you're interested, Sienna and our cousin, Callum, will attend the Monaco Grand Prix," I say, causing his face to light up with joy.

His knuckles brush over the fabric of my suitcase where it sits on my bed, waiting for me to get the energy to pack. Hector has been nagging me to train with him again, but I've been neglecting my duties as a Formula One driver. My head's been fucked. I barely managed to keep myself hydrated, let alone go for a run or work out my muscles, which is one of the worst things an F1 driver can do. Any sort of weakness can be deadly. So, I'm flying to France for the next race of the season earlier than I have to. My performance coach is already there, ready to beat me back into shape. I'm about to have to endure physical exhaustion like none I've ever felt before, but I deserve it. At least if I have to go through physical pain, the emotional one might subside for a minute.

Then again, I've been in a constant state of torture for the past three weeks, and nothing has been capable of easing it.

I see Valentina in everything I do. *The sun sets?* My mind drifts to the day we spent together, honoring my mom's life. *Flowers at the grocery store?* I hyperfixate on the sunflowers, barely keeping the tears from dropping out of my eyes. *The waffles Jean keeps asking me to make?* I can't even make the batter without remembering the day I made them for Val, licking the syrup off her fingers.

For fuck's sake, I cried in the shower yesterday when the memories of us showering together overwhelmed my heart. I want her back. I want to wrap my arms around her, drop to my knees, beg her to forgive me, anything. But I'm still a mess. A mess she shouldn't have to clean up. A mess I'm doing my hardest to uncomplicate because I will do everything in my power to prove I'm the only one for her. Hell, I'm so close to figuring everything out, it's on the tip of my tongue. I just hope she'll take me back.

No matter how long it takes, I'll fight for her, prove how much I love her.

These past three weeks, I've thought about little else than the fact that Valentina is and forever will be the love of my life. She's my pitstop, and without her, I've been racing without an end in sight. Without a single break. Without a chance to refuel to prepare for the shit show my life is. I used to be so right for her. Now, I've become the reason she cries, the reason for her sadness. I blink rapidly, trying to ignore the stinging pain inside of me.

When I left, I thought it would take forever to find Sienna. I didn't think it would be this... *easy* to track her down. This should have taken me months, a year even, but it didn't. It took a week to find her, another to book a flight to meet her, and one more to wallow in my grief of everything I'd lost. If I'd known... fuck, I never would have left Valentina. We could have figured something out. We could have—

'Could' *doesn't help this situation, Gabriel.*

"Thank you for finding them. I don't think I would have been strong enough," my brother says, peeling off a piece of the guilt lingering on my shoulders.

"It was nothing," is all I manage to croak out because it wasn't all for nothing. I've made my brother happier. I've given us another shot at having family to reconnect with our mom. Not to mention, they are some of the nicest people I've ever met.

"Don't brush it off like that," Jean says and walks over to me, grabbing my shoulders in an attempt to capture my attention. I stare at the ground because if I make eye contact with him right now, I won't be able to act like the big, tough brother I've always been for him.

"Jean, let go of me," I say, but he shakes his head.

"No. You've always been there for me. You've always done all you could to be the best brother, even when I was a complete asshole to you," he replies, holding on tighter while I try to step away.

"Please, stop," I say firmly to prevent my voice from quivering. I'm a fucking mess.

"No. You need to hear this. You're a good person. Whatever happened between you and Val, it'll be okay. She loves you, and you love her. I know you'd do anything for her, to get her back, so don't worry. Everything will work out the way it's supposed to," my little brother says, wrapping me up into a hug I didn't ask for but have needed for weeks. My tears almost drop, but they only fall when four more arms wrap around me.

"We're all here for you, little racer," Domi says, and I let my feelings out in front of someone who isn't Val for the first time in years.

"You're not alone, you never will be," Nicolette adds, stepping back to grab my face in her hands. "You have all of us, Gabri. All four of us," she says, one of her hands slipping onto Domi's baby bump.

My pregnant aunt smiles comfortingly at me, taking my hand in hers to place it on her stomach as well. The baby, little Vivienne Juliette or Maxime Guillaume depending on whether it will be a boy or girl—named after the people we've loved and lost—kicks as soon as my hand touches Domi's stomach. A nervous laugh escapes me before more tears leave me and all of them start hugging me again. It's close to the comfort I need, but something's missing.

As much as I love them, they will never compare to mon tournesol.

I'm going to get her back.

CHAPTER 9
Valentina

IT'S THREE IN THE morning when my phone starts vibrating on my nightstand. I shoot up in bed and reach for it, worry settling in my chest. My half-asleep thoughts send me spiraling into worst-case scenarios.

What if something happened to Gabriel? What if it is Jean telling me Gabriel has been in a car crash, plane crash, anything crash? No, no, please, God, don't let anything have happened to him. I can't lose him.

"Hello," I almost scream into the phone, still panicking when I hear a woman breathe unevenly on the other side of the line.

"Valentina, I need your help," Annabel Rossi breathes into the phone in French, and I rub my eyes to wake up. "Please, Valentina. My sister isn't answering her phone and James left for France yesterday. You're the only one I have, please," she begs, but I'm already out of bed and on my way to my closet.

"Tell me what's wrong," I say, so I know what's going on.

"I think I might be in labor," she says, causing me to drop the jacket I just picked up.

Oh man, it's really happening. She's having my best friend's baby. I feel like vomiting, and at the same time, I'm giddy. The confusion is messing with my head, but a feeling of happiness settles in my chest. *I'm going to meet my best friend's baby.* I'm out of the door before a minute has passed. I should have probably washed my face and brushed my teeth but all I can focus on right now is getting to Annabel.

It takes me several minutes to get to her house before I knock impatiently on her door. She yells for me to come in, and I open it in a heartbeat. Annabel is sitting on her couch, her hand rubbing her stomach. She is breathing heavily, and her long brown hair is all over the place. There is sweat running down her forehead and tears streaming down her cheeks. It must be at least a hundred degrees in her apartment, which doesn't help either.

"Oh, thank God," she groans, her hand still rubbing circles over her huge stomach. I run over and squat down in front of her.

"Where's your hospital bag?" I ask, and she tells me it's in her bedroom.

My phone vibrates in my hand as I grab it, James' name flashing on my screen. My finger presses the accept button, but I never stop running around. I gather everything Annabel needs and lead her out of the house.

"Love, please tell me you're at Annabel's," he says with panic in his voice.

"I'm currently helping her in the car, which is why I have to hang up now, but I promise I will look after her. You have my word." He exhales into the phone, and I can't help but wonder how he must be feeling right now. Annie is having their son while he is in Le Castellet, working.

"Thank you, darling." He sounds relieved, but I know he's not going to be able to focus on anything else until I tell him more.

"You know I've got you," I tell him.

Annabel is sitting in the car, breathing irregularly. When we finally arrive, I take her arm and lead her inside with my heart still racing in my chest. I talk to the woman at the reception, and moments later, a nurse with a wheelchair takes Annabel into an empty room. Knowing she's already more taken care of than she was half an hour ago sends a wave of relief through me.

We wait for her doctor, who seems to be taking her sweet time to arrive. Seconds tick by until they turn into minutes, Annabel breathing heavily beside me when pain strikes. My hand is in hers as I ignore the sharp stinging in my fingers whenever she grabs them too tightly.

For a moment, my mind slips to Domi, Gabriel's aunt. I wonder how she's doing, how her baby is doing. I wonder if her doctor's visits have been alright, if she's in a lot of pain or discomfort. I wonder if she's ready to meet her baby, just like Annie is ready to meet Damian. Then, I shut down all thoughts relating to Gabriel's aunts because I wish I could see them, but I don't have the right to anymore. It makes me too sad to think about.

I sigh when the doctor appears in the doorway. Annabel hasn't had any pain for the past couple of minutes, and we were both getting nervous about what that meant. Doctor Helen introduces herself to me, and I shake her hand impatiently. I honestly don't care who she is as long as she makes sure the baby and Annabel are all right. Dr. Helen asks my new friend some questions about her symptoms before she reaches a conclusion, which sends another bit of relief through my whole body.

"It's false labor. Very common and nothing to worry about." Annabel looks at her doctor in disbelief.

"Nothing to worry about? It felt like my organs were going to fall out of my vagina, along with the baby, and you tell me it's nothing to worry about?" Even though Annabel is mad, she is mad in the sweetest way. She seems like the kind of person who never gets angry, yet here we are, and Annabel looks ready to rip someone's head off. I can hardly keep myself from smiling at her.

"I'll be back, Annabel, I'm just going to call James and tell him it was a false alarm." I wrap my hand around hers once more, and she smiles at me.

My shaking fingers tap on my phone screen, dialing James' number. After one ring, he picks up, and, for the second time tonight, he sighs.

"Talk to me, what's happening?" he asks and demands at the same time.

"She was experiencing Braxton Hicks contractions. I'm going to take her home now and stay with her until tomorrow," I inform him.

"Thank you, gorgeous. I don't know what I would do without you." There is silence from both ends for a minute, every single word my mind comes up with feeling like the wrong thing to say. "How do I deserve you?" he asks next, and I don't know why, but tears flood my eyes. "You mean the world to me, and I love you with all of my heart."

Why does it sound like he is confessing his feelings to me?

"Darling, are you there?" he says, and I snap back into reality. James can't have feelings for me, and I shouldn't allow him to say these things either.

"Yeah, I'm here. I have to go check on Annabel, but I'll call you again tomorrow." I hang up without telling him I love him, trying to ignore the stabbing guilt in my gut.

It's not fair that James loves me so much, and I love him, but it's not in the way he needs me to, in the way that would be a hell of a lot easier than how I love Gabriel. But I'm never going to fall in love with James. I am head over heels, wholeheartedly, and blindly in love with Gabriel Matteo Biancheri, which has never hurt more than it does now.

Annabel is still in pain when I help her into my car, so I go as slowly as she needs, making sure she's comfortable. We drive in silence for a few minutes, but eventually, she breaks it.

"I hope James is doing okay. I hate making him worry." I give her a compassionate smile. "I'm glad it was only false labor. I want James to be there when little Damian comes into the world," she says, and we both laugh a little. "Oh, they did an ultrasound to check if he is okay. Look." Annabel holds the picture of the baby up, and I glance at him before focusing on the road ahead of me again. "He's so beautiful, just like his dad."

I can almost hear the click in my head when I look at the picture. Annabel is in love with James. She has feelings for him, I have no doubt about it. When she says his name, I can hear the affection and how drawn she feels to him. If everything goes well, they might become a happy, little family. They might become what I always thought Gabriel and I would be in the future, once we'd both retire from F1 and have a family. I swallow past the lump forming in my throat, but it seems to be an impossible task.

"Val?" Annabel asks, and I mumble an 'mhmm'. "How are you feeling?"

"Fine," I reply and furrow my brows. "Why?" Her hand covers mine on the gear shift, briefly forcing my eyes to her. She needs to stop studying me with that compassionate look, otherwise, I'm going to start crying.

"Because there are dark circles underneath your eyes, you look like you're in constant pain, and, as beautiful as you are, you have looked much better." I let out a small laugh. "You know you can talk to me. I always have an open ear for you," Annie says and squeezes my hand. I bite the inside of my cheek in response. "Please, let me help you," she begs when I don't respond.

"There is a guy I've been in love with for three years," I admit, letting that thought float around in my head.

Three years of strong, uncontrollable feelings. I would smile if it wouldn't hurt so much. My heart aches in my chest whenever I talk about Gabriel. The urge to wrap my fingers around the necklace he gave me is almost irresistible, but I don't. Instead, I tell Annabel about our relationship and blink back the tears in my eyes when I tell her he left me to find his family.

"But he'll come back. I mean, he gave me this necklace as a promise. It has to mean something." I park my car in front of her house, and Annabel gives me an odd look. "What's wrong?" I ask, and she lets out a big sigh.

"Can I ask you something?" I nod, impatient about what is going to come out of her mouth. "Is the necklace enough?" She decides to elaborate when a confused frown spreads across my face. "I mean, is that necklace enough for you to know for sure he will come back? Is it enough for you to put your love life on hold, waiting for a guy who chose a life without you?" she asks, causing pain to shuffle through my system.

Her words land deeply in my chest, and they shatter everything inside of me. All of my hopes of him coming back and regretting his decision to leave. Everything turns to dust until I land on an answer that terrifies me.

"I don't know," I say, and the next thing I process is crying, sobbing, and choking on my own breath. He really left me, and I have no idea if he's coming back. The anger I thought I lost when I forgave him comes back stronger than before, and I want to punch myself for being so naive. More importantly, however, I want to scream at Gabriel.

Annabel is comforting me by stroking my right arm and squeezing my hand, but I don't calm down for quite a while. I've been so in denial to protect my feelings that I didn't look at the truth at hand. Every emotion comes crashing down on me. I don't even realize when we walk inside her house, or when I sit down on her couch. All I know is I'm mad at myself, I'm mad at Gabriel, and I'm embarrassed for having a breakdown in front of Annabel.

"I'm so sorry, Annabel," I tell her when she sits down next to me again. "You have enough to worry about, and I am not helping." I take the tissue she hands me and wipe away my tears.

"First of all, call me Annie. I think we are good enough friends for you to call me Annie, and secondly, you have done more for me than you will ever know. You brought James to me, you helped us find a name for our baby boy, and you got up at three in the morning to drive me to the hospital. Val, you have done so much. If I can help you just a little now, I will. I will do everything to make you feel better." She is such a sweetheart. Pregnant, anxious, and still willing to help me.

"You already have. Now, let's get some food for you and Damian," I say and get up from the couch. I'm not going to sulk when Annie needs me.

I make her some breakfast and occupy my mind with something other than Gabriel. It's only six-thirty in the morning but I'm starving. The last time I was up this early... Gabriel woke me so we could drive to Maranello and race a car on the track there. He got us food on the drive and made me laugh the whole way. Gabriel might never be coming back, and even if he does, how could I truly forgive him? He fucking left. He left like my mother did. He broke my heart and—

I have to focus on something else.

Adrian texts me to check in on Annabel while also reminding me that we have to leave in six hours to drive to France. I'm working exclusively with his team from now on, which is probably because Gabriel has vanished from the face of the Earth. No one from his team has spoken to him, I know because I overheard them talking when I was test driving. Adrian, on the other hand, has spent his entire summer break—a break most drivers use to relax and rejuvenate—working on improving his performance.

"Annie, where are you?" a woman screams in French, and I look around the corner to see who walked through the front door.

My heart stops beating as soon as my eyes settle on her tall, lean body, red hair, and bright green eyes. Her face is not one I'll ever forget, even if the first time I saw it was through Gabriel's drawing. He really did draw her perfectly. I don't know what the hell she's doing here, but I don't get time to overthink it when Annie speaks again.

"Val, come meet my sister," Annabel calls out, and my heart drops from my chest into my stomach. *Her sister? No, no, no.* This can't be happening.

Her gaze catches mine, something violent flickering in her eyes before she shuts it down and fakes a smile at me. Harlow takes a step forward, giving my muscles the urge to run away and never return to this house.

"It's nice to meet you, Valentina Romana," she says and holds out her hand for me. Every fiber of my being fights me on shaking her hand, but I do my best to be polite despite wanting to crawl under my covers and hide from what the fuck is happening right now.

"Nice to meet you, too," I mumble, inhaling deeply to get rid of the aching in my chest.

This is the woman who slept with the man I love. I'm not upset because Gabriel had sex with other people, I don't care that he did. My heart sinks at the thought that I hurt him, and she took his mind off of me. He isn't mine anymore, and I think seeing someone who touched him in the ways I long to do now is what has me on the verge of throwing up.

"I should finish breakfast," I blurt out when Harlow and I have been staring at each other for several seconds too long.

"Do you need any help?" Harlow asks, her expression wary and her smile still forced. She doesn't like me any more than I do her.

"Not necessary, thank you." I hurry into the kitchen without another word, my heartbeat still uneven.

When I'm finished, I tell Annie I have to leave since Adrian and I are driving to France and disappear before she can say anything else. Storming out of her house like this is terrible, but I can't stay. Annabel is looked after, and I need to go home, take a shower, and, most importantly, hug my brother.

I really need a hug from my brother right now.

CHAPTER 10
Gabriel

EVERYTHING FUCKING *HURTS*. THERE is not a single muscle in my body left untrained, but I'm nowhere near done with my sets today. Hector is pushing me harder than he ever has before. He's furious with me for the way I've been treating myself. He understands and sympathizes with my grief—he lost his mom when he was young—but he's angry at the state I'm in. At how weak I let my body get. When I tell him about the way I abused myself with alcohol, dehydration, and starvation, he barely holds himself back from ripping me a new one.

Most people would think he only cares because he's my performance coach and it's his job to make sure I'm ready to sit in my F1 car, but he genuinely cares about my well-being, and seeing me shredding everything we've worked for over the years upsets him. Understandably so. He also doesn't want me to be in pain, but grieving your mother's loss all over again after so many years brings unstoppable agony, especially as I try to process all of the new information I received.

Mom was adopted.

Carlos Klein is my biological grandfather.

Sienna Mannello is a kind woman who gave up my mother, but only so Mom could have a better future.

All of what's been happening has been torture, but I haven't felt this close to my mom in years. It's like I can feel the hole she left in my chest finally heal a little again after being sliced open without remorse.

The bullshit they tell you about grief getting easier over time? It's not true for every person.

My grief is like a living thing inside of me. Something that makes decisions for me when I want exactly the opposite of what it demands. Break up with Valentina. Drink to numb the pain. Fall into darkness. None of it were things I desired until it flared up inside of me and took down who I am as a person. It turned me into someone I don't recognize.

But...

I've slowly been starting to feel like myself again. Finding Sienna, feeling safe and loved with Domi, Nicolette, and Jean, and training with Hector, all of it has brought me back to myself. Taken me away from this awful monster inside of me and given me control of myself. With every run Hector takes me on, with every message I get from Callum and Sienna, with every reassuring gesture from my family, I feel stronger. Like I'm ready to wrestle the evil creature living inside of me into obedience.

"One more set. You're not nearly done yet, Gabriel," Hector says, forcing me to push past my limits.

My arms quiver as I curl them to start up again, but Hector merely frowns at my weakness. I should be able to do this, even if I'd struggle a little, I'm supposed to be strong. Before everything happened, I did these sets every workout session.

A groan of frustration escapes me, so I bite through the pain and push myself further than my body is comfortable with at the moment. This is punishment, I know it is, but it's one I deserve for the chaos I've brought into the lives of the people I love. This is good. This is exactly what I needed. To clear my mind and take back control. To fight for who I am. To be Gabriel again. I've been so far away from the man who is passionate about racing in Formula One, loves to draw, cares for people with his whole heart, and does what he can to be deserving of his dreams.

"Push! You can do it," Hector says, standing behind me to spot me as I raise the weights over my head.

"Fuck," I grunt, holding back a scream of utter exhaustion and overexertion.

It stays inside until I make it to the end of my set, and then the sound roars free, along with a stray tear I'm incapable of holding back. Hector takes the weights from me and places them on the ground, stepping around me to take my shoulders in his hands.

My breath comes out ragged and with a little wheezing sound, but that's mostly because something feels strangely good in my head now. It feels... free. As if the torment of the last few weeks has finally subsided to leave space for me to sort through my mess. As if I'm finally healing.

"You should have trusted me to help you through this, Gabriel," Hector says while I sag forward.

"I wasn't ready before," I admit, breathing through the waves of pain my exhausted muscles send through my body. We might have pushed it a bit too far today, but it's worth it. This sense of peace in my chest tells me I'm one step closer to feeling whole again.

Now, all I'm missing is Valentina back in my life, if she'll have me back in hers.

CHAPTER 11

Valentina

"T HE GIRL FROM G ABRIEL's sketchbook is Annabel's sister?" Adrian asks me in disbelief after I told him what happened this morning.

"Yes, so, you can imagine how fast I ran when I saw her." Adrian's hand wraps around mine gently while I use my other one to cover my face.

"You really can't catch a break, can you?" I let out a small laugh and study my brother's hair for a second. It's messier and curlier than usual, and, somehow, a darker shade than the dirty blonde we inherited from the mother who left us.

"Actually, that's not true. Leonard and I are having a meeting with some investors in a few days," I say, bringing a smile to his face.

"I am so proud of you." Simple words, but hearing them out of the mouth of the most important person in my life makes me happy. "Can I come with you?" I laugh a little before I assure him he can. Having him at that meeting will probably ease my nerves.

Adrian and I arrive at our hotel, and when I see James, all of my emotions, all of the turmoil inside of me relating to my heartbreak, it all just stops. Adrian stops in front of the entrance, and I sprint into James' arms. He's already waiting for me, a bright smile on his face. It's been almost a week since I've seen him. My arms wrap around his neck and his familiar scent radiates off him to fill my nose. I sigh in relief.

"I missed you, Val," he mumbles against my shoulder before he rests his face in the crook of my neck.

"I really missed you," I reply and tighten my grip on him. He had to leave straight away after my test drive session, meaning I haven't spent quality time with my best friend in almost a month. "Never leave me for that long again," I demand, but my voice cracks, revealing my emotions.

"I'm so sorry, but I'm here now." I nod, and James pulls back to look at me. He cups my cheeks, bringing a smile to my lips. Seeing him makes me happy, no matter how awkward things were over the phone last night. "You look exhausted," he tells me, and I laugh.

"Thanks, you look good, too." James does look very good. His blue eyes look healthy, no redness in them or any dark circles underneath. His blonde hair is shorter now, but it makes him look more mature. His long lashes seem somehow fuller, framing his eyes in a way that should be illegal.

"No, seriously, when is the last time you've eaten or slept?"

I think about his question for a little when I realize I haven't eaten much since training in Maranello ended. Only some crackers that help with my nausea. Nausea that appears every single time I think about Gabriel. I've also not slept well, but that has more to do with my inability to keep my mind from racing. Some part deep inside of me is convinced I can't sleep because I'm so used to being next to Gabriel, not having his arms wrapped around me keeps me wide awake all night. Another part thinks it's the feeling of loss.

"If you have to think about it, it's been too long," James scolds, and I give him a guilty smile.

"Let's get some food," I say.

Adrian walks up next to us and hands me my bag. James takes my hand, leading me inside while I revel in the comfort of my best friend's proximity. Adrian goes to check us in while James and I wait patiently near the elevators.

"I saw an ultrasound picture of your son, and it's the best picture I've ever seen in my entire life," I say, and he smiles at me.

"I felt the same way. Seeing his tiny hands, feet, and head on that paper made my heart fuller than it's ever been. It also scared the fuck out of me, don't get me wrong, but it made something inside of me just click." A proud smile crosses his face.

"What do you mean there are no available rooms? I booked a suite for my sister and me two weeks ago!" I walk over to my brother who is currently glaring at the woman at the reception.

"I'm sorry, sir, we're fully booked," she says, and I stare at her in disbelief.

"But I booked it two weeks ago!" Adrian is mad, *really mad*. We chose this hotel because it is the closest to the track, and now we don't have a room?

"Adrian, it's fine. I have a suite, an extra bed, and a couch. It's enough privacy for both of you." Adrian looks at James for a brief second before taking his credit card off the table and flashing the receptionist a scowl.

"Are you sure three of us in one room will work out?" Adrian asks, and James frowns.

"Yes, the couch and bed are in a separate room, and if you can't share a room with your sister, she can have my room and we'll share." Adrian lets out a short laugh and looks at me.

"You can share a room with me, right?" my brother asks, and I look at him with playful disgust.

"No, you snore like a pig," I playfully complain, and when James starts laughing, so do I.

"You're probably just hearing yourself," Adrian claps back, and I stop laughing. "Come on, piggy, I have meetings to get to," he says to me before he wraps his arm around my shoulders and pulls me close to press a kiss to my temple. I smack his stomach, causing him to let go of me.

"I'd rather walk with James," I say, and before I know it, James' arm is around me so he can drag me against his chest.

We walk toward the elevator, get in, and James presses the button bringing us to his floor and hotel room. My best friend takes my bag from me and brings it all the way to the room Adrian and I will be sharing with him for the next week.

"Thank you," I say, and he kisses my cheek.

"Anything for you." His gaze lingers on my lips a moment longer than usual before it shifts back up to my eyes. "So, what do you want to eat for lunch? And it better be a lot because I know you probably haven't eaten much since everything happened with Gabriel. I intend to change that," he says. A laugh bubbles out of me when he puts his hands on his hips as if he were Superman.

"Okay, Mr. Kent, get me a pizza and three burgers," I say, and he drops his arms to his side, an easy grin on his face.

"Much better," he replies before moving over to me and wrapping his arms around me again.

"What are you doing?" A laugh follows my words, but he merely places his cheek on the crown of my head.

"Making sure for myself that you're alright," he replies.

"I'm fine, James. I promise," I assure him, but he merely holds me tighter.

"I know you're not, but I'll do everything in my power to ensure no one will ever hurt you again."

He believes he has that power. I wish he did, but life isn't designed to be painless. It's made for us to experience in whatever way we're meant to. I don't regret falling in love with Gabriel. I don't regret getting kicked out of the F3 team I was driving for. I don't regret any of the decisions I've made. They brought me to where I am today, being the first female Formula One World Championship contestant. Pain, pleasure, grief, and happiness are all part of my journey, of who I am. I have a lot left to learn, but one thing I know for certain.

No matter how flawed my life may seem, all of its pieces are a treasure to me.

CHAPTER 12
Gabriel

Fuck, I never thought seeing her would tear my heart into more pieces, but there she is, standing with Adrian and our team principal. An easy smile occupies her full lips, sending a wave of longing through my system. I want to kiss those lips, the mouth that is as much my home as every other part of her. My fingers are itching to run through her curly, dirty blonde hair, to get stuck in several knots because no matter how much she brushes it, her curls tangle into them anyway. My chest aches to have hers pressed against it while my arms beg me to let them embrace her.

But I can't. She isn't mine anymore.

Ever since I started training again, my mind has been in a clearer space. Hector has pushed me past my limits, but it's made me stronger both physically and mentally. I'm still working on the emotional aspect, and it'll heal, too, as soon as I find a way to get Valentina to forgive me. I found Sienna and Callum. Carlos and I have gotten to know each other. Domi and Nicolette sent me an ultrasound of their little baby this morning. I worked my way out of the dark hole I was in. I can be good for her again. It may have taken one long and miserable month, but I'm praying she'll be able to forgive me.

My feet are about to bring me to her when somebody grabs me by the collar, yanking me out of my box and into my private room. My senses are on high alert as I try to figure out who the fuck put their hands on me, so when I'm released, I spin around with anger coursing through my veins. Unfortunately, the attacker shoves me backward before I can fight back. It only takes me another brief moment to realize it's Cameron.

"What the hell is wrong with you?" I blurt out, taking a deep breath to slow my heart rate.

"What the hell is wrong with *me*? What the bloody hell is wrong with *you*?" he yells, and I take another step away from him. *Shit.* Cameron's full of rage. "You don't call me for a *month* and then I find out you broke my girl's heart? I don't fucking think so. You better give me a great reason for why you did what you did. Otherwise, I'm going to punch you right in your pretty face," he threatens, and I sink onto the table where my performance coach massages me after the races.

There is a reason why I've avoided my best friend for the past four weeks. For one, he loves Val so much that I didn't want to put him in a position where he'd have to choose between her and me. Not to mention, he threatened to destroy me if I ever broke her heart, and while that was very appealing at some stages, if he killed me, I wouldn't have the chance to earn her forgiveness.

"You think I'm pretty?" I ask Cameron to lift the mood a little. I can't handle him being angry at me, so when the corners of his mouth twitch ever so slightly, it eases the tension in my chest.

"You know you're pretty, Gabriel. You're the pretty boy of Formula One," he replies, and it actually makes me chuckle. It doesn't feel right, so I shut it down immediately. "What's going on, mate? Tell me," Cameron says, and I let my shoulders fall in defeat.

"Everything's fucked up," I reply, dropping my face into my hands.

Then, I share everything with him. My best friend listens closely, surprise and shock lacing his features as he studies me. Eventually, he sits down and throws his arm around my shoulders. At least I didn't lose Cameron. Adrian checks in on me, too, every few days, something I know he only does because we've grown closer and neither one of us is capable of losing people unless it's necessary. He puts so much effort into our friendship, I don't deserve it in the least. I haven't responded to him since I left his house, but he keeps trying anyway. Because that's how good of a guy my rival and teammate is.

"What on Earth?" is all Cameron replies. "How's your headspace? Are you doing alright?" he asks after several moments of complete silence pass between us. I look up at him and suck in a sharp breath.

"I've never been in so much pain," I admit because I'm drained.

I've been running on reserve fuel, but that's slowly disappearing as well. All the grief in my life hit me when I found out about Carlos and Sienna. I've worked through it again, but it's drained me, especially because the biggest source of my grief is currently standing with Lorenzo Mattia. I can't even tell her how proud I am to see her in the team colors because I have no right to do so. She doesn't want to see me. She probably wants nothing to do with me anymore.

"I'm going to make things right somehow," I add when Cameron doesn't respond. The Australian stands up and steps in front of me.

"I understand why you left her, but the longer you stay away, the more unsure you're going to make her about how you feel. You fucked up by leaving, even if you did it to save her from getting distracted during the most important time of her life. Don't make her wait longer if you know you're right for her again," he says, and I nod along to his words because I know he's got a point.

"I know, but going up to her and saying 'I'm sorry I left' isn't exactly a great thing to do. She'll only hate me more," I reply, earning myself a sad look from him.

"Then get on your knees and fucking beg, Gabriel," he says, clapping me on the shoulder and squeezing it in an attempt to comfort me.

"That's exactly what I plan to do."

CHAPTER 13
Valentina

ADRIAN AND JAMES SPEND the rest of the day attending meetings and going to autograph sessions. Meanwhile, I spend my day with Lorenzo Mattia, discussing data and analyzing it. He's taken me under his wing, teaching me everything I need to know as a reserve driver during a race weekend. I'm having the time of my life, and so is Scarlette, who is still training under Adrian's race engineer, Chloe. They seem to be getting along well, and I can't help stealing glances at their interactions every chance I get.

"Are you enjoying yourself?" I ask her when we both have a moment to breathe. She gives me a big hug, but I catch a glimpse of her teary eyes and bright smile before her arms are around me.

"Thank you. This is everything I've ever dreamt of," Scarlette says, giving me one last squeeze before stepping back. Her happy smile brings one to my own lips. My eyes briefly skim over the scar running through her mouth, admiring the unique feature. Scarlette Roots is by far one of the most beautiful women I've ever laid eyes on.

"Thank you for joining my team. I can imagine your husband wasn't too happy seeing you leave his," I reply, and Scarlette flashes me a wicked grin.

"He was happy for me, and I took care of any upset feelings," she assures me with a suggestive wink. The corner of my mouth curls before I can stop it.

After we have lunch together, Lorenzo Mattia calls me back to Adrian's box, and Scarlette goes back to Chloe. I somehow manage to go the whole day without seeing Gabriel, which is as much of a relief as it is a dull ache in my chest. A bullet without a trigger to set it off. There are hundreds of Velocità Rossa team members, but he's nowhere to be seen.

Do I even want to see him? Yes, I want to see him. I want to kiss him, I want to be with him...

My anger for him hasn't subsided in the least, and my thoughts shouldn't linger on him or the way he used to make me feel. But... I miss everything about him. His laugh, his kindness, his lips. The way his heart was so big, I thought I'd never have to fear losing my place in it. I take a shaky breath and walk outside to get some fresh air. Lorenzo told me there is nothing left to go over today, which means I'm off until my brother or best friend is ready to go back to the hotel.

As soon as I am outside, I occupy myself by searching for things to do around the tents, like I used to do before I was offered the position of my dreams. It feels almost nostalgic to be back here, a feeling I revel in for once.

My phone rings, my brother's name flashing on my screen.

"Finally," I blurt out, and he chuckles into the phone.

"Miss me already? I know I'm awesome, but you are capable of spending an hour without me, aren't you?" he teases, and I find myself rolling my eyes with a slight smile.

"I meant finally I can go back to the hotel and sleep," I say, already making my way to his box.

"Sounds like excuses to me. You know you love me, don't even try to deny it," Adrian adds, and I decide to hang up, snickering to myself as I imagine his dropped jaw.

As soon as I get to Adrian's box, my heart shatters into a million more pieces. No matter how badly I wanted to avoid him, I should have known life wouldn't be so kind. Gabriel is standing next to his performance coach, Hector, and race engineer, Tomasso, discussing something as they point at the car. The uneven rhythm in my chest doesn't leave, it only worsens when his eyes catch mine. His gaze softens as he studies me, his shoulders slumping in defeat. Gabriel looks tired, as if he hasn't slept in days. His facial hair is longer and so is his hair, but he already let it grow out when we were dating. He knows I like it when his hair is medium length and curly, mostly because I used to love tugging on it when he kissed me everywhere. The reminder sends a wave of arousal through me that messes with my head.

How could I possibly be turned on and in pain while looking at him? Did my body not get the memo? He broke my heart!

My feet bring me to James' box instead, and I cover my mouth to hold in the sobs. I hope being with him puts enough distance between Gabriel and me. I can't stand seeing him. It physically hurts to look at him.

James and I spend the entire evening stuffing food into our mouths and watching movies together. I don't even notice when I drift off into a deep sleep with James' hand on my hip and my head on his leg.

CHAPTER 14

Valentina

MY HEART BEATS VIOLENTLY in my chest as Leonard and I prepare for our first meeting with investors. We've been having meetings about our driver academy, 'Kids Like Us', since I agreed to become his partner. My time test driving didn't impact that, we simply called over Zoom where he presented his PowerPoints to me. If there is something this man loves, it's analyzing data, making statistics, and then talking about them. He loves working.

James walks into the conference room, a small smile on his lips. A grin slips onto mine as I excuse myself from Leonard's side to stand with my best friend. Something strange lingers in his gaze, but I can't quite decide if it's pain, adoration, a secret he's holding inside, or a combination of all three of them.

"Can we talk?" he asks, and I tilt my head to the side, curious.

"Since when can't we?" I ask, a little scared of the answer. He looks away embarrassed, his hand rubbing along the length of his neck. I take a step closer. "However, I would appreciate it if we could talk now because I have a very important meeting in about ten minutes," I say, and his eyes go wide.

"Yeah, yes, of course." James looks directly into my eyes. "You look very beautiful, by the way," he adds, his gaze trailing over my sunflower-pattern summer dress.

"Thank you," I reply with a smile, feeling nerves creep in because of the way he looks at me. "What's wrong?" I ask, gesturing for him to sit down at the conference room table. He merely shakes his head, clearly reconsidering what he wants to say.

"Nothing. I merely wanted to tell you good luck, remind you what an incredible woman you are," he says and closes the distance between us. "I'm so proud of you."

His hands slip onto my neck, gliding upwards until he cups my cheeks in his hands. Heat immediately soars into them.

"Thank you," I reply, my voice coming out in a strange croak.

I love him and the affection he shows me, but, right now, I'm not sure what he's going to do. He's looking at me like he wants to kiss me and is holding me the same way, too, but there is no way he'd do so now. I'm still heartbroken and still don't reciprocate the feelings he once had. He doesn't have them anymore, though, *right*?

"James, what the hell are you doing?" I ask, watching the way his lips are coming closer and closer to my mouth. Part of me wants to push him away before he can do something stupid, but another part of me is paralyzed by fear.

"Nothing," is his only answer before he presses a kiss to my right cheek and steps away again. "I'll see you later," James says, strutting out of the room like he didn't just confuse me beyond measure.

"Here," I hear Leonard say from behind me, holding out a fly swatter. My fingers wrap around the handle as a half-smile tugs at the corner of my lips. "To swat all the men away," he teases, and I can't help myself. I burst into laughter because not only is this situation ridiculous, but I love that he feels comfortable enough with me to make jokes now.

"You saw all of that, didn't you?" I ask, and his handsome features pull into a comforting smile.

"Yeah," he replies. I sink onto one of the chairs, dropping my face in my hands. A groan slips past my lips, making him chuckle beside me. "I know I usually give you racing advice, but I want you to know if there's anything else you'd like to talk about, I'm here," Leonard adds, and I tilt my head to look at him.

"Gabriel and I broke up. James was in love with me and might still be considering what just happened, and I don't have the energy to deal with either heartbreak. Mine or my best friend's. All of my attention should be on being a reserve driver and opening the driver academy, but they keep distracting me. It's draining," I admit in a rant, and, before I know what hits me, Leonard's hand is on my shoulder, giving me comfort.

It wasn't my intention to dump all of this on him, but I feel strangely comfortable around him. Part of me is about to mention the note I received, too, but he'd only worry when there is clearly nothing to be worried about.

"Why is this happening?" I ask, causing him to sit down beside me and lean back in the chair.

"Gabriel is an idiot if he broke up with you because everyone can see how well you complete each other. James, on the other hand, doesn't see it that way. He only sees how in love he was or is with you, and now that you and Gabriel aren't together anymore, maybe he hopes you two could work."

I don't like that idea at all.

"Gabriel is an idiot," I agree after a while of silence, and Leonard frowns in response.

"I was an idiot for a long time too. Fortunately for me, I found my perfect equal in every way. We had very rough patches, but they pass, if you let them," he says and stands up again, holding out his hand for me. "Love like yours and Gabriel's doesn't fade, trust me. I've known my beautiful wife since I was eight, and every day I fall more in love, not less. When you meet your true life partner, nothing is too broken that you can't fix." He gives the underside of my chin a comforting nudge, and I smile past the tears in my eyes. "Now, let's go bag some investors," he adds, and I let him help me up before slipping on my game face.

People start filling the conference room, and I forget how to breathe. Everything slowly becomes reality when Leonard and I stand in front of twenty people and tell them about our school. Adrian walks in five minutes late with an apologetic smile and a bottle of water in his hand, grinning proudly at us.

There are a few who are not on board, but the majority of the people in the conference room tell us it's a fantastic idea, and that they'd like to invest in it. By the end of the meeting, I'm beyond happy, and Adrian hugs me as he tells me how proud he is of Leonard and me. Lorenzo, who has taken a personal interest in this academy, congratulates us on the successful meeting.

Leonard gives my arm a quick squeeze before rushing out of the room to get to a team meeting, leaving me alone as I gather all of my things. I attempt to make my way out of the small room when I see him.

It's been twelve hours since my gaze attached to his beautiful face, but this time, I want to stay and see what happens. It seems like he wants to talk to me, but I'm not sure he will. Before everything happened between us, I used to be able to predict how conversations would go. Now, after he and I had a talk I could have never foreseen, I can't anymore.

Gabriel takes a long step into the conference room, stopping my breathing. I hate how much I miss him, his face, his smell, his kisses, our conversations, and the affection he showed me. I miss reading together, watching him sketch, taking showers together, or anything else we used to do. I miss being with him.

"You look breathtaking," Gabriel says, and tears instantly fill my eyes. I fight them back with every ounce of strength I have. "Your meeting was fantastic, by the way, I was listening to the whole thing." I'm unable to move or say anything, no matter how badly I would like to yell at him. "Aren't you going to talk to me?" he asks after a couple of moments of silence pass between us.

"No," I simply reply because it's the only word my lips can form right now.

"How have you been?" That's when my mind regains all the strength it usually has.

"That's none of your business." I watch his face fall before I go back to gathering my things from the table. I have to get out of here. The dull ache in my chest is too unbearable.

"You're right," he mumbles and rubs the back of his neck with his hand. He looks uncomfortable, which is why I decide to turn to him, face him head-on, and confront him about what I need to say.

"Just leave me alone, Gabriel. I don't need this right now. My life is moving in the right direction, and I don't need the heartbreak you bring into it." I push past him, my shoulder pushing him out of the way, but he grabs my wrist to stop me from leaving.

"I'm so sorry, ma chérie. You have to believe me. Please. I've been a mess, but I'm better now. I'm better for you, and I'm so deeply sorry it took me this long, but I mean it. Let me prove it to you," he begs, and it takes everything out of me to ignore how right it feels to have his hand on my skin. To ignore how badly I want to wrap my arms around him and sob into his chest.

"Gabriel, please, let go of my wrist," I say, and he drops it right away, tears filling our eyes at the same time.

"What can I do to fix this? Please, baby, tell me," he begs again, and I let the tears fall down my face.

"I don't know," I reply honestly.

I rush out of the office while part of me wishes he'd chase after me.

CHAPTER 15
Valentina

A NOTE SHOWED UP at my hotel room this morning. For a moment, seeing it made my heart drop out of fear, but, after reading it, that same organ merely beat faster to pump pain through my veins.

I miss you, ma chérie

It's all it said, but it didn't have to say more for me to want to burn it until his words turned to ash. Instead, I folded the note and pressed it to my chest because, despite how angry I am, I miss him, too, and anything from him is better than nothing. It also means maybe there is a chance for us after all.

Now, I'm staring impatiently at the screens in my brother's box. He's currently in third place, battling Kyle Hughes, Grenzenlos driver, for second place. Gabriel is racing away in front, and my heart aches in my chest. It's his birthday today, and I should be celebrating with him, should have woken him up with the surprise I had planned. But no, I didn't even see him in person, nothing. All I've done is watch him on the small screens in the pit box.

My concentration shifts back to the race, and I watch James struggle in fifth place. I notice Eduardo is struggling in last place, and I'm sure he's going to retire soon. Cameron is doing well in sixth place, battling Leonard for it.

Gabriel finishes in first, Adrian comes in second, Kyle has a puncture and gets a DNF, James finishes in third, and I see Cameron finishes sixth, ahead of Leonard. I'm proud of all of my boys, sadly even Gabriel for some inexplicable reason. Seeing him on the podium, celebrating with James and Adrian makes me as happy as it rips a part of me to shreds.

I let out a small, inaudible sigh as someone's hand covers my arm. A short man with black hair waves me to the side. He seems familiar, but it takes me a brief moment of studying his face until realization dawns on me. I have no idea what he could possibly want, but I follow him toward the side anyway. My curiosity gets the best of me.

When we're far away from the cheering crowd, he turns to me with a worried look.

"Hello, Valentina, I'm Francesco, Gabriel's manager." I knew that, but I'm a little surprised he knows who I am. Gabriel never introduced us. "I'm sorry to ask, but what's going on?" he says, but I furrow my brows and shake my head. "Come on, Valentina, please do not lie to me. Gabriel has been off the entire weekend. Yes, he may have done well, but it scares me how much he is concentrating on racing. He started yelling at me, getting angry, and I didn't understand why. So, I'll ask again, what's going on?" I step back and process the information Francesco has given me. It takes me a minute until I'm finally ready to answer him.

"I don't think that's any of your business," I reply and cross my arms in front of my chest. I'm not in the mood for people to stick their noses into things that are none of their goddamn concern.

"It becomes my problem when my driver doesn't want to do anything to promote himself and the sport. All he wants to do is race, even though he is contractually bound to film one video per race week, just some kind of challenge." Francesco throws his hands into the air and looks at me with frustration. The middle-aged man is behaving unprofessionally, to say the least. His issues are not mine.

"Why are you talking to me? Why don't you ask Gabriel what his problem is?" I'm about to leave when Francesco makes me stop dead in my tracks.

"Because he's told me you are the love of his life, and you are the only one who knows him inside out. I tried talking to him, but he ignores me now." Without trying to hold it back, I let the tear fall from my left eye. I'm not even embarrassed to be crying in front of him, he's crossed a line that wasn't his to cross.

"Sorry, Francesco, I can't help you. I'm not who you think I am, I don't mean that much to Gabriel." The words taste wrong and foul in my mouth because I know he loves me. I know he left for me, no matter how fucked up it made everything.

I don't wait for Francesco to respond, instead, I simply walk back to the crowd. For the next hour or so, Lorenzo Mattia allows me to sit in on the post-race meeting while Adrian and James attend their interviews. We all go back to the hotel right after. We have to get up early to drive home. As nice as Le Castellet is, James and Adrian need to get back and rest, and so do I.

Being a reserve driver is more exhausting than I anticipated. I've been standing non-stop this whole weekend, processing more new information than I could keep up with, and on top of it all, Leonard and I were working on our project. Add my lingering heartbreak to the mix, and I'm ready to sleep for the next few weeks.

Before we go to sleep, Adrian vents to me about how annoyed he is because Gabriel seems to be faster at the moment, but he soon switches the topic when he realizes he brought up the wrong person. I know Gabriel's been faster, I have been watching him for months. But I have been studying both of them and their pace for a long time now.

It's why I have no idea who the hell is going to win the championship this season, but I'm dying to find out.

We leave at around eight in the morning. The guys are exhausted, a lot more so than I am. It's been a short night for them, but it's time we all get home. Evangelin and I are going to spend the day together as soon as I get back. She's texted me a couple of times, telling me she is very excited to see me. I miss my friend too. It's been almost a month since I've had some time for her, and it's weighing heavy on me.

Adrian, James, and I are walking toward the couches in the lobby of the hotel, waiting for the concierge to check us out. The last person I expected to see was Gabriel, leaning against the front desk, waiting for something. I'm staring at him for much longer than is appropriate, so his eyes find mine. He looks like he's in pain, making some shoot through my chest. It's not fair that I sympathize with him when he's the one who has caused me so much hurt. Yet, my heart flutters when he straightens out his back and walks toward me. I sit down hesitantly, but James and Adrian take the spaces next to mine, ensuring Gabriel won't be able to come anywhere near me without them being there for me.

"Valentina, can we talk?" Gabriel asks as soon as he is in front of me. His stubble makes my heart stop, his green-brown eyes make my head spin, and his curly hair makes me miss him.

"No," I reply, my voice firm and cold.

"Please," he begs, and I look at James, who is glaring at Gabriel. *Uh oh. Not good.*

"What would you possibly want to talk to me about?" I ask him, and he stares at me for a couple of seconds.

"About us." *No, no, no... no.* Not yet. I can't talk to him yet.

My wobbly legs bring me upright and right in front of him.

"You gave me this necklace and told me it symbolizes I'm your team, that I am as much your life as your career is, but we both know that's not true, so here." I take off the necklace with his car number on it, step forward, and place it around his neck. "It makes more sense for you to wear it anyway since you don't give a damn about me." I want to take it all back when I hear his heart shatter in his chest.

"I thought after all this time you would know you are truly and honestly the person I care the most about. You are the one person I love more than anything else in the world. I'm sorry I did this to us, that I brought so much hatred into your pure heart that you would say something like this, but I understand. I need you to be healthy and happy, and with me, you wouldn't have been, not until I found Sienna," he says softly. I bite my bottom lip to keep it from trembling.

"You don't know that. You ran before we ever had the chance to find out. You decided all of this by yourself when I loved you for years, through the hardest and easiest times. Through it all, I never stopped and I wouldn't have through this pain either," I say while his face contorts into an expression of pure pain.

"Loved?" he asks, and I realize what the hell I just said.

"Gabriel—" I start, but he merely shakes his head.

"I've lost you forever, haven't I?" *No, you haven't, but I'm so mad at you, I can't begin to think properly.* "I'm sorry, mon tournesol, so sorry. I will keep apologizing until you know that I'll never want anyone who isn't you. That I will fight for you until my last breath because you're everything to me." He takes an unsure step toward me, but I let him. I even let him take my hands in his because I miss him so much, I crave any contact from him. "I love you, and I'm so sorry I wasn't right for you," he adds, kissing the backsides of my hands before resting his cheek against my right one.

"You hurt me," I manage to croak out, and Gabriel nods against me.

"I know," he replies in French, sending tears to my eyes.

"I don't know how to forgive you," I admit then, causing him to suck in a sharp breath.

"I know," he repeats, and I blow out a heavy breath. "I just needed you to know all of this," he says and lets go, sending ice through my veins. "I'm sorry Francesco bothered you about me. It will never happen again." He stands awkwardly in front of me before giving me one last nod, as if he's acknowledging how broken we both are before leaving.

I sink onto the couch behind me, and James wraps his hand around mine.

"Jesus, my love, that was really intense," James says softly, and I lean my head on his shoulder. Adrian grabs my hand too, trying to comfort me. "What can I do?" James asks, and I look at him with my tear-stained face.

"Never leave me," I say.

"Unlike him, I'm never going to be able to leave you," he replies, and I flinch ever so slightly. *I completely forgot about his feelings. God, I'm so stupid!* But he simply kisses the top of my head, and I close my eyes before dropping my head back onto his shoulder.

"Yeah, me neither," Adrian chimes in, and I let out a small laugh.

"You don't have a choice, Adrian," I say and turn my head to look at him.

"True, that choice was taken away from me when I first held you in my arms. After that, I have sadly established this unbreakable bond between us," my brother says with a sigh, making me laugh. He smiles in response.

Adrian's smile is one of the most beautiful ones in the world. It's our mother's smile, I know because I've seen pictures of her. It used to frighten me how much I looked like her, how much Adrian and I did. Part of me is convinced that's the reason why Dad didn't spend time with us as we got older. We were a constant reminder of the love of his life.

"I love you," I tell my brother, and he grins at me.

"As you should," he says, and I nudge him in the ribs while a genuine laugh escapes my lips.

CHAPTER 16
Gabriel

MY BRUSH TRAILS OVER Valentina's face as I paint it on the canvas, hating for once that I'll never get her beautiful face just right. Her words replay in my head all day. She used the past tense of the word love, and it sent me spiraling into a constant state of panic. *Have her feelings for me really faded? Is she not in love with me anymore?* She's angry, as I knew she would be, but could she have fallen out of love with me because of it? Fuck, I hope not. I feel nauseous even considering that possibility.

Loved, loved, loved.

The same word repeats itself in my head a million times as I finish painting Valentina's lovely figure and face. I miss her with a fierceness I don't know what to do with. There has to be a way I can make it up to her, but it will take time. Time I'm more than willing to invest. Now that I'm not a mess on the floor of my room, battling my darkness, I'm in the right mindset to fight for Val, which starts with finishing this painting.

"A month! It took you a month to get your shit together. Why the hell are you not groveling at my sister's feet like you're supposed to?" Adrian barks as he storms into my room. I freeze mid-paint-stroke, confusing him. When his gaze settles on the canvas in front of me, his eyes widen before he immediately turns them away. "Oh God, is that my sister? Half-naked?" he asks, sounding nauseous. It almost makes me laugh. If I wasn't so upset, maybe I would.

"Yeah. I wanted to finish it for her," I explain and place the brush on the artist's easel. "Thought she might like it," I croak out, clearing my throat to get rid of the emotion building in it. "How did you even find me?" I ask to focus on something less emotional.

"I went to your old house first, but your aunts told me where to find you," he says, and I cross my arms in front of my chest as I study him.

A week ago, I moved into an apartment I would have considered my dream place a few months ago. Now, it's an empty space without any traces of Valentina. She would have made this a home, but that's probably never going to happen. If I'm being honest with myself, I never wanted to move in somewhere alone. I always wanted to move in with her. Somewhere, anywhere, it wouldn't have mattered. As long as Val would have been by my side, I'd have been happy.

"Gabriel, why did you ignore me for a month? Why didn't you let me help you?" Adrian asks, and I feel guiltier than before.

"Because I didn't even know how to help myself. How were you meant to figure out a way to comfort me when there was no way to make me feel better? My darkness would have rubbed off on you, and I didn't want that," I explain, and he gives me a knowing look. He gets it, he feels bad for me, but he's also still pissed.

"You know what families are for?" Adrian asks, dropping onto my bed and lifting a stray sock into the air with disgust on his face.

One thing I've learned about Adrian over the years is that he's very particular about cleanliness. His room doesn't have a speck of dust anywhere. His clothes are worn once and then washed so they always smell good. His hands are washed so often, I don't know how his skin isn't cracking from dryness. I already wash my hands more than the average person and struggle with that.

"It's just a sock. I'm pretty sure it's clean too," I reply, and Adrian raises both his brows at me suspiciously. "Can you just tell me whatever it is you'd like to?" I ask, and he flicks my sock into the hamper next to the bed.

"Families are for unconditional love. For comfort and strength. They help you get through the dark times, if you let them," he says, and I turn to look at my painting of Valentina. "But, you know what? I won't lecture you right now. You left, shit hit the fan, and now we have to figure out a way to get you back together. Okay?" My gaze shifts back to him, and I suck in a sharp breath.

"What do you think I've been doing for the last week?" He regards me with a suspicious look before his eyes accidentally shift back to the painting and he flinches.

His hand covers his eyes as he says, "Could you turn that around? I'm not exactly a fan of seeing my little sister like that." I spin it around, a pang of longing moving through me at the sight of Valentina's beauty. Maybe it's not the worst idea to take a break from looking at it, even if it pains me as much to stop as it does to keep staring.

"How the fuck did you even get into my apartment?" I ask, crossing my arms in front of my chest as I watch him lean back on my freshly made bed. His left hand raises into the air, revealing my aunts' set of keys dangling from his index finger.

"I told them I needed access to tell you to stop being a self-pitying idiot. After assuring them I'll use words not fists, they handed over the key, but I might still change my mind. It all depends on what you plan to do to earn Val's forgiveness. It better be fucking good because you messed up big time," he says, letting his arm drop and sitting upright again.

"I know."

"Like, in the concept of mistakes, if destroying the moon is a big mistake, you leaving my sister is a ginormous one. I don't know if she'll ever forgive you, but you need to start doing something about the pain you've caused. While I understand why you did it, now is the time for you to fix it. No more waiting, or you'll lose her forever," he says, forcing a stabbing sensation into my chest.

"You say that like I haven't lost her forever yet when she told me she *loved* me. She no longer does, and I'm not sure how to earn back her heart," I admit, feeling tears sting my eyes. I blink past them, but Adrian notices. He leans forward on the bed, his elbows on his knees as he flashes me a compassionate smile.

"It is not up to me to tell you how Val feels, but if I were you, I'd give hope a try. Because without it, you'll lose more than the love of your life. You'll lose faith in life itself, and then it's not worth living, is it?" Adrian asks, and I raise a suspicious eyebrow at him.

"For someone as pessimistic as you when it comes to love, you sure are a hopeless romantic in the form of a wise old man," I tease, causing Adrian to let out a laugh. It dies out quickly, leaving a serious expression on his face.

"For my family, I'd become anything they need me to be. I know what Val, James, Cameron, and Leonard need me to be. What do you need me to be for you, Gabriel?" he asks. I step in front of him, placing one hand on his shoulder.

"I need you to be who you are, Adrian, because you're a damn good friend, and I really need one of those right now."

CHAPTER 17
Valentina

A BOUQUET OF SUNFLOWERS showed up on my doorstep this morning. There was no note, nothing at all to let me know who sent it, except for the single daisy placed in the center. Gabriel is the only person apart from Adrian who knows daisies were my grandfather's favorite. I know he's trying to make amends, trying to piece together the shards of our broken hearts through these small gestures—by sending me flowers and sweet notes, even by talking to me—but I still don't know how to let go of my anger.

I placed the flowers in a vase and put them next to my bed, unable to toss them out when they're a reminder of how deeply he loves me.

"But don't you think the light pink will fit better with the kind of clothes I'm going to sell?" Evangelin asks, and I raise a contemplative eyebrow. She's decided to invest some money into the store and expand it. Since business is booming, she's got a surplus and high demand, the best conditions for expansion.

We have been trying to pick the right color to repaint the store with, but we haven't been able to decide whether to paint it a light blue, a pineapple yellow, or light pink.

"I really like the yellow, though," I tell her, and she looks at the colors again.

"Well, I think we can get rid of the blue. Maybe we can both get the color we want. The lower level could be yellow, and then the second level could be pink, or vice versa," she suggests, and I smile brightly at her.

"I'd love that, but it's your store, so it's your decision to make." Evangelin stares at the yellow color for a little while before she looks around her store with an intensity I've never seen before. A memory slips into her eyes as she takes in her surroundings.

"You know, Carlos won his first race driving in a yellow Formula One car, and pink has no significance in my life. Yellow makes more sense, and I know it will make him happy, too." I try to hide my smile, but it comes out anyway.

After we're done, Evangelin invites me to go to her house and have some dinner. She tells me to ask Adrian to join, which I do with a smile on my face. Naturally, he doesn't hesitate to see Carlos. Evangelin and I make some tortellini, and Carlos helps by making dessert. Adrian arrives right on time for dinner and falls into a casual conversation with the world champion. They talk about his weekend, and Adrian's face lights up when Carlos tells him how proud he is of him. Those are the best words he could have ever said to my brother, and I know Adrian is going to use them as motivation to get better and faster. During dinner, I can't help but stare at Carlos a little more than I should. I don't understand the anger I feel for him, but the worst part is, I also feel some degree of gratitude. It's fucking with my head. How can I be so upset with him for hurting Evangelin and at the same time grateful because his biggest mistake brought the man I love into my life?

Carlos catches my glare from across the table, giving me a compassionate smile. He knows I blame him, and I can't hold back the wave of emotions washing over me. I excuse myself before walking toward the door that opens to the veranda. I step outside to let fresh air fill my lungs.

"Valentina," I hear Carlos say from behind me.

I wipe away the tears so when I face him he doesn't see how upset I am. Obviously, it doesn't work, and more tears flow from my eyes. The small man takes a step in my direction, smiling like he's in pain.

"You know, child, I was in the same situation with Gabriel three weeks ago. He was very angry with me, he started yelling, blaming me for bringing all of this into his life, for creating a battle within himself, and, most importantly, for ruining what he had with you. It took a while of him screaming at me until he finally settled down and just cried."

I wrap my arms around myself and let out a sob of frustration. Hearing how much pain Gabriel is in does nothing to ease my own. Carlos puts his hand on my arm and rubs it up and down to comfort me.

"Gabriel said something to me, and I think it was meant for you more than it was for me." Carlos grabs hold of my arm instead of rubbing it to make sure my attention is on him. "'I love her more than anything in this world. It's meaningless without her. Racing, winning, being the king of the fucking Formula One world, all of it means nothing if she falls out of love with me.'"

He must have known how important it was if he remembered it exactly. I don't even realize when my knees give in, and I sink to the ground.

"I'm sorry I brought this pain into your life. I never expected when I slept with Sienna that so many years later there would be such extreme consequences," Carlos adds, and I sniffle in response. I'm sure he didn't, but I would never wish he hadn't done it because I need Gabriel, as much as I might not want to admit it.

"How can I forgive him? I know I want to, he's in as much pain as I am, but I don't know how to bring myself to forgive him for choosing something he didn't even know existed."

Carlos leads me to a bench I hadn't noticed at the side of their pool. The plants around us are blossoming, and the red and pink flowers complement the green bench. Focusing on them settles my heart into a normal beating rhythm.

"Forgiveness is a fickle thing, my dear. To this day, I don't understand how Evangelin forgave me. She shouldn't have if you ask me, but I'm the luckiest man because she's my world. I would be nothing without her. I think forgiveness is a decision we make. You have to want to forgive the person who's hurt you before the healing process can start," he says, and I wipe my eyes, a blush of embarrassment settling on my cheeks.

"I'm sorry I made a scene." Carlos gives me a small smile.

"I'm sorry I made your life this complicated," he replies. I let out a small laugh, and he joins in.

"No, you haven't. Well, you're a small part of it, but it's a collection of events that caused the situation I'm in," I say because as mad as I am, I don't want Carlos to take all of the blame. He doesn't deserve it.

We walk inside together before he settles down on the couch. Adrian slips out of the kitchen with Evangelin, laughing together about God-knows-what. My brother winks at me before he steps over to Carlos, so they can watch highlights from last week's race, discussing what Adrian did well and what he could improve.

"How are you feeling?" Evangelin asks, taking my hand in hers.

"I'm fine," I reply with a small smile, for once meaning my words. Evangelin tightens her hold to lead me to a small room that looks like an office. Shelves fill the walls, stacked with binders over binders.

"I want to show you something," she says, grabbing my attention.

She pulls a photo album from the shelf on the right, which reminds me of the one that stands in Gabriel's room. The one that holds books he bought for me. I shake my head and focus on the picture of Evangelin and Carlos on the front of the photo album. The sight brings a grin to my face.

After looking through the album for a minute or so, she stops and points at a picture of a young man who looks almost exactly like Gabriel. The only difference between them is the boy in the photo has a much longer and fuller beard than Gabriel and is quite a lot shorter.

"That was Carlos when he was twenty-five years old. Handsome, no?" Evangelin says with a bright smile. I let out a small laugh and stare at the picture. It is unbelievable how much Carlos and Gabriel look alike. "That's why I knew exactly who Gabriel was when I first saw you with him. It's hard not to see the resemblance." I run my fingers over the picture.

"This is unbelievable," I say, at first not noticing I switched to English, but when I do, Evangelin says something that makes my mouth drop.

"But fucking cool too," she replies in English, and we both laugh.

She shows me more pictures of Carlos and herself, and then we rejoin her husband and my brother in the living room. Adrian, my sunshine of a brother, wraps his arm around my shoulders and presses a kiss to my temple. He's been giving me more affection since Gabriel broke up with me. I think it's his way of reassuring me that, no matter what happens, he will always be here.

CHAPTER 18
Gabriel

VALENTINA BEING THE RESERVE and test driver of the Velocità Rossa team, my team, is proving to be more painful than I ever thought it would be. Every fiber of my being was ecstatic when I found out her dream was finally coming true. If anyone deserves a seat in Formula One, it's her. But I can't deny that constantly seeing her wherever I go during race weekends or when Lorenzo Mattia demands my presence in Maranello is torture. Torture and relief at the same time. It's a combination I never thought I'd feel, but it's impossible not to be in pain and sigh happily at the sight of her smiling at Adrian next to his F1 car.

"Hi," I manage to say after joining them, but Val merely shoots me a wary look before turning to check where Lorenzo is. He asked us all to be here because there's something important he'd like to discuss.

Adrian smacks my stomach and violently jerks his head in Val's direction, reminding me of the plan we made a few days ago. Beg. Beg for another chance. Beg for her forgiveness. Beg for the life I so desperately want: Valentina and me until the end of my time in this life.

"Ma chérie, I—" I'm cut off by Lorenzo Mattia's voice.

"Ah, thank you for coming, all of you," he says in Italian, and I can't help but smile a little when Val responds in the same language. A language I was teaching her.

"It's an honor to be here." She forces a smile, but it crumbles as soon as her eyes meet mine. I hate that. I hate how her gaze, which used to hold nothing but love and admiration for me, now reveals the pain I've caused. I hate myself.

"There is a new upgrade on the cars for the overtaking setting, and we need two drivers to try them out. Valentina will be one of them, and Gabriel will be the other. I want her to get used to these kinds of situations in case she has to step in at any point during the rest of the season," Lorenzo explains, causing my heart to beat faster and faster with every word.

Val and I are supposed to test out an overtaking upgrade, which means we'll be racing each other.

She's going to be driving Adrian's car.

I'll be in mine.

And, fuck, I'm absolutely terrified.

During races, I don't care who's beside, behind, or in front of me. My goal is to win, and I do anything I'm allowed to overtake or keep my place. It doesn't matter if it's Cameron, who I've been best friends with for years. It doesn't matter if it's Adrian, who I care about like he was my brother at this point. It wouldn't even matter if it was my actual brother. I don't hold back or get scared. I simply get the job done.

This? Racing against the love of my life, even if it's merely to test a new upgrade, has my veins pumping liquid fear to every part of my body. This is dangerous and while Valentina is a phenomenal racer, I don't trust us to make it out of this with both cars intact. Not while we're hurting. Not while she probably hates my guts. Not while I don't want to make her even more upset with me.

"Okay," is Valentina's only reply before she walks away, obviously ready to put on her fireproofs and racing suit. I chase after her without a moment's hesitation.

"Tournesol, we should talk," I say, fighting the urge to touch her elbow and spin her around. If she decides to talk to me, it should be because she wants to.

"Yeah, I agree." I can't lie, I wasn't expecting this response in a million years, but my heart flutters with hope as she spins around.

She looks ready to rip my head off, but I know my woman. Val won't yell at me now. She's going to focus entirely on the task Lorenzo has given us.

"Don't take it easy on me. We race like we're rivals, aggressively but respectfully. Got it?" she asks, and I give her a few, small nods.

I'd never dream of taking it easy on her. For one, she'd know and hate me for it. And also because I would never disrespect her, especially not like that. Underestimating her racing ability is a dick move, one too many people have pulled on her over the course of her life. I will never be one of those assholes.

"Can you take it easy on me, though?" I joke, hoping it will relieve some of the tension between us. When the corner of her mouth twitches, I can tell she's trying to fight off a smile. One I desperately crave.

"You're not allowed to make me laugh," she says, crossing her arms in front of her chest and pulling her lips into a thin line.

"Why?" I take a step toward her and almost smile from relief when Val doesn't take one backward in response. But she doesn't have to. Her next words are a barrier, keeping me from moving any closer.

"Because you don't deserve to hear my laughter right now."

Her words are a thousand cuts to my heart, but she's right. I don't deserve her laughter, her love, *her*. That'll never change how much I crave her, though.

"We have to get ready, Gabriel. Lorenzo is expecting us," she says and spins around.

"Tell me to stop begging for forgiveness, mon tournesol, and I will leave you be. Tell me there is no chance for us left, and I will respect your decision. Tell me to stop chasing you, and I will. But you have to tell me. You have to rob me of hope if no part of you wants me anymore, otherwise, I'm going to keep begging. I'll fight for you, for us. I'll never stop, chérie, not until my dying breath because there is nothing and no one more important to me than you," I rant, stopping her dead in her tracks. Her back is tensed, and I battle with the urge to wrap my arms around her. "Tell me to stop if you're done with me forever," I add and wait.

Nothing happens for a moment. Valentina stands in front of me, her short frame still tense from my words. My heart aches from palpitations, reminding me just how badly I want her to tell me we'll be okay in time. We'll figure it out. But she says nothing. The love of my life walks away without a single word, and I can't help the hope blooming in my chest.

She didn't tell me to stop.

And I'm going to keep fighting until she's back in my arms where I desperately need her.

My car feels heavier today. *I* feel heavier.

Maybe it's because Valentina is right behind me, using my slipstream to gain speed over me.

Maybe it's because I'm so proud of her that I can't quite contain the excitement bubbling inside of me.

Maybe it's because I won't take it easy on her, and my competitive side is fighting with my love for her.

Either way, it doesn't matter. Valentina made a specific request, and I have no intention of going against her wishes. So, I push myself harder, taking the corners wider to block her from overtaking me. The new update still has a few kinks in it, but once the team works them out, I think it will help us gain a lot of speed and prevent rapid tire degradation. For now, however, I have to focus on keeping the beautiful woman in my biggest rival's car from slipping past me. She's aggressive, too. Not in a dangerous way, but in a way that makes me grin from ear to ear. Valentina pushes me far, almost off the track. I manage to stay ahead of her as we go into the fourth corner again. We've been racing for seven laps already, so only three more to go until we're supposed to head back into the pits.

"Try setting four," Tomasso says into my earpiece when Val pushes me far again.

"Okay, but I don't think I can stay ahead of her for much longer. She's taking risks, and they're paying off," I say, but there is no other response from my race engineer. He's letting us figure it out for now.

We make it to the main straight with Valentina's car coming closer and closer until she swerves to the side to be next to me. We're on the same level, but she brakes later than me, again taking a risk that works because she's ahead now. She races by me, and I'm so mesmerized by that beautiful move she pulled, I almost forget I'm supposed to be chasing her down now.

"Fuck," I curse, but the smile on my lips betrays how I truly feel.

I press down on the throttle, trying to close the distance between us, but it's no use. Valentina is pushing the car in a way I never could and, honestly, I'm too mesmerized to do more than watch her flick dirt onto my visor like I knew she would one day. Part of me still can't process it's already happening now. It gives me the urge to wiggle in my seat from pride and happiness.

At least until I remember I don't deserve to share her success anymore.

"Gabriel? What's happening?" Tomasso says, and I realize I've slowed down a lot from the realization.

Tears sting my eyes while I drive the car back to the pits, jump out of it, and rush to the private room reserved only for me. Hector tries to make it inside, but I've locked the door. My broken heart is burning in my chest as I sink to the floor, panic numbing my body.

Pain and grief are interesting sensations. One tells me I'm alive and that's why I'm experiencing it. The other has me so numb, I might as well be dead.

So, all I can do is cling to the pain of the broken heart I'm responsible for.

CHAPTER 19
Valentina

THE BABY'S ROOM LOOKS incredible. James outdid himself. The walls are painted a pastel orange, Annie's favorite according to him. The crib he chose is plain white, but the mobile hung over it makes up for the simplicity. It has stars attached to it in all kinds of colors. There are about fifty toys in the small room, and the changing table is the same color as the crib, yet the colorful blanket on it, again, makes up for it. The carpet on the ground barely covers the wooden floor of the room, but it looks soft and comfortable. So comfortable I walk over to it and let my bare feet feel how smooth it is.

James and Mia walk into the room with two boxes of diapers, and I smile at them.

"So, what do you think?" my best friend asks, his lips pulled into a serious line.

"I think it's beautiful. Damian is going to love spending time at your place." James wraps his arm around my shoulders as we admire the room.

"I hope so. Although, it will be a while until he can sleep over, but when he can, the room is ready for him." I wrap my arm around his waist and rest it on his hip.

James and I have been spending a lot of time together recently, but I've also been spending a lot of time with Annabel. We're becoming good friends, and with every day she is overdue, she seems to want to spend more time with me. It's probably because she likes my cooking. Annie is getting even more irritated and uncomfortable. Every hour she screams at her stomach, saying 'I'm going to rip you out by your beautiful, tiny feet.' I've also not seen Annabel's sister since that one day at their house. Apparently, *Harlow* flew to England to visit their parents.

James' phone vibrates in his pocket, and since I'm standing so close to him, it vibrates against my leg, too, making me giggle.

"It's my phone," he defends, but I hadn't even thought about it like that. I laugh even harder. "'Ello, Annie," he says into his phone with his usual thick English accent, and I let go of his waist so he can move around the room, something he always does when he is on the phone. "Okay, I'll do that. See you later. Bye." I stare at him for a couple of seconds, and he smirks at me. "What's up, darling?" *There it is.* He always calls me every sweet pet name in the book, but he never calls other girls by anything other than their names. I know why. James has never been in love with anyone else, only me...

"Nothing," I say and walk over to the crib. "I can't believe there is going to be a tiny human lying in this, a tiny human Annabel grew in her stomach... Jesus, that's really strange to think about." He chuckles and steps next to me.

"Tell me about it."

Something inside of me wants to scream because I'm getting impatient to meet the little guy. It's interesting to see how much I've grown to love this child that isn't even born yet. I'm impatiently waiting to meet him. I want to be an aunt... *am I even going to be considered his aunt?*

"James, have you ever thought about what I will be to the child?" I ask, rubbing my arm uncomfortably. A frown appears on his face, but it leaves soon enough.

"You'll probably be his favourite aunt, the person he goes to when Mum and Dad are being jerks, the one he goes to for advice he's uncomfortable asking me or Annie. No matter how much you tell your child you want them to be comfortable talking to you about everything, there will be things he rather wants to talk to his aunt about." I'm about to cry when he points at me and scowls. "No, don't fucking cry, you're going to make me cry." I swallow down the tears but the ones that were already in my eyes fall down my cheeks. "Val," he complains but hugs me anyway.

"I can't help it."

"Come on, I gotta go over to Annie's, and you're coming with me. She said she doesn't want me to come unless you're there. However, I feel inclined to tell you

I don't know if Harlow is going to be there. I know she's back from England, but I'm not sure if she's at the house."

"I'm not going," I say, and he frowns at me. Just the slight chance of seeing her makes my stomach turn upside down. It's not Harlow's fault. She's probably a wonderful person, but seeing her isn't exactly a pleasant experience.

"Please, darling. Annie asked for you, and if I don't bring you, she's going to stare at me with that upset frown where her eyebrow twitches uncontrollably."

Oh, he already knows her different frowns? Interesting.

I smile at that new information and assure him I will come.

While James changes into something that isn't covered with paint, I let my mind roam to Gabriel. My thoughts are constantly consumed by him, what he's doing, whether or not he found the family he is looking for, or even if he has smiled recently. It's absurd I haven't been able to bring myself to stop loving him.

Then again, how is a person supposed to stop loving their other half?

My heart is pounding against my ribcage and without thinking, I take James' hand for comfort. The possibility of seeing Harlow makes me nervous, probably more nervous than I have been in a while.

"Darling," James says and pulls me back into reality. "I know seeing Harlow is painful, but you'll never move on if you don't face your fear. You are the one who taught me that, remember?" I roll my eyes before I take a deep breath.

"Yeah, yeah, blah, blah, blah," I mutter, and James chuckles.

He knocks on Annie's door, and I forget how to breathe when Harlow answers it. Her smile fades when she sees me, making things worse. She doesn't want me to be here either. Harlow greets James, then me vaguely before stepping aside so we can walk inside. The smell of freshly baked cookies fills my nose combined with... *mahogany?* It almost smells like Gabriel's home when he bakes. It's highly unsettling...

Harlow bumps her shoulder against mine, and, even though she apologizes, I have a feeling she did it on purpose. *So, she does know who I am?* God, I'm reading into things again. Harlow probably just accidentally bumped into me and stopped smiling because she doesn't want any people around. Annabel, on the other hand, starts smiling brightly when she sees James and me.

"Valentina," she squeals when I hug her. "Thank you for coming. It means a lot." Tears flood her eyes, and she starts waving her hand in front of her face as if it would stop them from falling from her eyes.

"How are those mood swings treating you?" James asks her, and she growls at him.

"Shut up. You try to carry this baby and deal with all of the hormones at the same time. My ankles are swollen, my back hurts, and I can't go one fucking hour without having to pee."

Oh... Annabel is really angry. I've never seen her like this, which is most likely why she catches herself and mumbles an apology. I don't think she owes him one, and neither does my best friend. James sits down on the couch next to her and takes her hand in his. She leans her head against his shoulder, and I try my best not to smirk. This is all I want for him. A woman who loves him. I don't know if she is in love with James but Annabel has hinted at it for a couple of weeks now.

Annie, James, and I spent the rest of the day playing games and trying different methods to get the baby out of her. The complaining of wanting the baby out has gotten more frequent, and every time Annabel looks at her stomach and says the infamous sentence, 'I'm going to rip you out by your beautiful, tiny feet', I feel worse for her. I can't even begin to imagine how painful, weird, and awful it must be for her to still carry the baby that's a week over the due date.

The false labor has been happening a lot, too, causing her even more distress. James and I try all we can to help the baby on his way. Naturally, he is also worried she's going to go into labor when he's racing this weekend, but there is nothing he can do about it. Damian is going to come whenever he wants to, even though we took an hour-long walk, we ate the spiciest food I have ever eaten—it burned everything inside of me and it's going to continue to burn everything for the next three days—and I made Annie a special tea she bought.

The rest of the afternoon passes in a blur, and James drops me off at my place in time for dinner with Adrian. I furrow my eyebrows when I see a gigantic package in front of my door.

"What's that?" he asks, and I shrug before I turn around and look into his eyes.

"I have no idea."

I say goodbye before getting out of the car and walking toward the abnormally sized package.

With every step that I take, my heart beats faster.

With every step that I take, I am surer and surer what it is.

With every step that I take, I want to run as far away as possible.

Do I have it in me to open it?

CHAPTER 20
Valentina

By the time I reach my room, my arms feel like they're going to fall off. The canvas is heavy, but I am also out of breath because I'm nervous about removing the cover. I can't believe he finished it. My fingers poke through the thin paper, and I rip it off the canvas. I gasp when I see myself.

Gabriel made me look so beautiful. Every stretch mark on my body is defined on the canvas, he made my eyes sparkle somehow with the love I only ever felt for him, and my hair looks incredible, every curl drawn with precision and care. I lean it against my bed and let it rest there as tears run down my cheek. My eyes are still concentrating on the flawless piece of art, but I eventually have to look away when the pain overwhelms me.

It's been over a month since Gabriel broke up with me, but nothing stops the gut-wrenching pain that continues to linger in my chest. No matter how much I distract myself, no matter how much I focus on something else, my thoughts always come back to the guy who chose to leave me.

How dare he send me this now?

How dare he hurt me like this again?

Did he mean to hurt me with this?

I can't know what his intentions are, but I look inside the paper to find any clue, to find a note or a letter. There's one attached to the back of the painting, stealing my breath. My fingers are shaking as I pull it off the back and flip it around. His beautiful handwriting is on the front in the shape of my name, and I choke on my own breath.

Ma Chérie,

The first thing I am going to tell you now is I love you. You may not believe me because you think I left because I didn't love you anymore, but that's not true. You are the person I love the most in the whole world, and I had to leave to make sure you wouldn't hate me. I have lost people and watched them die and disappear right in front of my eyes. Ever since I was little, I always had hopes and dreams of one day having my own family. I hold this dream very close to my heart... It gives me hope, it brings me happiness, and it helps me when I feel sad. So, you understand how important that dream is to me. My career is too, I probably hold it just as close as the other dream, but I am living this one already. Racing in Formula One is my reality while having my own family seems so far away. And I am okay with that, at least I used to be because you gave me hope this would also become a reality. I told you you're my future, I told you how I see us in ten years, but now, I've lost it all. I found my grandma, and it helped me to keep from spiraling further into my grief, but I'd rather be in darkness with you than in any promise of light without you. I'm sorry I had to leave to figure it out. I'm so sorry.

This painting is for you, ma chérie. I finished it for you. It feels wrong for me to keep this when I was the one you offered yourself to, and I hurt you. You were vulnerable with me, and you let me in. I'm sorry I broke us apart. You have no idea how many tears I've shed while I finished painting you. All I wanted was to feel my arms wrapped around you again. During last week's race, all I kept seeing in my head was you. I needed to win for you. I needed to push myself to be the best for you, which is ridiculous because you don't even want me anymore. Not that I don't understand, because I do. I deserve all your hate and anger.

You're the only woman I have ever been in love with, and you will forever be the only one. You're my dream. I'm the biggest idiot to ever walk on this planet, and we both know it. If I was smart, I would have never let you go in the first place. Yet, I was foolish enough to believe maybe you could forgive me more easily for this than if I tore you down into the darkness with me. I'm so sorry I chose to chase something that wasn't you, I'm sorry I left you when I know I'm not the first to do so. I'm sorry I was foolish enough to believe leaving you would be better for you than sticking around and doing my best. But most importantly, I'm sorry because sorry will never be enough to make up for what I've done.

You're my everything, and I will chase your forgiveness until the day you tell me to stop.

I put the necklace into the envelope, hoping you will take it back and put it around that beautiful neck of yours, where it belongs. You're my life, you should have it. If you wear the necklace for the race on Sunday, I know you haven't decided to never speak to me again, if you don't, I'll know I have to try a thousand times harder to make you mine again. Hopefully, this letter already proves to you I love you, if not let me make it crystal clear.

I love you, I love you.

It will forever only be you.

Please, ma chérie, forgive me.

Only yours,

Gabriel

I hate him for writing this letter, for making me believe every single word written on these pages, and I most especially hate him for making me think I can forgive him. Somewhere halfway through this letter, I let go of my anger toward him, let myself believe he truly means it.

Why would he go through all of this trouble if he didn't? Why would he write those three meaningful words over a hundred times if he didn't mean them every single time?

He would have just moved on, but he obviously hasn't. He finished creating my painting, wrote me the longest letter I have ever received from anyone, and gave me back the necklace that is more meaningful than any piece of jewelry I have ever owned.

I twist the infinity ring on my finger from side to side, hoping it will tell me what I'm supposed to do now. My head is telling me to take it slow and not rush back into something with Gabriel, but my heart is telling me to drive my ass to his house, kiss him passionately, and lie in his arms until sunrise. But this time, I know I have to listen to my head. If I don't, it's only going to end up getting worse. Maybe Gabriel and I just need to spend a little more time apart... maybe we need to start over... I have no idea what the right move is.

What the hell am I going to do?

CHAPTER 21

Gabriel

TODAY IS ONE OF the worst days for Valentina of the year. Today is the anniversary of her grandfather's passing. So, the first thing I did when I woke up was go to his grave, clean away all the dirt and moss, and place a bouquet of daisies in the flower holder beside it. Knowing Val, she'll go to visit it today, so I wanted everything to look nice for her.

Valentina also has her little things she does to honor the person who passed, but I didn't get those for her. She told me she likes to get their favorite foods and drinks herself because it makes her feel connected to them again. Instead, I asked Adrian to give her an extra long hug from me when they're at the graveyard tonight, watching the sunset. God, even thinking about it makes me long to be near her, spend the day with her so I can comfort her myself. I know it's my own fault, *I know*. It doesn't make it any easier.

To occupy my mind, I called Hector and scheduled an extra-long workout session. I've been improving a lot recently, getting stronger, faster, and more endurance, but it's also why my body aches with pain with every step I take. It's a welcome distraction, and Hector seems proud of me for putting my career first. I am, after all, the leader of the Drivers' Championship, and there are only six races left this season.

Adrian and I are head to head. A lot can still happen, but I'm training to win. Every hour I have available—which means almost all hours now that Valentina and I are broken up—I spend with Hector to improve my times. I train in the simulator, in the gym, and outside where I go running. Anywhere I can. And always when it comes to the point where I have to push myself to keep going, I hear Val's voice.

"You can give up if you want, you can throw it all away and pretend your dream never existed, but if you clench your teeth, scream at the top of your lungs, and go through with it, you will end up more than happy with yourself."

She told me her grandfather used to say those exact words to her, and they're all I hear nowadays. When I'm racing or training, it's always this phrase that keeps me going. My dream is to be the World Champion. A World Champion married to the first female World Champion in the history of our sport. A dream I may have lost forever.

Fuck.

"Gabriel," Hector says, dragging me out of my thoughts. "That's enough." He takes the weights out of my hands, and I realize I've been doing too many reps without a single break in between them. My arms suddenly feel like bricks.

"Sorry," I mutter and run my hands through my hair, tugging on the roots out of frustration.

"I know you want to push yourself but remember your limits. Sometimes, it's good to listen to your body."

My performance coach stands in front of me with his arms crossed in front of his chest. This bond between performance coach and athlete is incomparable to anything else. I trust him with all my pre-race procedures, making sure I have everything I need, and in general, taking care of me while we train to improve my performance. He's also a good friend at times, making me laugh when I least feel like it. On the other hand, he can be a real piece of work sometimes and quite overbearing. He means well, but it makes me feel like my entire life revolves around racing, and a lot of it does. The problem arises when it impacts my time with the people I love.

"I know, but I'm fine," I lie, attempting to pick up the weights again. Hector stops me as he places both hands on my shoulders and shakes his head.

"No, you're not, but, lucky for you, backup should be here right about—" He doesn't get the chance to finish the sentence.

"G'day, boys. Someone called for a pick me up, so here I am," my best friend says as he struts toward me wearing sunglasses that are way too big for his face and a shirt with my face on it. I can't help but burst into laughter at the sight.

"Where the hell did you get that?" I ask, wiping away the tears of laughter. Cameron gives me a disappointed look.

"Please, I had this custom-made, and all eyes have been on me today. Thanks to you and that face of yours, pretty boy," he explains and drops onto the bench where I'm sitting with a smug smile. "Now, what can we do to cheer you up?" he asks, and I'm evil for what pops into my head.

Truly evil, but if he's offering...

"Anything I want?" I ask, turning my head to him with a sad expression all over my face.

Cameron places his hand on my shoulder before replying, "Anything." Fear crosses his face when a mischievous smile curls my lips.

"I think you should get my moon tattoo matching on your ass." All the teasing is what drives me to say this, but he barks out a burst of laughter in response.

"Ah, fuck, why'd I agree to anything?" He keeps laughing until he slaps his thigh and stands up. "Fine. Let's go. I did promise you we'd get it matching back then." I can't believe he truly means it, but he's already through the door before I can ask him if he's kidding.

We end up going to the best tattoo parlor in Monaco, but I tell Cameron to get whatever he wants. He chooses to get a rose along the length of his side. While he's getting tattooed, I look through the designs available, my heart lurching at the sight of a sunflower and sun combined in a single drawing. I swallow hard, tracing the delicate lines with a lump in my throat. Getting this tattoo would be impulsive. If Valentina and I don't get back together, this will be a constant reminder of everything I've lost. But also a reminder of everything I felt, had, and got to experience.

My phone rings while I contemplate getting this design tattooed on my skin for the rest of my life.

Valentina: Thank you for today.

I get the tattoo with a smile on my face.

CHAPTER 22
Valentina

Gabriel Matteo Biancheri. I want to kiss him and kick him and scream at him because I love him so much while being beyond mad at him. He keeps doing these incredibly sweet things, even sending me new drawings daily, and I can't help the way my anger fades more and more with each gesture. Part of me is still stuck on what happened at the track when we were supposed to race, but after I overtook him, Gabriel stopped the session and disappeared. Another part is stuck on the way he cleaned up my grandfather's grave to ensure it would be perfect for me a few days ago. All parts of me are stuck on *him*. On the feelings my heart still harbors for him, no matter how much time passes or how upset I am.

I fucking hate feeling this way. Lost, conflicted, and angry with him and myself. He wants me back, and I should be able to forgive him. He's shown me how much I mean to him, but I can't move on from what happened so easily.

Gabriel left in the same way my mother did.

But he came back.

And he only disappeared because he spiraled into darkness he didn't want to pull me into.

I have no idea what I'm going to do.

"Okay, today is about endurance. Are you ready?" Daniel, Adrian's performance coach asks, and I smile up at the Irish man. He has brown hair and brown eyes, is tall and broad, and has a gorgeous smile. I've always found him quite attractive, but he seems unaware of his looks.

"I'm so ready. I can't believe we've never done this before," I say mostly to my brother, who is currently stretching to show off his muscular chest to a group of girls who are ogling him. He flashes them a knowing, cocky smile, and I raise both my eyebrows at him. "Do you have an off-button for your flirting setting?" I ask, bringing my brother's attention to me. He grins like he doesn't have a single worry in the world.

"Not really, especially not when beautiful women are watching me," he replies with a simple shrug, bending forward to "stretch" but in reality showing off his ass. I roll my eyes and suppress a laugh because, I must admit, Adrian's impressively good at making people fall at his feet with his charm and good looks.

"How about a friendly competition to get your head to focus on the task?" Daniel says, and I shift my attention to him. His arms are crossed in front of his broad chest as he watches my brother and waits for a response. Adrian raises a single brow at his performance coach.

"What competition?" He's intrigued. I can hear it in his voice and read it in his face. Us Romanas are too competitive to pass up on this kind of opportunity.

"Whoever manages to swim twenty laps first wins me as their performance coach next year," Daniel says, causing my mouth to drop so far to the floor that I have to be careful not to step on it.

"You can't do that!" Adrian protests, but Daniel merely shrugs. He's trying his best to contain a laugh, I can tell.

"Actually, I can. My contract ends next year, and we haven't renewed it yet." If I didn't know better, I'd think Adrian might start crying.

"Are you unhappy with me?"

"Very much, yes," Daniel teases, so my brother takes a step closer, poking his coach in the shoulder.

"Well, too bad. You're my performance coach, *my friend*. I'll win and you'll have to stay with me." Adrian jumps into the pool two seconds later.

Daniel and I chuckle before the tall man lifts and throws me into the water. Adrian is howling with laughter when I resurface, and I can't help but grin as I flip off an amused Daniel. This is exactly what I needed. A day with my brother to enjoy myself and forget about all the worries in my life. To forget about Gabriel, even if it's impossible. At least consciously I can suppress thoughts of him.

"On three!" Daniel starts.

Adrian turns to me and mouths 'You're gonna lose'.

"One."

I smile as I get ready to beat him in this endurance test.

"Two."

My heart races with a familiar sense of anticipation.

"Three."

Adrian and I push off the pool wall at the same time, but I take my time. It's not always about who is the fastest. Endurance means taking your time, reserving your energy so you'll make it to the end. Yes, in this challenge, it's about who'll come in first, but Adrian is going so fast that he'll need a break soon. I won't need a break. I'm pacing myself well, something that's very important in Formula One when it comes to tire management too.

Halfway through, my brother takes his predicted break. I catch up with him until we're both only a couple of laps away from the twenty-lap goal.

"What lap are you on?" my brother screams breathlessly, forcing a giggle out of me.

"19," I call back, and he lets out a squeal of panic.

He ends up overtaking me right before the end, but I'm breathing too hard to care. This was fucking exhausting. My muscles are burning, protesting any further movement. Usually, we do endurance in the mornings, but today we decided to do it after a two-hour simulator session and some weight training. Swimming is a fun, new alternative to the running we normally do, and I can tell Adrian enjoyed it too by the way he's floating in the water at the moment. A smile is on his lips, one of happiness and content, most likely because he won.

"Alright, enough for the day, you two. You need your energy for tomorrow's workout session," Daniel says, and, for the first time in my life, I feel like groaning at the mention of training. I'm too tired.

My hands push me up on the rim of the pool, my body heavy and sore as it slumps on its back. Daniel stands over me with furrowed brows and a small grin, extending one of his hands to help me up. I take it gratefully, letting him pull me onto wobbly legs.

"Here, it vibrated while you were in the pool," he says, handing me my phone.

My heart sinks as I read the message on my screen.

Unknown number: No matter how hard you train, you will never be good enough. Stop now before your arrogance gets you killed.

What the fuck is happening?

CHAPTER 23
Valentina

I HAVEN'T TOLD MY brother about the two anonymous messages I've received. I haven't told anyone. The person hasn't outright threatened me, so I don't feel the need to worry him, even when my mind has been stuck on all the stupid W's you learn about in school.

Who is doing this?

Why are they bothering me?

What do they want?

Where am I safe from this harassment if not when I'm racing my car... or even at home on my phone?

When is it going to stop?

Paranoia has me checking my shoulder everywhere I go. In the grocery store. At the gym. At *Rush*. No one's watching me, but I can't help feeling as if someone were anyway. I'm so on edge, even Envangelin noticed something was off yesterday. All I could do was pretend I was nervous about the race weekend.

I blocked the number that contacted me, but what's to stop this person from messaging me on different apps? At least they don't know where I live, or I hope they don't, so they'll leave me alone in my home. It's what I keep telling myself to keep from panicking more than I already am. Being hated in this sport is nothing new, so neither is getting hate messages. When I was younger and still racing in Formula Three, people cyberbullied me and one person even wished I'd die in horrible crashes. I've been playing with the thought that it's the same person from before, but it doesn't explain how they'd have access to Adrian's F1 car. Someone from my brother's team put the note in it, but I suppose they could have been bribed to do it.

A groan leaves me at the realization of knowing nothing but needing to know everything to settle my racing mind. Instead, I de-install all of my social media apps and stare at my phone screen, preparing myself for all the things I have to do today.

After I book an appointment with my gynecologist to get an IUD—hoping it will help with my painful periods—I call back Annabel. She tells me to come over, at least that's what I think she is saying. It's hard to decipher since she's out of breath and her words barely make any sense. All I understand is something about her wanting me to come over and then something about dancing.

Half an hour later, I knock on Annie's door, and she screams for me to come inside.

"Oh, good, come join me. I'm dancing to get this little piece of... beautiful human out of me." I let out a short laugh, and she smiles at me. "I've seen a lot of videos, so maybe he'll want to come out if I continue to bounce like a ping-pong ball," she says, and I laugh again before joining her in the middle of her living room.

I do my best to not start crying with laughter when Annie starts dancing. She's bouncing up and down, just like she said she was, and I follow her lead. After a while of laughing, crying, and choking on our own breath, we sit down on the couch.

We relax for a little longer while Annie informs me she was at her doctor's office today to check on Damian. Even though he's overdue, everything looks perfect, sending a wave of happiness through me. All I want is for the baby to come out healthy and happy, and for Annie to feel the same way, although I know she isn't right now. She is in pain, impatient, stressed, and struggling to get the baby out when nothing is working.

"I'm so uncomfortable, and I don't know what to do with myself. This baby needs to get out," she growls, and I take her hand to comfort her.

"He will, don't worry, but until then, let's go take a walk." I get up from the sofa and hold out my hands for her, waiting until she slides hers in mine.

The hot air envelops my body as soon as we step outside. Sweat starts dripping down my back while the sun burns my skin.

Annie and I walk for a while when I hear an odd howling noise coming from somewhere near the rocks next to us. Naturally, my curiosity gets the better of me, and I move toward where I think the sound is coming from without thinking.

"What is it?" Annabel asks while I investigate.

The howl continues, my eyes roaming the ground until I find a beautiful puppy. It looks like a German Shepherd mixed with a Husky, terrified and hiding behind one of the rocks. It looks at me with its bright blue eyes, and I hold my hand out so it can sniff it. He almost jumps into my arms when I try to pick him up, clearly desperate for anyone to help him.

"How long have you been out here?" I whisper, and he starts wagging his tail when I hold him against my chest. My heart breaks when he cries as he tries to get closer to me.

"Oh, he's so small," Annie says, and I walk closer to her so she can see him, but he only nuzzles against me when I bring him near Annie. "Well, I guess he only wants you," she says with a laugh. I look into the puppy's eyes again, the little creature trembling because of how frightened he is. His ribs are standing out, his nose feels dry, and his eyes are half-closed now.

"We have to go to your place. He needs some food and water, Annie."

She nods, and we walk back as fast as we can. The puppy is sleeping in my arms by the time we arrive back at Annie's house, but sadly, Harlow is back, too. When she sees me and the dog walk through the door with her sister, she scrunches her nose in disgust and frowns.

"Take that dog and leave." I raise my eyebrows and look at Annie for help.

"He needs food and water, Harlow. They're staying until he's had both."

The other sister groans and moves off the couch before stepping toward her room and slamming her bedroom door. Annabel rolls her eyes. The little fellow is still sleeping in my arms when I fill some water for him and Annabel smashes up some plain crackers, which she mixes with some vanilla yogurt. When he smells the food, his eyes fly open, and I put him down so he can eat.

I don't know who put this little guy on the street, but it makes me so sad. I wonder what kind of horrible fucking human is capable of leaving behind an innocent creature to fend for itself. This dog was about to die if I hadn't found him, I'm sure of it. I study him for a few minutes, noticing all the different colors he has. He has a white line drawn from the top of his head down to his snout where it paints a big circle all around his nose. His chest is also completely white while the rest of his fur is a mix of brown, black, and grey. His paws are white and his legs are the same combination of colors as most of his fur. Although they seem faded, it's probably the dirt from being outside.

"So, what are you going to do with him?" Annabel asks, and I shrug.

The little guy struts toward me when he is done with his food and lies down in my lap. I can't explain this bond he's established with me, but I feel honored. He seems to feel safe with me, which is enough to bring tears to my eyes.

"I'm going to take him to the vet, get him checked out, and then, I don't know." I look at the puppy again to find him sleeping.

I say goodbye to Annie and do exactly what I told her I would do. I'm going to make sure he gets better.

The vet informs me the puppy doesn't have a chip that could tie him back to anyone. He tells me he is in serious need of more food and water. After a few more tests, the vet determines he's about three months old. The nameless puppy doesn't seem sure of anyone but me, so I stay close to him as much as I can. Two hours later, I finally get to take him home.

Apparently, the puppy has something called leptospirosis, a bacterial infection that travels through the bloodstream, but luckily not a severe case of it so a round of antibiotics will cure him in no time. I pay the bill, more than I have ever paid at a doctor's office, but as long as the little guy gets to feel better and gets to be healthier, it's worth it.

I go to the local pet store and buy everything he could possibly need. Food, a leash, a harness, treats, some toys, a crate where he is going to sleep, pee pads, and some shampoo so I can wash him when we get home. My mind is in protection mode, even if keeping him seems like an impossible want at this point in my life. All I want is to make sure this dog is safe from getting hurt again.

The little guy is sleeping peacefully in the passenger seat as we make it home. He opens his eyes slowly, and I watch his mouth attempting a big yawn. It may be the sweetest thing I have ever seen in my life.

After a long bath, his fur looks spotless and the colors are finally richer. I'm also sure I've finally decided on a name for the sweet boy, but I want to talk to Adrian before making any decisions. After all, this is also his home. The impatience for him to get home has me bouncing my leg up and down. Adrian texts me he'll be home soon, but it does nothing to ease this uncomfortable feeling in my chest. I'll do everything I can in my power to convince my brother to keep him because I won't trust another person with his safety.

The puppy and I cuddle while I dry his fur, both of us waiting for Adrian. He seems a lot more energetic now since he's had more food and water.

"Val, what did you want to—" He cuts off when he sees the puppy lying in my lap on the floor. "Who is this?" he asks in the highest voice I've ever heard him use. His features soften, and my brother drops down on the floor. Slowly and carefully, he scoots closer to the dog who moves further away from him.

"He's very distrusting, don't take it personally," I assure my brother, and he nods with a defeated look on his face. I tell Adrian where I found him, that I took him to the vet and anything else he might want to know about the little guy.

"A stray puppy? Here in Monaco?" I shrug and pet the puppy's head.

"I can't explain it either. I'm guessing someone brought him here from somewhere else and just left him to die on the side of the street." We both stare down at the nameless dog.

"You know dogs are a lot of work, Val. We'll be traveling, so he'd have to stay with someone else while we're gone. But if you want to keep him, I'm going to support you as much as I can. I'm going to help you." I nod and stare into my dog's blue eyes.

"I don't think I have a choice about this anymore, Adrian. He was left. His parent left him defenseless on the side of a random street. I can't give him to a shelter where I don't know if he'd ever get out. I can't give him up for adoption because who knows what the new owners would do to him. I need to raise him to make sure nothing bad is going to happen to him again. He and I have some weird connection, as if he knows he can trust me. I know how it feels to be left. Mom left, and now, Gabriel left. How can I leave this little guy when he and I are the same?" I don't even notice the tear fall until Adrian wipes it away.

"So, what are we going to call him?" Adrian asks to distract me.

"I want to call him 'Chase'," I tell Adrian, and he furrows his eyebrows.

"Why 'Chase'?" Adrian holds out his hand, and Chase sniffs it with the highest level of precaution.

"Because everyone chases after something, whether it is small things or one big dream. I chased my dream, you chased yours, James followed his, and this little guy was screaming from the top of his lungs because he was chasing a new home. We all chase one thing we need desperately, and we do so until we have it forever." Adrian smiles at the puppy that is now getting closer and closer to him.

"Chase... I like it." I smirk at him, and he grins at me before focusing on my son again.

"By the way, next week you're going to have to take Wednesday off. I'm getting an IUD, and I need you to come with me," I say. Adrian is too distracted by Chase to listen to me, so I slap his arm to bring his attention back to me. "Hello? Can you please come with me?"

"Yes, of course. Sorry, he's just so cute." I chuckle, and Adrian goes on, saying, "Yes, you are, yes, you are," in the same voice people use for babies.

Chase is going to be a perfect addition to our small family, I know it. Grandpa used to have a golden retriever when we were little, and I loved that dog. This, however, is going to be very different. Chase is my son, my responsibility, which means more work, more restrictions, but also more love. This is going to be good for me. I'll find a place for him when I have to go to work. Maybe I can hire someone to stay at the house with him. Evangelin might watch him. I remember her telling me about the dog she used to have a few years ago.

Everything will work out, I'm sure of it. And I don't just mean with Chase.

CHAPTER 24
Gabriel

"I can't believe I'm here. I just can't believe it," Callum says, and I force a smile.

He's been saying those same two sentences for the past two days. At first, I thought it was sweet, but now, I want to punch him in the face. There is a limit to how many times I can hear him say the same thing. Sienna seems to notice my irritation with my cousin, which is why she squeezes my arm.

I decided to bring both of them to my home race because Jean gets to spend some time with Callum and Sienna this way as well. He's been doing so since the day they arrived in Monaco and having a great time getting to know them, too.

"Callum, we all know you're excited, but dial it down a bit, please," Sienna says, and I mouth a 'grazie'. Again, she squeezes my arm as we keep walking through the pit lane.

My mind roams back to Valentina, where it is almost every single second of every single day. I haven't seen her once this weekend, and I'm getting worried. Adrian wouldn't tell me where she is either.

It's been a couple of days since I sent her the canvas, but I haven't gotten a response from her. Part of me was hoping she'd at least scream at me, demand why I wrote her a letter and sent her the canvas, but another part knew she wouldn't respond. She's too mad at me to text me, but I wish she'd at least tell me if we're on the road to finding our way back to each other. It's too big of an ask, so I don't push her, but I wish for it anyway.

I lead Callum and Sienna toward my box, and that is when I finally see her, standing in front of the screens, discussing something with her brother. My body freezes as I look at her, keeping me from walking to simply study how beautiful she looks in the long dress she is wearing with a slit on the right side. It displays her beautiful, thick legs and the rest of her body wonderfully. Normally, she wears jeans and a team shirt, but not today. Today, her curves are highlighted by a dress so fitting to her body that it makes my hands twitch to touch her. I mentally slap myself so I stop concentrating on her and focus on walking again. Qualifying is in two hours, and I need to warm up.

"My God, she's beautiful," Callum says from beside me, and I finally feel my legs again.

"Yes, she is. She is the most beautiful woman you will ever meet, inside and out, and if you are smart enough to realize it, maybe you'll be smart enough not to let her go." Callum switches between looking at me and her.

"Sounds like you're in love with her." I look at him, my heart aching in my chest. With every second I look at Val, it gets harder for me to breathe. It also gets harder to resist the urge to punch a wall to punish myself.

"I'm more than in love with her. She's *everything* to me, and I thought she would be able to forgive me for the decision I've made, but how could she? I wouldn't." I look back at her to make sure she is really not wearing the necklace. She isn't, but I pray to God she wears it tomorrow.

"So, she's available?" Callum asks, and I have to count to ten to calm down. The wall wouldn't deserve my violence, but he sure as hell does right now.

"You touch her, or even go anywhere near her, and you'll find out just how angry I can get outside of a Formula One car." Callum looks at me with confusion.

"Why? She isn't yours," he insists, and I nod.

"No, she isn't, but I am going to fight for her. No matter what it takes."

"Then go get her," Callum tells me, and I realize what he was doing all along.

He's right, I can't sit around and wait for her to speak to me. Not when I promised her I'd chase her. When she told me not to stop fighting.

I love her more than life. All I have to do is keep proving it to her.

CHAPTER 25

Valentina

GABRIEL'S BEEN STANDING OUTSIDE of Adrian's box, staring at me, for the past few minutes. I'm uncomfortable, but not because he's staring. I'm uncomfortable because something deep inside of me wants him to come over to me, grab my face in his hands, and kiss me. It's wrong, but right and wrong don't matter anymore.

When he disappeared, I felt like a sunflower looking for the sun. Turning everywhere to get even a glimpse of him to brighten up my life. One glance at him, and it seems like my petals stand taller and the warmth returns to my soul. It's not fair because he hurt me, but he's been in pain, too. Holding his decision against him forever when he did it with the best intentions isn't fair either.

The emotional turmoil inside of me amplifies when he starts walking toward me. Unfortunately, anger takes over, but not because I'm mad at him. I'm mad because no matter what I do, I love him so much, it hurts.

"Come with me, please?" he begs, his green-brown eyes pleading with mine.

"Don't you have to get ready?" I ask him, anger evident in my voice.

"No, I have to talk to you first." I don't move an inch, simply stare at him. "I'm going to stand here until you agree to talk to me. I don't care if I miss Qualifying." I give him a 'yeah, right' look, but he takes my hand in his. Goosebumps shoot down my spine, and my knees go weak at the warmth of his touch. "I'm serious, Valentina. I'm serious about proving everything to you. You are my first and only priority now. Fuck everything else, tell me what to do, and I will do it. Anything you want." He seems genuine, forcing my walls to lower an inch, but I'm too angry to think past my feelings.

"Anything, huh? How about going back in time and not leaving when times got rough? How about instead of writing me a letter, saying the words to my face? How about not making promises you obviously cannot keep? Huh?" The letter thing stings me because I love that he writes them. I love how old-fashioned it is. I love how *Gabriel* it is.

"I'm sorry!" he screams, catching everyone's attention. "I'm sorry," he repeats in a much quieter voice.

Tears shoot into his eyes, so I take him to an empty room. I don't pay attention to what room it is, but it's empty; the only thing that matters right now.

"What do you want me to do, Gabriel? What the hell do you want me to do? You left me. You hurt me, and I don't know how to trust you not to leave when times get tough again." This hits him hard, I can see it in his eyes.

"But I came back," he protests in a quiet voice.

"But you left. I let you in, and you misused that trust by doing the one thing I am most afraid of: you abandoned me. Yes, you came back, but you hurt me and—" He interrupts me.

"Then let me repair it. You know I love you, and I'll do everything to show you that I can't live without you." I sit down on the chair next to me because I don't have the strength to stand anymore.

"I know you love me, that isn't the problem," I whisper, and he kneels in front of me, my favorite pair of eyes in the world staring at me. "How do I know you won't leave again when times get tough, Gabriel? What if, God forbid, we lose someone else? Will you leave me again because you don't want me to carry your burden?" I ask, but he shakes his head.

"Ma chérie, this was a horrible situation. Everything was on the line for you, and I was a mess. I couldn't drag you down, but I didn't know what to do, so I left. I'm so sorry. I made a mistake. I truly thought it would be for the best," he replies, keeping his hands by his side. "You're everything to me. All I've ever wanted was to be everything for you."

"Those are just words, Gabriel, just some pretty words." He nods and his hands slip onto my thighs. I don't tell him to remove them because I enjoy the warmth spreading through me. The problem is, the slit of my dress is exposing the skin on my thigh, and one of his hands is there, confusing my body.

"Yes, they are just words, but—" I have to cut him off this time.

"No, Gabriel, let's also not forget about the fact it took weeks for you to come to this 'conclusion', and only after you found your family. So, if you hadn't found them, would you still have come back?" He stares at me in disbelief.

"Yes, I would have. Baby, as soon as I left your room, I wanted to come back. I know this must be hard to believe, but none of the choices I've made in the last month have felt like my own up until a week ago. My head was so fucked up, I didn't feel like myself. I couldn't see past the grief inside of me, so my mind convinced me leaving you would be the better choice. I thought I was protecting you this way."

"I know you didn't mean to cause harm, how overwhelmed and in pain you were. But you shouldn't have left. You should have trusted me to balance this situation with my career and help you through this at the same time. Your mental health would not have been a burden for me, Gabriel, nor would it have torn me down," I say, causing tears to fall from his eyes.

He drops his head onto my thighs, and his hands move to the side of my legs. This position is much more intimate because he's surrendering himself to me. He's giving up any power he has, and he has voluntarily done so. I slide my hands into his curly hair and start playing with it. I miss doing that.

"Please, forgive me. Please, mon tournesol, I need you." And my walls drop. They are completely down now, leaving me to be as vulnerable as him.

"I can't forgive you."

His head shoots up, sadness in his features. He loves me, he truly loves me, and I don't want to lose him. We're not perfect, but we are what the other person needs the most in this dark world. All of the notes, apologies, letters, and drawings. What more can I ask for? He's done nothing but prove to me, over and over since he came back, he loves me. He needs me. He can't live without me and will do anything and everything in his power to fight for me.

There is no way I could ever let him go.

"Yet," I add after ten, painful seconds. My hands rest on each side of his face, and my thumbs wipe away the tears falling from his eyes. "I can't forgive you just because you tell me what I want to hear," I say, and the smile he gives me warms my heart. I miss it, this perfect smile of his with dimples and hope glistening in his eyes.

"I will do everything in my power to make you feel safe and loved. And then, I'm going to make sure you don't ever regret that choice." He presses a kiss to my thigh, and I have to control the whimper threatening to leave my lips.

"Everything, huh?" He nods and stares into my eyes.

"Everything," he promises, and I smile.

"Take me on a date, one where I can bring my son."

Gabriel's eyes go wide from surprise, reminding me he doesn't know about Chase yet.

"My dog," I clarify, but he still seems confused. "I will tell you on our date," I say, and he puts his hands back on top of my legs.

"A date?" There is so much hope in his tone, bringing a smile to my lips.

"We have to start somewhere, Gabriel." We need to take it one step at a time.

"Okay, I'll arrange it all and on Monday, how about that?" he asks me, and I realize I'm still holding his face in my hands. His perfect face.

"I can't on Monday, I'm having lunch with Evangelin," I tell him.

"Then Tuesday," he suggests, and I smile.

His face turns contemplative as he stares up at me, still on his knees.

"Please, will you put your necklace back on, ma chérie?" he begs, and I trace his bottom lip with my thumb for a moment.

"I already did," I say and twist the necklace so the charm falls to the front. I'm wearing a dress that has a neck halter which is probably why he didn't see it. Or maybe he saw the necklace but he didn't think it was the one with his charm. But it is his, it's always been his, it's only ever going to be his.

"I really want to kiss you right now," he whispers, and my smile fades.

"Well, you gotta go drive first."

"Does that mean I'll get a kiss after?" he asks, pushing his bottom lip forward.

I don't know how we got to this point, but I prefer this over the chaos that's been going on. Two people as broken as we are, are bound to make a lot of mistakes. The only thing stronger is the bond between us. When I get up in the middle of the night because my mind is too hung up on the people I've lost, I need Gabriel by my side. He is the excitement in my life, the one I desperately cling to. The way he makes me feel is my own personal addiction.

"Your optimism is going to disappoint you this time." I get up from the chair, and he follows closely.

"At least we both know it would be a good kiss."

No point arguing with him on that. We've always been good together, I doubt what happened changed our chemistry, especially because the longer he touches me, the closer I'm getting to ripping his clothes off and taking what we need right here and now.

"Go race and good luck," I say instead, and he gives my cheek a slow stroke with the back of his fingers, smiling at me like I'm the most precious person to him in the world.

"I love you."

He doesn't wait for me to say it back, doesn't pressure me to respond at all. It seems like he just wanted to remind me before disappearing out of this room with the softest, sweetest 'bye' falling from his lips.

CHAPTER 26

Valentina

MY EYES DON'T LEAVE those small screens, not even for a second. Qualifying is always important because it determines from where the drivers are going to start in tomorrow's race. That is why it's nerve-racking, and I'm so focused on what they're doing, I jump in fear when someone taps me on the shoulder. Panic causes my throat to close as I divert my attention away from watching James, Cameron, Leonard, Adrian, and Gabriel.

The rational part of my brain tells me not to worry, it's probably just one of the mechanics or Lorenzo Mattia, but I've been so on edge during race weekends since the note and message, I can't help the fear inside of me. Waiting for the person to show their face or for another note to arrive. I know I'm probably being irrational about this, but I can't help it. I only hope this feeling will go away because I cannot work like this.

"Hi, I'm Callum. I'm Gabriel's cousin," a tall, extremely muscular man with stunning blue eyes, curly black hair, and a strong Italian accent says, holding out his hand. I shake it politely and smile at him. This is who Gabriel was searching for.

"I'm Valentina. It's nice to meet you, Callum." He grins at me, revealing a slightly crooked smile.

"I know, Gabriel speaks very highly of you." I shouldn't smile, but I can't help it.

Callum and I have a conversation about Formula One, while we study the times the drivers set per lap on the screen. Gabriel has an engine problem in Q2, causing him to fall out, something Callum and Sienna seem very upset about. I haven't met Sienna yet, but Callum pointed her out to me.

I watch Gabriel take off his gloves and helmet in frustration before he walks to his private room. He's upset, and usually, before everything happened, I would have gone to check on him, but we are not there yet.

My phone rings, and I see Mrs. Beaumont's name on my screen. I answer it quickly, worried something is wrong with Chase. However, she is simply inquiring where his food is, and I gladly let her know. Leaving him this morning broke my heart, but it's my job to be here, to learn with Lorenzo Mattia, so I had to. Luckily, Mrs. Beaumont loves dogs and was more than happy to dogsit him for me.

Callum walks over to Sienna and puts his hand on her shoulder with a bright grin. They seem like kind and good people, making it hard for me to stay mad at Gabriel. Yes, he hurt me, but he did to find them, and not just for himself. Jean looks happier than he's been in a while, and I think, no, I *know* having them here is going to be very good for him. Jean is a person who needs a big family, and a lot of love, which isn't a bad thing, it's just something I will never feel. I am happy to have my small family, and even though there is a new addition on the way and Annie has made her way in as well, I wouldn't go out and look for more. I have a hard time letting people in already, I can't imagine searching for someone to have that struggle over.

Gabriel joins Sienna and Callum for a few minutes until Eduardo comes over to talk to him. The hairs on my neck stand up as they start arguing over God-knows-what. Eduardo pulls Gabriel out of my sight, and I can tell whatever happens next is not going to be good.

"Fuck," I mumble under my breath as I follow them.

A strange feeling in my gut is telling me to check on those two before they do something irreversible. Another gut feeling tells me they're two grown men who can make their own decisions. However, the only thing that could cause them to fight at this point is me because neither of them interfered with the other's Qualifying and the only thing apart from racing they have in common is a past relationship with me.

When I reach the door they walked through a minute before, I hear screaming.

"Stay the fuck away from Valentina!" I hear Gabriel bark, and I'm paralyzed.

"Why? Because I had my tongue down her throat and she whimpered my name? Are you fucking jealous, Gabriel?" I hear a loud thud and rip the door open.

When I take in the sight in front of me, I let out a relieved sigh. Gabriel hit the wall, not Eduardo.

I stand in front of the Spaniard and push him away from Gabriel.

"What the fuck is wrong with you?" I ask Eduardo, my heart beating rapidly against my ribcage. His light brown eyes focus on me, nothing but fury in them. "I can't believe I ever let you touch me. What kind of a person shares such details about a woman to the guy who is in love with her? You disgust me." Eduardo grabs my wrists in his hands and tightens his grip until I wince in pain.

"You push me again, and I'm going to make you regret it, Valentina. It's not my fault you're such a little slut," he says before he pulls me close and traps me against his chest. I step on his foot to get him to let go of me, but Gabriel is the one to shove the Hawke driver so hard, he falls to the ground.

"And if *you* touch *her* again, I'm going to make sure it's the last thing you do." Gabriel takes my hand and leads me out of the room before I get the chance to confront Eduardo about his immature behavior.

"What the hell was that? Who started it?" I ask him as soon as we're alone.

"He just came up to me and started making inappropriate comments about you. Then, when I told him off, he said he needed to talk in private. I don't know, Val, I don't know what's wrong with him, but no one, and I mean no one, is allowed to disrespect you." He was protecting me... Gabriel will always protect me. I suck in a sharp breath because how could I ever doubt that?

"I have to go shower. Feeling his hands on me made me nauseous," I say, not very subtly changing the topic.

"I wanted to hurt him when he touched you. I should have," he says, and I look at his handsome face to comfort myself.

His stubble is back to the normal length, the one I love, his curly hair is a bit longer, but perfect to drive me crazy, and his green-brown eyes are as bright as ever.

"I'm sorry about this. God, you don't know how sorry. I'm trying to make everything fall into place, but there are things, no matter how much I want to control them, which just don't—" He's hyperventilating, which is why I cut him off.

"Gabriel, this wasn't your fault. It was Eduardo's. But it wasn't yours. You were just trying to protect me."

Before I can overthink things, I wrap my arms around his sweaty body and sigh when his familiar mahogany scent fills my nose. He hesitates at first, but eventually, I feel his arms around my shoulders, too, one of his hands cupping the back of my head.

Maybe it's foolish of me to rush into this. Maybe I shouldn't have agreed to go on a date with him or touch him. Maybe I'm making the biggest mistake of my life, but I couldn't care less right now. One date doesn't mean we'll get back together. It merely means being away from him when neither one of us wants distance anymore is unbearable. This doesn't mean everything's rainbows and sunshine, but it also doesn't mean I haven't taken a big step in letting go of my anger. Because I have. I think most of it dissipated when I saw Jean smiling at Callum and Sienna like they're the best thing he's seen in a long time.

So, I lean even more into the hug, relishing his warmth and scent and touch for as long as my heart allows before it aches again.

This hug means more than the rest of the world would ever be able to see. This is us taking one step toward each other after having taken a hundred steps backward.

"Don't you have things to take care of? Responsibilities to uphold?" I ask when neither one of us makes a move to get out of the hug. Gabriel strokes his hand down my spine and then trails it back up again, causing me to melt into his chest even more.

"I don't care. Nothing else matters, only you." I feel his lips brush the side of my head, sending warmth through my chest that reignites the heat I always feel when he's touching me. It's not desire entirely, no. It's flames of love, belonging, *longing*, and so much more.

"Your team is going to be furious if you miss the interviews," I remind him, but he merely takes the smallest step back to cup my face and look me in the eyes. The need to meet his gaze is overpowered by my eyelids falling shut to enjoy the softness of his touch.

"I'd never give another interview if it meant I got to have another moment like this with you." The sincerity in his voice almost brings me to my knees.

"I'll reschedule my lunch with Evangelin. I'd like to go on our date on Monday," I say, and Gabriel smiles at me.

"Okay, mon tournesol, Monday it is." I smile at him, and he puts his thumb on my cheek, tracing circles with a look in his eyes that says he can't quite believe he's touching me. For a brief second, I think he's going to kiss me when he stares at my lips, and he does, but only on the cheek. It leaves the skin there tingling.

It turns out Kyle and Jonathan got first and second place, Adrian was third, and James was fifth. Cameron ended up in seventh. Lorenzo Mattia asks Adrian, Gabriel, and me to stay after the session, and I can't help but feel nerves creeping in when he approaches me with a contemplative frown on his face.

"How did you feel testing the car during the summer break?" he asks, my brother and Gabriel slowly approaching. They're deep in conversation, Adrian looking at his teammate with surprise all over his features.

"Confident," I admit, not because I'm full of myself, but simply because while testing, I felt great. The car and I just clicked, as if I've always been meant to drive it. Lorenzo finally smiles at me, easing some of the anxiety that was building up in my chest.

"Good. I spoke to the engineers who were working with you, and they all told me you had something they've never seen before." My mouth falls open, but I decide to wait for him to tell me instead of asking. The way my heart races, it's surprising I'm still standing. My boss smiles proudly. "'Raw talent that's been molded into skill through dedication like no other' is what they told me. That's the impression you made on the entire team," he says, and I can't help the way my mind wanders to the note someone from the team must have put in the car on the first day of summer training.

Maybe I didn't win everyone over, but even having a few people who don't really know me supporting my joining the team is a huge win.

"I'm very proud of you, Valentina, and I know your Nonno and Papa would be too," Lorenzo adds, sending tears straight into my eyes.

"I hope so," I reply, looking at the ground to hide the betrayal of my emotions in my eyes. Lorenzo places a gentle hand on my shoulder, and I instinctively lift my head again to see his soft smile.

"I know so. Your Nonno and I knew each other for a long time, and you've already accomplished more than he thought this sport would allow you to. It was never about your talent, only about the opportunities you got," my boss explains, taking a step back and placing his hands on his hips. "Now, I would like for you to drive in the second free practice session of next week's race weekend. It will help you gain experience, further familiarize you with the car, and make you an even better driver overall, in case you need to step in this season."

It's almost impossible to keep my heart from skipping several beats. I'm a professional. This is what they signed me on for, but part of me still feels like placing a hand over my mouth to cover the shocked O-shape it wants to morph into.

"Thank you for the opportunity," I say, doing my best to keep the quiver out of my voice.

Lorenzo Mattia keeps me on a strict workout schedule, including training in the simulator. He wants me to be prepared to step in at any time during the season, and I'm more than happy to do exactly as I'm told. After all, it's my reputation that's on the line if I reserve drive and then come in last because of my performance.

"Don't be nervous," he says with a little chuckle. I try to return the sound, but it comes out high-pitched and wonky. Lorenzo smiles at me knowingly before turning to Adrian and Gabriel. I hadn't even noticed them standing beside us until now.

"Gentlemen, I assume you heard my announcement. All I have to figure out is which car Valentina will be driving, and then I'll get back to you," he says.

"Let her drive mine," Gabriel says at the same time as Adrian tells Lorenzo that I should take his free practice session.

"I'll let you know once I've made a decision," Lorenzo adds before walking away with another proud nod my way.

Adrian lets out a victorious roar before picking me up and jumping on the spot. He drops me back on my feet to plant a wet kiss on my forehead and then wraps his arms around me.

"I'm so, so proud of you!" He squeezes me until all the breath is knocked out of me and then lets go to turn to his teammate once more. "You should tell her what you told me," Adrian says. He nods his head my way, a secretive look on his face. Gabriel smiles from ear to ear as he turns to me, my brother leaving so we're alone.

Gabriel takes my hand to bring me a bit closer to him, and I move without thinking. He tugs a strand of my hair behind my ear, trailing his index finger along my jaw as he stares into my eyes with those beautiful green-brown ones of his.

"A reporter approached me today, asking if you were interested in giving an interview about being the first female reserve driver in the history of Formula One," Gabriel says, my gaze stuck on his full lips as he speaks.

"Are you serious?" I ask, bringing the tips of my fingers to my lips.

"Yes. I gave her your contact information, so you should be expecting an email from her in a few days," he says, but I'm flinging my arms around his neck before he's even done talking.

The thing about falling in love with a friend is that, no matter what heartbreak occurs, they were your friend first. Gabriel was my friend before we dated, and I like that we're slowly getting our friendship back, even if our romantic relationship isn't back to what it was before he left.

"Thank you," I say as I step out of the hug, my hands remaining on his neck.

The distance between us is minimal, barely a few centimeters, but I can't bring myself to stop touching him. My torso is firmly pressed against his hard one, relishing in the heat and smell of him. It would be so easy for him to kiss me, and I would let him. I would kiss him back as fiercely because I've been craving his taste since he left. I caress the skin on his neck before trailing my fingers all the way to his cheeks, slightly pressing my thumbs into the spots where his dimples usually appear.

"I've missed your touch," he whispers before dropping his forehead against mine. My eyes close in response as his fingers pulse on my hips, squeezing me until I'm even more pressed against him.

"Did you?"

"Yes. I would have begged for it on my knees if I thought I'd get it back that way," he says, and I almost smile at the fact that it's exactly what he did this morning. He begged for me, on his knees, vulnerable and ready to give me the entire world if I asked for it.

"Hmmm," I let out, inhaling once more to smell his mahogany scent and then pushing off, ignoring the way my lips tingle with the need to kiss him. Gabriel watches me with nothing but love in his eyes, and I wish I could freeze this moment in time to show the entire world how he looks at me. "I'll see you tomorrow, Gabriel," is all I say, turning around to leave when his next words stop me.

"I'll earn it again," he blurts out, causing me to freeze.

"Earn what?"

"Being called 'mon soleil' by you."

I leave the box with a grin on my face.

When I arrive at home, Chase celebrates my return with a spin and then jumps into my arms. It's only been four days since I found him, but he's already looking much healthier. His bones aren't sticking out as much as they were before, and he's running around a lot. I hand Mrs. Beaumont the money we agreed on for today, and she pets Chase on the head before squeezing my arm and leaving my house.

I sit down on the ground with Chase and play with him for a while. My mind keeps roaming back to what happened today, to all the events, and I can't stop it from running around like a five-year-old high on sugar.

Next week will be my first free practice session.

A journalist wants to interview me about my accomplishments.

Gabriel and I are going on a date soon.

I kiss Chase on the head before letting out an excited giggle. He bites my jacket sleeve and tugs on it until I finally give in and remove it, something falling out of its pocket and onto the ground.

It's a note.

My heart skips a beat.

DON'T UNDERESTIMATE WHAT I'M WILLING TO DO TO GET YOU OUT OF FORMULA ONE.

CHAPTER 27
Gabriel

"Hi, chérie," I say from behind her, a bouquet of sunflowers resting in my hand, a sketch of her in the other. Valentina spins around at the sound of my voice, a small smile tugging at the corner of her mouth.

"Monsieur Biancheri," she says with a teasing gleam in her eyes. I want her 'mon soleil' back, to hear the words from her lips again. *I want to be her sun again.* "Are those for me?" she asks, her bright green-blue-brown eyes on the sunflowers in my hand. Something seems a bit off in them today, but my next words seem to make her feel better.

"Actually, they're for Adrian. Have you seen him?" I ask, and she smacks my arm in response, chuckling softly. "Of course they're for you. Tournesols pour mon tournesol," I say, and she snatches them from me, staring at her favorite type of flowers.

"And that?" she asks, wiggling her eyebrows at the paper in my fingers.

"This?" I reply and lift it up, the drawing still facing me. Val nods, curiosity on her soft features. What I wouldn't give to kiss her all over. "This is a drawing of the most beautiful woman in the world, the first female Formula One champion in a few years," I say, and she rolls her eyes like she always does when I say something cheesy. I hand it to her, watching a look of awe cross her face as she studies the drawing of her dancing in the rain.

"This day is burned into my memory," she whispers, running the tips of her fingers over the paper.

"And mine. It was one of the best days of my life," I admit because I drew this *from memory*, and it is perfect. Well, as close to perfect as I can get it.

"Of course it was. You were with me," she says with a smug smile. Good God, she's so beautiful, cute, and sexy at the same time. I shake my head to refocus. "Don't you have to go prepare for your race?" Valentina asks, but I merely reach out to feel the charm of her necklace against my skin.

"Thank you for wearing it," I reply, and she lifts her hand, wrapping her fingers around mine and the charm. Her heart rate picks up, making her chest move up and down more quickly than before.

"You should stop touching me," she says, but I don't. "Gabriel," Val breathes when my mouth moves closer to hers.

"I miss you," I whisper, resting my forehead against hers instead of kissing her. I'm not allowed to do that right now. I'm not certain she'd like to feel my lips against hers.

"Gabriel," Valentina says more firmly, pressing her hands against my chest and pushing me backward. She's so magnetic, it takes every ounce of strength for me to step away. "You can't kiss me yet," she says with a little smile. Hope. There is so much fucking hope inside of me, I might burst.

"But I want to," I reply, making sure she knows I need her. She can never forget how much I crave her.

"Gabriel," she whimpers when my hands move to her hips, her bottom lip slipping between her teeth as heat colors her cheeks. God, knowing she still reacts to my touch like this, knowing she still wants me, excites every cell in my body.

"I can't wait for our date tomorrow," I say, feeling the fabric of the team shirt she's wearing against the palms of my hands. "I have something amazing planned," I say with a happy grin.

"You need to get ready for the race," she says because my woman is all business. *Almost. She's almost mine again.*

"Okay. Will I get a kiss after the race?" I ask, and she gives me a nudge, turning away but not before I catch her content smile.

"Bye, Gabriel," is all she says before giving her attention to Lorenzo Mattia again.

Valentina Esmèe Cèlia Romana. Velocità Rossa Formula One reserve driver. Future Alfa Adrenalina driver. Future World Champion. And love of my life.

She overwhelms me simply by existing, and I wouldn't have it any other way.

CHAPTER 28

Valentina

THE WRITING ON THE note has haunted me ever since I found it yesterday. Whoever wrote it was close enough to put it in my pocket, but the only person I saw near my things yesterday was Daniel, Adrian's performance coach, and Cameron. Neither of them has a motive to threaten me.

I'm doing my best to disregard it because it shouldn't frighten me, but I'd be lying if I said I wasn't terrified.

Whoever is writing these notes doesn't want me in Formula One.

I haven't told Adrian, James, or Gabriel because they'd only worry when it might be nothing to be concerned about. People like this are usually all talk with nothing behind it, and I'm never alone long enough to be in any actual danger. At least that's what I keep telling myself.

James could tell this morning that something was off with me, but I distracted him by talking about Annie and Damian. He started rambling over how excited he is to finally meet his son, and I smiled the entire time he was speaking.

The race is about a quarter done when my phone starts ringing in my pocket. I take it out and go to a quieter spot to answer the call I'm receiving from Annie.

"What's wrong?" I ask as soon as I hit answer. She moans a pain-filled cry into the phone, and my heart stops beating.

"He's coming, he's coming now!" she screams, and I'm convinced all the color leaves my face. My God, the baby is coming, and James is nowhere near finishing his race.

"Okay, I'll call an ambulance and meet you at the hospital. It would take too long if I came to your house first," I say, trying to control my breathing.

Annie agrees, and I hang up so I can call an ambulance to pick her up. I have no idea what to do first or next, so I decide to go to James' manager and tell her as soon as James finishes his race, he needs to go to the hospital. I tell her to say 'Damian', which James and I agreed is the code word for Annie giving birth to their son.

His manager cannot just pull him out of the race. This is James' job, and he has to go through with it, no matter whether Annie is giving birth to their child or not. That sounds quite terrible, but it would be dangerous to tell him in the middle of the race since he wouldn't be completely focused on driving his car. That's not something we can do.

Lorenzo Mattia releases me of my duties for today, so I run toward the parking garage and to my car. I stopped thinking somewhere between the phone call and talking to James' manager. My mind is focused on making it to Annabel safely but also as fast as possible.

It takes me too long before finally running inside the hospital and toward the lady at the front desk. She lets me know Annie is in room 105.

I find Annie bent over, her hands on the bed, her arms stretched out, and groaning in pain. Her eyes find me, and I watch her take a long, deep breath.

"Thank God," is the first thing that comes out of her mouth. "The midwife told me I'm at six centimeters, which means I'm going to have to start pushing soon. I don't want to, I can't." I roll up my sleeves and walk over to her to rub her back.

"I'm sorry, Annie, but I don't think you have a choice. This baby is coming whether you want it to or not. You just have to remind yourself you've been impatiently waiting for him and this is what you want. I can't imagine how much pain you must be in, but you can do this. I know you can. Damian needs you to," I say and continue to rub her back.

"Okay, I can do it, I can do this." She leans forward again and concentrates on her breathing. The thought of Damian is giving her strength, I can see it in the way she's fighting the pain with everything she has.

The midwife comes back into the room to check on how far along my friend is. Apparently, Annie is already at ten centimeters. I forget how to breathe because this is actually happening. Damian is going to come now, even though James isn't able to be here.

"You have to stay with me, please, Valentina. I can't do this alone."

Alone. Annie shouldn't have to go through this by herself, and there is nothing that could drag me from her side.

"Oh God, oh God, oh God," she keeps repeating. I keep telling her to breathe, and she keeps telling me to shut up. I'm as clueless as a father would be in this situation because I have no idea how to pull out of the bubble of oblivion. "It hurts," she cries, and I take her hand in mine.

"I'm right here, Annie, and I'm not going anywhere. You don't have to do this alone. I'm here." She squeezes my hand and more tears fall down her eyes.

When it's time to start pushing, she grabs my other hand and puts it on our intertwined ones. Everything is happening way too quickly, but I try my best to keep my mind present. If I drift off because I think about James or Adrian, I'm not going to be able to focus on Annie, and she needs my full attention right now.

The midwife mentions something about Annie having rapid labor, which explains why everything is going as fast as it is. They have to be more careful now, but they don't give me more information.

"This fucking sucks," she says, and I let out a small laugh.

I refuse to look at where Damian will come out of because I know it will scar me forever. So, I just stay by Annie's head and run my hands through her hair, massaging her head. It seems to make her feel better during the breaks when she doesn't have to push.

After an hour of her screaming and pushing, grabbing my hands and almost breaking them, the room is filled with screams that are not hers. The doctor holds up Damian, and I've never been so weirded out and joyful at the same time. He has red goop all over him, and his wrinkly features are formed into a frown. He's screaming at the top of his lungs, and I watch as the doctor looks at Annie.

"Who is going to cut the umbilical cord?" she asks Annie, and I feel her squeeze my hand.

"I want you to do it, I'm too tired."

Since I don't want to argue with her, I go over to the doctor and take the scissors I'm handed. It surprises me how difficult it is to cut it, as if there was a guitar string in the middle of the cord. Eventually, I manage, and Damian is taken away to briefly get cleaned up. My eyes drift back to Annie, who has hers closed. She reopens them when Damian is given to her. Tears fall down her cheeks, and a brilliant smile decorates her face. I can't stop happy tears from falling down.

"Could you hold him?" Annie asks me once we are back in the room from before. Damian has luckily stopped screaming and is now sleeping in Annie's arms. "I need to rest." Hesitantly, I take the small baby into my arms, supporting his head and body. "Thank you for everything, Val. It means more to me than you will ever know." I want to tell her she is more than welcome, but I can't find words. Damian's small face has captured all of my attention.

As soon as I sit down in the chair next to her bed, Annie falls asleep. I study Damian's features and use my index finger to touch his small cheek. His tiny hand lifts into the air, and he puts it on my lips, not on purpose, but just by chance. His nose is so small, his lips are so thin, and his eyes look like they are shut with little force, as if he is about to wake up. But he doesn't.

I hum to him, and minutes later, he opens his ocean-blue eyes to look at me. He is most definitely James' son. He has his nose and eyes, and he is the most adorable, smushed-faced child I have ever seen. *Why do I love him so much?* He's not mine, I didn't give birth to him. *So, why do I have such a strong connection to him? Is it because he's James'?* I have no idea... All I know is I need to protect this child with everything I have.

Relief washes over me when James finally walks through the door. His eyes scan the room and stop at Annie before he keeps searching to find his son in my arms. James steps over to me slowly, and when he reaches us, he sinks to the ground.

"James Landon, I think it's time for you to meet your son." Tears flood into James' eyes, which brings some back into mine. "He's been impatiently waiting for you." I place Damian in his arms and press a kiss to James' head. "I'll be outside," I say and leave the room.

CHAPTER 29

Valentina

THE FIRST THING I do is let out a long sigh. Then, I call Mrs. Beaumont and let her know what happened, but she informs me she is not under any circumstances mad at me for keeping Chase at her place for the night. After she hangs up, I put my phone back into my pocket and run my hands through my hair. I feel like I need a hug.

I find a chair close to Annie's room and just sink down on it. I drop my face into my hands and let out a nervous laugh. The next thing I feel is a gush of wind before someone settles beside me. An all-too-familiar hand rests on my neck before I have the chance to check who it belongs to.

I turn my head to stare into his green-brown eyes.

My good God, I want to get back together with Gabriel. I want to wake up next to him. I want to comfort him when he doesn't do well in races. I want to take care of him when he is sick. I want to be the one who loves him unconditionally, and I want to be the one who gets to say: he's mine.

His hand moves from my neck to my hair where his fingers rest on my cheek and the back of my head. My eyes close in response to his warmth and gentle cupping. I love his touch. It's made for me and me alone.

"You're here," I mumble as his thumb caresses my skin.

"I thought you might need me. I ditched the interviews. You are more important." He put me before his job, and I can't imagine the consequences it will have for him. Not even Adrian is here.

"How is Annie?" he asks me, and I tell him she is resting and recovering.

"How was your race?" He smiles brightly at me, his thumb continuing to caress my cheek.

"Adrian won, I got third place, James came in fifth, Kyle got second place, Jonathan fourth, Eduardo didn't finish," he says and stops so he can grin at me. I smile, too, because that asshole deserves to DNF a couple of times. "Cameron got sixth and Leonard eighth."

Gabriel tells me about all of the other drivers, but I'm not listening anymore. His full lips have caught my attention, and I am fighting with myself. I know I shouldn't kiss him, but I want to. I want to so badly, I cannot tear my eyes from them.

"Val, please stop doing that." I force my gaze to his just to notice his attention shifting between looking at my eyes to my mouth. This is not good.

"Sorry," I mumble and turn my head away, but he tilts it back to him with his index finger.

"I don't think you want to kiss me right now. I think you're tired and confused, which is why I won't kiss you, but know this, I want to, more than I want to do anything else."

I've never felt more clear-headed, though...

"There is something I need to tell you." He is still holding my face with his index finger, but his thumb went back to gently caressing my cheek. "Harlow has texted me again, and she is trying to go out with me. I told her no, and I asked her to leave me alone, but she keeps creating new social media accounts to message me," he admits, forcing me to suck in a sharp breath.

Gabriel and I aren't dating right now, which means he is free to be with whoever he wishes to be, but we all know he wants to be with me, he's made it clear. I just need him to remember he's mine. All mine.

Before I can stop myself, I lean forward and bring my lips to his. It doesn't matter who else I kiss, it never feels like *this*. It never feels like their lips were made for me. The way Gabriel's always envelop mine, the way he knows how I like to be touched, it all screams he is the one for me.

"Why did you do that?" he asks, and I wipe away the tear that rolled down his cheek.

"To remind you that even though we might not be together right now, it doesn't mean my feelings have disappeared. They haven't. They are still here, waiting to be expressed in every way possible."

"I thought you didn't love me anymore," he whispers before he rests his forehead against mine. I notice he's closed his eyes, and it looks like he's enjoying how close we are, that his breath and mine have become one.

"It would be easier if I didn't." I run my index finger over his rough stubble. "But how am I ever supposed to let go of how I feel when I know this won't come again." I pull back to look at him, seeing those beautiful dimples of his. "I missed them," I tell him, my fingers running over the imprints in his cheeks.

"You're the only one who brings them out."

I bite the inside of my cheek while fighting the urge to kiss him again. Instead, I take his hand in both of mine and lie my head against his shoulder.

"Thank you for coming," I say in a quiet voice because I'm too tired to speak louder.

"Thank you for kissing me," he replies, and I let out a small laugh.

Soon after, the exhaustion of the day sends me off to sleep.

"Why is my sister's head on your shoulder?" I hear Adrian ask, but I don't open my eyes. I'm too curious to see where this conversation will go to reveal I'm awake and listening.

"Because I am the luckiest man to ever walk on this planet," Gabriel replies, and I fight the urge to smile. "And because my left arm is completely numb now, which I deserve. I think it's her way of getting revenge," he jokes, and I hear Adrian chuckle briefly.

"Listen, Gabriel, I don't want to do this whole older brother talk with you. I've been supportive of you getting her back, but I need to say something not so pretty this time. This doesn't even come from a brotherly perspective, merely from a person who loves Valentina."

Adrian stops and inhales loudly.

"My sister has the biggest heart of anyone I know. She's been hurting a lot recently, yet she still managed to forgive. Val is even taking care of a stray puppy, which is a shit ton of work. I mean, this dog has been peeing and pooping in the house at least twice a day, but she's managed to train him, somewhat, to do his business outside. Anyway, that's beside the point. The actual point is I trusted you. I trusted you would treat her right, and you have betrayed that trust."

Adrian pauses again, and I wish I could see what his face is doing. I also wish I could see Gabriel's expression.

"You made a mistake, and it means you have to do everything in your power to make up for it. And when you do, do not, and I mean *do not ever* let her slip through your fingers again. I don't think she will forgive you one more time," my brother finishes before readjusting in the seat next to me.

Gabriel takes a deep breath, I can feel it by the way my head lifts with his shoulder.

"Don't you think I know that? Don't you think I know I am walking on the thinnest ice? I know, Adrian, and I am terrified. She gave me another chance to prove to her I'm good for her, and I know I am. I'm just an idiot who made a wrong decision. But, when we were together, mate, we were happy. We were so happy. I will do everything to get back there. There is nothing else that can make me as happy as she makes me, not finding long-lost family, not winning races, nothing. Nothing comes close to the way I feel when I'm with her. So, I don't need you to tell me I have to be careful because I know. I fucking know, and it terrifies me."

My hand, the one which has been resting in Gabriel's, is suddenly squeezed tightly by his.

"I don't know how to prove to her I love her, I need her, and that she's the only one for me." He takes another deep breath, and I control the tears.

"All she wants is for you not to do the same thing our mother did. Stay, that's all she'll ever want from you," my brother says.

Adrian is right, it is all I want. It's all I've ever wanted.

"I'll never leave her again. If I'm sure about one thing, it's that. She is where I am supposed to be. Valentina is my home."

CHAPTER 30
Gabriel

My fist connects with Adalene Beaumont's front door before I patiently wait for her to open it. Valentina told me Mrs. Beaumont took Chase to her place for the night since we all left the hospital late. She told me she'd get him in the morning, but I have another surprise planned for her, and after everything she told me about her son at the hospital yesterday, I want him to be there when she wakes up.

"Gabriel Biancheri," Adalene Beaumont says as she stands in front of me, smiling from ear to ear.

"Good morning, madame," I reply, giving her a polite nod.

I've known this woman since I was a child. She was friends with my grandparents before they passed. I hadn't seen her in years, up until Valentina and I started dating and I was at her house often enough to run into Mrs. Beaumont frequently.

"Come in," she says, stepping aside to let me pass. "How may I help you?"

"I'm here to pick up Chase and take him home," I reply at the same time as a little puppy walks up to me, uncertainty in his gaze. I drop to my knees, warmth spreading through my chest at the sight of him. "Val told me you're cute, but, man, you really are," I say to the little guy and hold out my hand for him to sniff.

At first, he takes a step away from me, but as soon as he sniffs my hand and lets me pet his head, something clicks. He starts wagging and jumping into my arms, licking my face. Thank God. I needed him to like me. Chase is important to Val, which makes him important to me. Plus, he's fucking adorable.

"Gabriel?" Mrs. Beaumont says, reminding me she's still here, too. I straighten out my back and take the leash she hands me. "I like you. You've grown into a good man, but don't ever hurt my girl again," she adds, and I feel a wave of pain hitting me hard and right in the chest.

"Never again," I promise. I hand her some money for watching the puppy and smile with appreciation.

Chase and I leave without another word spoken between Mrs. Beaumont and me. We make a quick stop at the flower shop before heading to his home where Adrian opens the door for us. Excitement lights up his features at the sight of the newest member of his family.

"Oh my gosh, you're home," Adrian says in a high-pitched voice as Chase jumps up and down against his legs. "I've missed you, little bear," he goes on, and I cross my arms in front of my chest with an amused grin. When my teammate and biggest competition for the championship catches it, he clears his throat. "I like him, okay? He's adorable," is all he says in a normal voice before grabbing his keys and leaving. "Val is going to love what you have planned," he adds with a pat on my shoulder.

I hope so.

Chase runs up the stairs toward Valentina's room without me having to bring him. I simply smile as I step into the kitchen, turning on some music, and getting to work. It's been over a month since I've been able to make this breakfast, but the memory of her loving every bite has been replaying in my mind for too long. I need to see her happy again, and this is the first step of my plan to give her the perfect date. My first step to giving her the perfect life... *with me.*

Before everything happened, Valentina and I were talking about our future, spending the rest of our lives together. When I was looking for an apartment, I looked for one that fit both of our needs because I want to live with her. I don't know if she would have left her grandfather's house, but I would have asked her anyway. It wouldn't have mattered where, as long as she and I got to come home to one another. The fantasy of it plays through in my head, and I start moving along to the music in response.

"Gabriel?" she asks, and my head snaps up.

Heat rushes into my cheeks, painting them a bright red because she caught me dancing in her kitchen. Ignoring the embarrassment, I bring a grin to my lips as I turn around to look at her beautiful face.

"Good morning, ma chérie. How did you sleep?" I put down the spatula in my hand before stepping around the kitchen island and toward her.

"Really well, I had a wonderful dream," she says, piquing my curiosity. Once I'm in front of her, I place a soft kiss on her cheek. I can't help myself. I crave any touch she allows me.

"You want to tell me about it?" My hands rest on each side of her face, and I can't breathe. Being this close to her again is setting every piece of my heart back into its proper place.

"No, because if I do, the dream won't come true." I smile at her in response.

"My mom used to tell me the same thing." My thumb rubs over her cheek before I turn back around to finish the waffles I was making.

"Did you bring Chase home?" she asks after she settles down on the chair at the island.

"Yeah, I thought you would like to wake up to his face." *I would like to wake up to your face...* I shake my head because this is neither the time nor the place to tell her there is nothing more I want than to live with her.

"Thank you for doing that. I appreciate it." I wink at her before throwing the finished waffle onto a plate.

"I want everything to go perfectly today, and it will," I reply as I add strawberries to the waffle and some whipped cream, placing it in front of her when I'm done. "Eat, and I will be back in an hour to pick you up," I promise, my heart racing as she looks up at me with so much love and fondness that it makes my fingertips tingle. She takes a bite as the words process. Surprise appears in her eyes a second later.

"You're not going to have breakfast with me?" she asks, tugging a loose strand of her hair behind her ear.

"No, chérie, I have to take care of a few more things, but I'll be back soon. Make sure you put on a bikini, you'll need one." My thumb runs over the corner of her mouth, catching the whipped cream stuck there.

"Thank you for breakfast," she says softly as I place my thumb into my mouth, tasting the sweetness of the cream. Valentina licks her lips while I fight the desire to kiss her and taste not just the waffle but also her. Nothing compares to the taste of her.

"Anytime, mon tournesol," I add and take a deep breath. "I got Chase a bone, in case you're wondering what he's chewing on." Her eyes drift to where her son is chewing on something on his bed, warmth appearing in her gaze.

"I can't wait to spend the day with you," she says when I'm halfway out of the kitchen, causing my body to freeze.

"If I do this right, I hope you can't wait to spend the rest of your life with me, too," I admit before stepping out of the door and getting to work.

CHAPTER 31
Valentina

WHEN I'M DONE EATING the breakfast Gabriel made, I place the plate in the sink. He already cleaned everything else he made dirty. Of course he did. He's Gabriel. Besides what happened, he's perfect for me. Annoyingly so.

Chase and I head up to my room while I wonder what the hell I'm going to wear. It has to be good. The first thing I do is shave every part of my body that needs to be shaved. I'm going to be wearing a bikini in front of him, and I feel more comfortable without body hair. I know Gabriel doesn't give a shit, but this is about my comfort, not his.

Once I am happy with the way my face looks, and the way my hair naturally curls down my back, I walk out of my bathroom and into my closet. Chase follows me everywhere I go, patiently waiting for me to get ready.

I put on the nicest bikini I own, a blue bodysuit with spaghetti straps, and a white skirt that falls loosely down my legs and hits just above my knees. It's a simple outfit, especially with the flip-flops I'm wearing, but I feel comfortable. Plus, Gabriel will think I look lovely even if I put on a garbage bag.

Chase is still sitting in front of me, waiting for me to go outside with him. I look at myself one more time, admiring the way his necklace fits so well with the outfit and how displayed it is. It was the first thing that caught my attention when I looked at myself in the mirror, and I'm sure it's the same way for anyone who looks at me.

My eyes drift to the canvas of Gabriel hanging above my bed. I never had the heart to take it down because I thought once I did, we were over. No matter how angry and disappointed I was with him, I didn't want to give up hope. All of his choices were to protect me, so I know I won't ever find someone like Gabriel again. He doesn't just understand me, we have a lot in common. He likes the same music as I do, watches the same movies and shows, likes the same food, reads the same books, feels the same things, has the same dreams...

I quickly check my phone to make sure everything is okay with James, and I'm relieved to see he sent me a text.

James: We're okay. Damian is crying a lot, but Annie has been sleeping while I tried to calm him down. She is rested for when I fall asleep hahahaha. Thank you again for everything, and when you have time, please come to Annie's house. There is something we need to talk to you about.

"Oh, Valentinaaaaa," I hear Gabriel sing an hour after he left my house, not one minute later. Chase and I have been waiting for him on the terrace for ten minutes, and impatiently so. "Ma chérie, come to meee," he continues, and I smile childishly. His voice is wonderful to me, although I'm sure it probably isn't to a lot of other people.

My feet bring me toward where his voice is coming from. He's standing outside my gate with a bouquet of... daisies...

"I'm sorry, I didn't mean to upset you. I remember you told me daisies were your grandpa's favorite flowers, and I wanted to surprise you."

"I'm not upset, Gabriel, you're just really sweet, and I can't believe you remember." He hands me the bouquet, and I take it from him before he presses a kiss to my forehead and I wrap my arms around his torso. His mahogany scent fills my nose, and I smile against his blue button-down shirt.

"I remember everything, mon tournesol." I continue smiling, although I would rather kiss him right now. "As much as I would love to stay like this, I have an amazing day planned for us, and we need to get it started before certain things... well, you'll see." I let out a short laugh, and he steps out of the hug.

Gabriel brought Nicolette's Audi Q8, perfect for Chase who has all the space he could need in the trunk. I make sure to take poop bags, his leash, some treats, and a toy. Gabriel assures me there will be plenty of water for him wherever we are going. He thought it all through to the smallest detail so far. He is trying everything in his power to seek forgiveness, even though I have already forgiven him. I'm ready to move on, especially after the way he woke me up this morning, the fact that he brought Chase home, the lovely daisies he brought me, and, most importantly, the fact that I love him with every piece of my soul. Simply watching him while he's driving makes my heart flutter.

His skin has gotten more tanned recently, his stubble makes him as handsome as ever, and his long lashes complement his green-brown eyes perfectly. Gabriel's curly hair is loose on top of his head. His lips are pinker than usual, and he has a constant grin on his face, showing off his dimples.

Five years ago, I would have never thought I would meet someone and think they are the most beautiful person on the planet, but now, it's different. I have met so many people, but no one compares. Gabriel is handsome to me, inside and out, and while he is also gorgeous to many more people out there, millions of fans for that matter, they don't know him like I do. I have his trust and his love. That's mine, and only mine.

"So, how are Sienna and Callum liking Monaco?" I ask him, and the grin on his lips fades.

"Are you sure you want to talk about them?" He's acting like it's their fault. It's not. They had nothing to do with what happened.

"Of course I do. Callum and Sienna seem like wonderful people, and it's not their fault decisions were made, and, you know, things happened." Gabriel's expression turns sad, and I take his hand from the gear shift to place it in both of mine. I don't want him to be sad. "So, tell me, how are they liking it here?" I ask again, my voice cheerful and my face showing a big smile. When he looks at me and notices it, he returns it.

"They loved it. They flew back to Italy this morning, but they enjoyed their stay, especially Callum. My God, Val, you should have heard him. 'I can't believe I'm here, I can't believe I'm here.'" I laugh a little, enjoying the sound of his rough laughter. I'm also reminded how much I love the way words roll from his tongue when he speaks English. "I was going crazy."

I can imagine. Gabriel is patient, but there are limits to it. He goes on to tell me about the weekend with them, and I listen attentively. My head rests against the headrest as I watch him closely. Eventually, he is done talking, and our conversation dies out, but we don't need to speak. The silence is as bonding as the talking.

Moments later, Gabriel squeezes my hand and breaks it again. "I can't believe James has a child," he says.

"Me neither. I also can't believe how much I already care about the kid," I admit, and Gabriel smiles.

"He's family, of course you do. I would be surprised if you didn't care about him. After all, you did spend a lot of time with Annabel, you were there when Damian was born, you were there for the false labor—" But I have to cut him off then.

"How the hell do you know all of that? I didn't tell you any of it, and it's kind of freaking me out." Gabriel chuckles, but I'm too confused to join in.

"I only know what James told me, and I asked him to tell me everything he could from what's been going on in your life. He did refuse to share anything that wasn't related to Annabel or Damian. He drew a line there." James is the most amazing friend anyone could ever have. "I was going wild not being involved in your life. I constantly wanted to know what you were doing, how you were doing, and how your training was going. Adrian filled me in a little too, if I'm already being honest," Gabriel says and smiles.

"Well, it is still pretty creepy," I tease, and he laughs.

"I'm sorry, I didn't mean for it to be."

He pulls my hand toward his mouth to press a kiss to the back of it, and then he lets me put our hands back into my lap. Gabriel bites his bottom lip and focuses on driving again while I concentrate on the way his lip looks trapped between his teeth. *Too handsome...*

"All right, ma chérie, we have arrived at our first destination." I look outside to see we are at the harbor front where all the expensive boats and yachts are. I would say 'I can't believe he did this', but I can.

I don't even realize when he gets out of the car and walks around the back to get to my side and open the door. He holds out his hand for me to take, and I remove the seat belt before letting him help me out of the car.

The air is hot and the sun burns my skin as soon as it gets a glimpse at me. When Gabriel closes the door again, I lean against it and pull on his shirt to get him closer. He grins wickedly, and my mind is no longer in charge. My body is doing what it wants, without listening to my head or even heart for that matter. Slowly, I let my hands drop from his shirt and move them under it. Gabriel sucks in a sharp breath when I rest my hands on his abs.

"Chérie, we—uhm—we should get going. I have something planned," he whispers, but I'm barely listening.

I pull his head down and step on my tiptoes so I can press a kiss to his earlobe. A moan leaves his lips, and I smile victoriously. God, I missed hearing those sounds, it's been too long. My hands drop down to his belt, and I pull his lower body against mine. His arousal presses against my stomach, drawing a low growl out of him.

"Val, I have some stuff planned." When my head starts working again, I pull back and run my thumb over my bottom lip. Gabriel watches me carefully, and I can tell he is trying his best not to rip off my clothes. His eyes betray him.

"Let's go," I whisper, and he nods, his gaze still focused on my lips.

CHAPTER 32
Valentina

WE GET CHASE FROM the trunk, and Gabriel takes my hand to lead us to a beautiful white boat with flowers drawn on it, flowers just like the ones on my helmet. It's small, yet big enough to hold at least fifteen people. There are two benches at the front of the boat, and I see the number nine on the floor of it. I smile at the personalization, and Gabriel squeezes my hand to show me the side of it. The name 'Le Tournesol' is written there in beautiful letters, in his handwriting style. He holds out the key for me, but I take it hesitantly.

"I can't drive it," I tell him, and he smiles at me.

"Well, you're going to have to learn because it's yours." My mouth instantly falls open.

"You bought me a boat?" I ask, my voice louder than intended.

"Yes." I can't even process what he's telling me. *Is he out of his mind? This must have cost a fortune!*

"Gabriel, this is—I can't—oh my God. What the hell? I don't know what to say." I don't even know why the hell tears stream down my face, but they do anyway.

"Nothing, baby, you don't have to say anything. This boat will be here for you." I nod because it's all I can do, and Gabriel wipes away the tears that escaped my eyes. "I didn't mean to make you cry," he whispers, frustration evident on his face.

"It's not your fault, I don't even know why I'm crying," I reply, and he gives me a strained smile.

"No more tears because of me, mon tournesol, I beg of you. I don't deserve any of them," he pleads, causing my heart to stop beating for a breath.

"You don't get to decide if you are deserving, only I do." My voice is gentle, but I'd very much like to shake him. "Besides, these are happy tears. You bought me a fucking boat, Gabriel. My emotions are everywhere," I say with a little laugh, the urge to pull him to me and press my lips to his so strong, I feel it all the way in my toes.

"You're everything to me, ma chérie. I'd buy this whole planet if I could, if it'd make you happy. Please, don't ever doubt that."

There is a battle storming in his eyes, one I'm not sure he can win. He wants to kiss me. It's taking every ounce of self-control for him not to close the distance between us and plant his lips on mine. He's put all the power in my hands by not making the first move, but he wants to. I can see it in the tortured way his eyes study my face.

Gabriel shakes his head a little, taking my hand and breaking the moment of tension that had my muscles tightening with anticipation. We kissed yesterday, and yet, it feels like I haven't tasted him in years. It's maddening.

Once he's helped me onto the boat, he reaches down to lift Chase off the ground and places him right beside me.

"Okay, ready?" Gabriel asks, and I nod.

Chase is excited and spinning around like a tornado. I'm just as excited as he is, impatiently waiting to go swimming in the water as clear as the sky. I leash Chase onto the metal on the side of the boat to make sure he doesn't jump in the water and walk over to Gabriel who is at the steering wheel. He smiles sweetly, his dimples carved perfectly into his cheeks, and I wrap my arms around him from behind. Instantly, his scent fills my nose, making me sigh in response.

"Are you happy?" he asks, and I bite my bottom lip, trying to hide my smile.

"More than," I reply, and he lets out a deep breath.

"That's all I've ever wanted." His hand covers my arms, and I finally smile as widely as I can.

"I know, but this is it. It's either all of it, the good and bad, or nothing. There is no more in-between, mon soleil." He shuts the boat off and turns around to face me. He's quite a bit taller than me, even if he isn't exactly tall, and I squint a little as I look up to meet his gaze, the sun directly behind him blinding me. Noticing, he moves us until he's the one with it in his face.

"I don't want in-between," he says. "I want us, Valentina, that's all I'm ever going to want," he whispers, and I put my hands on each side of his face.

"Well, what are you going to do about it?" I challenge, letting my hands drop to the waistband of his swim trunks, and he raises his eyebrows.

"If we weren't on a boat surrounded by more boats, I would make you come over and over and over..." He trails off, his lips dropping to my jaw. "Remind you that you're mine and I'm yours. Remind you there is no one who makes me feel the way you make me feel and the other way around."

He rubs his nose against mine, forcing a grin to my lips. His fingers pulse on my hips before he steps back with a frustrated groan.

"Let's go swimming before we create a scandal," he says, causing a little laugh to escape me.

Gabriel tugs on my shirt to try and pull it off, but since it's a bodysuit, it won't come off the way he is trying to remove it. He starts pulling harder, and I start laughing and squirming.

"What the hell is this?" He keeps tugging, so I smack his hands away, laughter leaving my throat.

"Okay, calm down," I say, and he looks at me with frustration in his eyes. I chuckle before pulling down my skirt to show him what kind of top I'm wearing.

"Oh, sorry," he says, a blush settling on his cheeks. He lets out a nervous laugh and rubs the back of his neck with his hand. "I've never seen something like that." I bite the inside of my cheek so I don't start laughing again.

"All you have to do is open the buttons down here," I say and take his hand in mine to guide it toward where they are. "And then you can pull it up," I whisper even though his finger is already running along the buttons, causing my muscles to lose all strength. My head falls back as he presses his index finger down against my clit, a whimper fighting its way from my throat and past my lips.

"Like this, chérie?" he asks, but my eyes are closed as my body enjoys his touch. Pleasure grabs hold of my body and before I can stop myself, I grind against his hand. "Harder?" I nod, my breath shaking.

"Oh God, Gabriel," I moan as he drags his finger over my covered pussy, pressing the heel of his hand to where my swollen clit demands attention.

"You have no idea how much I miss this, baby. How much I miss making you come while my name slips from the lips I could kiss until I die. How much I miss sinking into my perfect heaven between your legs. How much I miss *you*," he says, leading me under the roof of the boat where we're a little more sheltered. Not enough, but I don't care right now.

All I can focus on is the way he plays with my clit through the thick fabric of my bikini.

"I'm sorry I denied us this. I'm sorry I was an idiot. I'm sorry I ever made you think my decisions weren't out of love. Because I love you. So much. I'll never love anyone or anything as consumingly as you," he says in French, his voice quivering with overwhelming emotions.

Pleasure might be clouding my brain, but his words tear me straight back to reality. I gently grab his hand and pull it away from my pussy, lifting it to my mouth to press a kiss to his wrist. His eyes fill with remorse as he studies me like I might disappear if he blinks too hard.

"You thought you were protecting me, making the right decision. I don't want to hold on to anger because of it anymore, Gabriel. I want us to move on, work through the pain of the past, and fight our demons together. I wish you'd have trusted me to be able to handle your darkness, but I know if the roles were reversed, I wouldn't have put you through it either. I cannot fault you for making the same choices I would have."

No matter what anyone says about the man standing in front of me, the truth remains: he has a pure heart. It fights with darkness more often than not, but the bright light inside of him somehow manages to win every single time. Expecting him to handle situations like finding out Carlos Klein is your fucking grandfather, that your mother was adopted, isn't right. I love him too much to put us through more pain. And what would it even be for? Pride? Having to be right when both of us already know leaving was the wrong decision? It's pointless, especially when it's clear he's my endgame. He's it for me and always has been.

Gabriel takes a step toward me and presses his forehead to mine, seeking comfort as my words process in his mind. His lips find my cheek a moment later before he wraps his arms around my upper body and nestles his face in the crook of my neck. His mahogany scent creeps into my nose until I barely contain my sigh of happiness.

"I have a question," he says after a while of silence, bringing a smile to my lips.

"Uh oh," I reply, attempting to lean away, but he holds me close to him.

"Can I try taking off that ridiculous top again?" he asks, and I burst into laughter.

"If you can manage," I tease in response, forcing a snort from him.

Gabriel undoes the buttons and then pulls the bodysuit off my chest, leaving my breasts to bounce free in the not-very-supporting bikini top. He sucks in a sharp breath at the sight.

"Fuck's sake," he curses under his breath, one of his hands reaching out to rest under my left breast and on my ribs. His thumb trails along the skin there until a wave of goosebumps sweeps over my body, hardening my nipples. His mouth lowers a few centimeters as his eyes glaze over with desire. If I don't move away, I have a feeling he'll pull my nipple into his mouth and suck on it until I see stars, and we're nowhere near alone enough to let that happen.

"Come on, the water will cool us down," I assure him, although I am not sure it's entirely true. His lips still haven't touched mine, and it's driving me wilder and wilder by the second.

Chase lies down in the shade the roof provides while Gabriel hands me a bowl of water to give to my little boy. He takes off his clothes, and I groan ever so slightly at the sight. The muscles lining his back steal my breath. Then, he spins around to reveal a new tattoo he got on his ribcage. My brows furrow as a smile takes over my face. I take a step closer to make out what it is, my heart lurching at the sight of a sunflower and sun intertwined in one another.

"Gabriel," I gasp, but he merely follows my gaze to his tattoo with a smile. "You got this before we got back together?" A shrug lifts his muscular shoulders.

"You were already tattooed on my soul. I just wanted a visual representation, too," he explains, and I somehow fall even more in love with him.

My fingers trail over the simple lines, feeling the tug in my own soul that his has on mine. It's like my entire being is drawn to him, the kind of pull no one could ever resist. The tips of my fingers trail down his abs until goosebumps appear on his chest.

"Do you like it, mon tournesol?" he asks as my mind tries to process the fact that a part of me, of who I am to him, is forever tattooed onto his skin.

"I do, very much, mon soleil," I reply, looking up at him to see his easy smile.

My lips tingle with the need to kiss him all over, feel how hard he is, but I manage to jump into the water before the urge to kiss a line down his abs takes over.

Gabriel follows me, his cannonball spraying water everywhere. I turn to avoid getting any in my eyes but when I spin back, he's gone. A second later, his hands slip under my armpits and he throws me forward, water enveloping me. I push to the surface again to see Gabriel right in front of me, his curly hair wet and dripping water into his face. A smug smile plays on his full lips, bringing out a single dimple. I find it almost ridiculous how badly I crave to trace it, as if I haven't done it a million times already.

"If you'd like to touch me, chérie, please do. My body, heart, mind, and soul belong to you and every single part of them crave your attention," he says, effortlessly keeping himself above water. His bottom lip slips between his teeth as he watches my eyes and then my lips.

I can't help myself anymore.

My arms push through the water until the distance between us disappears, my limbs wrapping around him when I'm finally close enough. My fingers intertwine at his nape before I slide them into his hair and tug to bring his mouth closer. Gabriel doesn't hesitate. He presses his lips to mine and grabs me by the hips to hold me tightly against him. I moan into his mouth, unable to hide how good this feels, how good *he* feels. I don't know why, but my body seems to be more sensitive, more easily pleasured at the moment as long as it is Gabriel touching me. Euphoria blooms in my chest at the feel of my needy pussy rubbing over his hardening cock in the water, forcing another moan from me.

"Please, stop doing that," Gabriel begs, and I bring my lips to his earlobe. "Val, please, we are not alone out here, and if you make that little noise again, I won't be able to control myself," he warns.

"What if I don't want you to control yourself?" I ask, biting his lobe until a low groan escapes him.

"Then the rest of our day will go very differently than I've planned, and I'd very much like us to go to our second location," he says as his fingers dig into my hips. Part of me wishes he'd grab lower, give in to what we want, but another part is too curious about the mysterious *second location*.

"Okay," I mumble, pressing my cheek against his while we float in the water for a little longer.

It feels carefree being with him like this. As if there was no pain, no problems, absolutely no worry in the world. I could stay like this forever, right in the arms of my greatest love story while he whispers in my ear how beautiful I am over and over again.

And just like that, I wonder how I could have ever believed we wouldn't spend the rest of our lives being the other person's home.

CHAPTER 33
Valentina

CHASE IS ALREADY WAGGING and waiting for us by the time we get back on the boat. My chest fills with love and warmth at the sight, so I rush toward him and bend over to give my son the attention he craves.

"Val," Gabriel groans in complaint. I stand up straight, facing him with a confused smile.

"What?" I ask. He's frowning, almost pouting, causing the corners of my mouth to curl up even more.

"Put on some clothes, please," he says, his tone gentle and a little desperate. *Oh, that's his problem.* I laugh and assure him I will, in a second. My eyes drift to his hard cock straining against his swim trunks, and I smile at the fact that he's just as horny as I am. Then, I bend over again to pet Chase, who is still so happy to see me. Seconds later, I feel a gentle smack on my right ass cheek, sending a thrill through my body. "Put on some clothes," he repeats, his voice firm. My bottom lip slips between my teeth as I try to hide my smile.

"Hmmm," I say, my ass cheek tingling from his touch. I stand upright and grind a little against him, feeling his hard need pressing against me.

"God, chérie, you're going to be the death of me," he whispers, but instead of pushing me away, he glides his hands over my waist to drag me closer. A soft gasp leaves my lips as anticipation licks its way down my spine.

"I'm not the one pressing your cock against my ass," I defend, although my words are breathless. If there's one thing besides racing and drawing that this man is undoubtedly amazing at, it's finding ways to make my breathing hitch and desire pool between my legs.

"No, but you are the one I'll gladly die for," he replies, and I roll my eyes at his cheesy words like I've always done. The smile slipping onto my face, however, is completely out of my control.

"Still so corny," I mumble to myself as I spin around in his arms.

"Only for you, mon tournesol." He kisses the tip of my nose before reaching for my towel and wrapping it around me.

Watching his concentrated face, something so familiar and almost nostalgic fills me. *Longing.* I've felt it since my mother left, and then with every person I lost after. Longing to have them back. Longing to never have to let go again. Longing to feel whole once more. The closest I've ever felt to being complete again was when Gabriel held me, loved me, understood me, and supported me. Maybe it's the reason why I didn't simply move on because there is no moving on from Gabriel Matteo Biancheri.

Not when he makes me feel alive in a world of death.

Not when he's the sun to my sunflower.

My hands slip onto his back after he's done placing the towel around my chest, searching for a way to close the distance between us. His mahogany scent fills my nose, forcing me to fight back a sigh of relief because *he's really here.* We're okay now.

"I'm never letting you go again," I mumble into his chest. He leans back to cup my face. His eyes search mine before he slowly, torturously slowly, closes the distance and places his lips on mine.

"You are my home, Valentina Esmèe Cèlia Romana, you are my life." Gabriel drops down onto his knees and wraps his arms around my stomach. It will never fail to amaze me how willingly Gabriel places himself in vulnerable positions in front of me. Someone so determined not to get hurt again placing himself in my hands is something I'll do everything in my power to never take for granted. "I'm all yours, chérie."

He still doesn't see I've forgiven him. He doesn't see I love him too much to stay angry. For fuck's sake, he tried to prioritize my dream and me, even if it may have been the wrong choice. None of it matters anymore, so I can't help blurt out the one thing I want the most. The one thing I wanted when we were still together. The reason why I gave him a key and looked at apartments with him.

"Move in with me," I say after a few more moments of complete silence. This feels so good to say, the words falling off my lips with absolute ease.

"What?" he asks, confusion obvious on his handsome face.

"I want to live with you, in my grandfather's house. I want you to come home to me. I want you to call my home yours." A grin slips across my face, but he's too surprised to return it.

"What about what happened?" he asks, unsure of himself, of my words.

"I want you to move in with me, mon amour. I love you, Gabriel Matteo Biancheri and I want to live with you." Tears shoot into his eyes as he finally smiles back at me. Happiness takes over his entire being because I just told him I love him for the first time since we broke up.

"You love me?" he says, and I'm not sure whether or not it's a question or a statement. I merely lower myself until I straddle his lap, my hands moving to cup his jaw.

"I love you."

Before I can say anything else, he pulls my head down to his and brings his lips onto mine. He kisses every inch of my face until giggles escape my throat.

"Yes, yes, and yes. I want nothing more than to live with you."

He kisses me again, but this time it's different, it's more intimate. His hands are close to my breasts, and his tongue runs over my bottom lip before it disappears into my mouth.

"I'm never going to leave again, I promise," he says, and I believe him. I don't think either of us wants to go through this hell again.

"This is huge," I say.

"It is, it really is, but I know we can make this work, mon tournesol. I love you so much," he says, and I smile.

"I love you the same, mon soleil." Gabriel flashes me his set of perfect teeth and leans forward to bite the soft skin on my neck.

"Say it again," he says before he runs his tongue over the delicious ache.

"I love you," I moan because he's biting on my sensitive spot. "I love you, I love you, I... love... you," I say between kisses and nibbles. "Okay," I add and kiss him. "Let's go to the second location." Gabriel's lips find mine again.

"You're right. At least there I can touch you without anyone seeing." My whole body catches fire, but Chase lets out a bark, snapping me back to reality.

Gabriel clears his throat while I get up from the ground, pulling him up too. With a kiss on my lips, he goes to the steering wheel of *my* boat—that's going to take a while to process—and starts the engine again. I move over to Chase and play with him.

Monaco is beautiful, and the view from this boat shows exactly that. The old buildings decorating the skyline represent home to me, just like Adrian, Chase, James, Evangelin, racing, and Gabriel. My family is where my home is. The future often scares me, but when I look at Gabriel, I know I don't have to be afraid.

We arrive back at the docks where Gabriel parks the boat in its designated spot. I'm still in my bikini, which has mostly dried by now, and he changed into his boxers and shorts without me even noticing.

My boyfriend takes care of everything while I go to the car and change into the extra clothes I brought in my bag. The dress I put on doesn't require me to wear a bra, so I leave it off, hoping it will drive Gabriel wild. It is my favorite pastime, after all. Chase is patiently waiting in the back of the car, but *I'm* impatiently waiting in the passenger seat.

My man's eyes find my face as he gets in before they slowly trail down to my cleavage. The hunger in his eyes has me pressing my legs together and pulling his mouth to mine. My tongue plays with his until I'm aching to find a way to crawl over to his side. My mind is turned off, and my body is doing what it needs to do. I haven't been fully satisfied since Gabriel left because I can't fully satisfy myself, not the way he can. My hand drops to his bulge, but he grabs my wrist to stop me.

"Chérie, not here," he says, but I don't stop kissing him.

"I want you now," I whisper, and he loosens his grip a little so my hand can rub over him.

"Not here, chérie," he repeats, but he lets out a moan when I apply the right amount of pressure. "God, baby," he moans, grinding himself against my touch. "You have to stop, Val, you know paparazzi don't care about videoing intimate moments. They'll do it anyway and then share it with the world." I know he's right, which is the only reason I retract my hand. My whole body is on fire and aching. "Horny, are we?" I put my head against the headrest, close my eyes, and let out a long groan.

"You have no idea. I've been so aroused recently, it's absurd, and then the only guy who could help me with this wasn't there." I look at him again, and he wets his bottom lip with his tongue.

"I'm the only one?" he asks, his hand moving to my exposed thigh.

"Don't get cocky now, but yes, you are." But of course, a victorious smile spreads across his lips.

"My horny girl only wants me," he says, and I smack his arm playfully. The hand that was resting on my thigh, however, is moving closer and closer to my panties. "You have no idea how hot that is," he whispers, leaning in closer. He presses his nose to the hollow of my neck and inhales, forcing distance between us as a groan escapes his mouth.

Gabriel turns on the car and drives until we reach a large tree, parking the car under it so we're mostly hidden from sight. He spins toward me, grabbing my mouth in a fierce kiss. Every cell in my body lights on fire when he pushes his tongue back inside my mouth, tasting me until he groans with contentment.

"This mouth, Valentina, being away from it felt like every liquid in my body turned to dust," he says, cupping my face and tilting it to the side to lick along the length of my neck. "Being away from your skin was like my organs ripping themselves apart in protest," Gabriel goes on before sucking on the soft spot on my neck only he knows exists.

"Gabriel," I whimper, my clit giving violent, needy throbs, demanding his attention.

As if he could feel it, his hand slips under my skirt to cup my pussy.

"And this beautiful pussy, ma chérie, being away from it was like slowly dying of starvation," he says, rubbing the heel of his hand against my covered clit.

"Fuck," I breathe out, my back arching off the seat to get more contact. If I could, I would get on my knees and start riding his hand to find my release faster. Instead, I remain patient and let him stay in control.

"Tell me, baby, did you fuck your fingers when I wasn't there?" He presses his tongue to my soft spot to soothe the ache from his sucking. Pleasure erupts under my skin like little explosions of euphoria.

"Yes," I admit, wishing away my panties so his fingers could slide inside of me.

"But they didn't satisfy you the way I do." It's not a question but I give him another breathless 'yes' anyway. "You prefer my fingers, chérie, don't you?" he asks, and I nod and nod and nod. "And my mouth," Gabriel says, finally slipping his fingers upward until he's playing with the elastic of my thong. "But there's something you miss even more, isn't there?" He leans far enough back so that when he tilts my head his way, I can see the lust covering his features.

"There is." My heart hammers in my chest as he finally, *finally*, slides his fingers inside my panties.

"Tell me," he repeats, his fingers disappearing into my slick opening.

"Your cock," I blurt out as I buck against his fingers.

Gabriel lets out a satisfied hum, fucking me with his fingers and curling them inside me every time. He strokes my G-spot until I'm crying out his name over and over, my hand reaching for his wrist because the pleasure is too much. Too overwhelming. And at the same time, nowhere near enough.

My eyes remain on his while he takes his time bringing me to my orgasm, as if he wants to savor all of my sounds and the way I feel for as long as he can. A slight panic settles in my chest at the thought of anyone walking by and seeing him with his hand under my dress. That very same thought also dials my pleasure higher and higher until I feel my lower stomach tense. I roll my hips, chasing my orgasm because I'm so close. So fucking close.

"Val, you're so fucking hot and tight and wet, I want to drag you onto my cock and show you how hard you make me," he says, and his dirty words send a shudder of pleasure through me.

"Please," I beg, even if I'm not quite sure what for. I want to come on his cock, but I'm so close, I hope he doesn't stop fingering me either. His thumb trails over my bottom lip, which he pulls down only to watch it bounce back after he releases it. Then, he kisses me, breathing me in and groaning happily. Meanwhile, his fingers pick up pace, bringing me closer to the release I'm desperate for.

"Later I'm going to show you exactly why I'm the only one, let you ride me until you fall apart, but for now, come for me, chérie."

And I do. I come with a cry, my entire body trembling violently in the seat. Gabriel lets me grind myself against his hand to ride out my orgasm, and it doesn't stop for a while. All the built-up tension from the month without him releases in waves and waves of pleasure. Right as I think it'll stop, another wave hits me, one so hard I'm shaking everywhere. It doesn't help that he's still playing with my G-spot as I try to come down from my high.

"Seeing you come will forever be one of my favorite things to watch," Gabriel says as he pulls his hand out my panties only to slip the fingers he used to fuck me into his mouth.

Fuck, why is that so hot?

"I need my face buried between your legs later, baby, need my mouth on your pretty pussy." My body gives an agreeing quiver at his words.

Every piece of me is sated, so when I see the outline of his huge length pressing against the front of his pants, I have this desperate need inside of me to make him feel the same way.

"And I want my mouth on you now," I say, playing with the waistband of his shorts. "I want to suck your cock," I add, watching his cock press against the fabric like a prisoner trying to escape his very uncomfortable confinement. "Let me ease your ache, Gabriel." He lets out a string of curses in French when I undo his button and slide his zipper down.

"Fuck, Valentina," he curses as I lick my lips at the sight of his cock straining against his black boxers.

"Do you want me to stop?" I ask, my fingers itching to wrap around his length. Gabriel grabs my jaw with two fingers before catching my lips in a bruising kiss.

"Never."

CHAPTER 34
Gabriel

I've always known I don't deserve her. That became more abundantly clear to me after she forgave me. What's happening now? It's making it *even clearer*. Valentina Romana will forever be too good for me, but fuck if I'm not going to do my absolute best every single day to deserve her.

We've moved to the backseat so she's on the floor of the car on her knees, right between my legs. She's powerful, even in a position that should scream vulnerability, and I can't help but be more turned on. The way her slender fingers play with me, her colorful eyes staring into mine, her mouth pulled into a thin smile, all of it has me at her mercy. Especially watching her nipples pebble against the thin fabric of her dress because of how aroused she is. Aroused because she's holding my dick in her hands. Fuck me.

Val presses a single kiss to the head of my cock, sending a tsunami of pleasure through me until I shiver in the seat.

"I've missed having you inside me, even if it's just my mouth for now," Val says, and I'm so surprised by the way she's been talking dirty to me, I can't stop my cock from giving a happy jerk in her hand. "Hmmm," she moans, a satisfied little sound I feel traveling through me until it reaches the top of my head and tips of my toes.

"Chérie, I need—" I break off when she raises one of her hands and slides it under my shirt. Her nails drag down my abs, causing a happy moan to leave her.

"What, mon amour? What do you need?" She's playing with me like I'm her favorite toy, and I'm enjoying every torturous second of her slow touches.

"Your mouth, baby. I need your mouth on me." It's all I can focus on right now. Her perfect lips framing my cock, her tongue running over the length of it and coating me in her saliva.

The thought alone has me very close to coming apart.

"You need *me*, Gabriel. Don't ever forget it," she says, and while her words are serious, a playful smile crosses her face.

"How could I? An artist never forgets his muse, not when she's already immortalized herself in his work and soul." Her eyes sparkle with adoration before lust replaces it again as my bottom lip slides between my teeth.

"Am I your muse?" she asks, slowly pumping me now. My eyes flutter shut and my head falls backward against the seat, enjoying the pleasure washing through my veins.

"You're my everything, mon tournesol," I reply, my words turning into a low, guttural moan when she licks along the underside of my cock. "Fuck me," I blurt out, earning myself a slight chuckle from her.

"Shirt off, Gabriel, I want to watch your muscles flex for me," she instructs, and I don't waste a second. My fingers grab hold of the fabric, ripping it over my head and throwing it to the side. Usually, when we have sex, I'm the one who likes to be in control. Right now? I'm fucking ecstatic because of the way she's bossing me around. It's so sexy, it's making my already aching cock throb and leak with precum.

I don't know where her dominant side during sex came from, but I can't quite contain my excitement.

"You're fucking beautiful, Valentina. So devastatingly gorgeous. And mine. All mine." She gives me a smile in return, running her hand up and down my chest again.

"And who do you belong to, Gabriel?" Val licks along my shaft again until I'm quivering in the seat. My self-control is so far out of the window that I'm convinced it's in space by now. "Tell me," she demands, dragging me back into the moment. She takes me deep into her mouth, only pulling out once her gag reflex sets in. Fuuuuuck.

"I belong to you," I manage to croak out between moans and groans of pleasure.

"Say it again," she says before swirling her tongue around the head of my cock and making me see stars.

"I'm yours," I repeat, and she gives a satisfied hum while swallowing me down again. The sound travels through my cock until my balls pull even tighter. This woman is trying to kill me, and I've never looked forward to dying as much as I am right this second.

I'd die a thousand times at her hand if it meant being hers again.

If it meant moving in with her.

If it meant being with her until I die for good.

"You're mine," she echoes as she works me so wonderfully that my orgasm builds too quickly, too overwhelmingly. I barely manage to hold it off because I don't want this to end already. She's hardly touched me, and I can tell how much she's enjoying herself by the way little moans keep slipping out of her. By the way her eyelids flutter with pleasure. By the way I know her panties are already drenched again.

God, I want to touch her.

Valentina takes me deep into her mouth, switching between licking, kissing, and sucking me. My fingers curl around her hair, holding it back while her head bobs up and down. It's the sweetest type of pleasure I've felt since I left. Her hot, wet mouth taking me deep, her slippery and velvety tongue playing with my cock. The way she moans at the taste of me. Everything catapults me closer to the orgasm I so desperately crave.

"Are you wet, baby?" I ask when I notice her rolling her hips back and forth in search of some kind of friction. The hand she's resting on my thigh twitches as she nods. "Ah, fuck," I groan as her other hand slips from my cock to cup my balls. "Val," I beg because if she keeps playing with them, I will come quickly. Too quickly.

"Watch me touch myself, Gabriel. See what you do to me," she instructs as she slips her fingers low, finding her perfect pussy and playing with it.

Hearing the wet sounds of her fingers as they dip inside of her combined with the way she sucks me off and closes her eyes from pleasure sends me straight over the cliff. My cum shoots down her throat as my body trembles with an orgasm so intense, my vision blurs for a very long moment. Valentina swallows me down and keeps going long after my orgasm washes off, causing all of me to tremble. I curse and search for her face, trying to get her to stop while also not wanting her to. It's a strange sensation of pain and pleasure, as if another orgasm is about to ripple through already, even though I'm only half hard at this point.

"Val, please," I beg, so she lets go of my cock. It releases with a popping sound right as she cries out, her fingers pumping in and out of her frantically. I grab her mouth in a kiss, desperate to taste her pleasure.

"I love you," she says after opening her eyes and tilting her head to look up at me.

"Never stop telling me that," I reply and press a kiss to her lips again.

CHAPTER 35
Gabriel

THE DRIVE TO OUR second location is short, and Adrian is already waiting outside of the small building when we arrive. Valentina looks confused as her gaze catches her brother's figure, but I merely nod at my teammate as I slip out of the car.

"Did you make sure everything's in order?" I ask, and he gives me a smug smile. I wish I had his confidence sometimes. Other times, I'm glad I don't. I wouldn't be able to handle being this cocky.

"Yes, now let me get Chase," he says and steps toward the car, opening the door for Val.

They exchange a few sentences, and I finally watch curiosity and excitement cross her face. Adrian heads for the trunk to take Chase home. Meanwhile, Valentina and I are closing the distance between us, my hands lifting to cup her cheeks.

"I'm going to do something very cheesy and cliché, and I am going to cover your eyes, okay? Blindfold you like I did on our first friend date." We laugh for a moment, and I kiss her cheek before covering her eyes. "Ready?" I ask, and she nods in response.

We step inside the building and toward where the surprise is waiting for her. Valentina is patient, as always, while I do my best to avoid any spots she could stumble over. Once we're in place, I uncover her eyes, hearing a small gasp leave her full lips as she takes in the scene in front of us. There are sunflowers and daisies everywhere in the small room. Candles surround the blanket in the middle of it, and pillows rest at the top. Pizza boxes from her favorite restaurant are sitting on the blanket along with her favorite coffee. The room is dark, only lit by the candles and one small standing light in the corner of the room. It's intimate, just the way I planned.

"Do you like it?" I turn around, and she wraps her arms around me, my hands resting just above the small of her back.

"I love it," she replies. I grin while leading her to the blanket where we sit down.

Valentina and I start eating while she tells me about Evangelin and her expansion of *Rush*. I pay close attention to every single word, every detail she wants to share with me, and revel in the joy of hearing her tell me about her life again. It's one of my favorite things in the world.

Once we're done eating, we lie back on the hundred pillows I brought, and she finally notices the projector pointed at the white wall above us. Her eyebrows furrow, so I turn it on to reveal a slideshow of pictures of her and me, either together or only her. Every few seconds they switch, her eyes glued to them. The slideshow restarts when all the photos have been played, but Val takes the remote from me, looking through them once more.

"This is wonderful," she whispers. I press my lips to her temple.

"I'm glad you liked it. My friend rents out these rooms for the projectors and privacy," I reply, bringing a smile to her lips.

She snuggles into my side while I pull her even closer, enjoying her scent as it fills my nose. For the first time in weeks, my heart settles into an even, slow rhythm, one that doesn't send pain through my system with every beat. It's like, finally, I can rest again, take a break from all of the horrible things happening in the world to focus on the way Valentina buries her face in my neck to inhale my scent, too.

My pitstop.

"How are Domi and Nicolette?" she asks after a while of us reveling in how it feels to be back in each other's arms.

"They're busy building the nursery today. Jean is helping out, too, but he told me he's going out with his girlfriend tonight," I say, and her head snaps back to show me the shock on her features.

"Jean has a girlfriend? Since when?" she asks, leaning back even further to study me. I can't help but smile at the excitement in her gaze. This woman cares so much about my family and me, something that never ceases to amaze me.

"Since two weeks ago, I think. He's been rather secretive about it," I reply with a small chuckle and cock of my brows. Val grins like it's the best thing she's heard all week.

"I never thought I'd see the day," she says, settling back onto my chest and wrapping her arm around my stomach.

"Because he's so annoying? Yeah, it's a surprise anyone would willingly want to put up with him." She smacks my stomach in response, and I let out a laugh that pulls one right out of her, too.

"Damn you and your contagious laughter," she mumbles against my side, but I merely press a kiss to her forehead. Silence envelops us once more, but Valentina breaks it just as easily as before. "You're leading the championship. How do you feel?"

"Honestly, I'm fucking terrified," I say, accidentally squeezing her harder against me at the thought of the expectations weighing heavy on my shoulders.

"I'd be worried if you weren't. A lot is on the line for you, and my brother is a competitive racer. He won't give up without a fight," she replies, and, for a moment, I wish I could see the reason why she said it, why she'd add to my fear, but she answers the question before I have the chance to voice it. "But, speaking as someone who's been analyzing the data all year, watched you and Adrian fight it out on track, I think you have something Adrian hasn't quite managed to acquire. Something that'll help you win."

"And what's that, ma chérie?" I ask, barely managing to keep my breathing even.

"Taking this seriously and racing like your life depends on it. Adrian still hasn't shaken off the easy-going, overconfident act, and it's something he needs to work on if he wants to be World Champion. You don't win just because you're a good racer. You win because you *understand* the sport as much as you breathe it." She leans back once more to look me in the eyes. "And you, Gabriel Biancheri, have proven to the world over and over that there is only one of you out there, a rarity like none other. A racer with a heart so big, he knows when to shut it off a little to win." A mischievous smile crosses her lips before she kisses me and snuggles against me once more.

She's right. I can turn my heart off to win. No matter who races against me, I will do what it takes to get first place as long as it's within the rules. My determination gives me an edge, one Adrian doesn't have because he can't turn off who he is. It matters to him who he races against, and I often find that he backs out of fights earlier than I would on track.

"By the way, I'm getting an IUD on Wednesday. If I don't reply to your messages, that's why," she says, pulling me out of my trance. Panic grips me by the throat.

"Can I come with you?" I ask, and she looks up at me. I'm beyond worried, something she seems to sense because her fingers lift to my cheek to comfort me. My eyes close in response, and I can't help but smile.

"Of course. It's nothing serious, mon amour, nothing to worry about." I nod and open my eyes again, but only half this time.

"How come you're getting an IUD? Isn't the pill or shots or anything else working?" I don't like the idea of her having to get this procedure done.

"Mon soleil, you really don't have to be worried. Everything is going to be fine. An IUD is much safer, and it lasts five years. Trust me. There is nothing to worry about." She presses a kiss to my jaw to make me feel better.

"Chase is an incredibly beautiful dog, and I cannot wait to fight with him for his Mommy's attention," I say to switch the subject because having a panic attack about her procedure is not happening right now. It puts a smile on her lips before she leans her head against my chest again.

"There won't be much fighting, I promise. Chase will always have my undivided attention," she replies, and I huff out a laugh before tickling her. She bursts into a fit of giggles, but I don't stop, not until I'm on top of her.

"I can't wait to live with you," I blurt out, my hands pinning her wrists above her head.

"I can't wait either, which is kind of why I asked you." My little smart ass. I tickle her again but release her quickly. Her eyes catch my face, all soft features and happy smiles staring up at me.

"What are you thinking about?" I rub my thumb over her bottom lip, reveling in the plumpness.

"Um, I think I wanted to tell you something, but I honestly don't remember. All I can think about is your finger on my lip," she admits, causing a chuckle to rumble off my chest. My lips fall down to hers in an attempt to taste her feelings, the love she holds for me. It's a gentle kiss, and I fall into it as if it was a lifeline. *She's my lifeline.*

My phone vibrates in my pocket a second later, *one fucking second*, and I break our contact to groan into her neck. I pull it out of my pocket to silence it when concern spreads through my chest like hot liquid.

"Nicolette, what's wrong?" I ask, my voice shaking.

"Gabriel—" She cuts off, a sob coming through the line. "Domi was bleeding, and—we went to the hospital to check if the baby is alright, but—Gabriel, we lost the baby," she cries into the phone, stopping the world from spinning.

No. Oh God, no.

Nausea bubbles up in my throat when her words sink in and another sob travels from her end to mine.

"I'll be right there."

She hangs up right as my gaze travels down to Valentina where she's patiently waiting under me. Fuck. I can't breathe.

"Domi, she—uhm—she started bleeding," I start, her hand flying to her mouth when she realizes where this is going. "She lost the baby." My heart aches in my chest at the words.

"Come on, we have to go, your aunts need you, and you need to drop me at home—" I cut her off.

"No, please, I need you to come with me." Valentina gives me a small nod, placing her hand on my cheek for a brief moment before I get up and pull her with me.

I don't say anything else. My sole focus is on getting to my aunts to be with them while they go through something no one should ever have to experience. Valentina and I rush outside where I start fumbling with my keys, my hands shaking. Hers wrap around mine as tears fill my eyes.

This can't be happening. This isn't real. And I still cannot fucking breathe. *Why the fuck can't I breathe?*

"Gabriel," Val says softly, and I bite the inside of my cheek.

"I can't, Val, I can't. They were trying for so long, and they finally got what they wanted when they found out she was pregnant. My aunts are the sweetest people, and they were so happy when Domi got pregnant." The tears fall from my eyes, and I let them. She wraps her arms around me, letting me cry against her shoulder. I hate crying, *but this pain?* I can hardly bear it, and it isn't even mine.

"Come on, baby, your aunts need you," she coos after a moment of us hugging. I fight back the rest of the tears trying to claw their way out of my eyes, making her frown at me. "Let it out. It's okay to," she assures me, and I nod.

"I know, I just don't want to cry anymore." I've been crying a lot recently, reliving the grief of everyone I lost, living through the grief of losing Val, now this. "It's not fair," I whisper.

"No, it's not. In no way is this fair. All we can do is be there for your aunts and cry with them until there are no more tears left." She places her hands on my neck, caressing my skin there with her fingers. Mine are resting on her hips, my eyes focused on hers. "Tell me what I can do to make you feel better," she says, and I tilt my head to the side, my eyes fluttering shut.

"Kiss me and tell me you love me." She steps on her tiptoes a second later to kiss me softly.

"I love you, mon amour." We've been saying it a lot today, but I couldn't care less.

I love her, I love her, I love her.

She's the most important person in my life, and I finally got her back. It's the only thing keeping me breathing right now.

CHAPTER 36

Valentina

GABRIEL AGREED IT WOULD be better if I drove to the hospital since he doesn't think he can concentrate on the road right now. I can't even blame him, I'm barely able to concentrate on anything other than how badly my heart aches for Domi and Nicolette.

Gabriel takes my hand from the gear shift, presses a kiss to the back of it, and wraps both of his around mine, just the way I usually do with his hand. It makes me remember the time in the car when he was so touchy, he complained when I took my hand away. I asked him then why he was being so clingy, and he told me 'I'm nervous, and holding your hand comforts me.' He's nervous right now too, I can tell by the way he's behaving: his hands are squeezing mine tightly and his legs are shaking the whole car when we stand at traffic lights.

When we finally arrive at the hospital, I park in one of the last available parking spots, and we run inside. Gabriel is pulling me, and I do my best to keep up with him.

"I'm here to see my aunts. Dominique and Nicolette Biancheri." The nurse turns to look at her computer, and he shifts to me to give me a quick kiss, searching for comfort. When the woman looks at me, she says something that makes my heart drop.

"Family only. Girlfriends may not come in." Gabriel steps in front of me and glares at the woman.

"She's not my girlfriend, she's my wife," he says, and she mumbles an apology, avoiding both of our gazes.

She's my wife... I can't help my small smile, but it soon fades when we walk into Domi's hospital room and find Nicolette crying next to her wife, who is getting some rest after the worst day of their lives. Jean is leaning against the wall in the far back of the room, his left hand covering his mouth. His hair looks like he's been running his fingers through it over and over again.

Gabriel lets go of my hand and walks over to Nicolette while Jean moves over to me. He wraps his arms around my neck, and I fling mine around his waist. He needs this. I can feel it in the way he clings to me.

"Thank you for coming," he mumbles, and I force a smile.

"Valentina," I hear Nicolette say, and my heart breaks for her once again.

There is too much pain in her voice for me not to feel even the slightest bit of it. I open my arms, and the tall woman hugs me tightly as she sobs into my hair. I had no idea she liked me this much, but it doesn't matter right now. She keeps on sobbing, and I rub my hands over her back to comfort her. Maybe it's easier for her to let it out with someone who isn't directly affected by this grief.

We stay in the embrace for a few moments longer before she pulls back and wipes away her tears.

"Can I get you something?" I ask, and she tugs a loose strand of my hair behind my ear as if I were the one who needed comfort.

"No, belle, thank you so much for coming. I'm just going to get some coffee." I nod, watching her leave the room, Jean following closely behind her. Gabriel sits down in the chair next to his aunt's bed, and I step over to him. My hand slips onto his shoulder, and his wraps around my wrist before he turns his head to press a kiss to my arm.

"Tell me something nice," he says, probably to distract his head from all the dark thoughts entering it.

"You called me your wife," I say. Gabriel's green-brown eyes focus on my face, and he flashes me his dimples as he smiles softly.

"I guess I did. Sounded right, didn't it?" His eyes flutter shut as I press my nose to his.

"Yeah, it did," I admit in a gentle voice while leaning back, and he kisses my arm again. "Valentina Esmèe Cèlia Romana-Biancheri, that's quite a mouthful," I tell him, and he laughs.

"Yes, it is, but it sounds too right for us not to hyphen our last names." I squat down next to him, and he places his thumb on my chin, parting my lips. He shifts forward, presses his lips to mine briefly, and leans down to whisper into my ear. "Just imagine this: Mrs. Romana-Biancheri, we're done polishing your world championship trophy." I almost tear up when he says it.

The future holds a lot, and I hope it holds exactly what he just said. I finally realized what I want, I finally realized I do want children, as difficult as parenting is going to be. I want to have a big family, just like Gabriel. But not now, not anytime in the near future. First, I'll be World Champion. Then we can have our family. But his words make me realize I want to get married and spend the rest of my life with the one person I know I'll love forever. I'm young, but I have also been through so much it feels like I've been alive for a hundred years.

"When you move in with me, I want us to agree on something," I say, and he nods.

"Anything you want, ma chérie." His thumb runs over my bottom lip.

"No matter what happens, no matter how much we fight, I don't ever want us to go to bed angry with each other. If there is a problem between us, we'll sort it out right then and there. We need to be able to talk about things, otherwise, this will never work."

Gabriel's thumb moves to my chin again, and he lifts my head carefully.

"Okay, no more going to bed when we're angry with each other." I smile at him, and he kisses me again. When he pulls back, he winks at me before he brings his attention back to Domi. She's still sleeping, and I see Gabriel's legs bouncing up and down.

"Baby, why are you so nervous?" He follows my gaze to his legs, and I furrow my eyebrows.

"I'm not, I have to pee," he whispers. I bite my bottom lip to keep from smiling.

"Then go pee, I'll watch over her," I assure him.

Gabriel gets up and stretches before he kisses my cheek and walks out of the room. I take his place next to Domi's bed, checking my phone for notifications and see that Evangelin sent me a picture saying: *This would be really sweet for you and Gabriel.* I told her I was going on a date with him, and I cannot believe she sent me this already. It's two bracelets. They are both silver bands with a charm in the shape of a rectangle. The bracelet meant for him has a black charm with a blue stone next to the white words 'Her King' and a thin heart. The bracelet meant for her is the same thing except the charm is rose gold, the stone is pink, plus the words read 'His Queen' next to the thin heart. This is a beautiful gesture, but it's not personal.

After I put in the order of the personalized bracelets—luckily, I could change the writing—I place my phone aside and think of a way to give it to Gabriel.

"Valentina?" Domi says, and I snap back into reality.

"Yes, hi, hey, can I get you something?" I ask, panic settling in my chest. *Where the hell is Gabriel?*

"No, just, hold my hand, would you?" Tears fall from her eyes as I take her hand in both of mine.

"Of course."

She starts crying, tears of grief falling down her cheeks. My heart breaks for her. She finally got pregnant, she got familiar with that baby living and growing inside of her, she connected with the child, and now, she didn't even get to meet her or him. Domi is now a mother without a child, and it isn't fair. It's not fair that her baby was ripped from her before it even had the chance to let out its first cry.

"Take my mind off it, please," she begs once her tears have slowed. I stare at the ceiling for a second before I figure out what to say to her.

"I pranked Cameron a few months ago and got it on video. Would you like to see?" Domi nods eagerly, and I caress the back of her hand with my thumb while pulling up the video on my phone. "I'm still waiting for his revenge," I say, and she brings the smallest smile to her lips. I hold the phone out for her, and she takes it with shaking hands. A few moments pass before she lets out a small laugh.

"Oh my God, Valentina, you're evil for that. Where did you even get that mask of Adrian mid-sneeze?" she asks, still laughing. Then more tears follow, yet for that brief moment, she was smiling, and I'm glad I was the reason why. I squat down next to her bed, holding onto her hand.

"You're so, so strong, Domi. And you're not alone, okay? We're all here for you," I say, and she nods, sobbing into the room. Her hand covers her face as a pain like no other consumes her.

I place my hand on top of her head, running it over her curly, dark hair in comfort. Her brown eyes shed more and more tears until they slow. Using a tissue from the box that's resting on the table next to the bed, I wipe some of them away for her, dragging another small laugh from her lips. It's more of a tired sound than anything else.

"Thank you," she says, and I bring a comforting smile to my lips.

"Has anyone ever told you how beautiful of a crier you are? Because you truly are," I say, and a soft laugh leaves her lips.

"Thank you. I needed that," she says right as Nicolette, Jean, and Gabriel walk through the hospital room door.

Nicolette steps over to her wife to place a gentle kiss on her lips. I let go of her hand, and Domi mouths a 'thank you' as I step away. Gabriel wraps his arms around me from behind, his hands resting on my stomach as his face nuzzles into the crook of my neck. He kisses the skin there, making me smile at the ceiling, my eyes closed.

"Tu es ma vie," he whispers into my ear, and I melt. *You're my life.* "Thank you for making her laugh. We heard it outside, we just didn't hear what you said." I let out a small chuckle.

"It'll stay Domi's and my little secret." Gabriel kisses my shoulder, and I rub his arms with my hands.

There is a lot of pain in this room, but when I see Nicolette and Domi hold hands, Jean holding Domi's other one, and look at Gabriel, I also see a lot of love. The kind of love that's going to make sure those two wonderful women are going to be okay.

Not right now, not anytime soon, but they will be okay because they are not alone, they will never be alone.

"So, when are you two lovebirds going to make this official again?" Nicolette asks, and I look at Gabriel, wondering if he wants them to know what I asked him earlier.

"Actually, Valentina asked me to move in with her, and I said yes." Nicolette, Domi, and Jean gasp in excitement, and I'm surprised how quickly the mood changes.

"Congratulations," Nicolette exclaims, and I smile at her. "I'm so happy for you."

"About damn time," Jean says, and Gabriel laughs.

"Yeah, as if you had any faith in us," he replies, and Jean looks at him with an annoyed frown.

"I always had faith in Valentina, I just didn't always have faith in you," he tells his brother, and I feel Gabriel flinching next to me.

"Fair enough."

Nicolette falls into an intimate conversation with Domi, Jean is on his phone doing God-knows-what, and Gabriel is pulling me outside. He twists me around and puts his hands on my hips.

"Nicolette told me she wants to spend some time alone with Domi. I think she wants to grieve with her wife a little bit." I nod, and he twists my hips side to side. "I thought maybe I could sleep at your place," he says, and I smile.

"Of course. I'd love nothing more," I assure him, his eyes dropping to my lips.

"I want to feel as close to you as I possibly can." His voice is merely a whisper, and I know it's more about intimacy tonight than it is about desire.

"Me too," I say in the same tone.

He kisses me before mumbling against my lips, "Ma belle chérie."

CHAPTER 37
Valentina

GABRIEL AND I SAY goodbye to Nicolette and Domi, and Jean comes with us so we can drop him at home. The ride is silent, my hand resting in both of Gabriel's again. I'm driving, Jean is still on his phone, probably texting his new girlfriend, and Gabriel is staring out of the window. I think he's trying to process everything that happened.

"I loved the date you took me on today. It was beautiful, thank you so much." He squeezes my hand before he turns to look at me.

"Thank you for asking me to move in with you," he replies, his bottom lip slipping between his teeth.

"I'm really happy for you guys," Jean chimes in, and I glance at him through the rearview mirror.

"I'm happy for *you*. Gabriel tells me you have a girlfriend," I say, and he smiles like a little child. "So, tell me about her," I encourage him, and, even though I can't see it, I know he's blushing.

"She's gorgeous. She's from Spain, has curly hair, I mean the most beautiful curly hair with amazing volume, she is our age, she lives here with her parents and her two siblings, her laugh is sweet, she has brown eyes, bushy but perfectly shaped eyebrows, full lips..." He trails off, and Gabriel and I smile at each other. Little Jean has a big crush.

"Well, when are we going to meet Ana?" Gabriel asks, and my mouth drops. I squeeze his hand, but he simply shrugs as if he didn't just put a lot of pressure on his brother's new relationship.

"Okay, calm down, we've only been on four dates." I let out a little laugh, and so does Gabriel.

"No need to get defensive, little man," Gabriel replies in French, and I smack his arm playfully. "Hey! See what you did, you turned my girl against me." I smack my forehead with my hand, and Gabriel laughs. *My girl.* Doesn't sound as good as my wife, but I will take it.

For now.

We drop Jean at home. Gabriel goes inside to get his clothes and toothbrush before we make our way to my house. In front of it, Gabriel picks me up and doesn't waste any time bringing me to our bed.

At first, we don't do anything except hug each other. He holds me close to his chest, and I can hear his heart beating at an unhealthy speed. I don't know what he wants to do next, but I'm patient and in no rush to figure it out. Whenever he's ready, he'll let me know. I'll give him everything he needs.

"I want to have sex with you," he says, and his eyes concentrate on my lips. "Is that okay? Are you ready for that, too?" he asks to take some pressure off me while still looking for intimacy. This time, however, there is also desire in his gaze as it scans my face.

"I am. Take off my clothes," I reply, and his hand drops to my leg so he can take my dress in his grasp and pull it over my head.

Since I'm not wearing a bra, I'm almost completely exposed to him now. He takes my panties off soon enough, his fingers trailing over my naked body. Gabriel studies me, like he always does, finding crevices and moles I've probably never seen before. His touch lingers on the stretch marks on my breasts before he leans down to press kisses along them. Goosebumps spread over my skin as soon as his lips are on me, causing my eyes to flutter shut. I love his touch. I love how he worships me, as if he's never seen a body as beautiful as mine. The way he raises his hands to cup my breasts sends a wave of arousal straight to my lower belly, making my clit ache. His gaze is stuck on the tattoo on my hip bone. *Bon Appétite.* He smirks at it for a moment then continues his exploration. I reach for him, but he sucks in a sharp breath.

"Please, I need this. I need to touch you for a bit longer," he says, and I let my hands drop to my sides, palms pressing on the mattress. He cups my face as he stands up, leaning down to brush his lips against mine. "I need you, Valentina. God, I can't even express in words how much you mean to me," he says, pressing his mouth to mine more firmly. I lean back to respond.

"Then show me," I say, and he nods, bringing his fingers back to my body.

They explore every part of me. He runs them up and down, swirling them around my nipples, trailing them down my stomach, sliding them across my legs, and then pushing them inside of my wet and hot center. His lips claim mine to muffle my moan, my walls clenching around him. Pleasure seeps into my bloodstream until it's everywhere, in every cell of mine.

I need more.

My hands find his shirt, and I pull it up until it's over his head and on the floor. He moves between my legs instantly to kiss me again, not giving me enough time to pull his pants down and remove his boxers. He's gentle, and at the same time, he's getting more and more demanding by the second. His tongue pushes into my mouth as soon as I part my lips, and Gabriel moans loudly when his cock, hard and ready, presses against me. Hearing him moan makes me hungry. I want to hear the familiar sound over and over and over again.

My hand drops to his erection, and I palm him through the thick fabric of his shorts. Gabriel groans into my mouth before pulling back to remove his pants and underwear. My eyes fall to his tattoos, and I run my fingers over them. I missed his body, his defined stomach muscles, his muscular arms and legs, his neck, his lips, his scar on the side of his leg, his cock; I've missed every single inch of his body.

When he catches me staring, he smiles and places his hands on my angled legs. Having them on me, seeing him completely naked, it all sends more arousal to pool between my legs. Gabriel leans forward just to hover his lips over mine, but he doesn't kiss me, simply teases me while his hands work on putting on the condom.

"Ready, baby?" he asks, and I nod.

He slides into me, his lips still not touching mine, and my back arches off the bed so my chest presses against his. My hands grab the sheet under me as I let pleasure wash through my body. No one, no other person has ever been able to make love to me like this. No one ever will because Gabriel is one of a kind. My kind.

Finally, his mouth finds mine, but only for a brief second until his lips make their way down my chest and he pulls one of my hard nipples into his mouth. His hot tongue contrasts the cool air in my room, sending another round of shivers down my spine. I love it when he does that, love how the pressure from his gentle assault makes pleasure spread through my body. Combining it with his cock gliding inside of me over and over again at a delicious rhythm makes the sex mind-blowing.

I want to concentrate on pleasuring him the same way he is me, but I'm too overwhelmed by how good he makes me feel to do anything other than let him fuck me. He goes slow, but he hits the right spot inside of me with every stroke. We were made for each other. My pussy for his cock and vice versa.

"I missed you so much," he moans, and I let out my own sounds of satisfaction. "I missed being inside of you, feeling you wrapped around me." His words, his voice, and his hot breath on my skin all create more ways to make my body explode into a million fireworks.

I do my best to stay quiet just because I know we aren't alone in this house, but when the orgasm builds in my stomach, I have to cover my mouth and cry out the sounds I haven't since Gabriel and I last had sex. My body trembles and shakes with pleasure, my hands slipping into his hair as I fall apart and get put back together through a single orgasm.

Gabriel keeps thrusting, chasing his own orgasm until he finally spills into the condom in violent spurts I feel deep inside of me. He pulls out of me but not before giving me a long, loving kiss, making my lips tingle.

Then, he removes the condom and walks into my bathroom. I stare after him, admiring his ass tattoo, the moon on his moon. I laugh when I remember the story of Cameron and him, drunk at a parlor, getting stupid ideas and then putting those on their skin forever.

"Come take a shower with me," he says. I practically jump out of bed.

We wash ourselves, a little bit of inappropriate touching here and there, and then brush our teeth together before getting dressed to go to bed. We're spooning for a while when he breaks the silence.

"When do you want me to move my stuff here?" he asks, and I run my fingers over his hands.

"I want to go see James, Annabel, and Damian tomorrow, and then I agreed to meet with Evangelin. The day after is my procedure, for which you and Adrian will be there. I don't think I'm going to feel well on Thursday, so I won't be able to help you then either. So, maybe Friday? But that's so far away..." I trail off, trying to think of a way to make this work sooner. Gabriel chuckles into my ear and pulls me closer to his chest.

"Chérie, if it's okay, I can bring my stuff tomorrow. I don't have much except for my clothes and my bookshelf anyway. I'll leave the trophies and helmets at my apartment for now just because they have no priority. What does have priority is my toiletries and clothes." His lips touch my shoulder, and I spin abruptly.

"You found an apartment?" I ask, and he strokes my cheek with the back of his fingers.

"Yes, but don't worry, I can get out of the contract," he assures me, but I feel bad now.

"Are you sure?"

"One million percent." He kisses the bridge of my nose, making my stomach turn upside down. It's the sweet, gentle, and small gestures that make the difference between a temporary love and the kind of love you know you want forever.

"Thank you for coming back," I tell him, obviously not able to keep anything to myself. *Why am I still so willing to be vulnerable with him? Because I love him? Because I love him.* His features turn sad, and he looks away from me.

"Don't thank me for coming back. You should hate me for leaving."

"Yeah, I should," I tell him, and he finds my eyes again. "Why don't I?" I ask him, and he shrugs.

"I have no idea, but whatever the reason, I'm eternally grateful." Gabriel stares at me with the softest look.

"I'll tell you the reason. No one has ever loved me in the way you do, in that messy, chaotic, yet, overtaking, devoting, and loyal way. A part of me never wants to lose this love because it lives for it. You are my future, Gabriel. Now, don't get me wrong, if you hurt me like that again, or even worse, I'm never, ever going to let you back in again, but I also don't want you to live in constant fear of losing me. We are going to fight, we are going to get mad at each other, and I promise you I'm going to be right here with you while we figure out a way to make everything better again. As long as you are willing to stay and figure things out with me, we're going to be fine." His forehead drops against mine carefully, and he lets out a long, deep breath.

"God, chérie, I don't know what I would do if you weren't such a forgiving person." His hand caresses my arm, and he brings his fingers to my chin to lift my head to look at him. "I love you very much."

"I love you the same, mon amour."

He kisses me softly, and I smile against his lips. I could lie like this every single night for the rest of my life.

CHAPTER 38

Gabriel

"*Psssst.*"

"Go away," I whisper-scream because I'm half-asleep with Valentina wrapped around my body.

"Can't. Need to talk to you," Adrian replies, so I open my eyes, fighting back a sigh. I slip out of bed and walk toward where he is in the doorframe. "I'm so fucking glad you are wearing clothes," he adds when I'm in front of him, shoving him out the door. "Seriously. I know we're close, but I don't ever want to see your di—" I cut him off.

"Shut up. You're going to wake Val," I say, pushing him toward the staircase.

"Jesus. You should be in a better mood considering you just got laid," he says before cringing at his words.

"The love of my life took me back into her bed today. I couldn't be happier, except I'm not in bed with her, am I?" I reply, earning myself an apologetic glance over his shoulder. Chase comes trotting toward me, and I give him a quick pat on the head before focusing on my teammate again.

"I know you've had a long day. I'm sorry to bother you, but there's something we should discuss," he says, leading me outside onto the veranda. There are playing cards on the table along with two steaming mugs of... *hot chocolate?* I furrow my brows at him. "I was in the mood," he explains when he notices my confusion, flopping onto one of the chairs.

"Now so am I," I reply with a smile, joining him at the table.

Once we're sitting across from each other, both of us holding onto our mugs, he opens his mouth again.

"I'd like to switch places," he says, but I'm so lost, all I do is stare at him. "Valentina and I discussed you moving in months ago, and I told her whenever it felt right, she should ask you. It felt right for her today, but I never planned on staying here when it happened," he says, and guilt immediately takes over in my chest.

"Adrian—" I start, but he cuts me off with a smile.

"Can I be honest with you?" he asks, and I twist the cup a little on the table.

"Always."

"I hate living in this house," he admits, and my eyes widen in surprise. "Yeah, I know, it's just, everything here reminds me of my grandparents, of my dad. I think Val finds comfort in it now because she feels closer to them here, but I can't do it anymore. I need a place of my own, somewhere I can make memories that aren't tainted by the grief and loss this house holds," he explains while I take a sip of the hot chocolate he made. It tastes surprisingly good.

"So you'd like to move into my apartment?" I ask, and he gives me a small nod.

This is a heavy topic for him, I can tell. Adrian isn't the type of person who likes to get emotional around others, but he's found comfort in me because we share a similar grief. It's why he doesn't have to keep up his fun, happy façade. He can be himself, any version that suits his needs.

"Does Valentina know?" I ask, reaching for the cards to start shuffling.

I can't believe this has become something we do. I'm in bed with Val. He calls me to talk, so we do. We sit on the veranda and play cards. This seems so surreal, especially because we've known each other for years, and while we were able to spend time together, it wasn't something either of us actively sought out.

"Not yet, but I will tell her tomorrow," he assures me, his emotional turmoil darkening his eyes.

"You don't have to leave, if you're not ready," I say, but he merely shrugs.

"I'm twenty-three, Gabriel. I can't live with my sister and her boyfriend. You two need privacy, and so do I. I never bring home the women I sleep with because I don't want to disrespect this home with a hookup, you know?" he asks, and I nod because I understand what he means.

"The apartment is yours," I reply, and Adrian lets out a long breath, smiling at me.

"Thanks," he mumbles, staring at the cards I just dealt him.

"Hey, Adrian?" I say after a moment of silence between us. His eyes, twins of Val's, study my face expectantly. "I'd still like it if you came to bother me in the middle of the night so we can have deep conversations while playing cards." His features brighten at my words.

"Deal."

CHAPTER 39

Valentina

WHEN I WAKE UP the next morning, Gabriel is sitting at the side of the bed, sketching in his notebook. I don't have to check to know he's drawing me while I'm sleeping, his smile when he catches me looking proves it. I'm just glad I wasn't drooling because it would not make for a pretty sketch in his book of lovely images of me.

My eyes focus on his naked torso and then his scar coming out from underneath his black boxer shorts. Gabriel looks really good in his underwear, not as good as without any, but still very delicious. He puts his pencil and book aside to lie down on the bed next to me. I push off the mattress a little bit, just enough so I can kiss him to say good morning.

"Bonjour," he says softly, and I smile. I love it when he speaks to me in French, but I also love it when he speaks English and I get to hear his beautiful accent. Either language, either accent, either anything works as long as I get to hear his voice.

"Bonjour, mon soleil," I answer, and he kisses me again, this time more hungrily, more aggressively than before. "Hmm," I moan, and he bites my bottom lip before pulling back so his lips aren't touching mine but his breath is still hot on my face.

"I need more," he says, and I grin.

"Well, I have to get ready and see my son," I reply. He frowns, and I look into his green-brown eyes, wishing we could spend the whole day in bed.

"No fair," he complains.

I let out another laugh, about to kiss him again when someone knocks on my bedroom door, making me jump up from the bed. I take my robe from the chair at my desk and open it slightly, just enough to see Adrian stand behind it with an excited Chase next to him. My brother is smiling so knowingly, I cringe.

"Having a good time, are we?" he asks, and I playfully smack his stomach.

"What's up?" I ask. He looks down at his side where Chase is jumping up and down. I want to greet him so badly, but I don't want to open the door while Gabriel isn't dressed.

"Your son misses you," he says, and in that moment, Gabriel opens the door completely. finally allowing me to bend down and greet him. "I was wondering if you wanted to have breakfast, but it looks like I disrupted you in the middle of having it." I want to smack him.

"Well, mate, that's why you wait for us to come downstairs, so this doesn't happen," Gabriel teases back, and I get so annoyed with both of them, I tell Chase to come with me downstairs. He follows like the good boy he is, and I admire how much healthier and happier he looks.

"Gabriel said he needs to take a long, cold shower, but he'll be right down," Adrian says when he steps into the kitchen. "I took this little guy for a walk already, so no need to rush," he adds, and I turn to my brother, who is leaning against the island in the middle of the kitchen, sipping his coffee now.

"Thank you," I reply, and he winks at me. "I'm sorry I didn't discuss Gabriel moving in again. I know you said whenever it feels right I should ask, but I feel bad not speaking it through again," I say, but Adrian's face stays calm and cool.

"Having Gabriel here is going to make you happy, I know that, and I completely support him moving in here." *God, I love this guy so much.* "But there is something you should know. I'm going to move out and into Gabriel's apartment." Well, he ripped the band-aid right off, didn't he?

"Okay," I reply, fighting back the tears.

"Come here," Adrian says, placing his coffee cup on the island and opening his arms for me.

"I don't want you to leave," I say and fling my arms around him. My face presses against his chest, inhaling his comforting scent.

"I won't be far away, Val, and if you need anything, I'm one call away," he promises, but this? Him moving out after we spent our entire lives living under one roof together, it feels like my insides are about to implode. Then again, I can't have both. I can't live with Gabriel and Adrian. It isn't fair to my brother to expect him to live with a couple, no matter how big this house is.

"I love you," I say, and he squeezes me tightly.

"I know you do. And I love you, so much." He kisses the top of my head, not ready to let go of me yet. "I hate that you're growing up," he whispers, and I let out a short laugh followed by some stupid tears.

"I hate how quickly time passes," I reply, his hand running up and down my back to comfort me.

"Me, too, Val. Me fucking too." We stay like this for a while longer until he makes a farting noise right into my ear, and I push off, a laugh escaping me.

"I have to head over to Annie's soon, so—" He cuts me off.

"Oh, can Chase stay with me again?" A smile dances onto my lips.

"You really like him, don't you?" Adrian nods and squats down right before he calls Chase to him. The little guy comes running toward him all excited.

"Are you kidding? I love him. He's such a sweetheart." I knew it, I freaking knew bringing Chase into our lives was going to be the right decision.

"Okay, you can take care of him, but tomorrow, he's all mine." Chase comes to me as soon as I kneel on the ground.

Adrian may have spent half the day with him yesterday, but Chase still looks at me with different eyes. I wonder if he knows I saved him, or if he feels the same connection to me as I feel toward him.

"I'm going to take him to the beach to try and get him used to the water." He skips out of the room with Chase a second later.

With my head still shaking and a grin on my face, I prepare a light breakfast for Gabriel and me. I make some pancakes with a couple of blueberries, strawberries, and bananas and wait for my boyfriend to come back downstairs to eat with me.

The second I finish breakfast, Gabriel strolls toward me only wearing his swimsuit. I'm confused because I thought he was going to shower but don't mind his body on display. Quite the opposite. He gives me a big kiss and thanks me for making him food. The mint from his toothpaste is delicious, but it also brings out my next words.

"You want some orange juice to go with that toothpaste?" I ask, and he scrunches his nose.

"That's disgusting," he replies, and I laugh. "Will you go swimming with me?" Gabriel asks, covering his mouth since it's full of pancakes and fruits.

"I can't. Annie and James have something important to discuss with me, and I want to see Damian," I reply, and Gabriel gives me a playful frown.

"I want you to go swimming with me," he complains, and I shove the last piece of food in my mouth before standing up and placing my plate in the sink.

"The only reason you want that is to undress me in the pool and fuck me in the water," I say, earning myself a smug smile from him.

"Actually, I was thinking about putting you on the edge of the pool, stripping you bare, and burying my face between your legs to lick that pretty pussy until you come on my face." *Holy shit.* I swallow hard, my clit throbbing in response to his words. "You better go get ready. Annie and James are waiting for you," Gabriel adds, getting up and moving to where I am in front of the sink. "I'll do the dishes."

My mind is in a haze, but I somehow manage to get ready and put on some jeans and a crop top. It's still warm here in Monaco, even though it's September. Gabriel is outside in the pool when I come back downstairs. I walk through the glass doors onto the veranda, watching him smile brightly as he takes in my appearance. I'm so glad he's moving in, that this will be what I get to see every single day, *his beautiful smile.*

"Come here," he says, but his mischievous grin prevents me from obeying.

"No, baby, I don't have time to get pulled into the pool," I reply, and he laughs.

"You know me too well." Of course I do, I know him like the back of my hand.

"I will call you when I am on my way back from Evangelin's. She wants me to help her out in the store for a little." He pouts, so I walk closer to him. "Are you going to speak to Nicolette and Domi later?" I ask, watching a contemplative expression cross his face.

"I'll call them, but I'm pretty sure they want to be left alone for a while," he replies, so I give him a comforting smile.

"If you do speak to them, give them my love," I add, bringing a soft smile to his lips.

"I love you, chérie."

I pucker my lips before I blow him a kiss. I don't want to leave, I want to stay here, swim in the pool with him, have a lot of scx, and eat lots of food. But I have to keep up with my responsibilities.

I can feel his eyes on me, making me add a little swing in my step. He lets out a low whistle, sending heat into my cheeks and between my legs.

This man.

Chapter 40

Valentina

Harlow's car is in the driveway when I arrive at Annie's. I don't know why, but she bothers me a lot more than she should. Maybe I should tell her off, but I'm not that kind of person. I swallow down the anger. Today is not about starting a fight with the girl who doesn't know boundaries, today is about family and love, and I cannot wait to see little Damian. I can't control my excitement when I think about seeing him again.

I knock on the front door, and to my freaking luck, Harlow opens it right before she groans and rolls her eyes. She doesn't even bother telling me to come inside but simply throws the door in my face again, leaving me to stand on the other side of it angry and absolutely annoyed. *Okay, that is it!* I am done with her. I've been nothing but nice, and I am not going to let her treat me so poorly.

Once again, I knock on the door, but this time, I don't stop until she opens it again. "What the hell do you want?" she screams at me, but I stay composed because I know if I lower myself to her level, it's only going to get ugly.

"Listen, I've had enough of your rude behavior. I am friends with your sister, I was there right next to her when the baby was born, *I cut Damian's umbilical cord*, and I heard his first screams. I was there when your sister needed me most and know she would love to see me now, since she's been texting me nonstop about coming to her place to discuss something important."

Harlow's face is flaming red, but she knows what I'm saying is the truth.

"Now, I'm going to ignore the fact that you continuously hit on my boyfriend when he has made it clear to you he is not interested. I'll ignore it because you are

Annie's sister, and I don't want anything to make this whole situation even more complicated. But I will ask you to stop texting Gabriel because he's mine. *Only mine,*" I say, and she almost growls at me before a wicked smile covers her lips.

"That's not what he said when he fucked me all night long. He fucked me over and over again, your name not leaving his lips once, and then in the morning, he told me he had a lot of fun and that we should do it again. That he wants to feel my lips wrapped around his cock again."

I am about to attack when James appears behind Harlow and shakes his head. He mouths the words 'not worth it', and I swallow down my anger. I take a step closer to her, thankful we're almost the same height, and lower my voice.

"He may have fucked you once at a low point, but listen carefully now, it's never going to happen again. The only woman who gets to touch him is me, no matter how much you want him, you can't have him," I say and step back again.

The stupid smile from before leaves her and before I know it, her hand connects with my face. I feel the burn of the slap against my cheek immediately. It takes me a second to swallow down the tears and ignore the flashback of my aunt doing the same thing to me for years of my life. James is rapidly approaching, but I raise my hand to stop him. Then, I straighten out my back and face her again.

"Thank you for that. I'm going to file a report against you, so be on the lookout for that." Without another word, I walk past her and toward James.

He wraps his trained arms around me, and I let his familiar fresh scent fill my nose. I could start crying, but I don't. Aunt Carolina no longer has that power over me, not even through the terrible memories, and I sure as hell won't give it to Harlow.

I feel James' lips against the top of my head and let out the long breath I've been holding back. Then, I hear the front door thrown shut and flinch. James lifts his hand to the back of my head, rubbing it to comfort me.

"It's okay, she left." Once again, I let out a deep breath, and he pulls back so his ocean-blue eyes can study the red mark on my face. His pink lips form a frown, and I put my hand over his. "I almost just lost control," he says, and I laugh.

"How's Damian?" I ask to talk about anything else.

"Don't switch the subject, not before you tell me how you feel and if you're alright. And not before you tell me what I can do," he begs, his gaze searching my face until a wave of emotions storms through me.

"Everything's fine. I want you to tell me how Damian's doing so I can forget what the hell just happened." It seems to be a good enough answer for him because a small smile slips onto his face.

"He's amazing, Val, he's just perfect. I mean, yes, he's crying almost the whole night and his shit smells terrible, but other than that, he's absolutely perfect." James takes my hand to lead me into the living room where Annie is sitting on the couch and Damian is sleeping in his bassinet. When she sees me, a weak smile covers her lips, and she gets up to hug me.

"Val," she says, and I can see she is still in pain. Giving birth must seriously be a bitch. "What happened to your face?" she asks, worry spreading over hers.

"Oh, nothing for you to worry about. So, tell me, how are you?" I ask instead because there is no way I'll tell her what Harlow did.

"I'm in a lot of pain. Sitting is uncomfortable and everything inside of me aches," she replies. "But it's worth it. I mean, look at him," Annie adds after I give her a worried frown, pointing at her son's bassinet.

My feet bring me over to him while part of me is in disbelief that only two days ago, Damian was still inside of Annie. I look at the child's small features, his small hands, his small feet. His eyes are closed, his pacifier is in his tiny mouth, and his hands are next to his stomach. I would do anything and everything to protect him from any harm this world bears, and I finally know why. I said it to Harlow, and now I know. I was there when he was born, I cut his umbilical cord, I heard his first scream. I got attached to him when he was placed in my arms and I was one of the first people who ever got to hold him.

"He's perfect," I whisper, and James smiles.

In that moment, Damian opens his eyes and stretches his arms into the air, as if he wants to be lifted out of his bassinet. James picks him up and puts him in my arms. I support his head and hold him close to me as my best friend leads me to the armchair where I'm supposed to sit. I do as I'm directed as carefully and slowly as possible.

James and Annie sit across from Damian and me, watching us closely. There is that 'something' they want to talk to me about, and I really hope they would get it over with.

"How would you like to be Damian's godmother?" I almost gasp at Annie's question. Happiness spreads through my body until I can't contain my feelings anymore.

"I would love that!" They want me to be his godmother, *me...* and here come the tears.

"Oh, Val," James says, but I can't stop crying because I'm so damn joyful. I feel trusted, loved, respected, dependable.

"I would love to be his godmother," I tell them, and they both smile at me.

"Fantastic because we are planning to have him baptized in two weeks, and we want you to speak on his behalf and bring him to the front to be baptized, along with Adrian who we are going to ask to be his godfather," James says with his thick English accent, and I still can't bring myself to stop smiling.

My eyes shift back to Damian, whose tiny fingers reach out to touch my neck in his sleep, and I feel like I'm about to cry all over again. This isn't at all what I thought they'd want to discuss, but it's definitely the best thing they could have ever asked me.

I'm going to be a godmother.

CHAPTER 41
Gabriel

"WHAT THE HELL HAPPENED?" Val and I say in unison, panic flooding my chest. Somebody slapped her. Somebody slapped Valentina, and all I see now is red.

"What the hell happened to *me*? What the hell happened to you? Who did this to you?" I ask and close the distance between us.

My hands lift to her face as I cautiously place them on her neck and jaw. My eyes scan the red mark on her cheek, sending nausea into my chest. Sadness occupies her features as she studies my naked face. I shaved. For the first time in years, I shaved my stubble, but I didn't think it would upset her, not this much anyway.

"I told Harlow to back off, and she slapped me when I told her you'd never sleep with her again," Val explains, forcing the color to drain out of my face. My jaw ticks in response to her words while ice runs through my veins.

"I'm going lose it," I blurt out, but Val grabs my shoulders to calm me.

"Relax. I filed a restraining order, and they took pictures of my injury. James was also there so he could be a witness if one was needed. I'm fine," she assures me and puts her hands on my hips.

"I'm going to make sure she never comes close to you again. I can't believe she slapped you." My eyes grow darker again, so she pulls me closer by my hips, kissing me. It distracts me from my anger, but only briefly. I pull back because I never want my lips against Val's when negative emotions are flooding through me.

"Mon amour, I promise, I'm fine. Let's just have a nice evening and discuss the fact that my stubble is gone," she whines as she places her fingers against my cheeks.

A chuckle escapes me, so I decide to let go of my rage and give her a long hug instead. Her scent, something just Valentina, fills my nose.

"You don't like it when I shave?" My face is buried in her neck, making my words sound muffled.

"No, I love the stubble. You without the stubble isn't really you. It's like your trademark. How could you shave your trademark?" she asks as if it's the most horrible thing I could have ever done to her. I can't help but chuckle again, leaning back to stare into her light eyes.

"You don't find me attractive anymore, mon tournesol?" I challenge, but she merely rolls her lips.

"I didn't say *that*," she mumbles, crossing her arms in front of her chest. "You are handsome, Gabriel. So handsome that I just can't resist—"

Valentina cuts off abruptly to place her lips to mine with eagerness and need. A groan slips past my lips as my hands drop to her ass and grab tightly. She moans into my mouth, seeking proximity, so I pick her up without warning. Her whimper travels down my spine, my blood rushing straight to my cock.

No part of me is patient enough to bring her upstairs.

I carry her toward the lounge chair next to the pool instead, moving between her legs. I nibble on her bottom lip, desperate to taste more of her watermelon flavor. Her legs wrap around my hips as I thrust my hard cock against her, making her cry out. I almost crumble from the pleasure.

"No, bring me upstairs, I don't want Adrian to walk in on us," she says, but I'm greedy for her moans and rub against her again. Val cries out, grinding herself against me.

"Adrian is sleeping at my apartment," I say and kiss her on the lips. "We…" I continue and kiss her neck. "Have… the… whole… house… to ourselves," I add between kisses, trailing them down her body until I'm close to that pretty pussy I've been fantasizing about all day. "I want you to be as loud as possible. Don't hold back when you scream my name." Because it's only ever going to be my name from her lips. No one else's.

I unbutton her shorts, needing her naked right this second. My cock is begging me to thrust inside her as soon as possible, but my mouth wants a taste first. *What to do, what to do...*

"That depends on how good you'll make me feel," she teases, and I lick my lips in response.

I rip off her shorts, and she lifts her ass for me to help. The only thing covering her is a black, lace thong. My mouth waters at the sight of her, my fingers tingling with the need to reach out and run over her soaked panties. I bring my hands over her ass instead, spanking it the way she likes before soothing the ache with a more gentle touch.

"I love your ass," I say, placing one more smack on it. Valentina moans from pleasure, the sound going straight to my cock. "I told you to be loud," I remind her, placing a third slap on her slowly reddening ass cheek. She screams for me this time, and fuck if it doesn't make me harder than I already was. "That's my girl," I praise because it always makes her toes curl. This time is no different.

"Please," she begs as I drop to my knees in front of her.

"Tell me what you need," I say, my fingers curling around the waistband of her panties and tugging them down.

"Make me come on your mouth," she replies as her eyes watch her underwear drop to the floor, and I spot her tattoo. I don't fucking hesitate.

I press my tongue flat against her pussy, dragging it all the way up to her clit where I use the tip to circle it. My eyes catch her removing her shirt and bra, making my cock twitch against my shorts.

"Play with your nipples," I instruct in French, and her moan comes out before she even does as I ask. My tongue moves back against her warmth, her sweetness making my taste buds come alive.

"Gabriel," she whimpers, grinding herself against my mouth. I press a kiss to her clit before sucking it into my mouth, earning me a scream of pleasure. *Fuck, yes.* "More," she begs, and I do it again before running my tongue down her pussy and letting it slip inside of her.

"You taste so good, Val, so fucking good," I say, eating her out like my life depends on it because it does. It's been way too long since I've done this.

"I'm so close," she says, rolling her nipples between her fingers. I groan against her clit, sending her right over the edge. "Fuck, fuck, fuck," Val breathes, her back arching off the lounge chair as the orgasm makes her shake.

"Your breasts are my heaven," I say, still speaking French, and she tugs on my brown, curly hair.

"Take your clothes off," she commands, and I rip my shirt over my head. Her hands move to my stomach as a content smile crosses her face. "I love your abs," she adds while I slide my pants and boxers down, taking my cock into my hand and rubbing slowly. God, that feels good. Valentina has me so worked up, relieving the pressure even a little helps me breathe.

"I need to be in here," I say, still pumping my cock as I slide two fingers into her wet warmth.

"Condom, Gabriel, now," she instructs, lifting her arms over her head on the lounge chair. I grab the foil from my pocket, sliding it down my sensitive length while she watches.

"How do you feel about not using a condom after you get your IUD?" I ask, and she grins at me.

"I've thought about that a lot," she replies while I align myself with her entrance, anticipation rolling through me. "I want to. I want it all with you," she whispers as she grabs me by the neck and brings my lips to hers.

"I would love to feel you without a condom," I say against her mouth, thrusting inside of her a moment later. "For now, I'll fuck you like this." I lift her leg onto my right shoulder and push her left one to the side, opening her wider for me. It lets me go deeper, bottoming out fully, and fuck, it's heaven. Everything with Valentina is heaven. "God, you feel so good," I moan while she gets louder and louder for me.

My thrusts are hard but slow, and I love the way she arches against me with every pump. Her movements meet mine in perfect harmony as we both chase our pleasure. The build-up in my cock threatens to take charge and blindside me with an orgasm, so I slip out of her completely, dropping back onto my knees to use my tongue to play with her clit again. Another orgasm shatters through her, making me grin so brightly, my cheeks burn.

I bring my cock back to her wet entrance, thrusting inside harder and faster this time. I angle her hips upward, making sure to hit her perfect spot. My mouth connects with her right nipple, sucking on it until she moans. I don't last much longer after that.

A few thrusts later, I come so hard, I'm groaning louder than before. Wave over wave over wave of pleasure consumes my entire body as the orgasm takes me straight to paradise. The outer-body sensation gets me so high, I can barely breathe. I collapse on top of Val without meaning to, feeling her shake from her third orgasm. Coming with her, feeling her walls wrap tightly around me as she falls apart, will forever be one of my favorite things in the entire world.

I carry us inside and onto the couch in the living room, feeling her sweat and mine mix on our bodies. We're both in need of a shower, but I couldn't give less of a shit right now. All I want to do is to hold her, at least for a little.

"Want some water?" I ask when my throat feels a bit dry, realizing she might be thirsty, too. I grab both of us some water, watching her empty the glass before handing it back to me with a little grin.

"Can you scratch me between my shoulder blades?" she asks, and I place my cup on the table to turn to her.

"Of course, ma chérie."

She tells me to go a bit lower, then a bit more to the side, then a bit higher. She laughs when I simply use both hands to gently scratch her entire back. She sighs loudly, clearly loving every second of this.

"I don't know why, but I really enjoyed that," she admits, and I let out a small chuckle.

"I'll scratch your back whenever you want me to, baby."

She grins at me in response, but the red mark on her cheek has caught my attention again. I bring the back of my hand against it, doing my best to keep my breathing even. To distract myself, I drop my hand to the F1 car charm hanging between her breasts, my number carved into the material.

"I miss your stubble," she says, and I burst into laughter.

"My stupid facial hair really means that much to you?" She nods, so I shake my head.

"Imagine it like this: what if I cut my long, curly hair short? It would seem weird to you because you love it like this, don't you?" It's my turn to nod then as I bring my fingers into her hair and play with her curls. She's so fucking gorgeous, sometimes it hurts to look at her.

"Fine, you win, I'll grow it back and never shave it again." That earns me a content, little grin from her.

God, I'm so wrapped around her finger, it's frightening. Perfectly so, too.

CHAPTER 42
Gabriel

VALENTINA IS SLEEPING IN my arms, a hot water bottle pressed to her lower abdomen. My fingers run up and down her arm while I fight back the nausea from her whimpers. Before, during, and after her procedure, Val has done all she could to be strong, but it must have hurt like nothing she's ever felt before. And I'm utterly useless. I'm doing my best to comfort her, but I wish there was more. I wish I could take her pain away.

"God, stop frowning. You look horrible when you frown," Adrian says from his chair beside the bed. He brought it up here earlier so he could stay by his sister's side. He's worried about her, too.

"I can't help it," I admit, placing my cheek against her head.

"She'll be fine," he says, and I give him a slight nod, my arms tightening around Val. "I can't believe you're leading the championship instead of me. That's fucking annoying," he says, crossing his arms in front of his chest and pouting like an upset child. It makes me smile at him.

"Anything can still happen, Adrian." It's true. The season is far from over.

"Hmmm," Valentina whines in her sleep, sending a dull ache through my chest. I hate this. Her fingers grip my shirt harder, so I stroke her hair.

"It's okay, ma chérie, I'm here," I whisper and press my lips to her forehead, right where her eyebrows furrowed together and creases appeared. Her muscles loosen up again as she nuzzles her face into my chest.

"What is it you see in my sister that no one else can give you?" Adrian asks, and I cock an eyebrow in response. "To me, my sister is the most amazing person in the world. I know why I love and need her, but I'm curious to know why you do. What goes through your head when you look at her?" Adrian elaborates while I look for the right words to answer his question.

"For as long as I can remember, people just disappeared around me. Left and right, people I loved my entire life simply vanished from it, and I was so angry at the world for taking them away from me. That anger consumed me. I was mad at everything and everyone around me, and I threw myself into racing because it was the only thing that made me happy."

My hand stops moving, but Val's nose nudges me in response, so I keep going, scratching her back in the way she likes. She's awake. I know she is.

"When I met Valentina, all of the rage became more bearable, and eventually, for the first time in years, I wasn't angry anymore. Just looking at her face calmed me, even if it was just on the surface. Then, I got to know her, got close to her, and it faded internally. I'm not as mad at the world anymore. She saved me, Adrian, and now she is it for me. She is my life, she is what matters most to me in the world."

Her breathing hitches, letting me know she's listening. My nosey tournesol.

"So, when you ask me why she is the one for me, it's because she's the one who makes everything in my life better. I wanted hope for a better future, and she brought all of it to me. There is no other explanation I can give you," I say, my voice getting smaller and smaller with each word.

"You know, watching my baby sister go and find her path in this cruel world is the hardest thing I have ever had to do, and there have been a lot of terrible things I've had to go through. Valentina is the most important person on the planet for me and seeing her hurt over a stupid guy is not something I want to witness again. Don't make me regret trusting you with her happiness again," Adrian warns, and I let the corners of my mouth lift ever so slightly. I feel Chase move at the foot of the bed, groaning in complaint.

"I love her, Adrian, more than I will ever love anyone else, except for maybe our children," I say and shake my head. "It's so stupid, why am I thinking about having children with her already?" I admit while a rogue laugh slips out of me.

"Your whole life and our whole lives have been far from normal. You want to have kids because you love Valentina, and you want to spend the rest of your life with her. I get it, but please, for all of our sakes, don't rush this. You having children is not something either of you is ready for, and neither am I," Adrian says with a shudder, and I nod. I agree, I'm nowhere near ready to be a dad.

"Don't worry, mate, I'm not trying to have a baby now, and even if, the IUD is going to fend off all of me."

"Good, good. TMI, but good to know." Adrian gets up and walks out of the room before I brush the hair out of Valentina's face.

"How long have you been listening?" I ask, but she pretends to be asleep instead of answering. "Stop pretending, about halfway through my conversation with Adrian, I realized you weren't breathing as evenly as you do when you're asleep, and your hand was squeezing my shirt harder and harder." She grins and attempts to sit up, but a wince escapes her in response. "Easy," I say, so she drops her head back onto my chest.

"Sorry, I just couldn't help myself. Adrian asked a very interesting question, and I wanted to know what you would say to him," she admits, and I place my hand back in her hair to play with it.

"You did save my life, ma chérie, and I am not ashamed to tell you that right to your face. You make me happier than I've ever been, and I intend to hold onto you forever."

"I'm really glad you moved in," she replies, making me grin. "I'm also really glad you opened up to my brother about how you feel because what you just said were the best words I've ever heard in my entire life." The pad of my thumb runs over her cheek as I study her face.

"I'm going to get you some food and water," I say, but she whines in protest.

I kiss her once before slipping off the bed. Her warmth immediately vanishes, leaving me cold.

I spot Adrian walking out of the house with a box full of his things. He's slowly been bringing his belongings to my old apartment, especially when Valentina isn't around to see it. He doesn't want to upset her any more than she already is about him moving out of the house.

I've also been bringing more of my things here these past few days, but Domi and Nicolette offered to store my trophies and helmets until Val and I figure out where to put them. Apart from that, my aunts have hardly spoken to me since they lost their baby, still trying to process what happened.

Chase is on my spot when I return upstairs with some food and water while Val is cuddling him close to her chest.

"I'm gone five minutes, and he already takes my place. How unfair," I tease, bringing a wonderful, bright smile to Val's lips.

"Finders keepers." I let out an annoyed huff before placing the things I brought on her nightstand and slipping my arms around her from behind. This way, all three of us are lying together.

"Where are we going to hang the painting of you?" I ask after a moment of silence. I haven't seen it once since Val and I made up, but now that we're back together, I wish I could constantly look at it. Not because I'm impressed by my skills, but because Valentina is so beautiful, a painting of her should be admired.

"For now, it is going to stay in the room next to our bedroom." She turns her head to look at me, an idea blooming to life in her eyes. "Why don't you take it and use it to paint? I know you've always wanted to have your own room for it," she suggests, and I can't help but smile.

"That would be great, mon tournesol. Thank you," I say and kiss her, but she pulls away as pain slices through her body again. "I'll take care of everything, just rest, baby."

CHAPTER 43
Valentina

IT'S BEEN A FEW days since my procedure, and I feel much better. Occasionally, some cramps torment me, but I'm taking painkillers and the excitement of the day makes the ache a distant sensation. Today is my first free practice session in Formula One. It's also the day Leonard decided to tell me that he convinced three more investors to become part of our project, so it's difficult for me not to bounce up and down in my seat a little.

Lorenzo announced I will be taking Gabriel's session, and my boyfriend has been standing beside me the entire time, chatting with Scarlette, my race engineer in training, and some of the other mechanics. The helmet he got me is perfectly snug on my head, and I can hear his voice through the headset in my ear. The balaclava digs into my skin, but I love it too much to care. The marks I'll be sporting afterward for a little will make my chest swell with pride. Because I made it. I'm in a Formula One car. Reserve driving for the most prestigious team in the sport. I've fought hard to earn the team's respect, and I got it. Every single person I've met here treats me like they would any other reserve driver.

"Take a deep breath," Gabriel's voice comes through my earpiece, and I do as I'm told. It settles my nerves and reminds me of what Leonard told me a few months ago.

"If your biggest struggle is how nervous you get, you'll be fine. You may not be able to overcome it, but you can use your breath to ease the effects. Deep breaths will slow your heart rate, allow your mind to focus on something else, and bring much-needed oxygen to your brain."

"It's free practice, so enjoy the car. Take the pressure off yourself. Have fun," my boyfriend says, and I can't help but smile. He sounds so serious even though he's telling me to take things easy. I think he's nervous and excited for me, too.

"Don't worry, I'll be careful with your precious baby," I tease, patting the steering wheel of his car while looking up at him. Gabriel frowns as he squats beside me, grabbing my helmet where the clasp rests against my chin.

"You better because I have no idea what I'd do if something happened to you," he replies, placing a kiss on the helmet where my mouth would be.

"I'm sorry I stole your session," I say after he leans back again, but Gabriel shakes my head from side to side.

"Don't be. I'd give you all of my sessions if I could." And I don't doubt it.

Gabriel is currently leading the championship by ten points. Ten points is nothing in this sport. One race could put Adrian at the top and Gabriel right into second place. Luckily, the Velocità Rossa drivers have a bit of a buffer between the Hawke and Grenzenlos drivers. I don't know why or how, but Velocità Rossa has been dominating this season, despite Grenzenlos' long reign, which only ended this year. Last year, they were still on top, almost winning every single race on the calendar.

But Adrian is his biggest threat. Their cars are identically fast, and so are the drivers. I still don't know who is going to win, but I'm itching to find out. I want my brother to win as much as I want Gabriel to win, I can't help it, and I'll be happy and sad with either outcome. Everything is still on the table. I just hope that no matter who wins, their friendship won't break because of it.

"Ready?" Scarlette asks, and I shift my attention back to the here and now.

"I am," I reply, pulling on my gloves and concentrating on my breathing. I'll have to tell Leonard how right he was. I'm calm, focused, and prepared for anything.

My mind is balanced.

My body is balanced.

My emotions are balanced.

It's not a race, but my grandfather used to tell me that it didn't matter if it was a race, Qualifying, or free practice. As soon as you slipped into the car, you had to be able to shut off the world around you. Tunnel vision on what you are doing. So, once my gloves are on, I wait for the go-ahead to turn the car on. Tomasso, Gabriel's race engineer, gives it sheer moments later, sending a wave of shivers down my spine.

For a second, I let myself imagine this was Qualifying. I let myself think I'm on my way to set a fastest lap time to get me on pole. It's hard not to when this comes close to everything I've ever wanted in my life. Become a Formula One driver. Win a championship. Make my father and grandfather proud.

I shift gears and press down on the throttle, making my way through the pitlane and toward the track. Free practice for a driver means seeing how the car does on the track, finding ways to go faster, in which ways to take corners, and so on. These sessions are all about familiarizing yourself with the track and testing its limits. For me, it's a chance to improve my confidence in the car in case I have to race this season.

I'm having the time of my life. Over the summer break, I spent hours in this car, but there is something about the fans in the grandstands screaming as I drive by that sends my heart into a frenzy. They want me here. No matter how many times I've been told I don't belong, how many times people still tell me I don't, fans are cheering on the car that's sporting my number at the moment.

Most of the drivers, teams, and sponsors are still not on board with having a female racer compete starting next year, but I'm determined to leave them all dumbfounded and guilt-ridden. The only people in my corner are my family, and the people from Velocità Rossa, Alfa Adrenalina, and—unsurprisingly since Leonard raced for them for so long—Grenzenlos.

I will charm the rest of them soon enough, though.

Tomasso calls me back to the box after about ten laps to make some setup changes. The tires are not degrading as quickly as the ones from the other teams, bringing a proud grin to my face. In my Formula Three days, I was known as the tire queen. I managed mine so well, they always lasted longer than everyone else's. Even when they were barely hanging on for dear life at the end of a race, I managed to get the car over the finish line in one piece.

An hour later, we've made several more changes, tested out a new component the team implemented this week, and ran the car about thirty laps. It's more than the average, but there was a lot to figure out. I park the car before getting pulled into the box by the crew members. Gabriel places his hand on top of my helmet as soon as I'm close enough, grinning from ear to ear like he's never been prouder. I jump out of the car to get swept into his arms, but someone else grabs my elbow first.

"Has anyone ever told you red is your color?" Andrea asks, and I let out an excited squeal before wrapping my arms around them. I don't care how sweaty I am and how disgusting my racing suit probably is. I missed them a lot. "It's good to see you, too, Valentina," they add right as I lean back. Andrea places their hands on my shoulders and squeezes while I fight back the tears.

"I'm so happy you're here," I say, knowing it's not usual for someone of Andrea's position at the academy to travel all the way to Hungary for the Grand Prix weekend. They have responsibilities to train the members of the academy almost all year round. "How are you in Mogyoród?" They give me a big smile, their brown eyes scanning the surroundings before focusing back on me.

"I wanted to see my favorite student ace her first free practice. I'm happy to report I got exactly what I hoped for," Andrea replies, and my grin stretches even wider.

"Are you staying the weekend?" They give me a sly grin and an excited nod. "Then I'm taking you out to dinner," I add while pulling my sweaty hair out of my face and into a messy bun.

"Sounds like a plan. Maybe tomorrow at seven? I have a few meetings with Lorenzo to attend too," they say, and I assure them that works perfectly for me.

Andrea leaves a moment later, their eyes getting stuck on my bag where it rests next to Gabriel for a few seconds too long. I furrow my brows in confusion, but Daniel doesn't give me a second to linger on it as he grabs my attention with a bottle of water, a snack, and the towel I brought today.

"I hope you don't mind. I didn't go through your bag, only grabbed the towel from the top," he says, his smile easy and genuine. My furrowed brows remain in place, catching even Gabriel's attention. Worry crosses his face, but I force a smile as I shift my attention back to Daniel. Something is off. I feel it, but until I look through my bag to find what I think will be there, suspicion is all I have.

"Thank you for bringing me all of this. You didn't have to." Daniel has been very kind to me these past few weeks, training me and taking care of me after days like today. He's acting like my performance coach, even though he's Adrian's... and I shouldn't doubt him. I shouldn't *suspect* him to be the one writing me those notes.

"It's my pleasure. Do your breathing exercises, and I'll see you in a bit for a stretching session," he adds with a bright smile before walking away. Gabriel is right in front of me the first chance he gets.

"What's wrong?" he asks, placing his hand on my cheek as he searches my face for an answer. I cup it to lower it gently as I step towards my bag with shaking hands. Nausea builds in my throat as I fumble through my things and find a note sitting at the bottom of it, my name scribbled in an all-too-familiar handwriting.

LAST WARNING, VALENTINA. GET OUT OF YOUR CONTRACT FOR THIS SEASON AND NEXT YEAR, OR I'LL BE FORCED TO TAKE A MORE DRASTIC APPROACH.

YOU DON'T WANT TO FIND OUT WHAT THAT MEANS, I ASSURE YOU

I refuse to sink to the floor, to reveal how deeply this terrifies me. Was it Daniel? Was it someone I don't know or haven't thought about yet?

Daniel, on the other hand, has no reason to like me. He's my brother's performance coach and friend, but he's not mine. He could be faking being nice, and still hate me for making my way into this sport.

It could have been someone else.

Not knowing is sending me down a spiral I don't know how to come out of again. My head feels dizzy and I'm nauseous.

As much as I wish it wouldn't affect me because I've received these kinds of messages my whole life, this person *touched my bag*. This person has access to my things. This person is threatening to take more drastic action.

"Ma chérie, I need you to breathe." Gabriel's voice fills my ears, bringing me back into the moment for long enough to hand him the paper.

I should have told him before, should have told Adrian and James, too, but I didn't want to worry them. It should have been something I figured out on my own, but I have no idea what to do anymore. Ignoring this person won't make them go away.

What the fuck am I going to do now?

CHAPTER 44
Gabriel

EQUAL PARTS OF RAGE, worry, and fear consume me. I'm holding notes which threaten the well-being of the love of my life. Notes someone was close enough to place where Valentina would find them. A shudder runs down my spine. I don't know if it's because I'm terrified or because of the anger building inside of me. Jean was right when he said I've always had a problem controlling my emotions.

When I get deeply sad, I fall into darkness I never know how to make it out of. It's what happened when I found out Carlos was my grandfather.

When I fall in love, I do it with every single fiber of my being. I give myself to the person I love, protecting them from everything, including myself, if necessary.

When I get angry, I get so ragingly.

Right now, I don't know whether I'd like to wrap Valentina in bubble wrap, lock her in a room with me, and hold her to my body to ensure she's safe and protected. Or find whoever has been threatening her and rip off their heads. Both options are very appealing.

Instead, I take a deep breath and turn to stare into the same green-brown-blue eyes I watch open every single morning and flutter close at night.

"What would you like to do about this?" I ask my sunflower, but she barely looks at me.

Adrian has refused to let go of her hand since he read the notes and messages she's received over the past few months. He keeps his gaze on me, trying to have a silent conversation. I can read him well, so making out what he's saying is easy. *I'm going to kill whoever did this.* I nod in response because I'll help him bury the body.

Part of me is clinging to hope this is just someone who doesn't want Val in this sport and is trying to force her out by scaring her, but I can't be sure. I can't dismiss it either. If it was only messages, like the ones I've received on social media more times than I could keep count, I wouldn't be this concerned. So many people choose hate over love for reasons I'll never understand, but this situation goes far beyond someone hating Valentina for being a part of this sport. This person wants her *gone.*

"Ma chérie, you need to tell me what you'd like to do, or Adrian and I will hunt down whoever is harassing you and make them regret ever even looking your way." Adrian gives me a firm nod in response, but, no matter how badly I'd like to do that, this is Valentina's decision. I will not steamroll over what she wants because I'm having trouble seeing beyond how upset I am.

"I'd like to get this person to stop. And I want to know if I'm really in danger," she says, snapping out of her thoughts and straightening out her shoulders. "Maybe we can talk to Lorenzo Mattia to see if the cameras in the garage caught who did it," she suggests, and I realize she turned off the emotional side of her brain to let the logical and rational one dominate this situation. I still have to figure out how to do the same thing.

"I'll speak to him. We will find out what happened," I promise her when, all of a sudden, Cameron bursts through the door, one of his hands grabbing the collar of one of the mechanics on my team.

He's young, maybe my age if I'm not mistaken. He has brown eyes and blonde hair, a pale skin tone, and a slender frame. I've seen him a few times, but never for long enough to find out his name. I'm also pretty sure he only started working with my team this year.

"What the hell are you doing?" I blurt out, panic finally filling my chest when I realize how terrified the young man looks.

"This is Sebastian. He's the one who's been leaving the notes for Val," Cameron says and releases the mechanic with a slight push into the room.

The guy's eyes almost pop out of their sockets when Adrian stands up and pushes his chair backward simultaneously. My teammate steps toward him, his hands balled at his side.

"How the fuck did you find him so quickly?" I ask, already standing up to prevent Adrian from breaking this guy's nose.

My hand wraps around my teammate's arm while my eyes catch Valentina standing up and closing the distance between herself and the man who's been threatening her.

"Tournesol," I warn, but her attention is fixated on the man who is trembling now. Sebastian looks terrified the closer she gets.

"Why, Sebastian? I know you don't want to hurt me, so why write those notes?" she asks, and I realize they must know each other. His brown eyes scan her face with regret and shame. Something about this entire situation feels extremely off to me. Sebastian doesn't strike me as the type of person to go through so much trouble to spread hate and fear.

"Because you don't belong here," he replies, and I watch Valentina visibly flinch as if he'd smacked her. "Formula One is a man's sport. A woman has no place in it," Sebastian adds, and the hate in his eyes now takes away my previous doubts. He put the notes for her to find, I'm sure of it. The only thing I'm not sure of is whether he is the only one who feels this way, or if I have to convince Lorenzo Mattia to fire half of my team for not wanting Val here.

"No, *assholes* have no place in it. Too bad for you, you're one of those. I'll have your ass fired and banned from every single race in the future." Adrian grabs Sebastian by the elbow and leads him out of the room.

Cameron wraps his arms around Val in a reassuring hug—reassurance for himself that she's going to be okay and reassurance to her that everything will be alright. He doesn't let go for a minute, whispering things in her ear I can't hear because I'm not supposed to. My best friend places a single kiss against my girl's temple, then moves over to me to grab my shoulders.

"Next time something's wrong, you come to me. I'm sick and tired of you two keeping important shit from me. I'm older and wiser than both of you. Trust me to help you handle these things," Cameron says, his eyes shifting between Val and me. He's only five years older, but he did just find Sebastian in record time.

"How the hell did you—" I start, but he slaps my shoulder before I can finish the sentence.

"I demanded to see the footage as soon as I heard what's going on. Lorenzo Mattia was more than happy to go through it for me, and within twenty minutes, we knew who it was. What do you think the security cameras are for, Gabriel?" he asks, and I roll my eyes at the smugness in his voice.

"We were going to do the same," I protest, but, for the first time since we became close friends, I feel like a child in his presence.

It also doesn't help that I'm still terrified Val was in any kind of danger, even if it turns out it was someone who's braver leaving notes than they are facing the person they threatened. I don't think Sebastian is a threat we have to worry about, especially now that the entire Velocità Rossa garage probably knows it was him. There is no need to be worried anymore.

So, why is there a feeling in my gut that this is far from over?

CHASE

Part Two

CHAPTER 45
Valentina

Sebastian was fired immediately. It's been a week since his last note, since Adrian, Gabriel, James, Cameron, *and Leonard*—fuck, he was pissed when Adrian told him—found out about the messages I've been receiving. All five of them gave me a lecture on never keeping something like this from them again. Because I felt so guilty for scaring them all, I simply nodded through all of their speeches. Well, Gabriel didn't really give me a lecture. He kissed me over and over and begged me to never hide anything like what happened from him again. Not that I would.

Sebastian may have not been a threat—I saw him catch a spider and bring it outside when all of the other mechanics wanted to kill it—but who knows what could have happened? My attempt at not making them worry turned into them all getting furiously mad at me. Even Evangelin and Scarlette gave me earfuls when they found out how reckless I was about these messages.

It was stupid, yes, and I learned from my mistakes now. If it happens again, which I fucking hope it doesn't, I'll send out a group text to make sure everyone knows.

It's also now been over a week since my procedure, and I feel a lot better. I powered through the rest of the Hungarian race weekend where Adrian won, Gabriel came in second, James in third, Cameron in seventh, and Leonard in eighth. My brother and boyfriend are merely three points apart in the championship, which is nothing. One race could put Adrian on top and Gabriel into second place. If they keep this up, they will be challenging each other for the title until the last race. Not to mention, with every race I spend training under Lorenzo Mattia's guidance, I get ready for next season. I'm also still training in the simulator, like today.

After my whole body aches from exertion, I take a shower and throw myself into work. Leonard sent over some things for the driver academy, asking for my opinion. Lorenzo also sent me more contracts that I have to look over for my seat next season, but I forward them all to James, hoping he can help me with them like he helped me with the first one.

The Formula One grid is currently undergoing a lot of changes in its drivers. I've been given more funny looks from the men racing than I care to remember. Some of the lower team drivers haven't gotten a renewal for their contracts, so they shoot me daggers with their eyes because I, a woman no less, took one of the seats they wanted. Jonathan Kent is one of them. I've never liked him, and he's never acknowledged my existence, but now that Grenzenlos hasn't given him an extension, he seems to hate me more than anyone else on the grid. Eduardo also hasn't gotten a renewal yet, but he's been avoiding me since everything happened, which is more than fine by me.

Halfway through my workload, Annie calls me, wanting to discuss some things about Damian's baptism. She sounds off, but when I ask her what's wrong, she assures me it's nothing. I don't press either. Annie's probably sleep-deprived and exhausted. Having a baby is one of the hardest jobs.

"You know, I'm more than happy to babysit Damian if you need the night off." James, Gabriel, and Adrian are all not in Monaco at the moment, taking care of some business. Adrian and Gabriel are at a team dinner in Italy—they invited me, but I didn't feel like going after what happened last race weekend—and James is in England, visiting his parents.

"Thank you, I'd really appreciate it if you came over," she says, and I assure her I will be right there.

I get Chase ready to go and help him into the trunk of my new Velocità Rossa SUV. A few days ago, it showed up at my front door with a note from Lorenzo Mattia.

Dear Valentina,

You have not only exceeded all of my expectations, but your presence in our team has brought a lot of positive attention to our sport. Take this as a token of our gratitude and thanks for all the hard work you've put in. And as an apology for what a member of our team put you and your family through.

With love,

Everyone At Velocità Rossa

P.S. I wanted to get you a sports model, but Adrian told me you have a dog now, so this SUV was the best fit.

"Come on," I call out to Chase, helping him in the car before opening the door to the driver's seat and settling down in it.

Everything about this car feels right to me. It's not the Mustang my grandfather cherished above every other car and that I love so much now, but it's one hell of a vehicle. It roars to life, the power underneath my fingers exhilarating.

Damian is the cutest baby I've ever seen in my entire life. His ocean-blue eyes look exactly like his daddy's, and his tiny nose is shaped just like James'. The little fella in my arms is a duplicate of James.

I study his features for a while. Annie is taking a nap on the couch, probably for the first time since before he was born. Damian starts fussing around in my arms, and when he cries, I panic.

What if he wakes Annie? What if I can't calm him? Does that make me a terrible aunt? What if that means I will be a terrible mother?

Before I can spiral into my own thoughts, I focus on the fidgeting child in my arms. I hum a soothing melody over and over again until Damian goes back to sleep. *Thank God.* Maybe I won't be such a terrible aunt. I'm actually quite impressed with myself.

I place Damian in his bassinet and sit down on the other couch. Annie's house is a complete mess, and I wonder why she doesn't stay at James'. I'm sure he wouldn't mind, and he has a cleaning person who comes to his house twice a week.

I wipe the floor, remove all of the trash, wash the dishes, wipe away the dust, and simply clean anything that looks dirty to me. Since her sister doesn't do shit, the least I can do is help. With James in England, and Damian screaming the whole night long, Annie has too much to do with too little help. I feel terrible I haven't been there more, but I plan to be now. At least when I'm in Monaco.

Damian starts crying again as soon as I sit down on the couch after an hour of cleaning, and Annie wakes up to walk over to him. She picks him up and sinks back down onto the couch, breastfeeding him. She hasn't talked to me much since I've come to her home, but she's also been asleep most of the time.

As soon as she's done feeding him, she asks if I could burp him. I take Damian from her, put a towel over my shoulder like she instructs me, and pat his back until he burps. Meanwhile, Annie is in the bathroom, taking care of her needs for once. I put him back down in his bassinet and remove the dirty towel from my shoulder, bringing it to the laundry. When Annie comes back, she sinks down on the couch and lets out a sigh.

"I'm so tired," she admits, and I move to the space next to her. "Thank you for cleaning up. I don't know how to repay you," Annie says, and I hug her.

"I'm here for you for whatever you need. There is nothing I wouldn't do for little Damian," I reply, and she hugs me tightly.

"I know. It's why you're going to be the best godmother." I smile at her and press a kiss to her cheek. This girl needs some love and affection. She looks exhausted and tired, so I keep hugging her. "Thank you for being here for me. It means more to me than you will ever realize." I place another kiss on her cheek and hold on tighter.

"Always."

CHAPTER 46
Valentina

FINGERS... DELICIOUS, FAMILIAR FINGERS are running up and down my leg. I'm pretty sure I let out a moan in my half-sleep trance as I reach for where I feel them on my legs... my hairy legs. The ones I didn't shave because I was too lazy last night. I open my eyes to find Gabriel staring right at me.

"Mon amour," I say and wrap my arms around his neck. His mahogany scent fills my nose, and I let out an involuntary sigh. It's strange how much I need him, want him, even crave him. His hand keeps running over my leg, and I pull away, covering myself with a blanket.

"Why are you hiding from me? I already felt your hairy legs," he teases, and I swat his arm.

"I thought you were coming tonight," I complain, and he chuckles again. The rest of the world vanishes as I stare into his green-brown eyes and at his stubble, which has finally grown back, *thank God.*

"I'm sorry, chérie, I couldn't wait. I just wanted to come home to you." *He just wanted to come home to me...* Warmth spreads through my chest in response.

"Let me go shave quickly," I say, but he pulls the blanket off my body and pins me down on the bed.

"Valentina, I crave you. Your legs, your pretty pussy, your armpits, they're all beautiful, shaven or not," he says, and I grin at him. It's not just about him seeing me unshaven, it's mostly about my own comfort, as it should be. Right now, however, I couldn't give less of a fuck, not when he's pressing his rock-hard cock against my aching clit.

"Okay," I reply, and his lips envelop mine. *Finally.*

I wrap my legs around his hips and enjoy the warmth of his tongue as it enters my mouth. Moans, needy and desperate, slip out of my mouth and into his. His cock pushes against me even harder in an instant. God, I love it when he wears sweatpants and I get to feel his thickness against my pussy. My hands move to the zipper of his jacket, and I pull it down so I can take it off right before pulling his shirt over his head.

"Oh, yes," I say as I run my fingers over his hard body, but he simply smiles, showing off his beautiful dimples, and removes the pajama dress I'm wearing. I'm only in panties underneath, but he rips them off my body soon and lowers his head between my legs. Right before he kisses me, he looks up at me with a sexy smile.

"So wet and ready for me. Do you know how beautiful that is?" he asks, but I blush and lean my head back.

"Are you going to touch me or just smile at me?" He shakes his head, but the grin stays on his lips.

"Baby, I'll touch you until you can't take it anymore, if that's what you want." That's exactly what I want, and I push his head down toward my clit.

"Fuck me," I say, and he does exactly that.

His hands run over my breasts, squeezing my nipples. I cover his hands with mine when his mouth moves to the inside of my thigh. He pulls me to the edge of the bed so he can get better access. Gabriel runs his tongue over my legs, and I shiver in return. His index and middle finger trace the outside of my sex, teasing me. I squeeze my breasts since his hands left them, kneading them until pleasure seeps through me. Gabriel puts my leg up on his shoulder right before his fingers slide inside of me, and I moan at the top of my lungs when he sucks on my clit. He curls them inside of me every single time he slides in. When his tongue flicks over my clit, my hands drop to his hair, and I pull on it, grinding against his mouth. We keep that steady rhythm until I fall apart, his lips moving from my pussy up to my breasts where he tugs one of my nipples into his mouth.

Gabriel reaches inside his pocket to pull out the condom, but I take it away from him and throw it on the ground as I pull his neck down.

"I want you bare, Gabriel," I whisper, pushing my lips against his.

"Fuck," he groans and makes quick work of his pants.

He nibbles on my neck and massages my tongue with his for a moment, obviously trying to make sure I'm ready for him.

"Please, Gabriel," I beg because I'm still needy for him.

He slides into me at a torturously slow pace, but once he's all the way in, I'm full and letting out a soft moan. It does feel different, quite a lot different, and I know he feels the same way when he reaches for something, anything to grab and hold onto. The sensation of his skin against mine sends small explosions of pleasure through me. There is no barrier between us, nothing at all as my walls squeeze his cock in absolute content.

"God," he moans, and I bring my hands back into his hair. "Shit, fuck," he breathes, both of us reveling in the feel for a moment.

Gabriel wraps my legs around his hips, and I tug on his hair, letting sounds of pleasure leave my lips. He slides back out, then pushes back in, and the more he does it, the more I realize how much more I enjoy sex without the condom. All my senses are heightened, and everything feels more... intense.

"You're fucking perfect, chérie," he says, his thrusts hard and merciless, just the way I like.

"Yes! Oh my god," I breathe, and he lets out a low grunt on top of me. His thumb circles my clit until I fall apart, too overwhelmed by the sensation. "Gabriel, fuck," I breathe out when he keeps going. "Give me a moment," I beg, and his movements freeze. I suck in a sharp breath, letting things slow.

"Can I spin you around, baby?" he asks, kissing my cheek and forehead. I nod, and within a second, I'm on all fours. "Hold on," he says and gestures at my headboard, guiding my hands there.

"More," I say when I'm ready, feeling him slam inside of me right after.

My whole body trembles but he keeps going, fucking me hard and fast. He gives my right ass cheek a firm smack before grabbing both of them and going deeper and slower. The change in speed makes my head spin, especially when he increases it again, moaning into our silent room. My name leaves his lips right as another orgasm washes through my system and he spills inside of me. I feel his cock pulsing as my walls clench around him, his cum filling me.

"Fuck," he says, completely out of breath, pulling out and running his thumb over my entrance. I sink onto the bed and turn around grinning up at him. "I never had sex without a condom, and it felt a little too good," he admits. "If I wasn't already addicted to you, I would be now."

"Me, too." Gabriel stares into my eyes, all love and lust for me. "I think we should try again. Over and over until we're perfect at it," I say although we both know we already are.

"Sounds like a fantastic idea, but I'm going to have to postpone it until tonight because I have a special day with you planned, and we have to leave in an hour," he says, eyes focused on my lips.

Gabriel kisses me passionately before grabbing some tissues from my nightstand and cleaning both of us up. He drags us to the shower a moment later, and I follow happily, hugging him from behind once we're inside. He hums in appreciation, tugging me under the warm water and wrapping his arms around my chest.

"I missed you so much," he whispers at the same moment I say it. We laugh at how much we think alike, and Gabriel's hot breath against my neck makes me shiver.

"I'm never going anywhere without you ever again," Gabriel says and steps back from the hug. I frown and glide my hands onto his cheeks. "I mean it, chérie, I want to find a way to take you and Chase everywhere. Yes, I missed the little guy, too," he admits, making my heart warm in my chest.

"We can't always be together," I remind him, and he frowns in response.

"I don't like that," Gabriel says, and I let out a slight laugh.

"So, what do you have planned for today?" I ask. Gabriel grins wickedly.

"We're going to pick out my new car."

CHAPTER 47

Valentina

AFTER AN HOUR OF looking at ten different Velocità Rossas, Gabriel and I finally decide he should take the new Velocità Rossa 705 Bullet. The car is so sexy, I can't look at it without imagining having sex with Gabriel in it, on top of it, next to it, pretty much anywhere near the car.

"What are you thinking about?" he asks, sliding his hands onto my stomach as his front presses against my backside.

"Riding you inside this car," I admit, his fingers digging into my skin.

"Hmmm, later. I want that later," he says and kisses my shoulder. Shivers spread down my spine as heat pools between my legs.

"I would love to own this beauty," I say to distract myself from the way his body pulls me in, and Gabriel grins.

"Well, let me see what I can do about that," he replies, and I simply laugh because I assume he's joking.

Right after Gabriel signs the papers, I run my fingers along the smooth surface, admiring the glossy, shiny red color. He nuzzles my neck once he's done, and I let out a small giggle. He holds out the papers that show the contract he signed. Trade in his old car for this new one. At first, I couldn't comprehend why Gabriel would give up the car he loves so much, but he told me it's time, so I didn't question him.

Gabriel dangles the key between us, an easy smile on his full, pink lips.

"Here, you're driving it home," he says, and I don't know what I enjoy hearing more, the fact that he said I'm driving it or that he said home. Gabriel slips the key into my hand, and I gasp for air. *This is really happening, I get to drive this beautiful car.* I feel giddy. My Velocità Rossa SUV already excites every piece of me, but this? This is the kind of fast car I hope to own one day.

"Are you sure?" I ask, praying to God he says yes.

"More than sure. I trust you with my life, why wouldn't I trust you with our car?" *Wait, wait, wait, wait... wait!*

"What?" I almost scream, and he grins, his index finger pressing over his lips to tell me to quiet down. I would be pissed because he's shushing me, but I was being loud in a showroom where everyone is quiet.

"I put the contract under both of our names," he says, and I can't comprehend his words anymore.

"Gabriel, you cannot be serious. You just bought me a fucking boat and now you put both of our names on the contract of this sexy car?" I'm whisper-screaming, but Gabriel seems to be amused.

"Chérie, I barely paid a cent for it. I drive for Velocità Rossa, they would give me any car I want as long as I'm seen driving it on the street and promote it on social media. So, please, don't worry," he says and laughs a little. I, however, can't join him because my head is still spinning. "I put your name because I want you to own this car too, and the company said it's fine." His thumb caresses my cheek, and I calm down.

"I still don't think you should continue making big commitments like this without talking to me," I say, and he nods.

"You said you wanted it. Doesn't that count?" he counters, and I remember what I said to him earlier. "I thought it would make you happy. I saw how you looked at the car." His face falls a little, and his eyes drift to look at the car.

Well done, Val, well done.

Gabriel was just trying to do something I told him I wanted, and now I've made him upset. I'm such an idiot.

I step on my tiptoes to press a kiss to his lips, and his eyes fixate on mine with a soft intensity that warms my insides. I could have him look at me like that twenty-four hours a day.

"I love the car, and I love you, and it did make me happy. It's only because the boat was already a huge purchase."

"Val, I love you, and there is nothing I wouldn't do to bring a smile onto your lovely face."

"Can we make a deal?" I ask, and he cocks one of his perfectly-shaped eyebrows. The urge to run my fingers over it momentarily takes over, but I push it back down to focus on what I was going to say to him. "The next big purchase I want us to make is a house. Nothing else, just a house that is ours, where we create our own memories."

As much as I love living at Grandpa's house, it's always going to have those memories that haunt me everywhere I go. I can almost see him sit on the chairs at the kitchen island, or see him swimming in the pool he loved so dearly. That house is not mine, it's always going to be his in my mind, which is why I'm not planning on living there forever. It would be too painful.

"No boats, no cars, no planes," I warn, and he laughs.

"Okay, I promise." He kisses me swiftly before stepping back, showing me his dimple-accessorized smile. "What about a ring? Is that also a big purchase?" My eyes go wide, but I catch myself.

"No, because you're not going to buy me a fifteen-thousand euro ring! My ring has to be a hundred euros or less," I say, smiling at the conversation we're having.

"You cannot expect me to give you a hundred euros or less ring!" he complains, and I raise both of my eyebrows. "Before you start arguing with me, let me make you a counteroffer. Three thousand euros or less, just so it can be a good quality ring that will last you a lifetime." I want to complain, but this is so far ahead in the future, I don't want to argue over this.

"Fine," I say, and he takes my hands in his.

"Fine," he mocks me, and I smack his stomach, earning myself a chuckle before he wraps his arm around me and kisses my temple.

When we arrive at home, my eyes go wide at the image in front of me. Damian's Maxi-Cosi is in front of our house with bags and toys around it. He's lying in the shade, but I can hear him scream from inside of the car. He must be really hot, it is twenty-five degrees outside, after all. I jump out of the car and run toward the small child without hearing a word Gabriel is saying. I'm in protective mode now because Damian is screaming. I pull him into my arms to try and calm him down.

There is a letter addressed to me in the Maxi-Cosi, but I can't focus on that right now. Gabriel runs over to me to unlock the door, and we step inside to get Damian out of the heat.

"What the fuck?" Gabriel asks, and I shrug.

"I have no idea, I'm not supposed to have him today," I say, anxiety settling in my chest.

What the hell is going on?

Why the hell is he here?

What happened to Annabel?

"Here, give him to me and read that letter," Gabriel says, and as soon as I place him in Gabriel's arms, Damian stops crying.

I need to find out what happened to Annabel, where she is, and why Damian is at my house. There are too many things that are wrong at the moment, and I don't know which my brain should start focusing on. I feel like throwing up, crying, and screaming all at the same time, and I haven't even read the letter yet.

God, what is it going to say?

Whatever it is, it cannot be good.

My trembling fingers open the envelope with the utmost difficulty, and I take a deep breath before I start reading.

Dear Valentina,

I'm sorry to do this to you in a letter, but this way is the easiest. I can't tell you how sorry I am for putting this on you, but I'm a selfish person that never wanted to be a mother in the first place. All my life, I've known becoming a mother is not an option, but then I got pregnant with Damian, and I knew I couldn't just have an abortion. My parents would have disowned me, so I needed to come up with something else, something that would allow Damian to grow up while also letting me move on with my life and never look back. I can't believe the universe actually had you walk into my life to make the decision to leave that much easier.

Don't look for me, don't try to find me because I don't want to be found. I had this baby so he could live. I didn't have him to stop living. Please, tell James I'm sorry for all of it.

None of it was real. The Annabel you met is not the person I am. I needed to leave, and I needed to restart my life again without the baggage of having a son. He'll be better off without me anyway because he will have you. You are so much better for him than I will ever be, which is why I know this decision is the right one. James will make it work, even though his job will make it difficult for him. Then again, he will have you to help him with this whole situation. I sincerely hope you won't have *to give up your career for Damian either, but you'll want to put him first now. I know you. That's why I'm sorry.*

I told Harlow to back off and leave you and Gabriel alone, but I'm not sure she is going to listen to me. She is vengeful, I have to warn you, which is just another reason why I have to leave. There is nothing more I can say, there isn't an explanation I can give you that will satisfy you.

Just know I'm truly sorry.

Annabel

Annabel did what my mother did to Adrian and me, the one thing a child can never recover from. The feeling of being unwanted and undesirable, the feeling of abandonment and loss without ever being able to get closure for it.

I don't know what's worse, the fact that she is expecting me to become Damian's mother and give up my entire life or the fact that I have no idea what I'm going to tell my best friend when he lands in three hours.

The next thing I know, I'm pushing the letter into Gabriel's hand before running to the bathroom and throwing up everything inside of me.

CHAPTER 48
Valentina

"Chérie, can I come in?" Gabriel asks the moment I put the lid back on the toilet.

"No," I reply, but he comes in anyway.

"Damian is sleeping, and I just read the letter. I don't know what to say, baby. I have no idea what we're going to do."

We... He's right, this is not just on James and me, but it's also on him because Gabriel and I share one future.

I look at him with concern as tears fall down my cheeks. Before he can get closer to me, I rinse my mouth with water to temporarily solve the problem of tasting the vomit in my mouth. I'll have to brush my teeth later. For now, I need to talk to my boyfriend about what to do with my best friend's child.

"What the fuck are we going to do? How the fuck are we going to tell James Annie bailed? He's my best friend, Gabriel, and I don't know how I'm going to tell him his son's mother has been playing all of us for the last three months to get close to us and then leave. That's just sick, it makes me sick. I will never be able to understand how a parent can willingly leave their child, I just—"

Gabriel puts his hands on my legs, trying to comfort me. It's helping a little bit, but the situation is too terrible to find any good in it right now.

His thumbs caress my thighs, but he doesn't reply for the longest time, creating a suspense I wish away.

"I can tell him if that makes it easier," he suggests, and I give him a smile that doesn't reach my eyes.

Every time our lives go well, *boom*, something happens to turn them completely upside down again. We can't seem to catch a break, no matter what we do. At least we have each other to go through this. I haven't even had the chance to give Gabriel the bracelet I got him. I'm so mad, sad, and frustrated, I don't even know how to think in proper sentences anymore.

"No, mon amour, I need to be the one to tell him. James is my family, I need to talk to him myself, but I just don't know where to start," I say because it wouldn't be right.

I feel like I have to do this by myself, although I know if I say the word, Gabriel would do anything for me. I hear him sighing, so I place my hand on his cheek.

"I don't know what to do," I admit in a whisper, and he frowns.

"Neither do I. It was already a messed up situation because James is always traveling, but now it's even worse. And you shouldn't have to be the one who has to turn your life around to raise a child that isn't even yours." He's right, I shouldn't have to be the one, but for Damian and James, I would do anything. For my family, I would do anything and everything.

Even give up your dream career? my subconscious chimes in.

I feel like crying again because I'm selfish and that's the last thing I want.

"Let's just wait for James and Adrian to return, and then we'll talk to James. There is nothing we can do now anyway. Damian is his son, even if I'm to be his godmother, and he needs to be the one to make the decision about his son's future."

Gabriel nods right before he stands up. He holds out his hand for me, and I take it. Next thing I know, he's pulling me close and hugging me tightly. His fingers stroke along my back, his lips connecting with my temple as he kisses me.

"We're going to be okay," he assures me, and I let out the breath I've been holding since I saw Damian on the stairs.

Gabriel pulls back and attempts to kiss me, but I cover his mouth with my hand since he obviously forgot I just threw up. I quickly run upstairs to brush my teeth and pop gum into my mouth.

When I come downstairs again, I find Gabriel sitting on the couch with Damian in his arms. I never thought the first time I'd see Gabriel holding a baby while sitting on our couch would be under these circumstances. I never thought Annabel would be cruel enough to do something so horrific and terrible to her son. Ever since I met her, she seemed like the nicest person to ever walk on this unfair Earth, but now she turned into this heartless monster who left her son on the doorstep of someone she barely knew. I thought we were friends. I almost laugh at myself.

How could I have ever been friends with a person who hurt her child in the same way my mother did to me? How could I have ever trusted her when she is not someone that can be trusted? What does that say about me?

It says I am too gullible and too trusting. It says, deep down, I'm so desperate to expand my little family I don't judge people's characters in the way I should. I blow raspberries, and Gabriel frowns at me as if to say 'Shut up, I just got him to fall asleep again'. I smile at him and hold up my hands in surrender to show I'll be quiet.

I walk over to both of them and sit down on the couch next to Damian, who is sleeping peacefully in my boyfriend's arms. Gabriel and I sitting on the couch, holding a baby that is not ours isn't what I would consider perfect, but I still can't tear my eyes from the picture in front of me. I run my fingers through Gabriel's beautiful, curly hair, and he smiles the smile I could stare at forever. The dimples, the softness in his gaze, the love written all across his face, it's enchanting. *He's* enchanting.

We sit on the couch for a while, and I have no idea how I'm so calm. I should be freaking out considering the fact that soon, I'm going to have to tell James what happened. I almost growl thinking about it. I hate her, I hate her for doing this. That conceiving, backstabbing, lying shit-talker had to ruin everyone's lives just because she couldn't handle being honest. If she wasn't ready to be a mom, she should have spoken to us. We could have found a different way without her throwing us into ice-cold water.

I don't understand how Annabel could have acted this part as well as she did, I don't understand how anyone could play it so damn well. She made me believe she was sincere.

When the door to our house opens, my heart stops beating.

"Honey, we're home," Adrian and James scream in perfect harmony, and involuntary tears flow from my eyes in response. Gabriel looks at me with concern, and I quickly wipe them away. James and Adrian stroll into the living room, and James smiles brightly when he sees his son.

"Oh, I didn't know you would be here, bud," he says cheerfully, and I swallow down more tears. Before going to Damian, James comes to me and gives me a quick kiss on the top of my head. "Where is your mummy?" he asks when he takes his son from Gabriel's arms.

"I think you should sit down," I say, and Adrian stares at me with worry in his eyes. He can't even begin to imagine what I'm about to say, but I am convinced somehow, deep down, he knows what happened. He saw the pain in my eyes when Mom left. A similar one is playing in them now.

When we were younger, Dad shared the story of the day he told Adrian Mom left. Well, Adrian more or less figured it out by himself.

"She left us, didn't she? Why?"

Dad then always said to Adrian and me that he never had, has, or will have an answer to that question. Then again, how could he? Mom left him as much as she left Adrian and me, and I know it hurt him because it broke our entire family apart.

Adrian started taking care of me while Dad distanced himself from us. Yes, he still shared some things with us, but it was never the same after she left, it would never be the same again. There is a difference between a parent dying and a parent choosing to leave, I know because I've experienced both. One of those two leaves you always wondering why you weren't good enough or if there was something so fundamentally wrong with you they had to leave just to get away from who you are.

Now, for the first time in my whole life, I realize it isn't my fault. It wasn't because I wasn't good enough. Damian is more than good enough, yet Annabel couldn't wait to leave. It's never our fault, never, it's the fault of the person who decides to leave without as much as a goodbye.

"Damian was lying outside of my door in his maxi cosi when I came home, along with this letter," I say and hand James the paper I know is going to scar him forever. "I'm so sorry," I whisper, and Gabriel's hand wraps around mine, giving me the comfort I need.

With Damian in his arms, James reads the words carefully, anger washing over his face with each minute that passes, and I get more and more antsy.

"She left?" he asks, his voice cracking. A single tear rolls down his cheek before I watch his whole body get consumed by anger. "Gabriel, please take Damian."

My sweet boyfriend does as he is told, and James jumps up from the couch and runs out of the house. I'm not fast enough to catch up with him, so he's in his car and driving off just as I get outside.

"Fuck," I growl and run back inside to get the keys to my Mustang. "I'll be back soon," I tell Adrian and Gabriel. For now, I have to chase my best friend.

There is only one place I'm convinced he'll go, which is why I step on the gas and drive to Annabel's house.

Chapter 49
Gabriel

"This is not how a child is supposed to grow up," Adrian says as I shift Damian in my arms, making sure to support his head. This baby might be part James, who I dislike with a fucking passion, but he's pretty cute. Plus, it's not his fault his dad is in love with the love of my life.

"I know," I reply, staring into my teammate's bright eyes.

He's close to tears, and I realize he's reliving the trauma of being left as a child. He sympathizes with Damian as his heart hurts for the little child in my arms. I know because I wasn't left, but it fucking sucks to think about all the doubts Damian will have growing up. The same doubts I know Valentina and Adrian have to deal with every single day of their lives. Doubts two people as incredible as them should never have to deal with.

"Annabel is expecting Valentina to give up her career," Adrian mumbles as he reads the letter, and I give an agreeing nod. "I don't know why the fuck she'd put that pressure on Val and not on the father of her child, but okay..." He trails off, shaking his head. "This can't be happening. I won't let it."

Neither will I. Val will race for Alfa Adrenalina next year. She will not put a full stop to her life to raise Damian. If anyone has to, James does.

"We will figure something out, and if everything else fails, James doesn't have a choice. He will have to quit after this season," I say while Damian grabs a hold of my index finger.

How the hell can something be this small?

"Not necessarily. He could hire a nanny to stay with him," Adrian replies, but the thought of Damian staying with a nanny every single time James has work duties doesn't feel right. The little guy in my arms doesn't deserve it.

Some Formula One drivers make having a family work. They get married, have babies, and still manage to race every weekend to compete for the championship. But it takes a toll. Being away from their families isn't easy, so they rely on their significant other to raise and care for their children in the way they can't always do. With Annabel gone, Damian doesn't have another parent when James has to work, traveling the world for weeks sometimes. This isn't right.

"Yeah, I know, it's not a good solution," Adrian adds because I've been quiet for too long.

"Nothing is going to be a good solution, Adrian, this whole situation is a fucked up mess," I say and look at him again to see his eyes are on Damian. "Come, hold him. My hand is falling asleep," I lie because Adrian's been wanting to hold him since he found out what happened. He wants to comfort the little guy, even if Damian has no idea what the hell is happening.

"I've only ever held one baby before," he says, and I let out a laugh.

"It was Valentina, wasn't it?" I ask, and he grins like I've never seen before.

"She was all wrinkly, it was hilarious," he replies, and I chuckle. Sometimes I forget just how close those two are and then Adrian's eyes turn all soft as he speaks about her, making me realize Val is the person he loves most. She's always been. "I don't want Damian to grow up feeling unloved, passed around to any available family member. It's not fair," he says, rubbing his thumb over the little guy's cheek.

"Me neither," I admit, dropping my face into my hands. "How can people do this?" I blurt out without meaning to, Damian catching my attention when he starts crying in Adrian's arms.

"What did I do?" he asks, panic lacing his features.

"Nothing. He's probably hungry," I assure him as I stand up and fight off a smile.

"No, don't leave. I have no fucking clue what to do with him," Adrian begs, forcing a smile onto my face. I inhale deeply, smelling the true reason why Damian is crying. My teammate scrunches his nose before his eyes go wide.

"Not it," I say. Adrian lets out a string of curses while I laugh so loudly, I bend over at the waist to stop myself.

"Do you know how to—" Adrian cuts off, already standing up to get to the diaper bag.

"Yeah, mate, I know how. I'll show you," I say before both of us head upstairs to the bathroom.

CHAPTER 50
Valentina

WHEN I ARRIVE, JAMES is already knocking on the door to the most likely empty house. It takes me a second to get out of the car because I don't know if I'm able to calm him down. After another deep breath, I walk toward the angry man banging his fist against the door with too much force.

"James," I say, but he doesn't stop screaming Annabel's name and knocking on her door.

"Annabel, open the fucking door!" She isn't here. I know she isn't, but he's trying anyway because he's upset and desperate. Because he can't understand how a parent could be so cruel to their child. Because he's scared of what her disappearance will mean. Because he's hurting.

"Please, James," I beg, placing my hand on his arm, the same one he's using to knock.

"She's here. She has to be here! She can't be gone," he says, almost breaking down the door to get into the house.

"James," I repeat, this time keeping my voice a little firmer to try and pull him out of his freak-out trance.

"This isn't happening. This can't be fucking happening."

His words are followed by more of his knocking, so I wrap my arms around his stomach and hold on tight. Maybe it will calm him down, maybe it'll make him push me away, I have no idea. All I hope is that he needs this hug as much as I do.

Annie was my friend, someone I started caring about because I thought she'd stay. I thought she loved her son more than anything in the world, that she started caring for James, too.

She made me think she was falling in love with him.

"Val, I need you to let go of me so I can break down this bloody door," James says, making me hold on even tighter.

"She's gone, James. We both know it," I say gently, rubbing my hands along his stomach.

"No, she's not. She didn't do this to Damian, she didn't do this to *us*," he replies and keeps knocking, but his fists are slowing down as his chest trembles.

"We will figure this out together. You just have to take a deep breath for me. Can you do that?" I ask, turning my head until my chin rests against his back.

"I can't. Oh my God, I have to get back to Damian. He's all alone now, and I just left him. I left him with Gabriel out of all people, and I hate that guy—" James cuts off when he realizes what he's saying. I step away only to turn him around and grab his shoulders.

"Damian is in good hands. I know you don't like Gabriel, but Adrian is also home. They've got this if you need a minute," I assure him, but he's already shaking his head.

"No, I have to go to him. He needs me. I'm all he has," he says and storms past me and back toward his car.

"James, you're not alone in this. We're all here for you and Damian. I promise." He stops, his back tensing as his hand freezes midway to the driver's door. James seems to consider what to say as his mouth opens and shuts subtly a few times before his forehead drops against his car.

"I need to be with my son," he says and gets into his car without looking at me again.

Panic settles inside of me when I realize I'm all alone at the house where Harlow lives or lived, I'm not sure. Annabel said she's vengeful, and I'm not about to stand here and wait for her to get revenge on me for whatever twisted thing she thinks I did.

My heart races as I rush to my car, fear creeping into my chest until I'm out of the driveway and on my way back home. I shake my head to get rid of the sensation, my right hand lifting to where my heart is to massage away the feeling. Except, more panic fills my chest when I see Gabriel arguing with James on the front steps when I get back. Adrian is watching the argument unfold with his arms crossed in front of his chest and a scowl directed at his best friend.

Relief floods both Adrian and Gabriel's faces when they see me approaching.

"How could you just leave her at that house by herself?" Gabriel barks at James, his hand lifting to gesture to me.

"I don't understand what your bloody problem is, Gabriel," James says and attempts to step around my angry boyfriend to get inside and to his son.

"Harlow could have been at that house," Adrian replies, filling in the blanks and causing realization to dawn on my best friend.

"Fuck, I hadn't even thought about that," he blurts out before turning to watch me approach them. "I'm so sorry, my love, I wasn't thinking. I just wanted to get back to—"

"Your son. I know. I'm not mad, James, promise. Go check on Damian," I say and we watch James disappear before I take a deep breath. My hands run over my face. "You think that was helpful?" I ask my brother and boyfriend.

"You think it was helpful of him to leave you there by yourself?" Adrian challenges, so I shoot him a glare.

"Would you be thinking clearly after you just found out the mother of your child disappeared and left you to make impossible life decisions?" I say, and Adrian's gaze shifts to the ground, guilt clearly taking over.

They both stay silent, so I roll my lips for a moment, letting myself think about their perspectives too.

"Harlow wasn't there. She would have called the police on James for almost breaking the door down," I explain, but neither Gabriel nor Adrian look convinced.

"Does this even matter right now? My best friend is hurting. What do you think has priority? Getting pissed at James or helping him work through what's going on as a family?" My question leaves them both staring at me. "You're both being ridiculous, it was five minutes." I attempt to walk past Gabriel and Adrian, but my brother pulls me into a hug so tight, I can't breathe.

"We're just glad you're okay. Ridiculous or not, we were worried," he explains before pressing a kiss to my cheek and disappearing inside too.

A second later, Gabriel's arms are around me, pulling me close until my back is flush against his front. His lips attach to my neck where he trails kisses downward, stopping right at my soft spot and sucking it into his mouth. The moan I'm holding back makes my entire chest vibrate.

"I'm sorry, mon tournesol." His voice is soft and quiet, but I know he means it.

"That's a hell of a way to apologize," I say when his fingers trail over the waistband of my skirt, his mouth still sending shivers of desire down my spine.

"I didn't mean to add to this shitty situation. I was worried and let it out on James. I'm sorry." He's not trying to excuse himself in the slightest. He says it as it is.

"Let's go figure this out as a family, okay?" I say and turn in his arms. Gabriel's lips find mine immediately.

"Okay."

CHAPTER 51

James

I CAN'T BELIEVE SHE left. I cannot believe after everything we went through during these past months, she had the strength to leave Damian and me. What am I going to do? I have a racing career! I have my whole life ahead of me, I can't just drop everything! How am I going to finance my life? His life? Why did she just leave me to make such difficult life decisions about our son by myself? How could she do this to us? How could she do this to Damian? I don't understand, I don't understand, I can't understand. She gave me a choice about whether or not I wanted to be a part of Damian's life, so what if I had said no? What if I had made the decision not to care?

I don't understand how she just pretended this whole time to be someone she isn't. It makes no sense. I don't understand anything anymore. All I know is I don't want to do this by myself, I don't think I'm capable of it, but I know I'm probably going to have to. My parents have been unsupportive since they found out Damian existed, so they are not going to help me. Mia can't even take care of herself, and the only person I know is going to help is Valentina, and I do not want to put this on her. I love her too much to ask her to help me raise my son when she already does so much. Her racing school with Leonard. Being a reserve driver for Velocità Rossa this season. Training to be a bloody Formula One driver next season!

What the fuck? What the fuck am I going to do? I–I can't do this. What if I fuck him up? What if I make him a bad person? I'm not supposed to be doing this alone, I'm supposed to have someone to help me with this. I'm supposed to have Annabel! Why is this happening right now? Why is this happening to Damian? He shouldn't have to grow up without a mother. He shouldn't have to grow up with a father who will never be what Damian needs him to be...

Valentina and Gabriel walk into the living room, holding hands, and smiling at each other. It will never get easier to see how happy they are together.

I'm never going to love anyone more than I love Val. She's got my heart, one hundred percent. I hope I'm wrong because I know she'll never be more than my best friend. I will never be more than *her* best friend. She is never going to want me the same way she wants Gabriel. No matter how hard I try, nothing will ever change her mind.

I rock Damian back and forth to calm him, but also a little to calm myself. I've been freaking out since I found out Annabel left, and I shouldn't focus on Valentina right now. I should be focusing on what to do with Damian and how to create the best life for him and me. Maybe I shouldn't think about that either because I'm never going to reach a solution to make both of us happy.

Can we even be happy now that Annabel is gone?

I won't be able to do what I love anymore, and he won't have his mother to take care of him. Bloody fucking hell... I don't know what to do... Tears roll down my cheeks before I can stop myself, and I ask Adrian to take Damian for a moment. I'm convinced I'm having a panic attack, and I don't want to hold my son while I'm having a mental breakdown.

I run past Val and Gabriel to get somewhere, I'm not sure where. All my mind is focusing on is getting outside and breathing fresh air. It feels like I'm suffocating, like I can't breathe, and I need to find a way to get my lungs to work again. My mind has shut off completely now, and my concentration is on getting air into my lungs.

Why is this so hard? Why can't I breathe? Moments after I, apparently, dropped to the floor—something I only realize when I feel the rocks of the sidewalk underneath my fingertips—hands appear on my face.

"James, look at me," her beautiful voice demands, and I bring myself to look into her eyes, the same ones I've grown too used to. "One deep breath, and then another," she says with a firm tone, knowing I can't resist her. I would do anything she told me, anything to make her happy. So, I take a deep breath, then another, and then one more after that. When I finally get enough oxygen into my brain to be able to think again, I drop my shoulders and sigh.

"I'm sorry," I croak out and she sits down in front of me, a frown on her gorgeous face.

"Don't be sorry, I would be concerned if you didn't have a panic attack. Too much happened for you not to find a way to let out your fear."

She always knows the right thing to say, it's quite ridiculous. I wish I could kiss her right now, and I hate that her kiss would comfort me. It would take away the pain I'm feeling deep inside because Annie left. More tears stream down my face, and I admit the one thing that hasn't left my mind since I found out Annie won't raise Damian.

"I don't want to stop racing," I say, and a sob leaves my lips. I can't remember the last time I sobbed, but I sure as hell hate how weak I sound. Val runs her thumbs over my cheeks, and I let out another one.

"I know, James, but we'll figure this out. I'm going to help you in every way I can. You can stay here for now, both of you, and we will go day by day. One after the other until we're sure what to do next." There she goes again, telling me exactly what I need to hear. "Just stay here for now. I already asked Gabriel, and he's okay with it. Adrian will stay here for now to help out, too. Although they did say you will have to find a way to make it up to them for bringing a screaming baby into the house," she says and giggles, which makes me laugh, too. "You don't have to stop racing, I will take care of him as much as I can during the race weekend. For now," she assures me, but my eyes go wide, and the smile disappears from her face.

"No, Val, you are not putting your life on hold for me. I'm not doing that to you," I say, and she looks at me with an unreadable expression.

"Well, you don't have a choice. You are contractually bound to finish this season. Not to mention, I love your son with my whole heart, and I want to do this for him. Now, stop arguing and help me get up from this dirty ground," she demands in the cutest, bossiest voice I have ever heard her use.

I get up from the ground before I help her up as well.

"I love you," she says in the same way she always does, in the way that makes me want to rip my eardrums out.

"I love you more," I tell her.

We both know she can't argue with me on this because I love her so much more than she is ever going to love me...

CHAPTER 52
Valentina

A CRY FROM DOWN the hall almost makes me fall out of bed. My feet hit the ground first, which is good because it keeps my head from slamming against my nightstand. My heart is beating out of my chest from the shock of falling off the bed, and I see Gabriel sit up before turning in my direction to see what's happened. Chase is right next to him, staring down at my clumsy self.

"Ma chérie!" he says, and I fall to my knees, trying to slow my heart rate. "Are you okay?" he asks me in French, and I smile at him. Damian is still crying, and I have the urge to go see if James needs any help to calm him down.

"Yes, I'm fine, go back to bed," I reply, kiss him, and push him back down so he gets the sleep he desperately needs.

My feet bring me to James' temporary room, and I knock, hearing him tell me to come in. I open the door slowly to reveal an exhausted James and a screaming Damian. I rush over to them and look at my best friend, who clearly doesn't know how to help his little boy anymore.

"I'm really sorry. I tried to calm him, but he wouldn't take his bottle. I think he misses his mum," James explains, and I give him a compassionate smile.

"I understand that. When my mom first left, I cried every single night for over a week, according to Adrian. Then again, Adrian may not be a reliable source," I joke and make a small laugh leave James' tired lips. The circles underneath his eyes and the redness in them make my heart break. "Here, give him to me, I will feed and change him. You go to sleep," I demand, and he is about to protest when I cut him off. "Don't start, just go to bed," I warn, and he gives me a brief kiss on the cheek before he thanks me and lies down in bed.

I take Damian out of the room and downstairs where he won't wake up my grumpy brother or my moody boyfriend. Waking up early isn't a problem for either of them, not like it is for me, but waking up in the middle of the night is what makes both of them undeniably cranky. If there is one thing they have in common, it's this.

Damian calmed down after he took his bottle and is now fidgeting in my lap, clearly half-asleep already. I sing the same melody of my lyric-less song to him over and over again until he finally falls back asleep.

"I'm going to have to come up with words," I say once he's completely asleep. "Although, you seem to like it," I whisper, and his little hand lifts in the air, his pinky sticking out as he reaches for the ceiling. "You are definitely your daddy's son."

Already with the pinky, that boy...

"You know what, Damian, your mommy may have left, but I will never leave you. You don't deserve to live the same life I did. I love you so much, and I don't ever want you to feel like you are not the best thing to have come into our lives, that you are not the sweetest child James could have asked for, because you are." I run my index finger over his small cheek, and the hand that was in the air just a minute ago wraps around my pinky.

Yep, definitely James' son.

After half an hour of watching Damian sleep in my arms, I place him in the bassinet James left in the living room. I'm wide awake now, but I don't mind. I wanted to start reading again anyway, and at least now I'll have an excuse. I go back upstairs, get a book from my nightstand, and a pen so I can annotate it.

I start reading the first few pages and fall deeply in love. Not only can I relate to the main character, but I wish I was as badass as her. She lost almost everyone, but she is strong, and she shows everyone how tough her life has been while keeping her shit together. Then, a stupidly gorgeous guy comes into her life, and everything turns upside down.

Maybe my life should be written into a book.

After all, it's just as chaotic and messed up, and I also have the one guy who makes my heart race and jump, and causes my body to ache all over. So, when the main guy gets close to her in the book and then backs off again, I write 'Relatable' next to it, hoping it will make Gabriel smile. If it doesn't remind him of that day on the couch, then I don't know what will.

Damian fuzzes in his bassinet, and I walk over to him to make sure he's okay. His eyes, the ones he got from his daddy, stare up at me, and I smile at him. Thankfully, he isn't crying, only looking at me like he never wants me to leave. I know he doesn't understand, and I know I'm probably just imagining it, but it looks like he is begging me to stay with him.

I don't leave until his eyes are closed again.

By that time, it's five in the morning, and I hear footsteps coming down the stairs. A shirtless Gabriel comes walking into the living room, rubbing his eyes and searching for me. He looks adorable yet insanely sexy at the same time. His trained body is on display for me, and I'm ogling, just like I'm supposed to be. His tattoos are coming out above his blue boxers, which look amazing because they don't leave much to the imagination. I love that even though I've explored every inch of his body, I've seen every scar and birthmark, I'm still as attracted to him as I was when I first met him.

My eyes stick to the tattoo of the sun and sunflower he got for us a few moments longer than the rest of his body, a grin spreading over my face in response.

"Chérie, come back to bed," he says in French, and I melt into the couch. He's too tired to try and speak in English with me, just like he was earlier when I fell out of bed. "I want to cuddle," he goes on, and I put the book aside.

"I can't, I'm watching Damian," I say, and his eyes drift from me over to the small human in the bassinet and then he looks at me again.

With a sigh, he turns off the light and walks over to where I'm lying with my legs stretched out in front of me on the couch. He lies down with his chest on top of my legs, his arms at each side of me, and his head on my stomach.

"I don't sleep well without you," he says, still speaking to me in our mother tongue. "I hate waking up without you next to me." I run my hands through his hair and let out a small laugh.

"I know, I can't sleep without you either," I say, and he kisses my stomach before putting his head back on it.

"I love you," he says, and I smile. His curly hair is soft in my hands, and I wish we could stay here forever. "I love you more than the amount of stars there are in the universe, and unlike them, my love for you will never extinguish. Death is scary, but it is a lot less so when you have found the person you know you want to spend the rest of your life with. Even in death, we will find each other." *Woah, that's surprisingly deep considering he's half asleep.*

"I love you, Gabriel, I've never loved anyone like I love you, and I never will. You're mine, you'll always be mine."

My words don't compare to his, but I don't know what to say. Gabriel is the one who always says sweet things and makes my stomach turn upside down. Nothing I'll ever say can compare.

"Sleep a little more, mon amour. It's going to be a long day today."

CHAPTER 53
Gabriel

"MON TOURNESOL, PLEASE, GET some sleep. You're going to break yourself if you keep going like this," I warn, but Valentina is rocking Damian back and forth in her arms at four in the morning.

"I don't have a race tomorrow. You do. Go to sleep," she barks at me, so sleep-deprived, she probably doesn't even realize how harsh her tone was. I ignore it because my top priority is getting her back to bed.

Valentina's been running on three hours of sleep for the entirety of the race weekend because Damian has been waking her every hour. She refuses to let James wake up because he has to sit in a car all weekend and if something were to happen, she would never forgive herself. According to Val, she should be the one to watch him because it's not likely she will have to race tomorrow. What she doesn't understand is that all of her responsibilities as a reserve driver and Leonard's business partner are exhausting her enough as it is. Add a screaming baby that deprives her of sleep on top of that, she will faint from exhaustion sooner rather than later. Not to mention, that fucking jerk James isn't doing anything to stop her from destroying the emotional, physical, and mental balance she works so hard to maintain.

God, I fucking hate him.

"Let me watch him for a little," I say when he starts crying again. I can't believe we not only have to share a suite with an infant but also with his father and my teammate because they all want to be near the baby.

"Go to bed," Val says, her eyes red and puffy from the lack of sleep. I'm convinced she's also dehydrated, but if I point that out now, she might rip my head off.

"Okay, I've had enough. This has gone on for days, and I'm not going to watch you destroy yourself over a baby that is not yours!" I whisper-scream, and her eyes immediately fill with tears. Pain shoots through my chest at the sight. Seeing Valentina cry is one of the worst things in the world for me, but I can't let her keep going on like this.

"I'm all he has right now," she sobs, making the baby in her arms stir. He grabs a hold of her pinky, making her cry even more. I close the distance between her and me before dropping to my knees in front of the woman I love. I catch her tears with my fingers and then lift Damian into my arms where he sleeps peacefully.

"I understand why you're doing all of this, but you need to let us help," I say, but she shakes her head. *So stubborn.* "Yes, baby, you do. This isn't healthy," I say, walking over to Damian's bassinet and placing him inside.

"If you're tired and mess up during the race tomorrow, it could end badly, Gabriel. Please, don't fight me on this. It won't always be like this, just until we figure out what to do or until the end of the season. I know Damian isn't mine, but I was supposed to be his godmother, and that means if something were to happen to his parents, I would be the one to raise him. I know what I signed up for," she says, but I shake my head in response.

"Chérie, those are outdated expectations you cannot put on yourself. You have a career to think about," I remind her, sliding my hands onto her thighs. I can't stand to see her so tired. Every move she makes seems painful to her. Her head must be pounding.

"My career is fine. Betty watches Damian throughout the day when I'm at work," she says, her eyes barely open now.

Hiring a nanny, Betty, was James' idea. He wanted someone to babysit his son night and day, but no one was available for night shifts on such late notice. That's why the love of my life is currently in a horrible state. It's why I can't let this go on for the remainder of the season. Not for James and his son. Not for anyone.

"Let's go to bed," I say because I'm done arguing with her when we could be sleeping right now. "We'll speak about this tomorrow." Valentina gives me a single nod, holding out her hands as a way to ask me to help her. She can't even fucking get up by herself, that's how tired she is. I pull her up and against my chest, wrapping my arms around her.

"It feels like I haven't seen you in a week," Valentina whispers against my chest, and I press a kiss to her temple.

"Then let's go spend the rest of the night in each other's arms," I say, pulling her with me to our room. Once she's curled against me, I let out a silent sigh and claim her mouth with mine, desperate for her watermelon taste.

I know James and Damian just lost a very important person, but she shouldn't have to be the one to fill that role. It doesn't sit right with me. She has just started her career. We were planning on spending the rest of our lives together, starting our own family, and as selfish as it sounds, I hate seeing her play family with James. He's been in love with her his entire life, and seeing this, Val and Damian spending time together, is going to fuel his fantasy of ending up with the woman I belong to. I have to talk to him about taking the pressure off Val. I don't care how it affects his performance or what it will do to his third place in the championship. Valentina shouldn't have to be a mom to an infant she didn't choose to have. She's shifted her priorities, but she'll regret it one day. I'm sure of it.

James is the one with the big decision to make: race or raise.

I can't even begin to imagine how difficult this all must be for him, but he has to back the fuck off before I lose it.

A short man with tan skin and dark brown hair sings the Italian hymn at the top of his lungs, and I wish I could focus. I wish my mind wasn't stuck on the conversation I'm practicing in my head with James to make sure nothing that leaves my mouth will hurt Val's feelings. I wish I could concentrate on this race weekend since Monza means a great deal to the Velocità Rossa team. This is my first year with them and my first time at the Italian Grand Prix as a driver for the home team. If the situation we were in wasn't so fucked up, I might be able to enjoy the praise all the fans are throwing Adrian's and my way. We may not be Italian, but we speak the language, we wear the colors, and we are proud to be here.

"Are you okay?" my teammate asks as we walk away and toward our cars. Mine is in the first place spot while his is in second. James is right behind Jonathan and Kyle who hold places three and four.

"Have you seen Val?" I ask in return, causing his face to fall. "Then you know I'm not."

"Hey," Adrian says and grabs my arm before I can walk away. He holds out his hand for me and adds, "Breathe, race, and win, as long as it doesn't cost you a limb." The tension floods out of my shoulders because I'm still honored he'd say this to me when it's a family saying. Maybe I am family to him after all. I never felt it as hard as I do right this second.

I repeat the same sentence back to him and then rush through the crowd of crew members and drivers until I reach my car. It's time to shut everything else out. Focus on the strategy my team and I came up with. Race to the very best of my ability in the home country of my team.

There can't be anything more important than the championship, not while I'm racing at over two hundred kilometers per hour. People don't understand just how dangerous our job is until we crash into barriers at full speed and our cars explode. They don't realize it until one of us *dies*, but I never forget. I lost my best friend, when Maxime passed away during a race incident. There is no way I could ever forget that a moment of distraction, a moment like Maxime's, could be the end of my life. A life I plan on spending falling more in love with Valentina.

The race is exhausting. Sweat drips down my back and temples. Tire management is extra difficult today, and Adrian is making my life hell. He keeps staying in my DRS—drag reduction system—zone, giving him an extra speed advantage. Lucky for me, I'm one hell of a defender. He overtakes me close to the end, but I'm right there, staying less than a second behind him to get the DRS advantage, too. I overtake him again, finishing the last few laps with a groan.

It's unseasonably hot, and the heat is weighing heavy on my body. Along with having to use every muscle to withstand the G-force, my mind is at the edge of its capability. I'm exhausted, but I get one last boost of adrenalin to push over the finish line, earning my first win in Italy.

The crowd goes wild. I can feel the energy in my car during my cool-down lap and then again during my interview and the celebration on the podium. It's a one-two for Velocità Rossa here in Monza, the best possible outcome Velocità Rossa fans could have possibly hoped for. James managed to overtake Jonathan and Kyle, which means I have to look at his stupid face during the celebrations, making it very difficult to enjoy any part of it.

So, as soon as we're out of sight from the hundreds of cameras, I pull him to a private room. Complaints leave him, but I don't give a shit. We need to talk.

"What the bloody hell is your problem? I've got shit to do," he barks at me once we're all alone.

"You need to figure out how to take some of the pressure off of Valentina, and you need to figure it out *now*," I say, surprising myself by being calm and collected even though I feel like shoving my head through a wall. I hate James, and I hate speaking to him.

"Don't you think I know that? It kills me to see her so exhausted," he replies, and I almost roll my eyes at him.

"I don't care how it makes you feel because you haven't done shit about it. You can't give up racing? Fine. I get that, but you're costing Val the clear-headedness she needs to be a reserve driver. She just started her dream career, James. How could you let her put this on herself?" I ask, watching him shrink a little in front of me. Good. He should feel bad.

"I didn't *let* her do anything," he mumbles, and then it's too late. Anger like no other washes through me, and every plan to keep things civil flies out the window.

"Bullshit. And I'm done watching the woman I love do everything for you, including giving you the hope of becoming a little family because that's what it's all about, isn't it? You see her play family with you, and you love it too much to take raising a fucking kid off her shoulders!" I yell, and he stands up straight, rage in his eyes. He's angry now, too.

"And the only thing in the way is you, Gabriel. If you weren't here, Valentina would be mine," he barks, sending a wave of ice through my veins.

"I can't believe I was right," I say more to myself, rubbing my hands down the length of my face. "Unfortunately, you're her best friend, and I can't tell you to stay the hell away from her because that isn't my place, but let me tell you this," I say and step toward him, hating now more than ever that he's taller than me. It doesn't stop me from grabbing his fireproofs by the collar to get him close to me. He might be taller, but I'm stronger and angrier. "You touch her in any other way than a brother would, and I will show you just how little I care about you," I warn, and his eyes go wide. "Yeah, I see the way you long to touch her whenever she allows it. But let me make something clear. She didn't want you then, and she doesn't now. Get that through your fucking head," I say before letting go of him and leaving.

I'm done with him.

CHAPTER 54

James

"HAVE YOU DECIDED WHAT you want to do yet?" Valentina asks as she gives my son his bottle.

Even though I have no idea what the hell I'm going to do, I have to smile at the picture in front of me. Valentina and my son in her arms. This is all I've wanted since I was old enough to understand what having a family meant, what it meant to spend the rest of your life with someone.

She's with Gabriel, she's with Gabriel, she's with Gabriel!

I have to remind myself of this every hour or so because it's getting harder for me to realize she isn't mine. Val has spent a lot of time with Damian and me this past week, and I've enjoyed every second of it. Her presence has made the ache of Annie's leaving go away more and more. I was devastated before, but the drop-dead gorgeous woman in front of me has made everything better. Not that I cared for Annie in the way I do Val, or would have, but her leaving still hurt unlike anything I've ever felt because Damian lost his mother.

"Hello? Are you still with us?"

My thoughts snap back to reality, and I let out a short laugh. Gabriel would kill me if he found out what was going through my head. He already warned me once, and I can't say I blame him. If the roles were reversed, I'd lose it if he got close to Val like I have been.

"Yes, sorry. No, I don't know what to do yet. I want to keep racing, but I love Damian so much, it's just not an easy decision to make."

How could I ever decide? If I choose Damian, then I'm always going to blame him for ruining my career, that's the cold, hard truth. If I don't choose Damian, I'm always going to regret not watching my son grow up.

How could I ever decide? One way or another, I'm going to hate myself. If there was a way I could still race and see my son whenever I wanted to, it would be perfect, but that doesn't exist.

I never wanted to be a father in the first place, but I can't think about that now. I have Damian and that is it. Regretting sleeping with Annabel isn't going to change the decision I have to make. Not to mention, if I hadn't slept with her, I wouldn't have this little guy in Val's arms.

"Well, I hate to be that person, but you have to decide. I don't mind taking care of him, but I know it's hurting my relationship with Gabriel. This morning, I tried to talk to him, but he barely said a word to me. I don't like how this situation has affected him and me, and I'm sorry, but Gabriel is my boyfriend, and I haven't been treating him well," she says, and I know she's right. "And to be honest, I don't think I can keep this up for longer. Among the racing school, Damian, and my duties as a reserve driver, I have no time for anything else. I miss Evangelin. I miss Andrea. I even miss Lucie and Haru, who I was supposed to meet for dinner two nights ago, but I couldn't because you had a meeting," she says, the guilt in her eyes sending pain through me. She feels bad for telling me things I need to hear.

My inability to come to a conclusion has messed up everyone's lives around me. It's not fair of me to do that to them, it's not fair of me to break up Valentina's relationship because of my own selfish needs. *Although, it would make her single, and she might find comfort in my arms...* I pinch my leg to punish myself for even thinking that.

"You're right. I'm sorry I put you in this position," I say, and she wraps her free hand around mine.

"It's okay. I just have to fix this before I hurt him even more than I already have."

Her face falls into a frown, reaching every millimeter of it. If I didn't know better, I think she might start crying, but I know she won't do so until something actually happens. Valentina doesn't cry about things she knows for sure she can fix, that's why she never cried when we fought as kids. She always knew we'd make up again.

"He loves you more than anything else in the world, there is no way he'd ever leave you, not because of this," I assure her, but a painful look stretches over her face.

"He's left before, and we were fine then. Now, I'm pushing him away and barely talking to him. It's not fair, and he's mad. He has a right to be angry, but I need to fix this. I love you and I love Damian, but—"

"But you love him more," I interrupt her, and she looks at me with a sad smile.

"He's my future, James, he's the person I want to have a family with. Gabriel's the one who has understood me since we first met. The pain, the loss, the dark thoughts, the anxiety, the depression at times, the feeling of being lost, he's understood all of it, and he has loved me more for it. Nothing is ever going to be able to explain what we have because nothing like this has ever been put into words, which I love. He and I are messy, but I'll never be able to live without him." I know she didn't mean to, but she just broke my heart into a trillion pieces, *again*.

I hate how I can't be happy for her, but it also isn't fair. I've been at this girl's side since she can remember, and I've never been good enough for her because she claims I can't understand her. But she's never even given me a chance. I've always been a best friend to her, and it is all I'm ever going to be. I've tried everything to be more for her, but nothing has ever made me good enough in her eyes. I don't know what Gabriel has that I don't, and I'll never be able to understand.

But what can I do? Nothing.

Nothing, but be there for her like I have always been. I have bigger problems on my plate anyway, and I need to focus on my child. Val places him in my arms, and I watch as she walks back inside her big house.

"Love is a funny thing, Damian, and I can't wait until you're old enough for me to tell you how badly it sucks. Because it does, D, it really does. I hope you'll never feel this pain because it threatens to destroy you," I explain in a baby voice, the one I used to find so annoying, but now I'm always using. "I love you, but I don't think

I'm the right parent for you. You deserve a parent who doesn't think twice about giving up their career to raise you. You deserve someone better than me."

A tear falls down my cheek, and I hate that I can't be strong for him. His small face with his blue eyes looks just like mine when I was his age. I've seen enough baby pictures to know I'm right. I love him but I'm not old enough or in the right position to be a single parent to a child.

I never planned on being one.

My phone rings in my pocket, and I check my screen to see Mia is calling. I have no intention of picking it up, especially because she sided with my parents and told me to give Damian up for adoption.

They don't want to help me with Damian, fine, but I sure as hell won't be speaking to them ever again. They are terrible people all around, and I don't need them. I'm going to figure this out by myself, and I hope I will make the right decision.

If not, I will never forgive myself.

CHAPTER 55

Valentina

MY FINGERS PLAY WITH the material of the sexy outfit I'm wearing, and I have no idea whether or not I'm doing the right thing here. I feel awfully on display, and would it be for anyone else, I would go into my bathroom and put on some more clothes. I've never worn lingerie like this before, but Gabriel and I need tonight to reconnect. I feel so distant from him, it's making my heart ache. I made sure that James and Adrian went to James' house for the night so Gabriel and I could have the house to ourselves.

I look around the room to make sure all of the candles are still burning, and luckily, they are.

It's been fourteen days since Damian and James moved in, which means it's been ten days since Gabriel and I had sex. I was planning to seduce him, like I'm trying to today, three days ago, but then my period surprised me with painful cramps and heavy bleeding, and I did not feel anywhere near attractive. The good thing is my doctor told me it's completely normal if my period is unscheduled for the first couple of months, and if it's still painful. Otherwise, I would be highly worried.

I reposition myself seven times, rearrange the sunflowers twice, and take ten deep breaths. I'm impatiently waiting for Gabriel to come back from his meeting with Hector. He's been gone since this morning, and I've been working the whole day to prepare a nice meal, prepare dessert, and force my ass and breasts into this ridiculous outfit. I really hope I can make everything up to Gabriel because we have not been happy for too long. He hasn't even really kissed me, but then again, I haven't had enough time for him to kiss me long and hard like he always does. It's my fault, and I'm going to make it up to him.

When Gabriel finally walks through our door, he stops dead in his tracks, his mouth curling into a smirk. I sit up and onto my knees as I watch him closely, ready to tell him something I should have a while ago.

"I'm sorry about everything, mon soleil. I know I haven't been treating you right, and I'm so sorry." He tilts his head to the side, a tired smile on his face.

"Are you back?" he asks me, and I frown.

"Yeah, baby, I'm back." He's right, I wasn't here, not really.

"God, I missed you," he says, and I smile brightly at him. "You look so sexy," he compliments me, and I chuckle.

"Right back at you," I reply, and Gabriel walks over to me, putting his hands on my hips.

He looks handsome in his white shorts and blue polo shirt. His hair is messy, just like I like it, and his stubble is the perfect length to drive me wild. The beautiful color of his green-brown eyes looks more brown in this candlelight, but they're still stunning. Everything about him is stunning.

Gabriel pulls his bottom lip between his teeth as his eyes trail down my body and then up again. His hands drop from my hips to my ass, and he squeezes firmly.

"I missed your ass," he says right before his lips claim mine in the most aggressive way. I moan into his mouth when his tongue caresses mine, and I'm so grateful he's kissing me again, I melt right against his chest. I've missed his touch. "I want to rip this off your body," he groans, his finger running over the string covering my nipples.

"Do it. Do anything you want with me," I say, and he smiles victoriously.

"Oh, chérie, you shouldn't have said that," he says, ripping the fabric down and taking my breasts in his hands.

His thumbs and index fingers squeeze my nipples, and I let out a loud moan. I have sensitive nipples, so any kind of touch right now, especially since I'm horny, is going to make me dizzy with pleasure.

"I missed that sound," he says and leans forward to pull one of them into his mouth. His tongue runs over it and then his lips suck hard before he gives my other nipple the same attention. More moans leave me when his hand drops to my pussy, and he starts massaging my clit.

"So wet," he whispers, and I'm convinced he didn't mean to say it out loud.

"Fuck me from behind," I moan, and he grips my hips hard.

"Baby, I'll fuck you front, back, and sideways until I'm sure you can no longer walk tomorrow," he replies, and I bite my lip to keep from moaning.

His words are enough to make my body ache. The throbbing between my legs has its own mind as it makes my hand reach for his zipper and pull down his shorts. His erection jumps free from the containment of his boxers, and I lean back on the bed, spreading my legs wide for him. A beautiful smile appears on his lips, exposing his gorgeous dimples. My dimples. I haven't seen them in too long.

Gabriel pulls his shirt over his head, and I run my hand over my clit to tease him. I'm too aroused by his naked body, and he's not touching me.

Gabriel shoves my hand away, flips me around, and smacks my ass all within seconds. He pulls my hips close, and I'm on all fours when he slides inside of me. I grab the sheets and let out a loud moan. This position feels absurdly good. It's one of my favorites, and I think he feels the same.

"God, I love the way your pussy hugs my cock, chérie," he says as his fingers snake around my hip and settle on my clit.

Gabriel is groaning and moaning, which only makes this even better. His left hand reaches for my left breast, pinching my nipple.

"You're so fucking tight and wet, baby. So beautiful," he says as he shoves his cock into me with a brutal thrust that has me crying out from pleasure. I love it when he's a bit rougher, when he uses my body just like I told him to.

"You feel so good," I moan as my walls tighten around his hard cock, almost like I'm trying to keep him from sliding out because it feels too good when he's inside of me.

"Merde," he curses with a hiss.

He smacks my ass cheek again, making me buck backward in a move that meets his thrust perfectly. We both moan in response.

"Keep doing that, keep moving with me," he demands, so I comply, shifting to meet his strokes. He hits my sweet spot every single time until I'm shaking on my hands and knees. "You're such a good girl for me, Valentina, listening to my commands and taking what you need," he says until I'm trembling from his praise. "Impaling yourself on my cock feels good, doesn't it, tournesol?" I give an agreeing moan.

Waves of pleasure shoot through my body, and I orgasm before I want to. But Gabriel just keeps going, causing more pleasure to run through me as he keeps hitting the one spot inside of me only he reaches.

"I've missed you so much," he growls, and I let out a high-pitched moan. "Gabriel."

Saying his name only makes him go faster, so I say it over and over again until he moans my name more loudly than I've ever heard. His upper body curls around my backside as his speed increases even more, and he finally spills into me. His pulsing cock and shallow thrusts send another orgasm through my body until I tremble in his arms.

With one swift move, Gabriel spins me around, his cock shoving back inside of me as he kisses me like he hasn't tasted me in months. I kiss him back just as hard, enjoying the way he rocks back and forth ever so slightly.

"I'll never get enough of you," he says after a while of us kissing. I can feel him growing inside of me again as his mouth drops back to my left nipple to scrape his teeth gently over the sensitive skin.

"Is that why you're hard again already?" I tease, my eyes fluttering shut as my hands move through his hair.

"It's why I'm always fucking hard when I'm around you, Valentina," he replies, his head lifting just enough to show me he's smiling before he goes back to worship my breasts.

"That must be frustrating when we're in public and you can't do anything about it," I go on, moaning when he sucks my right nipple hard.

"Well, is it frustrating for you when you look at me and my mouth and your clit starts aching with the need to ride my face?" he asks, rocking his hips harder forward and making me suck in a sharp breath as pleasure builds inside of me again.

"Yes," I croak out, my back arching and ultimately shoving my breasts into his face. Gabriel doesn't seem to mind as he licks my pebbled nipple with a satisfied hum.

"That's what I thought. I see the way you look at me when we're working, the way you can barely stop yourself from dragging me somewhere private." I smile at his words.

"It's those damn fireproofs. They look too good on you." I tug on his curls when his mouth trails downward and his cock slips out of me. "No, come back up here. I still want you inside of me," I say, reaching for his now hard again cock, which is coated in both our cums. *Fuck.*

"So greedy," Gabriel says with a small smirk but gives me exactly what I want as he pushes back inside of me.

Before I know it, I'm coming so hard while riding him, my vision goes blurry and I collapse onto his chest while he spills inside of me, screaming my name. We quickly clean ourselves up before lying back down on the bed. Gabriel is beside me, completely out of breath. My hand moves onto his sweaty chest, and I grin at him. I've been so worried about us, but now, everything feels better again. We're going to be okay.

"What?" he asks with the same cute, joyful grin on his face.

"I love you," I say, and his facial expression goes soft.

"I love you so much, ma chérie."

"I'm so sorry about everything," I say again, and he bites the inside of his cheek. He seems to contemplate his words before deciding to ask what's bothering him.

"Do you have feelings for him?" he asks, sadness in his gaze. He's trying to read how his question makes me feel, but it's so absurd to me he's even asking this that I sit up in response, my eyes going wide.

"You know I don't. Where is this coming from, mon amour?" I ask, and he turns onto his back, studying the ceiling above our bed.

"Nowhere, just forget I asked," he says, but I'm a little upset now.

"Gabriel, tell me," I demand, and he sits up straight, staring at me. He shakes his head and I let out an annoyed groan before sliding off the bed. "If you don't tell me why you're feeling insecure, I can't reassure you," I argue, hating that we're in this position now. Because of me. Because *I* made him feel insecure.

"I need to know if I'm in the way," he mumbles, his head hanging low. *In the way? What is he talking about?*

"In the way of what, amour?" I ask, and he sucks in a sharp breath.

"Doesn't matter," he replies, but it does. It fucking matters if he feels less than the person I love the most in the world because he is. He took the spot right beside Adrian's, and he should never feel like less than everything to me.

"Dit moi," I demand because if he won't tell me in English, maybe he will in French.

"James told me I'm in the way of you, him, and Damian being a happy family," Gabriel says, and I'm out of words now.

"HE. DID. WHAT?" I ask Gabriel with the utmost anger. He cocks both of his eyebrows and stares at me.

"Apparently the only person standing in the way of the three of you being happy is me."

That is when a frown places itself on my boyfriend's sweet lips. He gets up to put his boxers on, and I walk over to him. Gabriel sinks back down on the bed, and I kneel in front of him, putting my hands on his thighs. He isn't looking at me anymore, so I tilt my head in the direction where he is staring at the floor.

"Am I?" he asks, his eyes meeting mine.

"No." I don't fucking hesitate to get the word out. "Look at me," I say, but he shakes his head. "Fine," I sigh and straddle his lap. He laughs and finally looks at me. I put my hands on each side of his face, caressing his cheeks where his stubble doesn't grow. "I don't want you to think you are standing in the way of James, Damian, and me being a happy family. He isn't the man I want, you are. I want to spend the rest of my life by your side, winning championships, raising children, and driving you wild in the same way you drive me wild. I'm sorry I haven't been here mentally, I know I haven't, but that is going to change."

I move off his lap and walk over to my nightstand, pulling out the box with the bracelets.

"You're my *everything*, Gabriel. You are the person I want to spend the rest of my life with. You are the one I want to race to the finish line with. You always have been," I say and hand him the box, my heart skipping a beat. Gabriel smiles as he pulls out my bracelet.

"That's a bit small for me," he says, and I let out a small laugh.

"That one is obviously mine. I mean it does say 'Son Tournesol' on purpose," I explain, and then it's his turn to laugh. He takes my hand in his, pressing a kiss to my wrist before putting the bracelet on.

"It's beautiful," he says, and I grin.

"Look at yours," I reply with excitement, and he pulls his out of the box.

He stares at it for a minute without saying a word. The words 'Son Soleil' are engraved in the charm.

"Marry me, Valentina," he blurts out, and I hold my breath. "I love you more than I will ever love anything or anyone else. Please, marry me," he begs, and I sink down on the floor again. I just told him I want to spend the rest of my life with him, and I do, I want nothing more, but this is a lot earlier than I thought he'd ask.

"We're so young," I say in a whisper, and he puts his bracelet on.

"I don't care. You and racing are the only happiness I need in my life. I intend to keep you both forever. So, let me say it again. Marry me." He's on the floor with me now, and I'm speechless. "Marry me whenever you're ready. For now, be my fiancée, so I can finally address you as more than a girlfriend because you've always been more. You've been everything," he says, and it doesn't seem so extreme anymore. I want to be his fiancée, I want to be his wife, but I fear we're both too young to even understand what it means.

"I'm sorry, but—" I start the sentence, and his face falls. "But you're going to have one clingy fiancée," I say and fling my arms around his neck.

We fall onto the bed together, laughing like the two people in love that we are.

"I love you, and I love the engagement bracelets, I think it makes us unique," he says, and I smile.

"Does this mean I'm not getting a ring?" I ask him, and he laughs. "Because I would be okay with that," I assure him while removing my hair from his face and kissing him sweetly.

"You'll get a ring, ma chérie. For now, take my boxers off," he demands, and I do just as I'm told. I want to celebrate our new status just as badly as he does.

And so we do, over and over and over again.

CHAPTER 56
Valentina

THE NEXT MORNING, I wake up naked and sore with Gabriel holding me tightly. I'm aching in all the best ways. A small smile spreads over my face, and I take a deep breath, smelling Gabriel's perfect, mahogany scent. I can't believe we're engaged... It's so weird even thinking about it. I'm engaged to someone.

No.

I'm engaged to the love of my life.

Are we too young? Probably. Does it matter? Not to me. No one is rushing us to get married, but this ties us together in even more ways. I want to be tied to him in all of them and him to me.

Gabriel's arms tighten around me, and I let out a sigh. I love being with him, and I'm relieved that everything is going to be okay again. Well, at least until I see James and rip him a new one.

How dare he say those things to Gabriel? How dare he make Gabriel feel so unwanted?

I never want Gabriel to feel that way. I love James, he's my best friend, but he's gone too far. I don't care that he's in a bad situation right now, he is not allowed to make Gabriel feel like this. I'm so mad just thinking about the conversation they had. My hands ball into fists as they rest against Gabriel's trained torso.

"What's making you this mad so early in the morning?" His voice is husky and sexy, just like I like it. I love his voice. It may be my favorite sound there is, except for the sound of a Formula One race car.

"Nothing for you to worry about, mon soleil," I assure him, but he cocks an eyebrow and looks at me with an inquiring look.

"It's James, isn't it?" I don't meet his gaze because I know he will see right through me. "It's okay, you know, what he said to me. Don't let it out on him," Gabriel says and runs his fingers over my arms.

It's meant to comfort me, but I still feel this anger toward James. If the roles were reversed, Gabriel would do anything to make sure I would never feel so insecure about our relationship again.

"I have to take Chase for a walk, and you need to get packing. We have to leave early tomorrow," I say, and he smiles brightly at me.

The Emilia Romagna Grand Prix is next on the schedule, and with the momentum of last weekend's race results, this one is bound to be great too.

"Okay, ma fiancée," he says and kisses me.

I slide off the bed and pull one of his sweatpants from the shelf and then onto my body. Gabriel is biting the inside of his cheek, probably to keep from smiling. His pants are a bit too long, but my ass is much bigger than his, making them tight in the back.

"Why are you so perfect?" he asks, and I look at my messy hair through the door in my bathroom mirror.

It's really not fair. When he has messy hair it's sexy, and I love it that way. When I have messy hair, I look like I just put my hand into an outlet and got electrocuted.

Instead of correcting him, I simply turn back around to look at him with a warm smile on my face.

"It's my superpower." Gabriel walks up to me and buries his face in the crook of my neck, taking a deep breath.

"Have I ever told you that you have the most wonderful scent?" I shake my head because it's all my body lets me do.

My hands move into his hair, and I enjoy the way his lips suck on my sensitive spot just above my collarbone.

"Hmmmm," is all that comes out of my mouth.

Words have left my mind and all I see is him. Only ever him now.

"Gabriel," I finally say, and gently push him away. His eyes are sleepy and his lips are nice and swollen from all our kissing. I spot a hickey on his neck that makes me bite my lip to keep from grinning possessively.

"What's wrong?" he asks, and I need a second to get my head to start working again.

"I, uh, I need to go talk to Adrian and James. I really need to talk to James," I say, remembering I wanted to do something not so great to him.

"I'm sorry I made you angry with him," he says, making me frown.

"You didn't do anything, mon soleil. He did," I say and press one last kiss to his lips.

When I reach the bottom of the steps downstairs, Chase starts wagging his tail like a helicopter, and I greet him like I do every morning. I kneel down on the floor and play with him. Only for a few minutes because my mind is too preoccupied with what I'm going to say to James.

I walk into the kitchen, anger finally starting to settle in my stomach when I see James at the kitchen island, eating his breakfast. Adrian is sitting right next to him, and they are having a quiet conversation. I can't understand what they're saying, but I honestly couldn't care less.

How the hell am I going to start this conversation?

"Hey, asshole, outside, now."

If I wasn't so mad, I would laugh at the fact that both Adrian and James turn around to face me. Both of them look at me with confused frowns, but after a few seconds, James' eyes go wide, and his face falls.

"Come on," I command, and he gets up before walking outside.

Adrian mouths the words 'what happened', but I don't answer. I simply follow my best friend outside.

"Who the hell gave you the right to tell Gabriel he's the only thing standing in the way of us being a happy family with Damian? Who? Because I sure as hell didn't, and it's my life you're messing with!" I bark, watching my best friend's shoulders drop.

"I'm sorry, babe, I wasn't thinking and—" I have to cut him off.

"That doesn't make it okay!" I rub my temples for a moment. "Why did you tell him that? Do you honestly think if Gabriel breaks up with me I will jump into bed with you?" His face shows anger then.

"It's never been about sex for me, Valentina, and you know that," he snaps at me, and I take a step back from him. He never uses my full name, unless he is angry at me or annoyed. Right now, I would say it's the first. "I'm sorry I said that to Gabriel, but I wasn't thinking clearly. My stupid heart isn't listening to my head at the moment," he explains, running one hand through his thick hair.

"Well, get it to listen. Gabriel and I are dating, and I'm not planning on breaking up with him, nor is he planning on breaking up with me. Get that through your head." I hate myself. I hate myself for throwing this at him, but I don't know what to do anymore.

"You know what, Valentina, I don't think we can be friends anymore. I'm in love with you, and I'm not going to get over it any time soon, especially if we live in the same house. I have to get out, get some distance from you," he says, and my world stops spinning. I can hear the rip as he tears apart my heart. "It's too bloody difficult," he mumbles, and I let the tears fall down my cheeks.

"You were the first person I said 'I love you' to that I'm not related to by blood, you were the first person who slept in my bed. You are the one person besides Adrian I have never feared would leave me, that is how blindly I trust you. You're going to walk out on me?" I ask, not even giving a single shit about how pathetic and selfish I sound.

"Yes, because my whole life, I've been selfless with you. Now, I have to be selfish." I let out a laugh that I don't mean one single bit.

"What the fuck happened to 'unlike him, I could never leave you'? Were those just pretty words to try and get me to fall in love with you? What was the point of making all of these promises if you were just going to leave me anyway?" I ask, my heart racing. He's not supposed to leave me. "I can't live without you," I add, tears now falling down my face.

"Well, figure it out because I can't do this anymore, my love. You are the person I wanted to have a family with, the person I wanted to fall asleep with and wake up next to, which is why I can't stand looking at you anymore. I need a break from us," he says, and I nod. Maybe if I let anger take over this will be easier.

"Fine, leave, just like everyone else leaves. I hope it's worth it to you to lose me forever." He closes the distance between us until I smell his all-too-familiar scent. It used to comfort me, now I fear I won't ever get to smell it again.

"So, *him* you forgive for leaving, but me you wouldn't?" I look up at the tall man, and I notice the tears that have now left his eyes.

"Yes, because, unlike Gabriel, you were there when *she* left. You know how much it broke me," I whisper, and James backs up again. He looks torn, and I don't know what to do either.

"What do you want me to do?" he asks, and his shoulders lift. "I don't know how to be near you without feeling this constant ache in my chest." My legs finally give in, and I sit down on the steps leading up to the house. I'm supposed to be happy. Gabriel and I just took a huge step in our relationship, but I'm nowhere near that.

"Stay, that's all I will ever want you to do, that's all I have ever wanted from anybody. Just stay. Love me enough to figure out a way to stay."

"Don't you get it? I love you too much," he says and lets out a small laugh he doesn't mean. "I have to leave for a little bit, can you forgive me for that?" James sits down on the steps next to me, and he takes my hand in his before pressing a kiss to the back of it.

"Will you come back?" I look at him with all of the pain I'm feeling, and he looks at me with all of his.

"I don't know," he replies, and I just nod. I have no idea what else I'm supposed to say or do. "Hey," he says and lifts my head with his index finger under my chin. "You are, and will always be, my best friend. I just need a little time to figure my life out."

His thumb runs over my cheek, and even though I shouldn't let him, I do. He needs this, and I would be lying if I said I didn't.

"I hate that you met him." James gets up, and I look at the floor.

"I'm so sorry I hurt you." I'm still not looking at him. The guilt I feel for breaking his heart is overwhelming.

"It's not your fault." Finally, I look at him, and I see he's pulling something out of his pocket. My eyes focus on the ring, and my heart stops beating. "My grandmother gave this to me before she died. I always thought you'd be the one to wear it."

No, no, no... He's got to stop showing and telling me stuff like this, it only makes me feel worse.

"I'm sorry," I say, and a sob leaves my throat.

"So am I. I'm sorry I have to go." He walks past me up the stairs, and I try to hold in my sobs. "I love you," he says, and I let another one out.

He disappears inside, and I grab my running shoes from next to me on the stairs. I don't stop running until I reach the one place I feel closest to the man I miss the most in the world.

CHAPTER 57

Gabriel

"WHERE THE HELL DID she go?" I ask James as soon as I come downstairs. He's picking up Damian's things and throwing them into a bag. *Oh no.* "You're leaving," I blurt out, catching his attention for the first time since I came downstairs. Tears are in his eyes, but he refuses to let them drop in my presence.

"Gabriel, your face is just about the last one I want to look at right now. Can you please fuck off?" he says and when Damian starts crying, his shoulders fall. He walks over to his son, picking him up gently and rocking him back and forth in his arms.

"Are you leaving?" I say, and he lets out a long sigh before nodding. "For how long?" I ask, scared of the answer.

"Until being in love with my best friend stops hurting so much," he replies, and I feel my heart drop for Valentina. *Fuck.*

"Don't do this. Trust me, all it brings you is more pain," I say, but he merely ignores me as he places Damian back inside his bassinet.

"You don't get it. You and Val are dating. You're probably going to marry her one day. Now imagine you weren't doing any of those things. Imagine you planned your life with her, but she was in love with me, *dating me*. Would you be able to be around her?" he asks, and I hate myself for what I'm about to say.

"No," I admit. "But you were supposed to be the better man," I say, and James lets out a harsh laugh. Adrian appears next to me, one of his hands sliding onto my shoulder and squeezing. He's telling me to let this go and leave so he can talk to his best friend.

"I'm not the better man, Gabriel. That's why she chose you," he says and grabs the bag, throwing it over his shoulder.

I watch him with disbelief because I remember once, after I left, he approached me and gave me so much shit for it. Asked me how I could do that to Valentina. Now he's doing the same fucking thing, and as much as I understand why, she's lost enough in her short life.

"You're punishing her for your own feelings," I blurt out, and Adrian pulls me to the side, pointing at the stairs.

"Go get dressed and find my sister. She needs you," he says, and I realize he's right. I'm wasting my time trying to convince James not to leave her when he's already made up his mind. There is no changing it now.

I make my way toward the staircase when I hear Adrian's voice again.

"I've watched you be in love with Val for as long as I can remember. You were ready to move on once, but then Gabriel broke up with her, and you got it in your head that you could make her fall for you, even when I told you not to," he says, and I know I should walk away, but my feet don't move. "You did this to yourself, and now you're letting it out on the person who deserves it the least, the person who prioritized your child over her own health. How could you do this, James?"

"I don't know. This feels like something I have to do," the Brit replies, and I sink onto the bottom stair, covering my face with my hands.

"You should be focused on your son. On what the hell you're going to do, not on breaking my sister's heart by taking away what you've given her all your life. Love, friendship, someone to go to whenever something was wrong. You let her trust you, even when you were already in love with her and she wasn't reciprocating your feelings. Help me understand why you would do that if you knew you'd never be able to get rid of them," Adrian says, and I almost gasp. He's not holding back in the slightest. He's calling James out on everything.

"I still had hope," James replies, and Adrian lets out a harsh laugh.

"Don't bullshit me. You've stayed all this time because you need her. You will always need her more than you're in love with her. You can leave now, but you better figure out a way to come back soon because you're not the only one to leave. You're taking Damian with you, and she loves him. She loves that little guy so much, she'd do anything for him."

As soon as I'm at the graveyard, I spot her dirty blonde hair flying in the wind. Her lips are moving, telling me she's speaking to her grandfather. I glance at Maxime's gravestone for a moment, nodding its way before taking in a wobbly breath and stepping toward Valentina.

"Gabriel loves me like no one else, and I love him with everything I am. I hope it will never change," she says, and I smile down at her. It sounds like she's been speaking for a while already, but I'm glad I caught this moment.

"It never will," I promise, and she turns around to look at me. Her eyes fixate on the flowers in my hand, tears filling them in response. "I'm sorry about James, chérie, I know how much he means to you." I walk over to the gravestone to place the daisies next to it. "I'm sorry," I repeat, and she gets up to wrap her arms around me. I take a deep breath and sigh in relief because I'm happy I found her.

"How did you know where I am?" she asks after a while of silence.

"I checked *Rush* before I figured out where you would go after losing a friend. You came here to mourn." Her eyes soften at my words, and I lose myself in how beautiful she is for a fraction of a second before refocusing on her pain.

"Thank you for finding me," she says, placing her hands on my cheeks.

"I will always rush to find you."

Her smile doesn't reach her eyes because they're too tired from all the crying, but she seems to relax a little at my words. I kiss her once more before dropping to one knee in front of her grandfather's grave. The gray, marble rock stares back at me, almost as if he was here.

"Monsieur Romana, thank you for raising the most wonderful human on this planet. Thank you for letting her walk into my life," I say in French, feeling Val's eyes on me. "I know you had something to do with that, and I will never be able to express just how grateful I am. She's forgiving and kind, and I have benefitted from that since the day I met her. I've done wrong by her, and I've hurt her, but her love makes me the luckiest man in the world. And I asked her to marry me yesterday. "

Valentina's hand slips onto my shoulder, and I spot the engagement bracelets we put on last night. I straighten out my back before placing one of my hands over hers and the other on the top of the gravestone.

"I know a lot of people still ask the parents or grandparents for their blessing to marry their child, but I believe it should be Val's choice. However, I would still want your blessing. I hope you would give it to me."

I stand up again, feeling her arms snake around me from behind and resting on my stomach. She's my happy place, my pitstop, my favorite person in the entire world. So, I run my fingers over the words 'Son Tournesol' and glance down at my own, the words 'Son Soleil' catching my eye. I love everything about it. I love everything about her, and I wish there was a way to make sure Valentina would never feel any pain again.

"I'm sorry I ran away without telling you where I was going. I just needed some time to digest the fact that James can't stand being around me anymore. I'm not sure how to process that." She sobs into my back, so I flip around and cup the back of her head, guiding her against my chest. Valentina breaks down in my arms, and I fight back the desire to find James and make him pay for hurting my sunflower like this.

"Let it out," I say, and she takes fistfuls of my shirt before screaming.

This is not just about James. I can feel it. It's for every single person she's ever lost. It's for the pain and grief she constantly has to live and deal with whenever something like this happens. And I will be right here, helping her pick up the pieces.

"Take me home," she says after a few more moments of silence.

"Okay," I reply softly, kissing her temple. I attempt to guide her away from this place, but she drags me back toward her to press her lips to mine. It's brief and sweet, and she pulls back just enough to make sure I hear her next words.

"Don't ever, *ever* forget that I love you. You're my safe place, my happy place, my everything place, do not forget that." A slight smile slips onto my lips, making her place her index fingers on my dimples.

"I'll never forget because it's what keeps me going more times than not," I admit, and Val looks up at me with her light eyes.

I'd burn the whole world down for her.

I'd count every grain of sand on the beach to see her smile.

I'd pluck a star from the night sky for her happiness.

"Let's get you home, you probably need your brother," I mumble before pressing my lips to hers one more time. By the way she nods, I realize I'm right. She needs Adrian, and I need to make sure she feels better again.

CHAPTER 58
Valentina

ADRIAN IS ON THE couch when we get home, but he's not alone. Nicolette and Domi are beside him with cups of tea in their hands. I haven't seen either of them since the day at the hospital. Gabriel told me they went away for a few weeks after everything happened, unable to sit in the house where they already built a crib for the baby they never got to meet. My heart aches for them, but when Domi gives me a small smile, it dulls it a bit. I walk over to where she is, wrapping my arms around her neck.

"Hi," she says, hugging me back as fiercely.

"I'm so happy to see you," I reply and lean back to smile at her. "I didn't know you were back. I would have invited you over for dinner," I say before turning to Nicolette and hugging her too. Not too long ago, I was a stranger to both of them, but now, I've become part of their little family. It's an honor I'm not sure I deserve, but I will take it.

"Don't worry about it, belle. We just wanted to come say hi and check on Gabriel and you," Nicolette explains and places her hand on my cheek, studying my probably puffy face. "What happened?" she asks quietly because Gabriel and Domi have fallen into a conversation of their own now.

"It's nothing for you to worry about," I assure her, but when I try to step away, she takes hold of my shoulders. My full attention is on her then.

"Did Gabriel upset you?" she asks, worry all over her face. I quickly shake my head.

"No, my best friend and I got into a fight and he left. Gabriel has been nothing but perfect, even when I didn't deserve it recently," I reply, a soft look crossing her face.

"You deserve the world, Valentina, and nothing less. It's something I've always tried to teach my nephews. Once you find your person, don't just say I love you. Show it. Prove it. Earn it."

I smile because everything about that makes sense to me. It explains why Gabriel does everything in his power to put me first, even if I don't like it. It explains why he's always so affectionate. It explains why he loves me like no one else could. He's always going to be the one to do everything he can to earn the I love you I'm more than happy to give him every chance I get.

"I know he's made mistakes in the past, but he has the biggest and purest heart of anyone I know," Nicolette adds, and I turn to look at Gabriel. His arm is around Domi's shoulders, pressing her against his side with his eyes closed. I notice Adrian staring at the water in his hands, something clearly bothering him. I'll have to speak to him later.

"Anyway, there is something we need Gabriel's help with. Would it be alright if I stole him from you for tonight?" Nicolette asks, and I grin at his confused face. He doesn't like the idea of leaving me tonight one bit, but I'm already feeling better, and I could use some time alone with my brother. I miss him.

"Of course. I will see him tomorrow," I say and walk over to where is about to protest. The struggle on his face makes me feel a bit uneasy. He doesn't want to go, but, at the same time, he wants to be there for his aunts. So, I simply press a kiss to his lips and throw my arms around him.

"I don't want to leave you," he says in Italian because he's been teaching me again since coming back, a little every day. He's also making sure Nicolette and Domi can't understand him.

"Ti amo," I say, and he melts against me. "Je t'aime." He kisses me. "Te amo." I kiss him. "I love you," I finish, having told him what he means to me in every language I know.

"Mon tournesol, mon coeur est à toi," he replies and kisses me one last time before following his aunts out of our home.

"God, you two are so in love. It's disgusting," my brother says, and I shake my head at him.

"Well, not everyone likes to have a new person to sleep with every chance they get," I reply and sink onto the couch where he is. He's laughing now, but I know there is something still bothering him.

"Why not? It's so much fun." I roll my eyes and settle against the back of the couch.

"What's wrong?" I ask when he goes back to staring at the glass of water in his hands. He shakes his head, unsure how to approach this topic. Not good. Adrian loves to hear himself talk. If he's hesitating to hear his own voice, then something's really wrong.

"Ever since we were little, I thought you were going to end up with James. He just seemed like the right choice because he gave you something I didn't think anyone else could give you. He gave you safety and comfort when you needed it desperately. That's why I was rooting for him to finally tell you how he feels, but he never did. Man, the amount of conversations I've had with him about you, it's ridiculous."

Adrian squeezes my hand, and I watch him as the tears flow down my cheeks. Great, now I'm crying again.

"I was so mad at him too because I never understood why he wanted to risk his friendship with you because of some stupid feelings he had, but I know now he didn't have control over them, as much as he tried."

I don't know what Adrian is trying to do because he's certainly not making me feel better, he's only making me feel guiltier.

"I always thought you might have some feelings for him, just from the way you were always talking about him and the fact you always wanted to spend time with him. But then you didn't, or at least you never allowed yourself to see them. You see, feelings are a funny thing, and I don't think anyone will ever really figure them out,

I at least haven't. I know you are one hundred percent sure about Gabriel. He's the right one for you, I see that now.

"When you met him, I finally realized you didn't need comfort and safety as much as you needed to feel alive. Death and loss have surrounded us since we were children, and you need what Gabriel gives you, you need to feel the life in your veins. Gabriel also gives you comfort and safety, but he gives you excitement, frustration, desire, happiness, spirit; he just makes you so full of life. That is why I want you to marry him, just like the two of you planned." My eyes go wide, and I stare at him with shock on my face.

"How did you know?" I ask.

"Gabriel came to me two weeks ago, asking me if you had ever mentioned how you wanted to be proposed to. I told him you never wanted a big, fancy proposal. I told him all you wanted was him." I put my other hand over his and smile at my loving brother, who knows me better than anyone else.

"So, you're okay with this?" I ask. Adrian shrugs, still focusing on the water.

"I don't care for the concept of marriage, and I'm not sure I ever want to get married. But I know taking risks is a part of life. There are some things you have to take the leap of faith for, and I think this is a good thing. Gabriel makes you happier than you've ever been, and there is no rush. You can get married tomorrow or in three years. Getting engaged just means you wanted to take a step forward. I may not get that because I don't fully know what I want yet, but it's not my decision to make. If you're happy, and if you're sure, then I will support you, even if I don't understand. You're so young, and I want you to go out and explore the world. Yet, I also know you have met the world countless times now, and I want you to explore it with the person you love. You need to live your life, and it's going to be a pain for us to adjust to this new part of it, but we can do it. We've survived everything else."

Adrian removes his hand from mine to wipe away a tear that has escaped his eyes. He swipes his hand on his pants before he puts it back between mine. My emotional brother, who has only ever shared this part of himself with me. At least to my knowledge.

"You've done a brilliant job. You are the best brother a girl could ever hope for, and I love you so much. I'm sorry for all of the complications and the chaos I've brought into our lives," I say, and he frowns at me.

"Don't be absurd," he scolds, and I let out a short laugh. "Protecting you is my job. Dad, Grandpa, and Grandma all trusted me with this, and I've been doing the best I can while still watching you go out and make decisions for yourself." I squeeze his hand and smile. "I have no idea how to be a parent, but I think you turned out pretty well," he says with a wiggle of his eyebrow. I let out a long laugh.

"Yeah, I turned out pretty well, and so did you. Life fucked us up pretty badly, but it's you who made it all okay for me," I admit, and he stares at me. His eyes scan my red ones, sadness creeping back onto his face.

"Okay, you know what, I'm going to keep you hidden, somewhere no one can find or hurt you anymore. Yeah, that's what I'm going to do," he says, and I laugh again. Adrian hesitates for a brief moment before telling me the one thing I really wish were true. "James is going to come around, I'm sure of it," he promises, but his eyes drift from my face as he does.

"Why are you lying to me?" I ask, and he tilts his head. His bright eyes, the ones that are mine too, stare at me, and I give him half a smile. "I've known you all my life. Don't you think I know when you're lying?"

"You're right, I have no idea if he'll come around. He has pretty strong feelings for you, and he's had them for most of his life. It's not something you can just get over, but I also know he wants to. You may think you need him, but he needs you more," Adrian says and pulls on my hands until I'm safely tucked against his side. "He will be back."

God, I hope so.

I can't lose another person.

"Val, Val," Adrian says while shaking me, but I don't stop screaming. "It's okay, I'm right here," he assures me, but I tremble in his arms.

The image of James' gravestone is imprinted in my mind, and I can't force it out of my head. The dream of him crashing into the barrier on the race track is what makes another scream leave my lips.

Adrian is trying to calm me, but it's not working. Nothing is working. I can't forget how James' car went up in flames with him still inside, just like it happened with Maxime years ago.

I open my eyes to see I'm all alone in my room. I didn't scream, I didn't do anything other than shoot up in bed and sit up straight. My heart is beating out of my chest, and I can't remember how to breathe. The fight with James just went to a whole other level. My abandonment issues triggering the trauma of my mother leaving is causing my dreams to be haunted by death and loss. The loss of my best friend.

Chase licks my hand when he sees how panicked I am, and I pet his head for a little, breathing steadily to slow my heart rate. I check my phone to see a message from Gabriel.

Gabriel: My aunts need me a little longer. They've asked me to move all of the baby stuff into the garage for now because it's too painful for them to do themselves. I will meet you in Italy a bit later than I planned, but if you need me, please call me. I hate that I can't be with you.

I do too, but Nicolette and Domi need him, and there is no question about where he should be. I had a fight with James. They're grieving.

Valentina: Take your time. I will see you soon.

I manage to fall back asleep, but my dreams are haunted by the death of my best friend. Over and over again. Until eventually I do scream, but into my pillow to make sure I don't wake Adrian.

CHAPTER 59
Valentina

ADRIAN STRUTS INTO MY room and rips the curtains open. I let out a groan before pulling the covers over my face. We arrived in Italy late in the afternoon yesterday, and I went straight to a meeting with Leonard. It went well. We've got more people interested in investing in the driver academy. Lorenzo Mattia also made me sit in Gabriel's car for a few hours, testing a new update for this weekend since my fiancé isn't here yet. In other words, I fell into bed late last night and am beyond exhausted.

"Man, I always wanted to do that," Adrian says in a chipper tone, and I pull my hand from under the cover to flip him off.

My eyes are sore, and I want to stay in bed for the rest of the day. Chase sniffs my head, and I let out a laugh. He makes me feel better. Dogs have a superpower, as if they understand everything that's happening and then try to take some of your pain away.

I remove the covers from my face again to pull Chase close to me.

"Come on, you can bring Chase. I talked to Lorenzo, and he said it's okay, you know, since Chase is potty trained and all." I let out a short laugh. "Go have some breakfast," he commands, and I grin at him.

"Did you order room service?" I ask, and Adrian smirks.

"Something like that." I cock an eyebrow, but he leaves the room without saying more.

Maybe he went out and got something to eat? Actually, I don't mind either way. As long as there is food, I'm happy.

I pull the covers off my body completely and slide into the slippers I brought from home.

"Chérie," the voice I've fallen in love with says, and I turn in the direction from where it came from.

Gabriel's wearing his Velocità Rossa team shirt and black jeans that make my body ache for him. The shirt fits so snugly, I let my mind wander to how his hard muscles feel underneath my fingertips.

He walks closer to me, sucking in a sharp breath when he stares at my half-naked body. The crop top and shorts don't hide much of me. Gabriel stops halfway through the door and takes a step backward again, as if he needs another moment to appreciate my body. He can have all the moments he wants as long as he's going to do something about the ache between my legs from his gaze.

"How'd you sleep?" he asks, and I smile at him.

"I missed you," I say, a yawn slipping past my lips. He chuckles in response before wrapping his arms around me and bringing me flush against his chest.

"No fucking more, Valentina. I'm going to stay right by your side until you get sick of me," Gabriel says, his lips attaching to my neck where he sucks on my soft spot. I whimper, my head falling backward as heat starts pooling between my legs.

"Good," I reply and moan into the quiet room when his thigh moves between my legs to press against my clit. "Fuck," I mumble, but he grabs the back of my neck and presses his mouth to mine to swallow the word.

"Grind," he groans, and I roll my hips against his trained thigh, whimpering against his lips. "Mine," he says, his tongue slipping into my mouth and massaging mine.

Gabriel's hands drop to my ass, and I moan into his mouth when he moves my hips for me, bringing waves of pleasure to my body.

"More, please," I beg, so he slides his hands into my panties and pinches my aching clit between his fingers. "Oh God," I moan, grinding against the ball of his hand while he slips two fingers inside of me.

"Need my cock in here," he mumbles before thrusting his fingers inside of me again and stroking my G-spot.

My stomach muscles tighten in response, my orgasm sneaking up on me. It takes hold of my spine, arching my back so my chest presses against Gabriel's. I shake and he holds me firmly, planting kisses along the length of my neck. I could get lost in moments like these, and, sometimes, it feels like I do.

The rest of the world doesn't exist when Gabriel fucks me.

"What do you want?" he asks when I unbutton his pants and slide my hand inside his boxers. My fingers wrap around his erected cock, and I smile against his lips.

"I want to feel your hard muscles underneath my fingertips before I dig my nails into your arms while you thrust into me." Gabriel bites my bottom lip before he lets go, picks me up, and wraps my legs around his torso.

My hand moves into his hair, and he slams me onto the bed before making sure the door is closed. He walks back over to me, and I tug on his shirt before he can move between my legs. Without hesitating, Gabriel rips it off and puts his hands on my knees. He thinks for a moment before leaning forward and pulling my shirt and panties off. I am completely naked by the time he focuses on my body again. His eyes drop to my breasts, and I grin wickedly as I lift my arms over my head, exposing my body completely.

"Hard in an instant..." he mumbles, and I run my tongue over my top lip. "Spread for me, baby," he says, and I do as I'm told.

He bites his bottom lip as he runs his hands over my breasts. A small moan leaves me, and I feel my nipples go hard under his touch. Gabriel smirks down at me, and I sit up to pull his pants down. I'm too impatient to wait as he explores my body. I want to feel him inside of me.

"We've got time, chérie, we only have to be at the track in an hour," he assures me, but I look at him with hunger in my eyes.

"Well, I'm impatient." I need to be as close to him as humanly possible. "Don't make me wait," I beg. Gabriel smiles at me and nods.

"Okay, I won't," he promises, taking my legs and placing them onto his shoulders. "But I need a taste first," he says, placing his tongue against my wet core and licking his way up to my clit. He hums in response, fucking me with his tongue like there is nothing he'd rather do in this world. "You taste so good," he says while I cry out from pleasure.

"Like what?" I manage to ask, my words coming out breathless.

Gabriel sucks on my clit once more and then lets his tongue slide into me before pushing off the bed and bringing his mouth to mine. My tastebuds light on fire as I taste myself on his tongue.

"Like mine," he replies and without breaking eye contact, he thrusts inside of me.

I hold onto his ridiculously defined arms as I try to keep my moans in. I don't want to wake up all of the other hotel guests, no matter how good it feels as he slides out and thrusts back into me.

"I can't get enough of this pretty pussy, baby," he says, pressing his mouth to mine. "Or these lips," he adds, sinking in hard and deep.

"Oh fuck," I scream, covering my mouth to muffle it.

"You like that, ma chérie?" he asks, thrusting in just as hard.

"Yes, yes, more," I beg.

He starts going faster, and I get overwhelmed by the pleasure. My legs wrap around his hips, and I do my best to meet his movements, but I just want him to pleasure me until I can no longer contain my screams. Gabriel moans into my neck, and I can't hold back the sounds of pleasure anymore.

"Just like that, Gabriel," I say, and he keeps fucking me at the same, steady pace. Fast and hard and deep. Over and over again.

I come hard, my body trembling once more in response to the overwhelming pleasure.

"I want you in my mouth," I blurt out when my mind is out of the pleasure haze.

"You want my cock in your mouth?" he asks with a smirk, and I nod eagerly.

Gabriel slides out of me, and I readjust on the bed to take him down my throat. As soon as he's inside, he wobbles over me. A low groan leaves him while I swirl my tongue around the head of his cock.

"Fuck, I'm gonna come," he moans, and I smile as I take him deep down my throat. His hard length pulses in my mouth before he finally spills down my throat. Gabriel grabs onto the headboard with a sound of pleasure so sweet, I wish I could have it on repeat for the rest of my life.

This is what I needed. Just a calm moment between us after everything that happened.

Gabriel slides out of my mouth, and my back pushes off the bed out of reflex. "More?" he asks with a wicked grin on his face before kissing me. "God," he says as he tastes himself in my mouth. "You're all mine, Valentina. All fucking mine, just like I'm all yours." I run my thumb over his bottom lip.

"Mine," I say, and he chuckles.

"What should we do now?" Gabriel asks, letting his mouth drop to my hard nipple and sucking it into his mouth.

"We've gotta go soon, and I need to shower," I moan, so he lets go of my nipple. I slide off the bed before I change my mind and stay with him. Gabriel stares at me, and I shake my head, a smile on my lips. "Enjoying yourself, are we?" I ask, and he chuckles, forcing his eyes to mine.

"Always when you're naked," he replies, and I walk closer to him. I put my hands on his thighs and move close until my lips are a centimeter away from his.

"You know, naughty men like you shouldn't even get to taste me," I whisper and watch goosebumps trail down his arms. With a smile, I go on. "Better not lose that privilege. I don't think you could handle never being able to touch me again." His hand lifts to my breast, and he runs it over my hard peak before I step back to break skin contact. Slowly, I walk away from him, and Gabriel falls backward onto the bed with a loud sigh.

"The things you do to me, chérie. I will never understand them." I chuckle but walk into the bathroom without looking at him again.

I take a shower and put on light blue jeans which fit snuggly. I add a thin line of eyeliner and mascara. Once I'm satisfied with my hair and makeup, I step out of the bathroom. I haven't decided what top I want to wear yet, but when I see Gabriel's team shirt lying on the bed, I'm tempted to put it on. He appears behind me and places his hands on my stomach. I lean back against his muscular torso, tipping my head against his chest.

"Can I wear your shirt?" I ask, and Gabriel presses a kiss to my temple.

"What kind of a question is that? Of course you can," he replies, and I grin.

Ever since giving me my necklace, he hasn't been as obsessed with making me wear his shirts, but he still adores it when I wear his clothes. He picks it up from the bed and turns it the right way around.

"Arms up," he whispers, and I do as I'm told. He puts the shirt on my body and flashes me his dimples once he's done. "I spoke to Lorenzo today, and he said we should do another hot lap." My eyes go wide, and he smiles. "I thought you might like doing it since you're not just a trainee at the driver academy anymore. You're our team's fucking reserve driver," he says, but I'm still speechless.

"Thank you," I reply, and he bites his bottom lip to keep from grinning in the same stupid way I am. It's no use, the grin comes through anyway.

"I love seeing you wear my number," he says, and I stare down at it, seeing the seven across my left breast.

"I wish it had mine on it," I admit in a whisper. Gabriel places his index finger under my chin to lift my head so that I look at him.

"One day, it will. You'll race for Velocità Rossa, I'm sure of it," he says, and I pucker up my lips to hide my happy grin. His finger wraps around the charm hanging from my neck.

"I love you, Gabriel Matteo Biancheri." He lets go of my necklace and takes my face between his hands.

"I love you the same, Valentina Esmèe Cèlia Romana," he replies, his lips meeting mine. I melt into the kiss.

CHAPTER 60

Gabriel

VALENTINA IS WIGGLING IN her seat from excitement. I know she's having the time of her life being the reserve driver for Velocità Rossa, but it doesn't include much racing during the season, unless it's for test driving or if one of the drivers gets sick.

Lorenzo Mattia called me yesterday and told me that the video of Val and me doing hot laps got a lot of positive feedback and then asked if we could film another one for the fans. I'd agreed in a heartbeat, especially when I remembered Valentina's happy smile.

"Almost there," I assure her, and she flashes me the same smile I was just thinking about. It lights my heart on fire.

Val tilts her head to look at Chase, who is standing in the trunk and looking outside the window. I've arranged for someone to look after him while we film our video.

I don't know when it happened, maybe during the two weeks Val and I didn't see each other much, but Chase and I have bonded. That little guy has become mon bébé. It's not something I've admitted to anyone. Maybe I should to Valentina, but I don't want her to think that I think I have any claim on this dog now. He's hers. I would never see it differently. I just love him. That's all.

"I'm nervous," Val says when we're almost there. I can feel her heart racing in her chest. A smile slips onto my lips when she wipes a drop of sweat from where it rolled between her breasts. Good God. Everything about my woman turns me on.

We step out of the car, and Val grabs Chase from the trunk. He shakes once then nudges my legs until I bend down and scratch his head. His tail is going wild from excitement, and I let out a happy laugh.

"Why are you nervous, chérie?" I ask in a soft voice to distract myself. My thumb finds its way onto her cheek, caressing her soft skin for a moment.

"I don't want to mess up," she replies, making me frown.

"Please, baby, you are a wonderful driver, better than any guy on any of the teams. You have nothing to worry about," I reply, and she snorts in response. I kiss her before she can tell me she isn't. I don't want to hear that shit right now.

As soon as our lips disconnect, we get overwhelmed by fans who have been waiting for me to arrive at the track. Val steps aside with Chase, and the longing to follow her almost takes over, but I have responsibilities.

I sign twenty different articles of merchandise, take fifty pictures with the fans, and smile until my cheeks burn. I like this part of my job a lot. Connecting with the people who support me is a feeling like no other. Recently, I haven't had many chances to give back to the community I have my current career status to thank for, so this makes me smile genuinely.

I make sure everyone gets at least a picture or an autograph before running to look for Val and Chase. I don't have to go far. They're both standing near the entrance still, Chase sitting and Val squatting beside him. A grin appears on my face as I join them again.

"Why didn't you go ahead already?" I ask and bend down to stop Chase from crying. He almost jumps into my arms.

"I wanted to, but Chase didn't want to leave without Daddy," she explains, and I feel my eyes go wide in awe. Joy overtakes every part of me.

"Really?" I don't know what's better. Him not wanting to leave without me or Val referring to me as his dad. "Awe, buddy," I say, addressing Chase, and the small puppy licks me across the face. I chuckle before standing upright. "When did I start deserving this new title?"

"Ask Chase, he's the one who decided." I shake my head, but the smile never leaves my lips.

"I adore you," I say, and one corner of her mouth lifts to form a smirk.

"I know."

She takes my hand in hers so I can lead her to the pit box. Valentina and I talk the whole way there. People are running around everywhere, just like they always do during the race weekends, and we talk about how she's going to be one of them next season. Running from one place to another. Like I do. Like Adrian does. Like Cameron, Leonard, and James do.

The job of a Formula One driver is hectic. Something she's about to find out in a few months, and that thought alone brings a big smile to my face. She made it. Valentina is going to be an F1 driver, and I've never been prouder in my entire life.

A friend of mine from the team takes Chase to watch him, but both Val and I look longingly after... our son. God, I'm going to need some time to wrap my head around how happy that makes me. Val's hand slips into mine, sending a bolt of electricity down my spine. I'm smiling for a completely different reason now.

"Ciao, Valentina," Hector says as he approaches us, and she holds out her hand for him to shake.

"Ciao, Hector. Come stai?" she asks, and I grin down at her. She's been picking up Italian quickly, and I'm proud. In true Valentina fashion, she spends every spare minute she gets looking over every vocabulary and grammar paper I write for her.

"Very good," Hector assures her, making a blush settle on her cheeks. No one should be as sweet as Val. "Are you ready to take the 266 Fuoco for a spin around the track?" Excitement lights up her face as she nods. Hector's thin lips stretch wide as he flashes her his white teeth.

"Yes, I'm very excited," she replies, almost bouncing up and down.

I'm curious to see how she'll be next season. If this will be her before every race.

God, I hope so.

"Good. They've arranged for you to race against Adrian, if you want. You'll get however many laps you need to familiarize yourself with the track."

I'm only half paying attention to him because I'm too happy about Val's reaction to listen. Then, I process my performance coach's words, and I barely keep my jaw from hitting the floor.

"We'll record everything, and I think it will be very good to get more younger viewers interested." The first female Formula One driver racing against her brother with her Velocità Rossa driver boyfriend beside her in the car is going to get a lot of attention.

I squeeze Valentina's hand once before slipping inside the building to grab the gear we're going to need. Because my team is incredible, it's already laid out for us. Some of my crew members walk up to me to talk me through everything I have to do once we're done. Again, I'm only half-listening because I can see Valentina standing near the car we're about to race in, and the biggest smile is on her lips.

"Are you ready, ma chérie?" I ask when I finally get to be next to her again, and she directs that happy grin at me.

A second later, it fades as her gaze focuses on someone behind me. Without turning around, I know it's James. The way tears, guilt, and pain fill her eyes tells me everything I need to know. She's been doing her best all morning, and probably for the past two days, to keep her feelings bottled up, but I know she's not okay. One of the most important people in her life told her he can't be around her anymore. He wasn't supposed to leave. Like Adrian, James was never supposed to make her feel this way. And I hate him more for it, for making Valentina fall apart but hide it to ensure she doesn't burden anyone else. But she just lost her best friend and godson indefinitely, and that hurts. It hurts so much, her breathing hitches until the pain crosses my chest too.

"I need a minute," she says and pats my arm before walking inside the same building I got our gear from moments ago.

It takes me a few seconds to put down everything I was holding to chase after her. She shouldn't be alone while she's hurting. So, I sprint inside, searching for her until I realize exactly where she is. I knock on the door to my private washroom, but she doesn't answer. I knock again, resting my forehead against the door.

"Chérie, open the door, please," I beg and hear the lock click a second later. I slide into the bathroom and settle down in front of her. An ache hits me right in the chest when I look at her tear-stained face.

"He left," she says breathlessly, and I nod.

"I know, mon tournesol, I know." She covers her face and sobs so loudly, the sound makes my bones hurt.

"He said he *couldn't*," she cries, and I pull her against me by her elbows. She flings her arms around me as we both stay on the floor. "He told me he would never be able to." I press a kiss to the top of her head while her breathing hitches and shakes.

"Baby, please, breathe," I say, and she does. It seems to settle her a little, but she's still crying, and I wish I knew how to make everything better. I want her happiness from earlier back, the smile of excitement.

"Everyone always leaves. My grandpa left me, my dad left me, my grandma left me, my mom ran away voluntarily, you left me—" she blurts out, hitting me like a shot to the stomach. Guilt slices through me until I'm nauseous.

"I did..." I trail off and let go of her arms. She has every right to bring it up, but it doesn't stop regret from filling me from head to toe.

"I'm sorry, mon soleil, I didn't mean to throw that in your face," she apologizes, grabbing my face in her hands. My gaze shifts back to her sad face, but there is a firmness in her features now, too. "I promise we're okay. It just means we're not perfect, which is a good thing. Perfect is unnatural," she teases, and I bring myself to smile.

"It's irritating how close to unnatural you are then," I say, and she gives me her typical eye roll before grinning.

"That was cheesy." I grab her face and plant my lips to hers, tasting her watermelon taste.

"It's what I do," I say once I pull back.

Val nuzzles her face into my neck, inhaling deeply before pressing a kiss to where a faint hickey is painted on my skin.

"I'll bring him back to you, I promise," I say after a few minutes of silence, and she leans away from our embrace, surprise all over her beautiful face. The face I love the most in the world. The face I hope is the last I will ever see before leaving this world.

"Why?" she asks, and I tug a loose strand of her hair behind her ear.

"Because I love you."

With James gone, I should be happy. It's not a secret that I hate him for how in love he is with Valentina, but this isn't about my feelings. It's about the love of my life deserving more than all of the shit she's dealing with. Val isn't just a good person, she is the best in my eyes. She's always taking care of others. Helping Evangelin in her store. Comforting my aunts. Being there for everyone she cares about. Pushing all of her needs and dreams aside to take care of Damian. Partnering up with Leonard to start a racing school for kids like them. Taking care of me in every way possible. It's not fair that she receives so much heartbreak in return. No one should have to go through what she's going through.

Instead of pointing all of that out to her to explain why I'm going to do everything I can to get her best friend back into her life, I simply wrap my arms around her again. My lips find hers, feeling her melt into my chest in the same way she always does. In the way I've gotten used to and the way I'll never be able to live without again.

Valentina is my other half. I would die for her. And a little part of me will have to in order to speak to James.

James Fucking Landon. God, I hate him more with every breath.

CHAPTER 61
Valentina

RACING AGAINST MY BROTHER is going to be exciting. With every lap I drive in the car, my heart races faster and faster. I feel much better than I did half an hour ago in the bathroom, and Gabriel is smiling proudly next to me as he watches me almost fly over the track. Being in this car with the man I love while I do something that is going to be my career is a rollercoaster of the best emotions. It feels like breathing. Adrenalin courses through my veins, and I'm thriving in this environment.

"Go a bit faster, chérie," Gabriel says, and I do as I'm told.

I'm confident enough on the track to drive faster now, and I'm getting closer to being ready to race against Adrian. It's a one-lap race, but it doesn't matter how long it is. What matters is that I want to beat Adrian's ass. When we were younger, we used to race against each other all the time, but never to this extent, never like how we're going to race against each other in the future.

How could I have ever imagined this scenario?

Grandpa did back then, and I'm glad we're able to make his vision come true. Even in death, I want to make him proud.

"I think I'm ready," I tell Gabriel, and he grins brightly.

"Okay, line up next to the other Velocità Rossa, then we wait for the go sign," he explains, and I nod.

My stomach turns upside down, and I can't decide whether I feel nervous or excited. It's both, definitely, I just don't know which is stronger at this point.

As I pull up next to Adrian, I let out an excited squeal. My brother waves to me, and I hold up my pinky. A slight pain shoots through my chest, but seeing Adrian laugh takes my mind off it.

"You got this, baby," Gabriel assures me and squeezes my hand.

I wink at him and concentrate on the light in front of us. *Red, red, red, red, red...* Go! I hit the gas pedal, getting a quicker start than Adrian. My reflexes have always made starts easy for me, and they are also why I was above average at them.

"Careful, there's a bump," Gabriel warns, and I slow a little to avoid driving directly over it.

Adrian is next to me, and I do my best to stay ahead. Sweat drips down my spine as I take the corner a little too hard, making Gabriel grab onto his door for support. I can't help but smile at the camera a little before refocusing on the track, taking the next corner a little less aggressively. Adrian is right behind me, but I'm pressing down hard on the gas, needing to go faster. A lot faster.

When we race over the finish line, Adrian is barely behind me, but enough to earn me the win. I won against my brother. I fucking won. A howl of joy escapes me as I bring the car to a stop and turn to look at Gabriel. He's smiling brightly, and I know that I have the same look on my lips.

"That. Was. Amazing!" he yells, and I laugh. "You were so good. I'm so proud of you." He sounds like a fan, and I love him for it.

I pull his head close and kiss him. It's difficult because we're both wearing helmets, but I manage to show him how much I love him before breaking the kiss for the sake of the cameras. Gabriel encourages me to go to my brother, and I do, jumping into his arms while the adrenalin continues to get me high.

"Well done," Adrian mumbles, and I laugh.

"You almost had me," I say with excitement in my voice, and he pulls back so I can see him nod.

"Yes, I did. But you were faster," he replies with a smile, but I'm barely paying attention to him. My mind is overwhelmed by everything that is going on, and I feel like shedding happy tears. Instead, I smile until my entire face hurts. "I'm so proud of you," he goes on, and I feel like bursting with happiness.

Yesterday's Qualifying did not end well for any of my guys. Gabriel got fourth place, Adrian got seventh, Cameron last, Leonard fifteenth, and James twelfth. This race has to go well for all of them, and I feel like throwing up as I watch the monitors.

The lights go out, and I'm unable to move. Gabriel gets a terrible start and moves into fifth place. Adrian overtakes Eduardo and pushes into sixth. James moves up to seventh, and Cameron gets pushed off the track and into the barriers.

For a few seconds, I forget to breathe, but when I see Cameron get out of the car unharmed, I inhale again. My eyes drift to Gabriel, who is now in second place. I don't know how he got there, but I almost scream with enthusiasm. Adrian is still sixth, and I wonder if he'll be able to overtake Antonio Henderson, who is less than a second in front of him.

A lap later, Adrian overtakes, and I clap my hands together. He's one step closer to getting to the top, although I'm not sure if he can make it this time.

There are 63 laps in this Grand Prix, and I gasp in surprise when Adrian finishes in first place. Pride overwhelms my body, and I let it show through a victorious scream. It may have been a lot of luck that got him up there, but he drove phenomenally too. Gabriel comes in third, which is still really good, and James is fourth. Adrian's and Gabriel's crew celebrate in their boxes, and I celebrate with them.

This season is unlike any other I've ever witnessed. My brother and boyfriend are merely two points apart in the Driver's Championship, both of them ready to snatch the title, but neither of them ready for this battle to be over yet. There are still a few races left, a lot can still change and turn, but James is too far behind to catch up with them if Gabriel and Adrian's performance on track remains this strong.

When everyone walks outside to greet the Velocità Rossa drivers, I join them and wait for my brother and fiancé. The first one to come is Jonathan, who seems upset that he lost. The next is Adrian, and he comes to greet me before going to the rest of his team. My hand lifts to my necklace when Gabriel pulls up.

Although he only came in third, he smiles brightly as he looks at me. He places his helmet on top of his car to walk over to me and kiss me in front of everyone. I kiss him back just as fiercely. He moves on to celebrate with his crew, and I grin.

The day goes by like any other race day does, and I enjoy spending the night with Gabriel and Chase in our hotel room. We're driving back home on Tuesday because Leonard invited Adrian, Gabriel, and me to a charity event he's supporting. He told me it doubles as a work meeting too since one of the richest men in Formula One will be there, and he'd like to get him interested in investing in our driving school.

Gabriel is playing with my hair while I rub Chase's belly. It's been a long weekend, and I hope James and Damian are doing okay. No matter how many days have passed, thinking about them still brings a lump to my throat. I swallow it down, but not before Gabriel notices the tears in my eyes. His finger moves under my chin so he can tilt my head up toward him.

"You're thinking about James." It's not a question, but I nod anyway. "I'm sorry," Gabriel says and scratches my back. I love how he does it without me asking now. "He'll come back, I'm sure of it," he says, and I tilt my head back to look at him. My fingers trail over his new tattoo, symbolizing our relationship, and his trails over the one on my hip absentmindedly. "Be a little more patient, mon tournesol." I nod as he rests his forehead against mine.

I don't want to be patient.

CHAPTER 62

Gabriel

It's not often that I can't control myself around Valentina. During work events, I can *mostly* turn off my dirty thoughts and focus on the task at hand. The problem with tonight is, this isn't work for me, and Valentina looks mouth-watering. She's straightened her usually curly hair, applied some dark shades of brown eyeshadow to bring out her eyes, and the long, red dress she's wearing hugs all of her curves so perfectly, I find myself staring at her ass more often than not. The slit in the dress exposing ninety percent of her leg isn't helping my body cool down either.

"It's a pleasure to meet you," Val says with a bright smile after Leonard introduces her to someone, but I'm standing with Adrian to let them do their thing. This is for the racing school, after all.

"You're an artist. There are like a dozen paintings around. How are you not admiring any of them?" my teammate asks, and I can't help but smile. Mr. Anti-Relationship can't comprehend that there is nothing better than looking at the person you want to spend the rest of your life admiring.

"None of them compare to Valentina," I reply, earning me a hurling noise from my future brother-in-law.

"Do you even hear yourself when you say stuff like that?" he asks, and I chuckle into my glass. I do hear myself.

"I cannot wait for the day you say the same *stuff*," I reply, nudging his shoulder with mine. "I really hope you get to fall in love like I have because there is nothing better in the world. No race win, no championship, no fancy cars, nothing compares," I say, my eyes finding Val's at the same time hers find mine. We linger there

314

for a while, our gaze heated with love and lust, and it takes everything out of me not to drag her somewhere private. Fuck. Now it's all I can think about.

"If you say so," Adrian replies, dragging me out of my lust-filled trance. I tear my gaze from Val to see him sipping on his glass of water. Then, his eyes catch someone from across the room before his lips curl into the seductive smile I've seen too often. "Bye," is all he says as he strides toward the curvy woman with short brown hair that caught his eye. I merely shake my head and grin at the ground.

That guy is going to fall in love harder than everyone else, except me, of course.

"Gabriel fucking Biancheri." *Somebody shoot me.*

"Your Slimyness," I reply as I turn around, facing the prince with white-blonde hair and bright blue eyes. Christian rolls his eyes at me, but I notice his older brother, Thomas, beside him nudging his brother's arm. "Your Highness," I say with a nod of my head. I met Thomas a few times during race weekends in Monaco. He's a big fan of Formula One.

"My favorite driver," Thomas says and holds out his hand for me. I shake it with a smile.

"It's a nice surprise to see you here," I reply, focusing entirely on the prince whose company I enjoy.

If I look at Christian's stupid face too long, I get violent thoughts, and I'm not entirely sure I could keep my fist from connecting with his face. He pushed Valentina off the karting track. He hurt her. And I would love to hurt him back for it. Instead, I take a calming breath and force a smile at Thomas.

"I'm here to donate to Leonard Tick's racing school," is all he says before excusing himself and leaving me to catch my jaw off the floor. Holy fuck.

"Yeah, I don't know why he'd do that either. It's obviously going to fail," Christian adds, but I'm not surprised. He's the purest form of asshole there is.

"You don't understand because you're neither a person of color nor a woman in this sport. Oh, and of course because you're disgusting," I say before leaving him where he is and walking toward Valentina.

She's holding out her hand for me, signaling she'd very much like me by her side. Her smile fades as she glances behind me to see the royal brat right where I left him.

"I was having such a wonderful evening," she whispers as I place my arm around her waist and pull her close to kiss her temple.

"I know," I reply, tilting her head back to claim her lips. "But Thomas is also here, and he's got some great news," I manage to explain even though I'm a little high on her after that kiss.

"Can it wait? We walked by a storage closet earlier, and I haven't been able to stop thinking about ripping your shirt off in there," she whispers, and I swallow hard. It shouldn't be possible, but my dick hardens in response to her words and the way she looks up at me through her thick lashes. "Then again, you look delicious in this tuxedo, and I kind of want you to keep it on while you fuck me," she adds, running her hand over my stomach. My muscles tense as all the blood in my body rushes to my cock until it's throbbing unbearably. Good God, this woman drives me wild.

"Press your back against me. Feel what you do to me, ma chérie," I say, and she obeys, humming in response to me pressing my cock against her. "Feel how fucking hard I am for you, only for you," I whisper, wrapping my arms around her stomach and making her gasp.

"Gabriel, closet," she begs, but we're interrupted by Leonard and Thomas approaching. Val's eyes snap back open as she does her best to refocus.

"Your Highness, it's an honor to see you again," she says and attempts to curtsy, but I hold her firmly against me. If Val moves right now, people are going to give me funny looks for the hard-on I'm sporting.

"Please, I told you, it's Thomas," the crown prince of Monaco says, holding out his hand for her to shake, which she does. "Now that you and Leonard are both here, I would like to formally inform you of my decision to donate to 'Kids Like Us'," he announces, and Valentina's mouth forms a beautiful O-shape.

"Really?" Val asks softly, and I start grinning from ear to ear.

"Yes. As soon as I heard you were on the project, I knew I had to look into it. I was impressed with what I saw, so I'd like to help you make this happen. If you're interested, of course," Thomas says, and Leonard, the man I've never seen smile in my entire life, beams at the prince.

"We're very interested, thank you, Your Highness," Leonard says, shaking the future king's hand.

Valentina attempts to do the same, but Thomas presses a kiss to the back of her hand instead. Something shifts inside my chest, but it's not jealousy. Not entirely anyway. It's just a voice saying, 'Back off'. I don't want Val to be uncomfortable and at the same time, my head is screaming 'mine, mine, mine'. It's fucking frustrating, but I guide her further against me anyway, both to protect her and silence the words in my head.

"Still trying to hide your excitement?" she asks in Italian, and Thomas smirks a little before turning toward Leonard. Well, he obviously speaks Italian. Fantastic.

I press my lips to her ear before responding, "I crave you," in French. Goose-bumps spread down her arms, and I smile at them. "I need to be inside you now, chérie, need you wrapped around my cock," I say, watching her breathing pick up pace as her chest rises and falls more abruptly.

"Gabriel," she whimpers when I press my now again hard cock against her back. My arms wrap around her as we step to the side to admire the painting of a horse surrounded by sunflowers.

"It's beautiful, don't you think?" I ask, wishing I could slip my hands under her dress and my fingers inside her right now. If there weren't as many people in here, I would. I would tell her to describe the art to me while I made her come over and over again. My cock aches in my pants at the fantasy, so I press her further into me to ease some of the pressure.

"Gabriel," she complains, and I hum into her ear. Pleasure blurs my vision for a second. "I need—" She cuts off when someone walks by us, but I make her gasp by rolling my hips ever so slightly against her ass. "God," she breathes, stepping away from me and turning around to show me her pink cheeks. I smirk in response. She's so turned on right now, I can't help but picture wetness dripping down between her thighs.

"What do you need?" I ask as I close the distance between us again, placing my hands on her cheeks. We're in a less crowded part of this art event, but people still give us funny looks as they pass. I couldn't care less.

"You."

I swallow hard once before grabbing her hand and slipping through the crowd of people to get to the storage room she was talking about earlier. It's unlocked, so I guide her inside, lock the door, and press my lips to hers with so much intensity, she whimpers a little.

"I've been hard since you put this dress on, Valentina. Do you know that?" I ask, guiding the straps on her shoulders down until her breasts are free from the containment. Her hard nipples draw me in, but I study her smug smirk for a second instead.

"I know," she replies, her hand sliding down to my groin before she palms me through my pants.

"Fuck," I mutter, and my hands fly to the wall behind her, trapping her between my arms.

"I need you," she says, increasing the pressure on my cock. "Inside of me," she adds, unbuttoning my shirt to slide her hands over my stomach, still one of her favorite parts of my body.

"Spread," I command, reaching my hand between her legs. Val obeys immediately, sighing with relief when my fingers make contact with her drenched panties. "Have you been this wet all night?" I ask, grinding my fingers against her swollen clit.

"Yes," she moans, and I drop my mouth to her hard nipple, sucking on it until she cries out.

"I know, baby, but you have to be quiet. I can't have everyone hearing the sounds that belong to me," I say, and she nods once before grabbing my face and planting her lips on mine. There will never be anything more fulfilling than kissing this woman. Never.

Valentina fumbles with the zipper of my dress pants, a frustrated groan leaving her when it doesn't budge as easily as she would like it to. I smile into our kiss, my tongue massaging hers as I take out my cock and then fist her dress in my hands to slide it up. Her panties come down, and then I'm inside of her, gasping at her warmth and wetness. I'm convinced this is what heaven feels like. Valentina is what heaven feels like, in every way.

"So good," she moans quietly, and I thrust back inside of her so violently, it makes her legs shake. "Oh," she gasps, her nails digging into my arms in response.

"Just because I don't want them to hear you doesn't mean I don't want your legs to shake when we walk out of here for all of them to see," I say, pumping inside of her with another hard thrust. A quiet cry of pleasure slips past her lips as she claws at my shoulders to get me closer.

"More," she begs, and I give her everything. I'll always give her everything.

I keep up my rhythm, fighting off my orgasm even though it seems impossible. She feels too good and her little noises only send me further toward the edge. Val is close, I can feel it in the way her body starts surrendering to the pleasure and her muscles relax, but when her walls tighten around me, I'm so fucking close, I have to pull out of her completely. She whines in response, but I distract her by kissing her senseless. My tongue slips back into her mouth as my finger drops to her clit where I rub tight circles. I swallow her moans with a hunger like never before.

"You're my fiancée, all mine," I say as I thrust back inside of her, the threat of my premature orgasm dissipated now.

"All yours," she agrees, and I grab her leg, placing it on my hip. Her head falls back as I fill her up over and over, hitting that one spot inside of her I know drives her crazy.

"You take me so well, chérie, like I was made for you and you for me," I breathe out because my words always bring her closer to her orgasm, and I need her to come right now. My orgasm is pulling everything tight in my cock and balls, begging to be released. "You like getting fucked knowing someone could hear, don't you?" A shy smile slips onto her face, and I bring my hand back to her clit, my pinky finding its way to the place where we're connected. It shouldn't feel as good as it does.

"Gabriel, I'm—" She doesn't have to finish that sentence because she's coming so hard, her body trembles against me. Her arms fling around my neck to hold herself up, and I drop my face into her neck as my orgasm finally hits, sending me into oblivion.

"Fuck," I moan as my cock pulses inside of her, filling her with my cum.

"Hmmm," is all she replies while I kiss her neck and do my best to regain full consciousness. Valentina's fingers play with my hair for a moment, and I can't help but smile. I'm happy. I've never been this happy.

"I love you," I say, reaching for the tissue box on one of the shelves near us and cleaning her up.

"I love you the same," she replies and giggles as I wipe the tissue over her sensitive pussy. My smile widens.

"I think we should do this more often," I blurt out, throwing the tissue into the trash can on the other side of the room. My feet bring me back to her, my hands tugging on the straps of her dress to put them back in place. I kiss the curve of each of her breasts up her neck until I reach her mouth where she's grinning.

"Have sex in storage rooms?" she asks, and I press a single kiss to the corner of her mouth.

"Have quickies," I explain, and she giggles.

"We have quickies all the time. Like this morning, yesterday before the race, last week before we had to—" I cut her off by wrapping my lips around hers, and she laughs out of happiness. "You just like that I'm going to walk out there on wobbly legs, and everyone will know what we did," she says, and I lick my bottom lip at her words.

"Yeah, but so do you," I reply, trapping her against the wall with my arms again.

"Yeah," she admits, her hands pressing against my stomach. "We should go," Val says and starts buttoning my shirt.

Once we're dressed again, we slip out of the room and walk back to where the charity event is taking my place. Adrian cocks a suspicious eyebrow our way before scrunching his nose in disgust. I let out a small laugh and ignore him while Val and I move back over to Leonard.

I spend the rest of the night smiling at the way her legs shake as she walks.

CHAPTER 63
Gabriel

My feet bring me to James' house, and I fight the urge to turn around and leave again. This is the last thing I ever saw myself doing, but I want to keep my promise to Valentina. I will do everything in my power to bring him back to her. James is family, and not only is Val suffering, but he is, too. He's been suffering ever since Annabel left him. No matter how deeply I despise him, I sympathize with him.

I take a couple of deep breaths before I can finally bring myself to knock on the front door. Ever since I met Val, he's been there too. He's her best friend, and I know if I was in a bad spot with Cameron, she would do everything she could to help make it right again. I also know she can't be the one to approach James. Looking at her clouds his judgment. Then again, he hates me, so I don't know if this will help.

Sweat drips down the side of my face while I wait for James to open the door. When he does, I no longer feel afraid. If anything, I feel bad for him.

His hair is all over the place, his eyes are bloodshot from the lack of sleep, and his shirt looks like Damian threw up on it a few times. It must have been days since he's had the time to shower.

"How can I help you, Gabriel?" he asks when I don't say anything. He's not angry or annoyed, he's just tired.

"May I come in?" I reply, and he nods, stepping out of the way.

His house is a mess. There are toys, towels, and clothes all over the place. Plates, baby bottles, and other dishes fill the sink, and James leads me into his living room where Damian is sleeping in his bassinet. I settle down on the couch, and James sits on the armchair across from me. I feel beyond awkward. He and I have never spent any time together, and now, without Val or Adrian here to help us make conversation, it feels unnatural.

James looks at me with high expectations, and I know I have to start talking now.

"I'm not going to beat around the bush, James," I start, and his eyes go wide, clearly surprised with how forward I am while he is in this state. "Valentina is hurting, not just because you left, but also because when you did, you took Damian with you. She has a strong bond with him, as you know, and I don't think it was fair of you to leave like this. I know you have feelings for her, and it's hard for you to be around her, but she's your family, for fuck's sake. You don't leave family, trust me, I know." I pause briefly because guilt and pain shoot through my chest when I think about what I've done. "Is being in love with her and leaving really more important than being her best friend?" He studies me with an angry look before standing up and pointing at me.

"Fuck you, Gabriel. You have no idea what it feels like to be in love with someone for almost your entire life and never being good enough for them!" he screams, and I suck in a sharp breath.

"You're right, I don't. But you know what I have been in love with my entire life?" James shakes his head, and I watch the anger fade from his face because he's confused by my words. "I've been in love with having a big family, and I used to have one, but over time, life made it seem like I wasn't good enough for it and took away almost every single person I cared about." He sits back down, guilt washing over his features. "You may have been in love with a person, and I with a concept, but nevertheless, I know how you feel. I know the pain, believe me," I explain, and James nods, leaning back against the armchair. "Let me ask again. Is being in love with Val more important than keeping her close by being family?" James' eyes drift to Damian's bassinet, and I take a deep breath. This is going better than I expected it to. Although I do feel like throwing up. I don't like sharing my feelings with anyone who isn't Val.

"Would you be able to be just friends with her?" he asks. I stare at him and place my arms on my thighs as I lean forward.

"No, she's the love of my life, and I could never accept being just friends. But you're the better man, James. You're the one who was supposed to stay. So, why did you leave her like I did?"

This one hits him hard. He is finally realizing what pain he's causing her. James was with Val when I left, he knows how much she suffers when she loses someone who is dear to her. I just need him to realize what's most important: family.

"It's really not fair, Gabriel. Why do you get to be with her?" He seems desperate then, and I let out a big sigh before I bite the inside of my cheek. I'm sweating so much at this point, I need to change my shirt.

"I don't know. I don't deserve her, but she saved me. I love and need her more than you ever will," I say firmly so he understands each word perfectly.

"It's time I let her go, isn't it?" he asks me, and I give him a compassionate smile.

"Romantically, yes, but come back to her as the best friend you know she needs, the one you know you need," I beg, sounding pathetic and desperate, the last two things I ever want to be in front of James. Yet, for Val, I would be anything.

"I can't come back. I'm too overwhelmed with Damian and Formula One. How can I deal with my feelings when I don't seem to have any time!" he says. This time, a bigger smile comes onto my lips.

"I have a solution for you." I stand up and walk over to Damian, who is awake and looking around.

"What is it?" James asks as I turn my head to look at him.

"My biological grandmother, Sienna, gave up my mother because she knew she wasn't the right parent for her child at that time of her life. It allowed my mom to grow up in a family with people who cherished her until the day they died. It was the hardest decision Sienna ever made, but it was the best thing for my mom."

After a moment of silence, I bring my gaze back to Damian.

"My aunts have wanted a child for years, and I promise you, they'd be the best parents to Damian. I'm also sure they wouldn't mind letting you see him on the weekends when you're in Monaco, so here is my solution: offer for them to adopt him. You can still be his dad, but this way you don't have to choose. You get to keep your career and give this little boy the life he deserves. Because that's what really matters here. Making sure Damian gets to grow up happier than the rest of us ever were."

CHAPTER 64

Valentina

I SIT IN THE little room next to my bedroom, which has now become my office and Gabriel's painting room, looking over some plans for the racing school with Leonard. We're doing a video call, discussing something I'm more than thrilled about. We're deciding on a date for when we're going to open the school.

It's been hard since James left, but I handled it better than I thought I could. It's been a little over a week, and I don't think I would be doing as well as I am without the school, Adrian, training, Evangelin and I working on her store expansion, and Gabriel. Especially Gabriel.

He's been doing everything in his power to make me feel better. From doing little things like rubbing my back and showing me all different kinds of affection, to the big things, like buying or cooking my favorite meals and organizing romantic dates in the park, on our boat, or simply in our bedroom. He's trying his best to make me forget how much I miss James and Damian, and most of the time, it works wonderfully.

After I've completed all of my work, I decide to take Chase for a walk. Gabriel told me he has some things to do, but he will be back by the time I've finished dinner. Tonight is my turn to cook, but it's early, and Chase has been such a good boy, waiting for me to finish work. I get up from my seat, and he stands quickly, his two-colored eyes studying my face.

"Let's go?" I ask, and he spins around once before jumping in the air and barking out of excitement. I shake my head, and we make our way downstairs. My brother sits at the dining room table, and I walk over to him with a smile. "What are you doing here? Homesick already?" I ask, and he grins.

"Maybe..." He trails off, paying more attention to Chase than me.

"You want to come with us? We're going for a walk," I say, and he places down his water and stands up.

"Yes, let's go! I've been meaning to spend some time with the little guy."

Adrian is such a good uncle, not only to Chase but also to Damian. When the baby was here, my brother changed his diaper, fed him, burped him, and pretty much did everything James asked him to do to help with Damian. There is no one like Adrian, and I am the luckiest girl to have him as my big brother.

"Okay, then, come on. I still have to make the pizza when I come back."

His eyes light up when I tell him I will make one of his favorite meals, Grandma's homemade pizza, and I grin at him. I remember when we were younger, it was all Adrian ever wanted to eat, but Grandpa made a rule to only have it once a month. He wanted us to base our diet on healthy foods, one very important aspect of being a Formula One driver.

Once we're out the door, Adrian takes Chase's leash from my hand and walks ahead, skipping like a little child from one foot to the other. I almost start laughing when Chase matches Adrian by adding a jump in his step. I take my phone out of my pocket and record them. This is a moment I want to document so I can keep it forever.

Adrian and I walk through our neighborhood for a little while before we make our way to a café. The temperature is pleasant since the sky is covered by clouds, but every now and then, the sun shines through, making me squint my eyes to see the ground in front of me. Chase and Adrian have stopped skipping, but they are still walking a bit ahead of me.

A stranger comes up to us with his dog, and we let Chase socialize with the golden retriever. The young man who owns Penelope, the two-year-old golden, makes conversation with us about Chase.

My eyes shift past him, and I see someone standing across the street from us, completely dressed in black and a hoodie on their head. I can't tell if it's a woman or a man, but I notice them watching us.

I take Adrian's hand and squeeze it to get his attention.

"What is it?" he asks me, and I tilt my head in the direction of the person who is still staring at us.

"You see them too, right?" I inquire, and Adrian lets out a short laugh.

"Don't worry about it, I'm sure it's nothing," he assures me.

I glance in the direction of the person in all black again, and I think my mind plays a trick on me when I see a strand of red hair coming out from under the hood because when I look closer, I see nothing. Only a black hoodie.

I shake my head and let out a hard laugh. Annabel's letter is messing with my head. 'She is vengeful, I have to warn you, ' Annie said in the letter, but Harlow wouldn't do anything with a restraining order against her. *Would she?* And neither would Sebastian. *Right?* I haven't heard from him since he was fired. The problem should have been resolved with him gone from the team and away from me. *Should have...*

"What if it's Harlow? Sebastian?" I ask Adrian, and I can feel him tense next to me.

"Okay, wait here," he says, before running across the street toward the creepy-looking person.

In my current state, completely freaking out it may be Harlow or Sebastian, I wouldn't be able to talk to whoever hides underneath that hoodie.

After a couple of seconds, Adrian reaches them, and they pull down the disguise to reveal someone I've never met before. When they take a selfie, I understand the female with long, brown hair must be a fan. I let out a long breath. *I'm being paranoid!* I've seen too many movies and read too many books.

"Not Sebastian or Harlow," I say when he's close enough for me to hear. He shakes his head and smiles.

"No, Val, it's neither of them," he assures me, and I let out another deep breath to calm my heart rate.

Adrian gives me a comforting hug, and we continue to make our way to get some coffee, not that I need it anymore.

I'm wide awake.

Gabriel texts me and lets me know he won't make it to dinner. I wonder what he's been up to all day, but he won't tell me over the phone. He assured me he will when he comes back home, and the suspense is killing me. The whole time while I cook, I let my mind play out each different scenario. I come to no conclusion. I even ask Adrian while we eat, but he's too in love with the food to pay much attention to me. He does the dishes as a thank you, and I go upstairs, my son following closely behind me after my brother leaves.

I'm on my bed with Chase, reading the last chapter of my book when I finally hear the front door unlocking and footsteps coming toward my room. I place the book on top of my chest and lean back, pretending to be asleep.

The door opens while I do my best not to smile, even though his presence has a way of bringing one to my face with the least amount of effort. I feel the bed go down a bit when he sits beside me, and then the book disappears from my chest. It closes before he clears his throat a little. Laughter is bubbling up in my throat, but I swallow it down.

"I have froyo," he says with a firm tone, and my eyes shoot open in response. Frozen yogurt from my favorite froyo place sits in his hand. Gabriel chuckles when I sit up straight and hands me the cup. "I knew you couldn't resist," he teases, and I press a kiss to his lips before digging into the sweet, cold, and delicious yogurt.

"You know me too well, Monsieur Biancheri," I reply, and he grins, his hand sliding closer to my thigh.

A serious look lingers on his features, and, after I take another spoonful, I hold my cup out for him. He takes some in his mouth before studying me.

"Amour, just tell me what you were doing all day. I can handle it, I promise," I joke to lighten the mood, but he stares at me with an intensity that lets me know I might not be able to handle it after all. I place the froyo down and give him my full attention.

"I was with James," he blurts out.

James is the last person I ever expected Gabriel to spend the day with. I prevent my jaw from dropping, although it takes a lot out of me to keep it in place.

"We are going to meet him at Domi and Nicolette's house tomorrow. I told him to offer for my aunts to adopt his son," he explains, and my heart lurches in my chest in response.

"What?" is all I manage to ask. Gabriel strokes his hand along my leg, the serious look in his eyes remaining firmly set there.

"Yeah. I was thinking about it for a long time, especially about Sienna and my mom, and I think this is the best thing for him, Damian, Domi, and Nicolette, if they decide it's what they want, too."

I feel like I'm going to choke on my own breath, but at the same time, it seems like I can breathe again. This is the right thing for Damian and James. James doesn't want to give up his career, and he's clearly overwhelmed being a single parent. In order for Damian to grow up in a stable and happy household, he needs to be with at least one parent, who will be unconditionally committed to him. This way he will have two, and Domi and Nicolette are the perfect women for the job.

"Why didn't you tell me?" I ask, too surprised to let it go. Gabriel looks away and places both of his hands between his legs.

"Because I didn't know if it was something James would even consider, and I wanted to make sure it was before telling you," he explains, his gaze trailing back up to my face.

"So, you just went to James to—" I cut off, not quite sure how to put my surprise into words.

"I wanted to check up on him, and when I saw he wasn't doing well, I told him he had another choice. One which will make everyone happy." *Gabriel went to James' place to check up on him?* I want to believe it, but it's a bit difficult, considering how Gabriel feels about him. I trust him, and if he tells me this is what happened, I have no reason to doubt him. But I do have reason to believe his intentions may have been better than what he is letting me believe.

"You were trying to convince him to come back, weren't you?" I ask, and Gabriel shifts his attention from the wall to my face. I reach for his hand, but, instead he gets up, removes his shirt, and holds out his hand for me.

"Let's take a shower," he says softly, and I take his hand so he can pull me off the bed. He drags me close and presses his lips to mine, but only for a brief moment.

Once we're in the shower, he doesn't speak to me. Gabriel concentrates on rubbing the shower gel all over my skin and then washing it off again. He moves onto my hair next, and I just stand there, watching him bite the inside of his cheek while he focuses on cleaning me. Something's on his mind, but I don't ask. I have a feeling he won't talk about it unless he starts the conversation.

He turns off the water and steps out of the shower, wrapping a towel around his waist before using another to dry his hair. He uses the same one for mine and gets a towel for my body. I attempt to wrap it around me, but he tells me not to do anything. Gabriel stands in front of me, regret shooting in his eyes when he looks at me. His arms wrap around my body, and I feel his grip tighten with every passing second.

"Mon soleil, talk to me," I finally say.

"I'm sorry," he replies, and I lean back to look into his beautiful eyes.

"What are you sorry about?" I ask him, scared he's going to admit he punched James. He places his forehead against mine, and I take a deep breath.

"Today I realized how much I truly hurt you when I left, and I won't ever be able to tell you how deeply sorry I am. I'm so sorry, ma chérie," he whispers the last part.

I place my hands on each side of his face and make him look directly into my eyes. He's been trying to avoid doing so, but I need him to hear me clearly now.

"You should have stayed, but I will tell you again: I have forgiven you. We all make mistakes, Gabriel, and we've made plenty in our lives. That is what relationships are about, it's what makes us different because we were able to work through our problems and find our way back to each other. Compared to other couples, we've had it easy! Look at Evangelin and Carlos. They've had it hard, and they're still together and so in love. It's because they know love isn't all happiness. It's about every single feeling you could ever feel. Love takes a lot of work, but it makes the hell we've gone through worth it. So, please, my love, forgive yourself," I say in French, without stumbling over a single word.

Gabriel stands up straight, causing my hands to drop from his face. He walks backward until his ass hits the white, porcelain sink. I close the distance and place my hands on his hard stomach.

"Thank you for being patient and letting me grow with you," he says, switching back to English, and I smile.

"Always, Gabriel," I reply and lean forward.

Instead of pressing a kiss to his lips, I press one to his cheek, teasing him. He lets out a short laugh and follows me back into our bedroom.

Only when we are in bed with his arms wrapped around me do I finally get the feeling he's calming down. His breathing is more even, and with my ear pressed against his chest, I can hear the steady beat of his heart.

"He'll come back. I'm sure of it now," Gabriel assures me after a while of silence. I look up at him, and he smiles. "Tomorrow will be a long day, but it will be a good one. I can feel it."

With those words, I finally fall asleep, dreaming of Damian and James.

CHAPTER 65

James

I shake Dominique's hand before Nicolette wraps her arms around me. Usually, I would probably step back because she's a stranger, but I need the comfort. I study her and her wife. Nicolette is tall with long, red hair and brown eyes. Her skin is pale and her frame is lean. Domi, on the other hand, is curvy with dark skin, brown hair and eyes, and full lips downturned in concern. Nicolette hasn't stopped smiling. I understand why Domi doesn't want to force a smile. She is in more pain than I could ever imagine.

"It's very nice to meet you, James. Gabriel has told us a lot about you," she says in English, although I can tell it's not her first language. Her accent is thick, but her English is perfect.

"It's nice to meet you, too," I reply and push the stroller forward so both women can meet my son. When Domi's eyes focus on Damian's face, they fill with tears.

"May I hold him?" she asks, and I nod.

I can tell she needs this, and I want to see how Damian responds to someone else holding him. Until now, exactly six people have held him. Annabel, the nurse in the hospital, Val, Adrian, Gabriel, and me. No one else, not my parents, not even Mia, since she is busy partying somewhere in the U.S. with some of her friends.

Domi picks up Damian, the little over one-month-old, and my son stays completely calm. Nicolette and Domi start talking to him in French, but I don't even have to understand them to know they are completely in love with him already. I can see it in their eyes.

Ever since Gabriel told me there is a possibility of Domi and Nicolette raising Damian, I have been racking my brain to try to find an answer.

I don't want to give up my son.

I don't want to give up my career.

I'm a selfish bastard.

These three things have been rotating in my head every few seconds, but they don't help me find an answer, they just make me realize what a fucked up person I am. I didn't want to be a dad at such a young age, but it doesn't mean I don't have a responsibility to my son to man up and figure this shit out.

Everything was so much easier with Annie. I hate her for leaving, for hurting our son. *Would I be abandoning him if I gave him to Domi and Nicolette? Or would I make his life better by giving him two loving and devoted mothers?* I don't know them well enough to decide this yet.

"Valentina and Gabriel are already here," Nicolette says, and Domi holds onto Damian as we walk into their small living room where Val and Gabriel are sitting on their brown leather couch.

As soon as she sees me, Val stands up, and I watch pain shoot across her lovely features. She dressed up today, for this very special occasion, and I can't tear my eyes off her. Val's hair is curly and falls loosely down her back, and her eyelashes are longer from the mascara she is wearing, but they frame her eyes wonderfully. The red dress she wears highlights her curves and makes it hard for me to breathe. Being near her hasn't gotten easier, but seeing the dark circles underneath her eyes and how pain-filled her expression is, pulls me close like a magnet. My feet bring me to her until I can wrap my arms around her.

"I'm so sorry," is all I can bring myself to say, and she sighs into my ear.

I hold onto her, and even though it pains me to know she'll never be mine, it can't compare to the pain I felt when she was out of my life. I *can* handle seeing her happy, I *can't* handle never seeing her again. I had no idea about any of this until I just pulled her into my arms and let her familiar, sweet scent fill my nose.

"I know you are. Everything was just too much, wasn't it?" I nod and hold on even tighter.

I open my eyes and see Gabriel smiling at us. It's a genuine smile, and it confuses me. He doesn't like me, and he especially doesn't like it when Val and I are close. Yet, here he is, smiling, *no*, grinning, while I hold on to her. If he can put her feelings first, then I sure as hell can, too.

I step back and place a loose strand of her hair behind her ear.

"Don't ever do this to me again," she warns and smacks me softly on the stomach.

"I'm sorry," I repeat, but she flashes me the smile I've had dreams about.

This woman may be the one I'm in love with, but she is also my family. I can't believe I left her and told her I didn't know if I could come back. There is no way I could have ever left permanently. I love my life with her too much.

We sit down, and when I look up again, Nicolette is the one holding Damian. Domi follows closely behind, and they sit across from us on a longer couch than the one Val and Gabriel sat on, which has the same material and color.

"Oh, he's smiling, James," Nicolette says, and I quickly make my way over to her to see Damian is in fact smiling. He lifts his hands and touches them to Nicolette's face, who is now pushing her bottom lip forward, probably because of how cute he is. I take a step back and take in the picture in front of me.

They look like a happy family. This is everything I have ever wanted for Damian. He is not even their son yet and these two lovely women are consumed by his presence. Domi and Nicolette have wanted a baby for a long time. They are ready and prepared to be parents.

I signal for Gabriel to follow me out of the room, and he follows without asking any questions.

"Have you spoken to them about it?" I ask him when we're alone, and he shakes his head.

"No, mate. I didn't want to get their hopes up if you didn't want this. It is up to you, no pressure from any side. You don't have to feel like you have to give Damian to them because they have no idea we are even considering this. It makes it easier on them, and it makes it easier for you." I definitely hate Gabriel less. He's a nice, thoughtful guy. If he is like this with Val, then I finally understand why she wants to be with him.

"Thank you, Gabriel. For everything. I appreciate it," I say, and he shifts his weight from one foot to the other.

"Don't thank me. I should thank you, if anything. I know it's difficult for you to be here, to have to make this decision. I'm really sorry." I've reached a new conclusion. This isn't Gabriel. It just can't be. It makes no bloody sense.

"What do you think I should do?" I ask him because I know Gabriel will help me find the right answer.

"Give him the future he deserves, with two amazing moms and a dad who would make the toughest choice because he knows it's for the best. I don't have to tell you any of this. If you're being honest with yourself, you've made this decision the second they held him," he says, and I nod.

I know what I have to do.

CHAPTER 66

Valentina

GABRIEL AND JAMES WALK back into the living room, and I feel my heart beating evenly, calming my whole body. Gabriel sinks down on the couch next to me again, but he stays on his side, not even holding my hand. He doesn't want to hurt James by showing off how happy we are. I watch James closely, trying to anticipate what he will do next, but I have absolutely no idea.

James settles down beside me, and I notice his shoulders rise and fall. He starts to shake, so I take his hand in mine because I know it will make him take a deep breath. As expected, my touch calms him as he looks at Gabriel's aunts.

"Domi? Nicolette?" Gabriel asks, catching their attention. They look up and focus their gaze on their nephew. "You remember how I told you Damian's mother left?"

Both women nod, and James tenses. He looks at Gabriel with gratitude in his eyes. James wasn't prepared enough to start this conversation, and somehow, Gabriel felt it.

"Well, it's been difficult for James to balance his career and personal life, which is completely understandable considering the circumstances. But there is something he would like to ask you two, since we know how long you've been trying to have a baby," Gabriel explains lovingly, and I grab his hand, too. Both women look at James with nothing but hope in their eyes.

"Would you like to adopt Damian?" James asks, and their eyes go wide before tears roll from the corners of them.

"What?" Domi replies, and Nicolette places her hand on her wife's shoulder.

"Damian deserves to have a stable home instead of always traveling with me. I know you will love him and take care of him in a way I can't. That's why I would like for you to adopt him with the condition that I get to see him on the weekends when I'm not racing, if that is okay," he elaborates, and Nicolette and Domi exchange an unreadable expression. It feels like an eternity passes before anyone speaks again. My stomach turns upside down while the anxious feeling from the silence takes over my body.

"That's a lot, and I don't know how this would even work," Nicolette eventually says, and my hope begins to fade.

"James, I just lost my baby. I can't risk you changing your mind once you realize you made a mistake," Domi says with sadness in her voice. James leans forward and rests his elbows on his thighs.

"I won't change my mind. As long as I'm allowed to see him, come to his soccer or baseball games or dance recitals, whichever he chooses, I will be happy. I am too young to be a father, and I don't think it's fair for Damian to grow up with a single father who will blame him for ending his career. Val is my family, and Gabriel is hers, which means you are also family. If you don't want this, I completely understand. There is no pressure. Just think about it," James offers.

"This is a lot," Nicolette repeats and exchanges another look with her wife.

"We've wanted to have a child for years, and now, we have the chance to adopt the most perfect little boy," Domi says in French to Nicolette to make sure James doesn't understand them. He gives me a confused look, and I force a smile. I have no idea where this conversation will end up.

"Yes, but this is happening so suddenly," Nicolette counters, although her expression becomes soft when she takes a look at Damian.

"But this is perfect. With James in his life, we can still go out on dates and have a couple of days just for ourselves. This is our chance to become parents now, Lette. Isn't this what you want? To give this child the best future it could have and relieve James of the constant battle within himself while we get everything we've ever wanted?" Domi says. Nicolette takes Damian from her arms and hands him to James.

"Are you sure about this? One hundred percent?" I hold my breath while James takes a moment just to look at his son.

"Yes, I am," he replies with a firm tone in his voice, and I grab Gabriel's hand.

"Valentina, you've been very quiet, belle. What do you think?" Nicolette asks me out of nowhere, and I almost stumble over my own breath. James hands me Damian, as if he was our talking stick now, and I look at his small face. I almost start to cry because it's been so long since I've seen him, and I love him so much.

"I heard his first screams, changed countless diapers, and watched over him while he slept to make sure he was alright. I had the happiness of taking care of him for a little while, and I can only tell you he's a wonderful child already."

Damian opens his eyes, and I use my index finger to touch his cheek. He reaches out and grabs my pinky, something he clearly inherited from his father, and I smile.

"James is a great person, he is just not ready to be a father, let alone a single one. He didn't sign up for it, and neither did Damian. As a child who grew up with a distant father and no other parent except my grandfather, I don't want Damian to go through this. But you shouldn't do this out of pity for him, you should do it because you want him," I go on, and Damian gives me a smile, too. I let a tear escape the corner of my eye, and Gabriel sits up straight, wiping it away. "If you decide this isn't the right thing for you, don't worry. I would do anything for Damian, and I will take care of him. We just know you've been wanting to have a child, and this little guy is looking for a big family."

Nicolette takes a deep breath and sits down next to Domi again. My eyes drift back to Damian, who is still smiling at me.

"I love you," Gabriel whispers in French, and I tilt my head to look at him. A big smile covers my face after I mouth 'I love you the same'.

"James, this is something we need to talk about in private if you don't mind waiting a couple of days," Nicolette says, and to my surprise, Domi nods.

Deep down, I know she is going to use those days to convince Nicolette. She has already fallen in love with Damian, and now, she wants her wife to drop her barriers and admit she feels the same.

"Of course," James replies and stands up. "Thank you for taking the time to meet us," he goes on and takes Damian from my arms so I can stand up, too.

Gabriel and I say goodbye to his aunts and then leave their house with James and Damian. I hug James goodbye before Gabriel and I start walking home. The evening air is chilly, and I shiver when the wind blows against us from the front. Without hesitation, Gabriel pulls his sweatshirt over his head and then steps in front of me to stop me from walking.

"Arms up," he demands, and I let out a soft laugh.

Once the hoodie is safely placed on my body, he presses a kiss to my nose and takes my hand to guide me home. I stare at the ground in front of me before I lift my head and look at Gabriel. His concentrated expression brings out his dimples. It is my turn to stop him then.

"Thank you for bringing him back to me," I say softly. Gabriel smiles at me for the first time in too long, and I can tell he is finally able to breathe again.

"I didn't do anything. It was all James."

We both know it's not true, but he doesn't want to take credit for it. Instead, he merely kisses me and continues walking. Eventually, he stretches his hands into the air before pain washes over his face. Concern settles in my chest.

"What's wrong with your back?" I ask and place my hands on his stomach. The wind blows through my hair, covering my face. Gabriel chuckles as he removes it and puts it behind my ears.

"I pulled a nerve," he replies. I take his hand in mine and lead him home.

Gabriel follows me all the way into our bedroom. It is still strange to call it 'our'. Strange, yet oddly comfortable and right. We have found each other in the midst of so much hurt and pain, and although it took a lot of work for us to get here, we are finally happy.

"Take off your shirt," I say when I walk over to my nightstand and pull out some cream to help with Gabriel's back pain.

"Yes, ma'am. Any other article of clothing you would like me to remove?" he asks teasingly, and I turn to him with the pain-relieving salve. He's smirking at me, and I shake my head with a smile.

"You are in pain, and you're still horny?" I ask in return, and he throws his head back in laughter.

"Always. You know what, I think your naked body would be the best way to forget about my pain," he says with a wicked grin.

I place my fists on each side of my hips and stare at him in disbelief. We've been having a lot of sex, which is why I don't even feel bad for rejecting him right now. Gabriel and I can go a night without creating the delicious rhythm that makes us both feel so amazing...

Focus, I scold myself.

"Lie down so I can put this on you," I say, ignoring his previous comment.

He pushes his bottom lip forward, but I simply point to the bed. Still pouting, he drops onto it. I pull his sweatshirt over my head before I straddle his back.

"Let me know where the pain is the worst."

I guide my hands from the top of his shoulders down to his lower back, pressing slightly down every now and then to find where he hurt himself. As I reach his lower back, he winces.

"There," he says in a strained voice, and I pick up the small, blue tube and place some of the white substance into my hands. I let it rest there for a few moments to heat it a bit and then lower my hands to where he told me it hurt.

Gabriel lets me massage him, the way my grandfather showed me how to take care of my own sore muscles. My thumbs go deeper while the rest of my fingers have more shallow strokes.

"Careful, ma chérie," Gabriel groans.

"I'm sorry, amour," I reply and kiss the part of his back I haven't covered in the salve yet.

I study his freckles and birthmarks. One of them almost looks like a teardrop. I shift my gaze to the cluster of freckles near his shoulder and run my fingers over it. Then, I spot a small scar right above the waistband of his boxers on the left side. I could study this man all day and still find new things about him.

"How does it feel?" I ask a few minutes later, and Gabriel slides his hand back to reach for my leg. I drop down next to him on the bed, and when he attempts to lie on his side, I tell him to let the cream dry and soak in first.

"Much better. Thank you," he says, and I lean forward. My left hand lifts to touch his cheek, and his eyes close in return.

Leonard and my racing school is opening soon, James has come back into my life, I will be able to see Damian more, Adrian is doing well in the championship, and so is Gabriel. My career is exactly where I always hoped it would be. I'm in love with and engaged to the man I've wanted to be with for so long. Things are going suspiciously well, which is why I'm not sure I trust it.

Gabriel's breathing slows, and his lips slightly part, letting me know he's asleep. I feel the urge to lean forward and press a kiss to his lips to show him how much he means to me. Butterflies appear in my stomach while I let the thought of his lips on mine linger in my head.

Thinking about growing old with someone is scary. There are so many reasons why we might not work, but none of them matter, especially not at this very moment.

CHAPTER 67

Valentina

GABRIEL AND I SIT in front of his phone, waiting for the call we are expecting in a few minutes from his aunts. It's been two days since we were at their house. My fiancé and I have been staring at each other for a minute straight, neither of us ready for what they are going to tell us. Eventually, he reaches out to take my hand, and I place mine in his. We both need the comfort of each other's touch. A warmth spreads through me, and I lift our intertwined fingers to my mouth. My whole body feels completely out of balance, which may also be because of the lack of sleep. It's hard to rest when I know my best friend is getting no sleep.

The phone is still not ringing. A minute passes and then another, causing Gabriel to eventually stand up and pace around the room to relieve some of the tension. I stand up, too, but out of reflex because he's standing now.

My anger starts boiling up again when I think about Annabel, who is probably living her best life now. Her selfish behavior caused problems she would never be able to imagine. Before she left, she didn't consider James' feelings for me. Or maybe she did and was hoping I'd have feelings for him too so we could be one happy family. I'm so angry just thinking about her, it makes me nauseous again. I pick up my glass and guide it to my mouth, hoping it will help soothe me.

The phone starts to ring on the table, and Gabriel reaches for it to answer as quickly as possible. He greets his aunts politely.

"Nicolette and Domi would like to speak to you," he says, surprising me. I take the phone from him with a confused look, but he only shrugs and shakes his head.

"Bonjour," I say into the phone, and I hear Nicolette sighing.

"Belle Valentina," she replies, and I feel my heart sink. "We have decided to adopt Damian."

Immediately, tears of happiness shoot into my eyes, and I walk over to Gabriel to place my hand on his arm. I nod when he mouths 'Yes?'. A big smile covers his face instantly, and I can see how relieved he is.

"But James told us something interesting we would like to discuss with you," she goes on in French, and I hold my breath again.

"Of course," I answer. I hit the speaker button so Gabriel can hear too.

"Although Damian is coming to live with us, we would still like you to be his godmother."

"Really?" I blurt out and exclaim at the same time. Nicolette and Domi both let out a sweet laugh.

"Yes, really. You are a very important person in Damian's life, and we want you to visit him and spoil him as much as you want. He is your godson, there is no doubt about it," she says, and I lean forward, covering my mouth with my hand to keep from sobbing into the phone. Gabriel takes it from me and pulls me close.

"She is very excited," he assures them, his hand playing with my hair and my own still covering my face. "Thank you both. Valentina will be the best godmother to ever walk this Earth," he adds, and I nod fiercely.

"Yes, I will," I tell them in my happy, crying voice.

"We have no doubt about it. You are family, belle, and very important to us. Without you, our Gabriel would not be who he is today. Thank you for everything you have done for us. The comfort you gave when we went through something so painful and tragic meant the world. Never forget how much this family needs and cares for you."

Life may have taken away too many of the people I've loved, but I've also never had this many people I care about. Evangelin, and even Carlos to some extent, Adrian, James, Nicolette and Domi, Cameron, Leonard, Chiara, Andrea, Scarlette, Damian, and, best for last, Gabriel Matteo Biancheri.

"Thank you," I blurt out right before we hang up.

Gabriel throws his phone on the couch, and I take a step back. He grins so brightly, it makes me a bit lightheaded. His dimples and full lips have a strange effect on me.

I feel like jumping up and down because I will still get to be Damian's godmother. Everything is going to be alright now.

Gabriel takes one of my curls between his fingers to put it behind my ear.

"Jump," he says as if he could read my thoughts.

I look up at him to see if he is joking, but he seems to be dead-serious. When I don't move, he takes my hand and moves me from side to side, making a small smile spread over my lips.

"Just jump," he repeats, and I do exactly that.

I jump up and down with so much joy, my heart feels like it will explode. Gabriel spins me around once, and I fall against his chest. I let out a laugh and then a sigh. These past few weeks were really hard, but all of this tension has suddenly disappeared.

After I've calmed down, Gabriel and I just sway to absolutely no music. He spins me around once more and picks me up from the ground. I wrap my legs around his torso for stability, and my lips attach to his. The familiar fire starts to burn inside of me, and my head spins when he slips his tongue inside my mouth. My hands slide into his hair, and Gabriel groans into my mouth.

"Upstairs," I moan when he squeezes my ass. He carries me all the way to our bedroom.

Gabriel shuts the door, drops me to my feet, and pushes me against it. The memories of the first few times he did this flood my mind, and I smile against his lips.

"What?" he asks, confused.

"You really like pushing me against the wall," I say and move forward to nibble on his earlobe. His hands slide down the wall from where he had them before.

"I like how I can pleasure you," he mumbles so quietly, I can barely hear him.

I trail soft kisses down his neck to make him moan again. Hearing the sounds of pleasure leave his lips makes me ache. I reach for his pants, but he grabs my hand and places it back against the wall. I smile because he obviously wants to be the one in charge in the bedroom. He likes to be in control here. And I like when he takes over.

CHAPTER 68
Gabriel

"A̲h, V̲a̲l̲e̲n̲t̲i̲n̲a̲, m̲y̲ l̲o̲v̲e̲. Come to me," Cameron Kion says, and she doesn't waste a second before running into his arms. He picks her up and spins her around like they haven't seen each other in years. It's been two weeks. They're both exaggerating, but I love them, so a grin spreads across my face anyway.

"Watch where you put your hands, Cameron," I warn because they're too close to her ass, and I don't care if he's happily taken by Elijah. His hands need to keep their distance. But, of course, Val whispers something in his ear, making Cameron laugh and smack her ass. Yeah, it's a good day to punch my best friend.

"God, you're right. He's so possessive," Cameron says to Valentina as he drops her back onto her feet. I roll my eyes at them.

"Protective," I correct, but he furrows both of his brows.

He raises his index finger to the height of her breasts, slowly guiding it there while keeping eye contact with me. Val is laughing so hard, tears are coming out of her eyes, but I pick her up and place her behind me before Cameron makes contact with her nipple. Not that he would have. He was trying to get a reaction out of me, and I gave in. I don't care. I don't like anyone else touching Valentina inappropriately, even if it's not meant that way. If that makes me possessive, so be it.

"You need to relax. Valentina is going to be a Formula One driver next year, and we slap each other's butts after races all the time," Cameron says, and all words leave me when I realize he's right. We do that a lot. I let out a small chuckle.

"Just keep your hands off my fiancée's ass," I blurt out, freezing in place when I realize what the fuck I just said. Valentina's hand lifts to my arm and squeezes it. We decided not to tell anyone we were engaged for now because we wanted it to be ours for a little, only ours. That's why this is not good.

"You're engaged?" *Great.* "Congratulations, kiddo," Leonard Tick adds and places his hand on her shoulder.

"*Congratulations?*" Cameron asks, and I frown at him. "More like, my deepest condolences, Val," the Australian says before directing an upset glare my way. "Why didn't you tell me you were going to propose?"

Cameron looks genuinely hurt while Leonard lifts Valentina's hand to look for a ring. His eyebrow arches in confusion, but my beautiful sunflower laughs and shows him her bracelet instead. As much as I love them, I need to find the perfect ring for her as soon as possible. I've been looking, but it's like trying to find the perfect seashell on the beach. They're hard to find, sometimes impossible even, and I need to find one for Val. A perfect ring for ma femme parfait. Something that shines as bright as her, that deserves to be on her finger.

"It just happened," I tell Cameron because I don't want him to feel like I kept this from him. He continues to pout before a big smile spreads across his face.

"I'm messing with you! I knew you'd ask her sooner rather than later." I can't help but return the look of happiness he's flashing me. "That's the best thing I could have heard today. I'm going to have a great qualifying session now," Cameron says and gives me one brief hug before kissing Val on the cheek and leaving the conference room. The same conference room Lorenzo Mattia asked Leonard and her to meet him in.

"Do you know what this meeting is about?" the Brit asks, but Val merely shakes her head.

"All he said was that it's urgent," she explains and settles down in the seat next to the one at the head of the table. A yawn slips past her lips, and it takes everything out of me not to walk over to her and kiss her.

"Well, it must have something to do with our school if he requested both of us to be here," Leonard states absentmindedly, not trying to explain anything to

Valentina but trying to figure it out for himself. "It's so strange," he mumbles, sitting down across from her.

"Lorenzo is a great person, Leonard, I'm sure it's fine," she says while I step behind her and place my hands on her shoulders. They're tense from the constant stress and pressure she's been under, so I massage the sore muscles, kneading until she melts into the chair.

"I'm sure you're right," he replies, his usual scowl on his face. My eyes drift to the clock on the wall, my stomach flipping at the time. *I'm so late.*

"Oh, fuck. I have to go meet Adrian for a pre-quali warm-up. He asked me if we could warm up together today," I say and lean down to kiss her lips. I don't want to leave, but, at the same time, it gives me an excuse to finally kiss her again. Before my mouth claims hers, she pulls away.

"You're warming up with my brother?" she asks and cocks an amused eyebrow. I pick up on her implication and smirk down at her in response.

"Well, I take what I can get, and since you're busy, your brother will have to do," I tease, making her jaw drop.

"You're sick. That's my brother," she says but bursts into giggles when I tickle her sides. "Fine, I'm sorry," she laughs, and I kiss her senseless until she's humming contently against my lips. "Be safe," Val calls after me, and I look at her over my shoulder before winking. I'm extra careful in my car nowadays, too afraid of losing the future I've been planning with her for a long time.

It's pouring outside. Team principals have been in contact with the FIA for an hour now. These aren't the right conditions to do Qualifying in, and everyone knows it, but... we're supposed to drive anyway. We've been told the rain will decrease in five minutes, so I'm in my gear, looking over at Adrian. A nervous smile rests on his face as he looks at me, and I know what he's thinking. This sport is dangerous enough during sunny conditions, and even though some drivers love to race in the rain, these conditions are near storm-like. Valentina's hand slides into my gloved one before I can climb into the car.

"I have a bad feeling about this," she says, but I can barely hear her through the thick padding of my helmet.

I grab the headphones with the microphone attached from my race engineer, catching a worried Scarlette's glance. With one nod toward my fiancée's future race engineer, I turn back to Valentina and place the headphones on her head so she can hear me better, too. Her bottom lip is tucked between her teeth.

"Everything will be alright," I assure her, and a little myself. These conditions... Maxime died driving in them. Everyone knows. It's why none of us can comprehend why the hell we'd be driving in them now.

"Gabriel—" she starts, but I place her hand on my chest to let her feel my racing heart.

She understands immediately. She senses my fear. She knows I share all of her concerns. So, instead of pointing them out to me again, she stands on her tiptoes and presses a single kiss to the front of my helmet, where my mouth would be.

"You've got this, mon soleil," she whispers, but I hear her loud and clear in my ears. Then she steps away from me and walks over to where Adrian is, hugging him fiercely.

My team demands for me to get my ass into the seat. Qualifying is about to start, and they have run out of patience with me. I apologize a few times then slip into my seat where my crew helps me get ready. My hands curl around the wheel for a moment, making sure it's attached properly while someone takes away the monitors resting on the front of my car.

Thick raindrops hit my visor as soon as I drive out of the garage. Fuck, this is going to be hell. I can barely see the track let alone the lights at the backs of the cars in front of me. This isn't safe. I don't feel in control of the car, which is by far one of the worst things a Formula One driver can experience when they're racing. There's a voice in my head, screaming at me to ignore everyone telling us to keep driving, to go back to my worried girl and assure her everything will be fine.

But before I can make it to the pitlane, the back of my car slips away, and I spin until my car hits the barriers and then flips over itself.

CHAPTER 69
Valentina

"I'm here to see my fiancé. His name is Gabriel Biancheri," I tell the lady at the reception of the hospital in Germany. My heart is racing in my chest.

After Gabriel's crash, they took him straight to the hospital. I wasn't allowed to see him and have received no updates. Adrian, James, Cameron, and the rest of the drivers fought to get the qualifying session canceled after what happened. The FIA agreed instantly. The session was postponed to tomorrow before the race, but it should have been done earlier. The love of my life shouldn't be in the fucking hospital right now!

Tears slip into my eyes as my breathing hitches. The woman at the reception looks up from her laptop screen to study my face. I look like a mess. I know I do. I haven't been crying, but I've been on the verge of it for an hour now, trying to get to Gabriel. Trying to find out if he's okay, and not knowing has been killing a part inside of me only the sight of Gabriel breathing and alright will bring back to life.

"Mr. Biancheri is in room 217," the woman says after another minute of silence, and I thank her a couple of times. Right as I attempt to walk away, she calls me back. "Take a deep breath, miss. Your fiancé is fine. He only has a mild concussion and a bit of whiplash. We tested for internal bleeding, but there was none. He's going to be alright," she says, and I feel a weight lift off my shoulders. My lungs are finally able to fully expand again as I breathe in all the way.

Gabriel is going to be fine.

"Thank you," I mumble.

My feet bring me toward his room, but I have to take a deep, calming breath before I'm able to touch the door handle and step inside. It doesn't matter that I know he is okay, seeing him attached to an IV and replaying the crash in my mind still makes me uncomfortable. I'm also nauseous and tired because my period hit me hard this afternoon. My cramps are more painful than ever before, but I don't have a moment to concentrate on them. I'm too concerned about Gabriel.

He's sleeping. My hand reaches for Gabriel's, and as much as I want him to wake up so I can yell at him, he doesn't. I lean forward and rest my forehead against our intertwined hands. I start sobbing quietly because everything comes back to me. My dad's accident, Grandpa's disease, Grandma's death, it all comes back, and darkness threatens to take over.

If I lost Gabriel, I have no doubt I would be consumed by it. There is a big difference between breaking up and losing someone through death. I lost my mom, but that pain cannot compare to the pain I feel every time I think about Grandpa.

More sobs leave me, and I start to cry for all of the people I've lost. I cry because my family will always mean the world to me. I cry for the little girl who is so traumatized by death, she can't even get it together in case the man she loves wakes up. Luckily, I'm so exhausted from the pain of my period and trying to keep from breaking down, sleep washes over me.

Gabriel is safe and okay. He was hurt, but he's not going to die like this.

I don't have to cry for him anymore.

"Chérie, wake up," his soft voice appears in my dreamless sleep.

It takes me a moment to realize where I am and what I'm doing here, but when I do, my eyes shoot open. I sit up straight and stare at him as my heart rate skyrockets. His eyes look tired, even though he probably slept until now.

"How are you feeling?" I ask and stand to place my hands on each side of his face. I bend down to press a kiss to his lips without giving him the chance to answer my question. This is my way of making sure he is okay, and when he kisses me back firmly, I know he is. Everything will be okay.

"I'm fine," he says when I pull back again. "My head is throbbing, but nothing I can't handle." I nod and sit back down. I pull his hand to my mouth and press a kiss to the back of it.

"You can't do things like this, Gabriel," I say. "They said they were checking for internal bleeding," I cry and drop my face into my hands.

I feel his fingers slide into my hair, and he massages my head to calm me. It mostly works, but a small part of me still can't process the day we've just had. We knew the track conditions weren't safe. All of us had a horrible feeling.

"Val, it's okay. I'm as healthy as a… what is the saying? Healthy as a horse?" I walk around the room to give myself an outlet for my restlessness.

The loss of his touch irritates me for a moment, but I also can't just sit any longer while he acts like nothing happened.

"Gabriel, please don't joke about this. You could have died—" I cut off and suck in a sharp breath.

"Formula One drivers get into crashes all the time, mon tournesol." He's trying to calm me, reassure me this is fine, but I'm a little angry now.

"I know they do, but not like this. We knew the track wasn't safe, and they didn't listen," I say, and Gabriel's features soften.

"Come here," he says and removes the blanket from his body just enough to signal for me to lie down with him. My feet bring me to him before my mind catches up. His arms wrap around me, and I sigh into his chest as he comforts me with his touch. "By the way, you're never allowed to be in a crash, ma chérie. I will put padding around your car so the others simply bounce off you," he says, and I burst into laughter at the visual image popping into my head.

"You can't do that. My car is going to be too heavy to even start," I reply, but he merely kisses the top of my head and chuckles in response.

"The doctor told me I can't race tomorrow," Gabriel says, and I stare up at him as my heart drops.

"Fuck. The championship," I say, knowing full well that if he misses a race and Adrian finishes first, my brother is going to lead the championship by more than twenty points. As proud as I am, it shouldn't happen like this, under these circumstances.

"You shouldn't be worried about the championship, Val. You should start getting excited about tomorrow being your first race weekend in Formula One," he says, and my heart stops beating altogether. If my heart rate was attached to a monitor, it would show me flatlining right now.

"I didn't even think about that," I whisper, suddenly overcome by nerves.

"Really? It's the first thing I thought of when I heard," Gabriel says with a smile, and I shake my head at him.

"Our priorities are clearly not aligning," I reply with a laugh, but he tilts my head toward him so our eyes meet. His features have suddenly turned serious as he regards me.

"You're my priority," he says and kisses me until I forget all about tomorrow and the pressure I'm suddenly under. "Now, let's prep you for tomorrow. You'll be driving my car, and even though you have been training on the tracks during your simulator sessions, this will be different. Luckily, you will have some time to get used to it during Qualifying," Gabriel says, and it finally all dawns on me.

I'm going to race in my first Formula One Grand Prix. Tomorrow. In less than twenty-four hours.

Good God.

"Let's talk strategies, tire management, and pre-race prep," he says all business-like, and I grin from ear to ear.

"Yes, boss," I reply, earning myself a little tickle.

I can't believe this is really happening. Everything I've dreamed about is finally coming true. I wish it were under better conditions, that Gabriel didn't have to give up a race for me to be able to do this, but happiness has set camp in my chest anyway. There is no removing it now, even if I'm freaking out because, fuck me, I'm a goddamn Formula One driver.

CHAPTER 70
Gabriel

VALENTINA IS FAST ASLEEP in my arms. The doctor released me after another hour in the hospital, and Val and I came straight back to the hotel room so she could get some sleep before tomorrow. I've talked her through every important detail, but it still feels like I missed some. I should have told her more, but I could tell her period hit her hard today. I sent Adrian to grab her some strong painkillers for tomorrow. I know Valentina would bite through the pain if she had to, but if there is any way to ease her pain, she has to take it. Racing in Formula One is too strenuous as is.

"*Pssst.*" I'm going to kill him.

"Not again," I whisper to myself as I slide out of the hotel bed and make my way to where my teammate is standing at the door.

"I've got the stuff," he says and holds up the bag of painkillers, a hot water bottle, and some other things I don't have the energy to identify. My head is throbbing from the mild concussion and my side is killing me. Not to mention, my neck aches from the whiplash. A Formula One driver with an injured neck? Not good.

"Thanks," I mumble and walk into the small kitchen of our suite.

"How are you feeling?" Adrian asks, his voice soft and worried. My hands freeze halfway toward the water boiler, and I turn toward my teammate to look into his worried, light eyes.

"I'm fine, mate, I promise," I assure him, watching him let out a heavy breath.

"That was one terrifying crash. I don't know if you know, but I was right behind you, saw it happen in front of my eyes," he admits, and my shoulders sag in response.

"Sorry," I mumble, trying not to picture the fear in his eyes or imagine the panic in his chest.

"It's all good. You're alright, and that's all that matters," he replies, once again reminding me what a good person Adrian is through and through. The only mean bone in his body is the protective one Valentina's safety and happiness bring out in him. Other than that, Adrian is one of the best people in this world. I can't believe he's part of my family. "Have you heard from your aunts? I can imagine they were terrified," he goes on while I boil the hot water for Val.

"Yeah, they called me a while ago. Sienna and Callum, too. They wanted to make sure I'm alright," I say and get lost in my head for a moment.

After the race weekend in Monaco, Sienna and Callum went back to Italy, but I've invited them to spend some time with Jean, me, my aunts, and Valentina after the season is over. My beautiful fiancée already made a dozen plans of things to do with them, like spending the day on our boat, going to *Rush* with Sienna, and showing Callum her simulator at home. There are many more trips she's planned, but the longer I linger on how incredible she is, the more scared I get about tomorrow.

"Listen, I know I don't have to tell you this, but I need to say this anyway," I start, capturing Adrian's complete attention.

"Talk to me," he replies, and I thank him internally for being so easy to confide in. For someone who hates to talk about his feelings to anyone but Valentina, he sure likes to open up to me.

"I'm worried about her," I blurt out, earning myself a confused scrunch of his eyebrows.

"Valentina is one hell of a racer, Gabriel. You don't have to be worried about her," he replies without hesitation, but he's not understanding me.

"She hasn't taken part in an actual race in a long time, and while she's the best racer there is, it takes some getting used to. She's been practicing and driving the car, but I'm afraid it wasn't enough to prepare her," I explain, and realization dawns on him.

"Are you doubting my sister?" he asks with a shocked hand pressed to his chest, and I frown at him.

"Of course not. All I doubt is how easily the other drivers will take it on her, which is not at all. If anything, they're going to be meaner and more aggressive toward her, and I can't even be there to take the heat for her," I say in a quick rant, making me freeze in place.

I love her. I know I love her more than anything, but taking the heat for her during a race? Fuck. It's a good thing I already asked her to marry me, otherwise, I'd be waking her up right now.

"I'll be there. James will be there. Cameron and Leonard. Don't worry, she'll be okay. We won't make it easy for her, of course, but we will keep her safe." That doesn't reassure me at all.

"We both know you can't, Adrian. That's not how this sport works, plus—" I'm interrupted by the voice I've come to love more than any other sound in the world.

"Plus, I don't want any special treatment! Gabriel, I know you're worried, but this is what I've been training for my entire life. It comes as easy to me as breathing. Please, don't ask for something I don't want," she says, and I let my head drop, the pounding in my ears not helping the worry in my chest. Combined, they make me want to throw up.

"I'm sorry, chérie, this is just a lot, and I'm worried. After today even more so," I say because if Val would be in the same type of crash as me—I've watched the recording of it—I'd lose my mind.

"Come to bed," she says, walking over to her brother and kissing his cheek before turning to me. She waits until I've filled the hot water bottle for her and then takes my hand and leads me back into our bedroom.

"Valentina," I say with a smile when she removes her shirt and then mine to slip it over her head instead.

"You need to rest," she replies, dragging me to our hotel bed as the front door shuts again. Adrian must have left. "You won't be able to protect me from this sport any more than I can protect you. Next season, you're not going to go easy on me. I know you're a championship-competing team and I will be in a mid-field one, but if we happen to be close together, do not hold back. I don't want that. If you treat me differently from the other drivers while we're on the track, I'm going to beat you up," she threatens, but it's so cute, I chuckle in response. I have no doubt she could kick my ass, but she would never hurt me. She loves me too much.

"You're my everything. It's going to take some time to get used to this," I admit, fighting off the anxiety in my chest. I lost Maxime in an F1 crash. I cannot lose Val like that. At all. God, my head hurts.

"And you're mine, Gabriel, but you're going to have to trust that I know what I'm doing," she says, curling her body against mine once we're tucked underneath the blankets.

"Again, I trust *you*. I don't trust the rest of the grid," I reply, helping her adjust her hot water bottle and then kissing the top of her head. Val is chuckling beside me, clearly amused that I didn't exclude Adrian from that list.

"Would you sleep better if I said I'll fuck up the start and be last for the duration of the race?" she asks, and I smile as I give her my bullshit response.

"Definitely." Val snorts

"Get some sleep. You have a race next week you need to be a hundred percent for," she says, but she's the one whose eyes fall shut first. Sleep overcomes her, but I can't rest. I'm too scared of her competing tomorrow, no matter how proud I am.

No matter how much I've wanted this for her, I've never been more scared in my life.

CHAPTER 71
Valentina

IT'S RACE TIME. QUALIFYING went surprisingly well considering this was my first time partaking in it in years. I set my lap times and managed to get third place, Adrian and James in the two places in front of me. Gabriel was so proud of me when he watched from his pit box, he kissed me as soon as I took my helmet off. I spent a few minutes with him until Hector, his performance coach, ushered me away to do some cool-down exercises and give me electrolytes. My body is already tired, but as soon as it realizes it's time to race, it goes into high alert. The mask I've practiced putting on for most of my life slips right back into place, and I shut everything out. Music plays in my ears as I get ready for one of the most important moments of my life.

My first Formula One race.

Scarlette squeezes my shoulder before I head off to where the German national hymn will be sung, my brother's arm slung across both of them when I walk out of the box. He doesn't speak to me, but I'm grinning at him, the people around us, the track under me, at everything. This is all I've ever wanted. To be at *my* race, standing with the other nineteen drivers before we get to do what we all love. Become one with the car. Feel the adrenalin course through our veins. Control the heavy machinery we sit in. Kick ass.

"Red looks good on you, darling," James says as he takes in my appearance. I smile down at my race suit, feeling like I'm invincible for the first time in my life.

"It feels good too," I reply, giving him a low five and doing my best not to explode from happiness. My best friend looks much better too, making this moment near perfect.

Near.

I miss Grandfather and Dad a lot today. If they were here, they would be so proud of what I've accomplished. Even if my relationship with Dad hadn't been the best, I loved him. I admired him. I wanted to be as good of a racer as him. As Grandpa, too. It's hard not to get lost in the grief as I listen to the woman singing the hymn, but as soon as my brother realizes my sagging shoulders, he inches toward me and grabs my pinky in his. One of his favorite ways to show affection and comfort has always been physical touch. James loves words of affirmation. Gabriel has many love languages, but one of his favorites is acts of services.

My love language?

I take after my big brother in that regard. I've always adored physical affection because there's something so irreplaceable about having someone's skin on yours. Platonic or romantic, there's nothing like a hug from the person you love. It was Grandma's, too. It's one of the only things I got from her.

"They would be so proud of you," Adrian whispers as we move toward our cars.

"I know," I reply right as Cameron sneaks up on me from behind and lifts me high in the air.

"Everyone watch out. Future Formula One champion coming through," he says, and I burst into laughter. "Oh, and of course the first female championship competitor," he adds, and I laugh even harder.

"You're impossible," I call down to him, but he barely acknowledges my response.

"Excuse me, may we have a word with Valentina Romana?" a reporter asks, a common procedure during the pre-race happenings. I spot my team working on my car not too far from here, but the man with white hair and pale skin isn't stepping away. He wants my attention, so I tap Cameron's fingers to signal for him to put me back on my feet.

"One wrong word, Anthony, and I will have you fired," my brother grumbles beside me, and I realize this is the same reporter he's complained to me about in the past.

"Ms. Romana, it's nice to meet you," Anthony says, ignoring my brother's warning and addressing me.

A nervous feeling creeps into my chest as I shake his hand and smile. Adrian stays close by, out of view of the camera but close enough to step in if he has to. I smile at him because even if I'm nervous, I can handle myself.

"How does it feel to be the only female racer among nineteen men? Nervous?" he asks with a smug smile, obviously trying to rattle me. I keep my expression light and happy, but on the inside, I have the urge to kick him against the shin and walk away.

"Honestly, it's just an honor to be here. I'm nervous and happy," I reply, taking a sip of the water Hector hands me. I didn't even notice him approaching us, but he's signaling for me to follow him toward the car now.

"I know it must be intimidating to be the only woman on the grid today. What position are you aiming for? Fifteenth or lower?" This question has my heart skipping several beats.

How. Fucking. Dare. He.

"I'm in a championship-competing car, Mr. Lombardi, so I'm aiming for the win." His cameraman lowers the big camera he's holding, so I step closer to Anthony. "Not to mention, I'm more than my gender, and I'd appreciate it if you treated me like any other driver here. You wouldn't ask a male reserve driver the same sexist questions, would you?" I ask, and every hint of his smug look from before vanishes. He stays quiet as I step toward my brother, glancing over my shoulder to throw an 'I didn't think so' look at him. Hector guides me toward my car with a proud grin on his face.

Then, everything starts passing in a blur.

Adrian comes up to me one last time to say "Breathe, race, and win, as long as it doesn't cost you a limb."

Leonard walks up to me and gives me some tips to help with pre-race jitters. He also reminds me of the breathing exercises he taught me earlier this year.

Hector hands me everything I need for the race, and before I know it, I'm in the car, sweating from nerves and the heat.

Tomasso, Gabriel's race engineer, and Scarlette are in my ear, reminding me of all the things I need to know for the start.

My head is slowly slipping back into its high-concentration mode, allowing me to shut off everything unimportant, like the doubts Anthony tried to implement in my head. Nothing and no one else matters right now.

For the duration of this race, it's only this car and me, and the nineteen other people I need to beat.

"Feeling alright?" Scarlette asks, and I can't help but smile.

"Feeling like the ruler of the world," I reply, knowing full well other people like the FIA can hear my response.

"There is no rain on our radar until later into the race," Tomasso says, and I nod, even though no one can see me.

The lights flash over us, telling us to take the formation lap. It's meant to warm our tires and take in our surroundings and the track conditions. It also helps me mentally prepare for what's about to happen.

The crowd cheering around us is like a confidence boost, one I soak in as much as I can. I never knew how long a formation lap could feel until right now when I'm almost impatient to get it over with. I want to start the race so the nervous feeling in my chest subsides and I can focus entirely on what I do best.

Race.

We all line up at our positions once more, Eduardo right beside me. Fuck. I haven't even thought about him starting in the position beside mine. I knew the Grenzenlos team took penalties for changing their power units, but I didn't think about everyone behind me. I only focused on the ones in front of me. Rookie mistake. I almost scold myself when I notice the lights above me turning on one by one. Now isn't the time to be upset with myself. It's time to start the race, and if there is one thing I do best, it's start.

Once the lights go off, I hit the gas, my reaction time near perfect. James and Adrian move toward each other, leaving a gap on the left I slide into. We go into the first corner together, but in order not to crash into one of them, I have to hit the break a little harder. Adrian stays ahead, but I'm side by side with James now. Sweat drips down the side of my face, the adrenalin in my bloodstream pushing me forward.

I manage to overtake my best friend and slide into second place. A sense of victory streams into my chest, but I push it aside. There is no time for celebrations yet. Not with Adrian leading and James and Eduardo right behind me. Tomasso is talking to me, telling me the gaps to the cars in front and behind mine. James is still in the DRS zone three laps into the race, but I'm pushing hard. I'll create a bigger gap while I chase my brother.

"Box, box," Tomasso says twenty laps into the race. I'm the first one of the front people to go in, but Tomasso wants to prevent an undercut—pitting early, using the fresher tires to close the distance between the front people so that when they pit, you'll be the one out in front.

James and Eduardo pit at the same time as I do, but my crew takes almost four seconds longer, erasing all of the hard work I put into creating a gap between me and my best friend. I curse under my helmet, waiting for the green light as I watch James slip past me. Eduardo is right behind me until I'm between two Hawkes. Fuck. I ask Tomasso what the hell that was, and he informs me one of the tires they brought outside was the wrong one. *How could that happen?* I don't ask. I'm too busy picking up my speed and trying to stay ahead of Eduardo. An aggressive and angry Eduardo.

In the fourth corner, he's right beside me, pushing me further and further off the track until I'm inevitably in the gravel. As he speeds past, I spin, a scream skipping past my lips. My car comes to a full stop and at least ten cars speed past me before I'm able to rejoin the race. I fucking hate him.

After what happened with Gabriel and him, I've done my best to avoid him as much as possible, but this? This was about more than trying to get past me. This was revenge. And I fucking hate him for it because now, I'm fifteenth. I'm in the same position Anthony thought I'd be in.

"Focus," Tomasso's voice comes through the headset, and I suck in a sharp breath. "He will get a penalty for that, and you need to fight your way back to the top, you hear me?" he asks, and I clench my teeth together, my molars grinding in response.

"Make sure he gets a penalty," I reply, but he assures me the team's on it.

Then, I get to work. Luckily, there is no damage to the car, and I get to race at full-speed after all of the drivers in front of me. One by one, I overtake them. One by one, I push my way back up to the top. I'm nowhere near finished fighting, and one asshole move by Eduardo isn't going to change that. I'm up in fifth place when it's time for the second pitstop of the race. This one is a lot cleaner, and I get right back to working my way upward. Tomasso let me pit earlier than the rest in hopes of an undercut, and by the time the last few laps come around, I'm back up in fourth place, right behind fucking Eduardo. I take a deep breath every single time Tomasso tells me the gap is closing.

"Striking distance is down to two laps," he says, and I give a wicked smile under my helmet. I'm going to get that son of a dick, and he's going to be royally pissed. Perfect.

Once I'm close enough to use the DRS and get a speed advantage, I line up right behind him, moving to the left to take the inside line at the last second. I overtake him with ease, but that wasn't the part I was worried about. There are five laps left, and I have to make sure I keep that place. So far, Eduardo hasn't gotten a penalty, and I'm not certain he will.

That's why I have to make sure I'm ahead of him regardless.

That, and of course to get my own bit of revenge.

He tries to overtake me a few times during the last laps, but I stay in front.

I take third place.

And I'm fucking ecstatic.

CHAPTER 72

Gabriel

"CAN I TALK TO her?" I ask Tomasso as soon as the race is over. My heart is beating out of my chest, it has been since the start. The incident between her and Eduardo had my blood boiling in my veins.

"Yeah, here," my race engineer replies, clicking a button so I can tell my beautiful girl how wonderful she drove.

"Ma chérie," I say, holding my breath to fight off the wave of emotion hitting my chest like a tsunami. "That was one of the best drives I've ever had the pleasure of watching. You were phenomenal!" She was. How she worked her way back up to the top was unlike anything I've ever seen before.

"I'm third," she says with a slight sob into the comms, and I grin from ear to ear.

"Yes, you are, but you know what else you are?" I ask, and something inside of me tells me she's shaking her head. "You've been voted Driver of the Day," I say, my cheeks burning from how bright I'm smiling.

Driver of the Day is a poll our fans can partake in, voting for the driver they think deserves that title the most for each individual race. Valentina being voted not only means that she's popular among the fans, but more importantly, that they all saw how badass she drove today. She raced like no one else, deserves this title like no one else, and the majority of the people know it.

"I am?" she asks, voice soft and uneven. We're both well aware this conversation isn't private. The FIA is listening, and, if someone decides this makes for good television coverage, they will play it for the millions of people watching.

"Yeah, mon tournesol, you did it. Eduardo got a five-second penalty too," I reply, but if it were up to me, he would have gotten a five-minute penalty and several race suspensions.

"Ha, jerk deserves it," she says in French, and I burst into laughter. *God, I love her.*

"Enjoy your cool-down lap and then come kiss me," I say, not giving a single fuck who can hear us. Everyone can know how wrapped around her finger I am.

"Yes, sir," she replies with a giggle.

This has quickly become one of the best days of our entire lives.

Valentina drives up to the third-place sign with Adrian and James next to her. I watch her get out of the car—*my car*, which only makes this situation a million times better—and rush over to her brother. He gives her a big hug, patting her back as he, I'm sure, tells her how amazing she drove. Not that he could have seen it, but he knows. James does, too. Everyone who knows her didn't have to watch the race to be blown away that she got third in her first-ever Formula One Grand Prix. If it hadn't been for her horrible pitstop and fucking Eduardo, she would have finished higher. I'm certain of it.

I'm impatient. My fingers are itching to grab Val's sweaty face and plant my lips against hers. She's ripping off her helmet before running toward our team. They don't hesitate to congratulate and hug her, and she soaks it all in, high-fiving every member and wrapping her arms around Scarlette. As much as I would love to leave her be and take her time, my hand wraps around her arm to pull her against my chest.

"Oh," she gasps, but I swallow the sound with my lips, kissing her with everything I got. Val melts against me, a smile on her mouth I can taste on my tongue.

"Marry me," I whisper against her mouth, and she giggles.

"I already said yes," she reminds me, flinging her arms around my neck.

"I know, but you're the kind of woman who deserves to be asked more than once," I blurt out, probably making her roll her eyes. She steps back, her hands on each side of my face and nothing but love in her gaze.

"When do I get to ask you?" she says, and I beam down at her.

"Whenever you want. I will always say yes."

Valentina kisses me once more before she squeezes my hand and runs toward where her brother and best friend are standing. James gives her one big hug, and I find myself not hating him as much as I did before. In a way, I think he and I... *bonded.* The thought makes me shudder, but, at the same time, that bond is responsible for him being able to breathe a little easier, and my aunts happy at home with their son. A son they're going to have baptized soon and Valentina will become the godmother of. A little baby that has gone through more in his few weeks alive than some people experience in their entire lifetimes.

My head pounds a little as the Monegasque hymn plays through the speaker, but I can't help the smile on my face when I see Val singing along to it, soaking up this moment. It may be playing for her brother's victory, but it's her home's hymn, too. This is as much her moment as it is his, maybe even a little more so because when Val is handed her third-place trophy, the crowd goes wild. Our team is screaming for her, and even from down here while she's up on that podium, I can see the tears glistening in her eyes. This overwhelming amount of support is hitting her right in the chest, and I hope she never forgets a single second of it because hardly anything compares to your first F1 race, especially if you end up on the fucking podium. I grin at that. Her first race and she's up on the podium... *Goddamn.* She's going to wipe the floor with all of us.

After all three of them spray the champagne—James and Adrian completely soaking Val as she giggles at the top of her lungs—Valentina comes right back to me, dragging me to the shower with her.

I'm on my knees a second later, fucking her with my mouth until she falls apart in my grasp. Then, I slip inside of her with her leg on my hip, ignoring the pain in my body from the crash and simply making love as we celebrate one of the happiest moments of our lives.

The first female Formula One championship contestant is moaning my name, and I'm on the verge of fucking giggling at that thought.

I'm so happy.

CHAPTER 73
Valentina

WE WALK UP THE front steps to our home, and I unlock the house door so we can step inside. Despite Gabriel's complaints, I carry his luggage the whole way. He's still recovering from his crash, and I may be exhausted like never before, but I'm not in pain.

"Would you like some water?" I ask him as he takes the first step with some effort.

The first day after the hospital, the painkillers were helping him, but today, he's struggling a lot with the pain. He also has some bruising near his hips and ribs.

"Not right now, thank you. I will just take a shower and then we can go to bed. It's been a long day," he says while walking up the stairs into our bedroom, and I follow closely behind. I know his bruises are bad, but if he wants to shower without me now, it must be worse than I thought.

"You never want to shower without me," I point out, and he takes a step back. His hand moves to the back of his neck and runs along there.

"Just for today," he mumbles, but I'm already taking my shirt off and walking into the bathroom. His eyes follow me with every step I take, and I know he wants to get in there with me. I can tell by the way he looks at me.

"Are you coming?" I ask him, and, as I was hoping, he makes his way into the bathroom.

"It's not that bad, I promise. It looks much worse," he assures me, but both of us know I will be concerned either way.

He pulls his shirt over his head, and I gasp. The large bruise, the size of a football, stretching from the middle of his stomach all the way down to his hip bone on the left side of his upper body is even darker than before. I cover my mouth with my hand and fight the tears. It *is* much worse than I'd thought.

"Soleil," I whisper and close the distance between us to place my hands on his stomach. I make sure not to touch the bruise. His hand lifts so his thumb can rest on my cheek.

"I'm fine, just a bit sore," he assures me, and I shake my head.

Formula One is dangerous, I've always known it. It's what keeps me up at night, knowing my family is always in danger when they get into those fast cars. There is so much beauty in it, but there is also a lot of pain. I wish I wouldn't have to worry about Gabriel, James, Cameron, Leonard, and Adrian every single race, but it's my job to. Their job is coming back to me in one piece.

As terrible as Gabriel's bruise looks, at least he is still here.

"Okay, come on, it is my turn to shower you," I say and guide him in.

I let out a small squeal when the cold water hits my skin. I wait for it to get warm before I let it run over Gabriel's head. My hands move over his body to distribute the soap, and I spot a small bruise near his kneecap. I press a kiss to it and then stand up a little to press the softest kiss to the big bruise on his stomach.

I knew letting him in was dangerous long ago, and not just because he is able to break my heart. It's because he has the ability to rip it out of my chest should anything happen to him. The mere thought of him being lost to me forever makes me nauseous.

I massage the shampoo into his hair, then into my own, just like he always does with me. I finally understand why he likes to do this. There is something special about the way he gives himself to me. Not to mention the way his half-closed eyes follow my every movement is intoxicating. It's absurd how sexy he looks.

When I'm done with washing us, we get out of the shower and ready for bed. Both of us are more than ready to just shut out the world and let our bodies and minds rest. Chase is already sleeping on the bed when we get under the blanket. Gabriel points out how big he has gotten, and I almost whine about it. He's growing up too fast, and I'm not ready for it, but he's never looked better. His fur is soft and full, he's the perfect weight for his age, and he's happy.

"Everything will be alright," Gabriel whispers against my temple after we've been lying in bed for a while.

"I'm sorry you're in pain," I reply, but he merely pulls me closer and kisses my lips.

"Don't be," he says.

"I'm excited for the baptism," I say to steer the conversation to something more positive.

"Me, too. I need to go see Evangelin for an outfit," he mumbles, already half-asleep. I grin up at him.

"Let's go together. I need a dress, too," I reply as he hums into my ear.

Long after Gabriel's finally asleep, I whisper 'I love you'. Even though his breathing is even and his heart rate has slowed, a small smile touches his lips, and I know he heard me. My hand reaches for his necklace, and I hold onto it as I drift off into a dreamless sleep.

CHAPTER 74
Valentina

GABRIEL LEADS ME THROUGH the church doors, and I'm mesmerized, just like I always am when I step into a building as old as this one. The Saint-Charles catholic church is over a century old, and even though it looks like many other churches, it's lovely. It is dark inside, but the light-colored walls and the stained glass with depictions of angels and Jesus bring light in. I pull down my dress, which already reaches over my knees, and readjust my scarf, covering my shoulders.

We pass the dark brown, wooden pews. The only people here are all three of Damian's parents, his godparents, Jean, and Adrian. I look up at the high ceiling and then at the pillars, which strengthen the church.

Finally, I let my eyes drift to Gabriel. He's smiling at his family, and I bring a grin to my face while I look at him. The blue suit he put on makes him look just the right amount of handsome for me to handle. We are in a church, after all. I wouldn't want to have unclean thoughts.

I'm definitely having dirty thoughts about him.

My arm is hooked through his. I have been holding onto his bicep since we stepped into the church. It helps with the nervosity. I'm about to, officially, be a baby's godmother, and not just any baby's, Damian's godmother.

"You look very handsome," I say before we reach our family, and he brings his eyes to me.

"You look intoxicating," he compliments me back, and I blush.

I pull on the blue fabric of my dress, and he winks at me. We coordinated our outfits for today, and unlike when Adrian and I accidentally dress in the same colors,

I am actually enjoying this. I wanted us to wear blue because it looks incredible on Gabriel, and he wanted us to wear blue because it brings out my eyes.

When we reach Nicolette and Domi, we give one another the two customary kisses on the cheeks, the bises, and then I walk over to James. I stand on my tip toes and fling my arms around his neck. His wrap around me with ease. His minty scent fills my nose, and I feel my cheeks burn because I've been smiling so much.

He is wearing a white dress shirt and black dress pants, and I know Gabriel feels overdressed. Adrian didn't bother putting on dress pants. He is wearing white jeans and a cream-colored dress shirt. He's not even wearing a tie, but it is annoying how well he pulls it off. It's the reason he gets away with such a casual outfit.

I greet Jean with a hug and notice how much he looks like Gabriel in the black suit he is wearing. Nicolette and Domi have also coordinated their outfits. Nicolette is wearing a red suit, and Domi put on a white dress with red polka dots.

"You both look lovely," I inform them. They smile at me, and Domi holds out her hand. I place mine in hers and she squeezes it.

"So do you," she replies. "Are you ready?" she asks, and I feel my heart skip a beat. Domi diverts her attention from me to look at Gabriel to direct the question at him too. I feel his eyes on me, and I nod when he asks me the same question without using words.

"Yes, we are," I reply for both of us.

I walk over to Damian's stroller and take him in my arms. He is wearing a white dress with a lace pattern at the top and bottom. It stretches in a single line. I smile at the little boy, who is wide awake and looking at me with his ocean-blue eyes.

An elderly man dressed in a white and gold robe walks to us and introduces himself as Father Julien. He speaks French and English, but out of respect for James, he will do the ceremony in English. Gabriel and I stand next to him on the altar and listen. We swear to protect Damian and care for him. I look up at Gabriel and he looks down at me.

Everything around us disappears for a second, and I realize just how much this moment means to me. I think about the broken girl I was before I met him. She would be so proud to see how much Gabriel and I've grown together.

We've become a force to be reckoned with.

"I baptize you in the name of the Father, the Son, and the Holy Spirit," Father Julien says and pours the holy water over Damian's head. The small child reaches for my pinky, and I do my best not to cry. I feel like he knows I will protect him with my life, no matter what it takes.

"I love you," I whisper to Damian, and Gabriel flings his arm around my waist to pull me close.

Father Julien brings the ceremony to an end, and I hand Damian to Domi. She smiles at him from ear to ear, and I feel Gabriel's lips press against the side of my head. He's still holding me close, and a big part of me feels guilty about how James might feel. But then I see him standing with Nicolette and Domi, taking his child into his arms, and I no longer feel guilty. He's happy now, and I don't have to hide that I am too.

As one big family, we walk outside. Gabriel walks over to Jean, and I link my arm through my brother's. I grin at him as he places his other hand over mine.

"You know, I get it now. Marriage, having children, and so on, I think I understand it. It is a way of bringing unlikely people together. James would have never dreamt of being close with Gabriel's family because of how he felt about you, but now, he's going to have a really close relationship with them. And you brought us all together, Val. We're a big family now because of you. I'm so proud to be your older brother," Adrian says, and I bite my bottom lip to keep myself from sobbing like an idiot because of his sweet words.

"You raised me well," I reply, and he looks down at me. His eyes show how emotional my words have made him, even though I barely said anything compared to him. I grin at him, and he looks away.

"I'm not going to cry so wipe that amused smile off your face," he jokes, and I let out a small laugh. My brother, the strong man who isn't afraid to let his emotions show in front of me, is embarrassed to cry in front of so many people he cares about.

We arrive back at Domi and Nicolette's house where a catering service has delivered food. The two women have also gotten a tent and arranged for a table with a white cloth covering it and plates and cutlery on top. There is another smaller table with silver gas stoves to heat and hold the food. Champagne bottles fill the table, and although it is only lunchtime, we have cause for celebration.

Gabriel and James pop two of the bottles, and everyone holds out their glasses for them to fill, except Adrian. Gabriel fills his and mine since they are in both of my hands and quickly gives me a kiss before filling Jean's glass. I walk out from underneath the tent and over to Nicolette's garden. She's clearly been working a lot on it. I see strawberries hanging from one plant and blackberries from another. Nicolette has also planted white roses and some sunflowers I'm sure Gabriel convinced her to.

"The sunflowers aren't quite there yet, but I expect them to blossom in a week or so," Nicolette says, and I turn to look at her.

"I'm sure they will be beautiful," I reply, and she smiles at me.

"There is something I would like to tell you," she says after a while of us admiring her garden.

I take a sip of the champagne and turn my whole body so I can give her my attention. Her brown eyes linger on me, and I take a deep breath I hope isn't visible. When people say there is something they have to tell me, it's not always good.

"Gabriel's mom wanted me to give his future wife something, and I think it is clear that you two plan to spend your lives together." I reach for my necklace out of reflex and smile.

Nicolette hands me a letter, and I can't help the warm feeling spreading through my chest. I finally know where Gabriel gets it from.

"She wrote this in case something were to happen to her. It was my idea because of what happened to my mom. She wrote one for you, and one for whoever will be cursed to marry Jean," she jokes, and I let out a small laugh, but it's not out of humor. My mind is still wrapping around the fact that Lilliana wrote this letter.

"Thank you for giving this to me."

If there was a single doubt in my mind about Gabriel and me, I would give it back to her and tell her to wait. But there isn't, so I don't. She gives me another quick hug before she goes back to her wife and presses a firm kiss to her lips. I smile at them but bring my attention back to the letter.

My heart skips a beat at whom she addressed the letter. Two simple words.

Gabriel's trésor.

CHAPTER 75
Valentina

GABRIEL IS FAST ASLEEP as I make my way into his painting room with Lilliana's letter in my hand. He put an armchair there so I can read while he paints. There is a lamp next to the brown, leather chair, and I sit down in it. I switch on the light and for a second, Gabriel's artwork catches my attention.

When he paints, he chooses to draw something related to me. I spot a canvas with sunflowers on it, another one with our boat, and another which is just a drawing of me in the same chair I'm sitting in right now. My eyes drift to the half-nude painting of me. He hung it next to the window on the right side. It is directly in his eyesight when he sits at his desk and creates his art.

I stare down at the letter for a few moments to gather the courage to open it. I thought I would never meet Gabriel's parents, but this feels like I am. I am scared of what else this letter will reveal. Scared, and excited at the same time. Gabriel's mom probably poured her heart out here, and I'm going to read what she had to say so many years ago.

At first, however, I don't have the strength to open it. I won't be able to unread or forget anything she said. I will memorize it all. Gabriel's mom loved him so much, she wrote a letter in case anything ever happened to her. My own mother didn't even bother to stay until I was old enough to remember anything about her.

I'm sad I will never get to meet Lilliana.

After several deep breaths, I rip open the back of the letter and pull out the piece of paper inside of it. Her handwriting is much like Gabriel's.

Dear treasure,

I'm sorry I didn't get the chance to meet you. I don't know why or what happened, but I'm deeply sorry. As a mother of two boys, I was looking forward to potentially having a daughter in my family. Gabriel always described his perfect wife to me, and I know you're probably much different. No matter who you are, where you came from, or what your demons are, I know you make him happy. Gabriel doesn't surround himself with people who hurt him. He is usually very good at reading them, but he's also very stubborn. I know he is a lot of work, but I'm glad you have the patience and love for him and have become his wife. I admire that about you. I'm grateful to you if you make him happy, and I understand why you get frustrated with him. When he was young, I often got angry because he was consumed by his racing career. I love how driven he is, but he needs to remember to live a life outside of it.

What I really wanted to tell you in this letter is thank you. Thank you for being everything he needs. Losing me must have hurt him deeply, but I hope you can help him work through the pain. I hope you don't feel the same one he does, but if you do, I'm sorry. I love being a mom, especially because my sons are the light of my life, and I wish I could be there through everything. I would love to meet you, and I hope you will never read this letter, but here you are, and I am gone. I pray you can heal him, but that is too big of a task to ask of one person. Being there for him is all I need you to do. Listen to him, be his rock, and love him unconditionally because that is how Gabriel loves. He wants to be open with the people he cares for, and he is not ashamed to be sensitive. I would like to think I had something to do with it. Whenever he cried, I wanted to make him feel like it's okay to show emotions.

Since I'm no longer around, I need you to do one thing for me. Tell Gabriel how much I love him. He needs to be reminded because I'm not there anymore to tell him in person. If it is too hard for you, you can also show him this letter. As a matter of fact, show him everything I've written. He probably wants to read my words and feel connected to me. I know Gabriel well enough to know he needs this. I couldn't bring myself to write a letter for him. It was too difficult. I never wanted to leave him, and I can't express how sorry I am that I'm no longer there to be his shoulder to lean on.

I wish both of you all the luck and health in the world. I hope you are happy together, like I am with Gabriel's father, and I hope you will get everything you dream of. You are the love of his life, and only you are entitled to read this letter and receive my wishes. I hope you have beautiful children and grow your family when you are both ready. I wish you everything good in this world, but remember, even the bad has a purpose in our lives. It makes us stronger when we come out the other end. Remember, relationships are difficult but when you've found the right person, you will want to make it work. If you don't want to make it work, you are not the right person. I know because Gabriel's dad and I have been through much in our years together, and we've always done our best to communicate and grow with each other. I'm not going to lie, marriage is difficult, but it is also one of the best things that has ever happened to me. I hope it will be for you too. You are lucky to have Gabriel, and if you are the girl I hope he found, he is lucky to have you.

I'm a mom, and I want the best for my children. He chose to marry you, so you are what is best for him, otherwise, Nicolette wouldn't have given you this letter. I asked her to meet you first, to see who you are deep within, and since she gave this to you, I know for sure you are the perfect woman for my son. Take care of him, please, and make sure he lives the life he deserves. I won't tell you he's perfect because he's not, but I am a bit biased when I tell you he deserves to be loved the same way he loves you. If you read this and think you love him more than he loves you, you're perfect. You are all I've wanted for him.

Thank you for taking the time to read this. It means more to me than you will ever know.

Lilliana

This must have been the hardest letter she ever wrote. Imagining a future where you don't exist just to make sure the person your son ends up with knows how grateful you are... I can't even process this.

I read over it a few more times before I fold it and place it back in the envelope. I can't believe how strong she was. I would never be able to write a letter like this, to put myself in a position where I have to imagine my child's life without me.

I run my hands over my face and let out a small sigh. More than anything, I wonder if Lilliana would have liked me, and a small part of me thinks we would have been good friends. I didn't know her, but this letter gave me a fraction of an idea of what she was like. She was a wonderful and loving mom, who would have done anything for her children. Lilliana is the kind of mother I hope I will be when it is my turn.

I just sit there, staring at the clock on the wall, and watch as minutes turn into hours. It feels like I suddenly have insomnia. I can't go back to bed and sleep because my thoughts are running wild, and I'm grieving a woman I've never met.

Gabriel and I went to bed at midnight and it is three in the morning now. I have spent the past three hours struggling to bring myself to read it, actually reading it a few times, and then trying to process her words. Nothing about this has been easy, but I'm so grateful to have gotten the chance to, no matter how heartbreaking it was.

"Mon tournesol?" Gabriel's voice says softly from our bedroom, and I wipe away the tears I didn't know I was crying.

"Yeah, I'm coming," I reply but he's already in the room then. He rubs his eyes and scans my face.

"Why are you crying?" The sleep is almost immediately knocked from his face, and he is on high alert now. "Did I do something?" he asks, but I shake my head.

Gabriel pulls me into the air and sits down on the chair before placing me on top of his lap. My legs hang over the armrest but my back rests against his chest. I hold the letter out in front of us so he can see his mother's words.

"That's my mom's handwriting," he says, and I nod. "Where did you get this from?" He searches my face for an answer, and I search his features for the pain I know he feels. His eyes reveal it.

"Nicolette gave it to me. Your mom wanted you to read it too," I inform him, and his gaze drops to the letter in my hand again. "Should I leave you alone with it?" He shakes his head and pulls me closer to him.

"No, I need you here, please," he begs, and I nod before giving him a soft kiss on the cheek.

I wrap my arms around his neck and nuzzle my face into the crook of it. I listen to his heart beating more rapidly now as he reads the letter, and I have no idea how I can make him feel better. My thumb runs over his cheek, which seems to calm him a bit.

Reading it already took a toll on me, and I didn't even know her. Gabriel loved his mother more than anything or anyone else in the world. I know because he told me this long ago when our relationship was based solely on friendship. Her loss broke him. She was the first person he ever experienced grief for, and even though she wasn't the last, she was the worst for him. I can't imagine how painful it must be to read her words, to feel like she is here when she isn't. I just hold on to him to make sure he knows I'm here when he's done reading and rereading it.

I don't know how he will react. He could let his sadness out in many ways. He could get up and leave to be alone for a while. Gabriel could start breaking things. He could push me away and close himself off from me because he can't deal with the sadness he is experiencing. There is much he could do, but I will be here to catch him if he falls, no matter which scenario he chooses.

He wraps his arms around me and simply holds me. I press a kiss to his neck, and his head drops onto my shoulder as he starts sobbing. I hum the melody of his favorite song into his ear to try and calm him. His grip on me only tightens while his sobbing slowly fades. He rocks us back and forth, probably because it reminds him of his mom, and I slide my hands into his hair to massage his head.

We stay like this for a while. Neither one of us speaks nor do we move. The tears I shed for him have dried, and so have his. Losing a parent becomes slightly more bearable to live with over time, but it does not get easier. The bullshit they tell you in the movies isn't true. You might learn how to live with the hole in your chest, but it doesn't shrink. It doesn't become less painful. Whether I want it to or not, even my own mother has left a hole in my heart.

I pull back to look at him, and his tired eyes find mine. I give him a small smile before I tell him something I've had on my mind since I finished reading Lilliana's letter.

"Your mom brought me to you. She knew I would be everything you could ever need. She knew I would always put you first, even when I shouldn't. She brought me to you because she knew I would stick with you through anything. I promise I will always be on your team, Gabriel."

I grab his necklace and hold it up ever so slightly. His eyes drop to it before he shifts his attention back to my face.

"I won't disappoint her. I love you the same way you love me," I go on, and another tear falls from the corner of his eye. I wipe it away with my thumb before running the back of my hand over his cheek.

"I love you so much," he says, and I lean forward to press a swift kiss to his lips.

"I know." Now more so than ever before.

I look at the modern wall clock Gabriel brought from his childhood home and see it is already five-thirty. I stand up and pull him with me.

"I want to go somewhere with you," I say and tell him to put on sneakers.

Gabriel and I follow the path Grandfather always led me down when we went for our runs, the same one Gabriel and I ran along what feels like an eternity ago. The pathway made of stone brings us to another one, leading down to the beach. Gabriel follows me silently. Everything around us is still pitch black, but it's going to change very soon. We remove our shoes when we reach the sand, and I spread out a towel in front of us so we can sit down. Any second now, the sun will appear and illuminate our dark world.

"You brought me to watch the sunrise?" he asks me, and I smile at the ocean in front of us.

"A while ago, I realized something that made me feel a bit better about my grandfather's loss, and I wanted to share it with you," I admit, and he studies me with an inquiring look. I tilt my head in the direction of the ocean just in time for the sun to appear from the 'edge of the Earth'. "Even though his sun has set in one place doesn't mean it won't rise in another. He's just looking at the Earth from a different perspective," I say more to myself than to him.

"I've never thought about it like that," he replies, and I take his hand in both of mine.

We watch the orange color light up the black sky, and then shades of blue appear everywhere.

"Being a part of your world is the best thing to have ever happened to me." I lean my head against his shoulder and smile.

The feeling is more than mutual.

CHAPTER 76
Gabriel

WE'RE THREE RACES AWAY from the end of the season, and Adrian has food poisoning. He's leading by fourteen points, so I know this is by far the worst thing that could have happened to him. No matter how much I'd like to win, I don't want to do it like this. I want us to fight for the title, like we're meant to. My teammate is strong, fast, and determined. We both fought to be here, earned a seat because we worked our asses off our entire lives. This is it. A chance for either of us to become World Champion for the first time, and, while it hopefully won't be the last opportunity, you never know in this sport. It's why we both want to win more than anything. It's why I'll do everything I can to beat him.

Valentina keeps checking her phone, waiting for an update from Adrian, who's at the hospital here in Singapore right now, fighting off a fever and trying not to throw up everything inside of him. I know she's excited that this race weekend, one of the most thrilling street circuits on the calendar, is hers now, but the worry for her brother dominates the sense of excitement. He'll be fine, the doctors assured us he'll be back to a hundred percent in a few days, but both of us seem unable to stop the concern from taking hold inside of us.

"I hate it when he gets sick," Valentina mumbles as she reaches for her balaclava, getting ready for Qualifying. She did a phenomenal job in the free practices earlier and yesterday, but I'm still a bit nervous. This is her first street circuit Qualifying in years. I want her to do well.

"I know, but I need you to get him out of your head. Tunnel focus, remember? You're about to sit in your car, and your entire focus has to be on staying away from the walls, okay, mon tournesol? The track is a lot tighter here," I say, even though she already knows. Even though she spent all of free practice familiarizing herself with this track and spending extra hours studying it at the hotel room, memorizing it. Every corner, straight, and zone until she could draw it with her eyes closed.

"It's just Qualifying," my sunflower tries to assure me, but it's not working.

Qualifying isn't a lot less dangerous than the rest. Yes, you don't have people up your ass, trying to overtake you, but it's full speed. Pushing yourself and the car to the limit to get the fastest lap. It's avoiding other cars on the track. It's—

"Gabriel, amour de ma vie, I'll be fine. Get out of your head," Valentina says, bringing me back from my spiraling thoughts. "You can't be a hypocrite by telling me to focus and then worry about me and distracting yourself," she says, forcing my lips to seal shut because, damn it, she's right. Val grins at me because she knows I just lost the ability to say anything, so I pull her into me instead, my arms coming around her waist and my hands resting on her ass.

"These fireproofs look deadly hot on you, ma chérie," I say, my eyes tracing the swells of her breasts covered only by the tight fabric. I can't help it. I take one of my hands and caress her left one with my thumb, making her shiver and lean into me.

"Not half as good as they look on you," she replies, rubbing along my torso until she reaches my neck to pull my head down.

Our lips brush against one another's, but she doesn't kiss me, only teases me. We're both standing here, clinging to each other with our race suits tied at our waists. It's a moment I wish I could capture in my drawings. Maybe I'll try.

I'll definitely try.

"Okay, you two lovebirds. It's time for Qualifying. I need Valentina in the car, now," Scarlette says, and I grin at the woman where she's standing in the doorframe of my fiancée's private room. We left the door open, which is the only reason why my head isn't between Valentina's legs right now.

"Coming," Val calls back and slips out of my arms while I'm distracted.

She turns around to kiss my lips once, and I fight every instinct in my body screaming at me to hold her again, to never let her back inside a car because I'm so terrified something will happen to my brightest light. The reason I breathe. It's irrational and stupid of me, but I can't help it. It makes me wonder if she feels the same way every single time I step into the car. If she's terrified out of her mind. We share the same grief, the same trauma, so the answer is probably yes.

"Let's go," Hector says, and I twist my head to see him standing where Scarlette was only a minute ago.

"Yeah, I'm coming," I assure him, walking out of the room to see Valentina laughing and chatting with Daniel, who's been taking care of her like he would Adrian the entire race weekend. I'm glad he's helping her, but I need to remind her to look for her own performance coach soon. She has to at least get to know them during the winter break.

"There's some light rain to be expected in about thirty minutes," Tomasso informs me, and I nod at my race engineer as I slip on my balaclava followed by my helmet.

I'm in the car at the same time as Val, and my eyes skip over to her to find her head already turned my way. She holds up seven fingers, and I chuckle as I hold up nine in return.

Fuck, I love her so much.

Qualifying is a mess. Jonathan Kent takes pole with me in second place, Kyle in third, James in fourth, Val fifth, Cameron sixth, Eduardo seventh, and Leonard in tenth. Fucking Eduardo impeded Val on her last fast lap, probably stealing her chance to win. Tomasso tells me everything about Valentina's lap times throughout and at the end to make sure I know exactly how she did while I can't look at the screens to see for myself. I appreciate it more than he'll ever understand.

"Eduardo will receive no penalty for impeding Valentina," Tomasso informs me as I rip off my gloves in the car.

Fucking Eduardo.

If I hadn't heard the rumors that he has no contract for a Formula One seat next season, I'd do everything I could to get him kicked out of the sport. I don't care who his dad is and how much money he has. I'd tell the FIA everything about his lack of sportsmanship and the way he behaves on and off the track. The amount of times he's pulled risky moves with me, if I got the footage together, I'm sure they'd side with me.

"Don't worry, Adrian's team and Mr. Mattia are already speaking to the stewards about Eduardo getting a penalty," Tomasso assures me, and I take a settling breath.

The number two place sign pisses me off, but so does the view of Eduardo parking his Hawke where places four to ten are meant to be. I think about dropping everything to speak to him, but Val beats me to it, throwing her gloves onto the nose of the car and poking him in the chest. They're both wearing helmets, which sucks because it means I can't see either of their expressions or try to read their lips. He's keeping his distance from her, and I do my best to focus on getting to the post-qualifying interview instead of rushing over to Val.

"Fucking cheater," Val spits in Italian, loud enough for me and everyone here to hear it. The crew members from our team snicker because they're the only ones who understood her. She storms off, bumping her shoulder into his, but Eduardo doesn't make a single move to retaliate. It's strange and extremely unsettling, but my attention shifts to Jonathan, who taps my shoulder to remind me I have responsibilities. He narrows his eyes at Valentina, distaste in his gaze, and I almost punch him in the face. He also didn't get a seat next year so far, and I'm sick and tired of them blaming Valentina for it.

"Yeah, I'm coming," I say with a warning undertone in my voice, fumbling with the clasp of my helmet when Valentina appears in front of me, still raging mad. I can see it in the way her shoulders shake a little from anger. She hates losing, especially when it wasn't her fault.

"He was slowing down on the track! In the middle of it! I had to abandon my last chance for a fast lap because of him," she explains in French, her voice revealing how upset she is. Her visor is up now, so I can see it in her eyes too.

"We'll make sure he gets a penalty," I promise, placing my hand on the underside of her helmet and tugging her close to me.

"I can't do this an entire season next year, mon amour," she whispers while I wrap my arms around her, not giving a fuck if people are waiting for me or how many cameras are on me.

"He doesn't have a seat next year, don't worry," I reply, resting my helmet against hers because part of me is too happy she's okay not to seek contact.

"He better fucking hadn't. He's been like this with you almost the entire season," she says and slips her hand to my ass to give it a firm smack. I startle backward a little, a chuckle breaking free when I see her grin. "What? Cameron said you do that all the time," Valentina explains before winking at me and leaving me dumbfounded. Leave it to her to take the tension out of this situation with ease.

Meanwhile, Cameron is booming out a laugh, waiting for her to wrap his arm around her shoulders and knock his helmet against hers. He loves her, probably more than he loves me at this point. I know tomorrow he'll do everything in his power to keep Eduardo away from her on the track because she has the faster car and because he doesn't want anything to happen to her because of that stupid asshole.

"Gabriel Biancheri," a female voice fills my ears, and I realize the interviewer is waiting for me to remove my helmet and join her in front of the cameras. I raise my hands in apology as I tear my eyes away from Val and Cameron swaying from side to side to a song they're singing.

I wish life wouldn't always find a way to rip me of my happiness because, in moments like these, I don't want to fear losing it all. But I should.

Because I always do.

CHAPTER 77
Valentina

EDUARDO DIDN'T GET A penalty, and I'm pissed. The stewards tried to tell me there was enough space for me to pass, and I only looked at them with utter disbelief because *what the fuck?* It's always worse when it happens to you, so Eduardo impeding me is probably not as bad as it felt in the car or looked on the screen. My emotions are involved, just like they would for any other driver in my position, but it doesn't mean he should get away without a penalty. Even Lorenzo Mattia agreed he should be punished, and, when it comes to racing, that man can keep his emotions locked away so tight, only the rational side of his brain is in action.

"Focus on your race today," my brother's voice comes from the other side of the phone. He's feeling much better today, which is a weight off my shoulders. He's not fit to race, but at least the fever is gone and he's managing to keep food down for now.

"Yes, sir," I reply with a teasing tone, and he snorts into the phone.

"I'll be watching the entire time, Val, cheering you on. I'm so fucking proud of you," he says, causing tears to sting my eyes.

"Proud of me for convincing you to eat the crab you said didn't smell good?" I ask, and he bursts into laughter on the other side of the phone.

"Yeah, good job. This way you get to race again." A smile stretches across my face, but Scarlette ushers me along, reminding me I have to be in the car in two minutes. "Breathe, race, and win, as long as it doesn't cost you a limb," my brother adds before telling me how much he loves me and hanging up the phone.

My eyes scan the crowd of crew members, drivers, and reporters. After the incident with Mr. Lombardi, the FIA has ensured no male reporter is allowed to interview me. That's why I can't help but grin when Eloise Bellamy from *Griffin Sports* approaches me with a fierce smile on her face.

"Ms. Romana, how are you feeling starting fifth today after you were setting the fastest times yesterday and then getting impeded by Eduardo Marquez?" she asks, and I'm surprised at how blunt she is. It's fantastic.

"Not great, but I'll fight my way to the top to battle it out with the Grenzenlos drivers and my teammate for the day." I notice Gabriel approaching with a devastatingly beautiful smirk and wonder how the hell I've managed to keep it from the world that he's my fiancé, not just my boyfriend anymore.

"What about endurance management? With the humidity here, it's always quite the challenge," Eloise goes on, and I answer her question, along with a few others she asks before giving me a warm smile and then leaving with her camera crew again.

"Red most definitely is your color," Gabriel says, causing a blush to take over my face. "Okay, new pre-race ritual, ready?" he asks, and I straighten out my shoulders to mimic his stance. "A kiss for good luck, an I love you just in case, and a hug because no matter what happens on the track, I want to spend the rest of my life with you either way." My perfectly corny man always manages to find ways to make me emotional.

"What if I cost you the win?" I challenge, fully aware of what his answer will be before he says it. But his words make my heart skip a beat anyway.

"All the trophies, money, and wins in the world mean nothing to me if you're not mine. You're my tournesol, and I'm your soleil. That's all I'll ever need." I wrap my arms around his neck, kiss him, and hug him before we exchange 'I love you's. I step back in time to see Hector approaching Gabriel with a little box, but my crew pulls me away from him before I have the chance to see what he was about to give him.

They usher me into the car, but once I'm sat, I realize my phone is still tightly clutched in my hand. As I'm about to hand it to Daniel, my screen flicks on from a message.

A message that has my entire body shaking with fear.

Unknown Number: If I were you, I'd get out of the car right now.

My heart accelerates in my chest as another message appears on the screen.

Unknown Number: I was never the real threat, he was...

He? Who is he? Daniel grabs my phone out of my hand with a scolding look, sending fear through me. It was Daniel, wasn't it? This whole time, he was the one orchestrating everything...

Except, he doesn't have a reason to do any of it, and hatred certainly doesn't make you take things this far, do they?

Fuck, my head is swimming as I pull my gloves on, unable to tell everyone I'm not racing just because of a message I received. Sebastian is probably only trying to mess with me.

Then, the last written message I received slips back into my mind.

Last warning, Valentina. Get out of your contract for this season and next year, or I'll be forced to take a more drastic approach.

You don't want to find out what that means, I assure you.

This person is obsessed with getting me to get out of my contract. This person wants me out of the seat at Alfa next season. This person is out for revenge.

They want me gone, and I don't want to know what lengths they'll go to in order to achieve it.

All of these thoughts circle in my mind as we take our formation lap. No part of me has time to acknowledge how beautiful the Singaporean skyline is at night, or how excited I am for this night race. No. I'm trying to figure out what Sebastian meant by telling me to get out of the car. My eyes catch a glimpse of Cameron in my left mirror, then I spot Eduardo.

Gabriel told me he doesn't have a seat next season.

A seat... a contract!

Oh my God, he blames me.

"Alright, setting one," Scarlette says, and I wish I could focus on the fact that she's the one speaking to me today and not Adrian's race engineer, but I can't.

Because it was Eduardo.

I have no proof, no evidence except for knowing who he is and how awful he's been to Gabriel and me in the past. He was trying to make me look bad by making me mess up during my race and Qualifying. He's been trying to get me out of my seat, but it hasn't been working. What lengths will he go to now?

I swallow the lump in my throat and try to focus on calming my racing heart as the lights slowly turn on above me. My engine makes a strange noise, but it's drowned out by all twenty cars revving as we wait for the lights to turn off.

I slam onto the throttle as soon as the lights disappear, but my car jerks forward, like something's not entirely right. It subsides quickly, but I still ask my engineers what the fuck that was. Driving Gabriel's car is a lot different than driving Adrian's. But this? I know something's wrong.

I can feel it.

"We can't see anything from our end," Scarlette says, but I'm busy fighting off Cameron behind me and trying to overtake James. But it's useless. My car is slow, and I end up between Cameron and Eduardo, trying to keep going even as I hear my engine crying in protest.

I manage to make it one lap before everything ends in disaster.

CHASE

My engine bursts into flames and my car spins out of control, hitting Cameron in front of me and taking out Eduardo behind me too. We hit the barriers, Cameron's car spinning and Eduardo flying over the boundaries and landing between them and the metal fence. My body jerks violently in the seat before my helmet knocks so hard against the car, my vision becomes blurry as my car flips several times before landing upright again.

A moment later, darkness consumes me, and the flames of my burning car in the mirror are the last thing I see.

CHAPTER 78
Gabriel

THERE IS NO EXPLANATION, no words that could ever explain the way my heart collapses in on itself at the image of Valentina's car up in flames. I don't think. I ignore every single person on my team as they scream for me to keep driving, to let the stewards help her because they're nowhere to be seen yet. They're still making their way toward her, but I'm right here, and I'm not about to keep driving when Valentina's life is on the line. She hasn't moved in the car, which either means she was knocked out or... I'm not going to think about the or. I'll get her out of that burning car. I will.

"Gabriel, stay the fuck in the car. Don't you dare get involved. You'll do more harm than good, and the FIA will suspend you for going against protocol," Lorenzo Mattia says through my earpiece, but I don't give a shit.

Panic has a hold of me, and I'm not going to stop until Valentina is safe and sound in my arms. I stop my car and jump out, running all the way toward her. My eyes catch a glance at Cameron's car, but it's not in flames. It's a relief I don't get to linger on because, while it's only the back of the car for now, fire is licking its way around Val's car.

"Fuck," I curse out, tugging on the steering wheel and throwing it to the side. Something explodes at the back, and I throw my body over hers without thinking. Luckily, the seat where Val is remains untouched.

Her body is limp inside as I wrap my hands around her arms and try to pull her out. Her seatbelt broke apart, but she's stuck somewhere else. I let out a frustrated scream, hoping it'll wake her up, but there is no reaction.

"No, no, no, please don't leave me. Please, ma chérie, don't you dare leave me," I beg, wincing as the heat of the flames brushes against my left side. Thank God for the fireproofs.

"Get her out!" I hear James scream before twisting my head to see he's running toward us too.

"I'm trying," I reply, doing my best to keep the quiver out of my voice because I'm too fucking scared not to be freaking out. "She's stuck somewhere," I explain loudly enough so he can hear me.

Valentina still hasn't moved, but the flames are closer to us now, so close, I can feel my racing suit heating until my skin burns.

"It's her left leg. Hold on," James says and maneuvers around in her leg space until I hear a pop. A second later, I'm able to pull her out and collapse onto the floor with Val on top of me.

"Mon tournesol?" I ask, but nothing happens. "Please, baby, please, wake up. I need you to wake up or give me a sign that you can hear me." I watch the marshals attend to Eduardo and Cameron before I look back at her, but she's still not moving. "Chérie? Wake up. Please."

I'm sobbing. She's in my arms, unresponsive and still, too fucking still. James drops to his knees beside us while I hold Valentina in my arms, rocking back and forth as more sobs leave my lips. Tears are wetting my balaclava while we wait for marshals to take her to the paramedics.

"Wake up, Val. Come on," James begs, just as I've been for the last few minutes. *Why the fuck is she not waking up?*

"Come on, baby, please come back to me. I need you. Please, please," I beg over and over, wishing I could take her helmet off. I'm too scared she injured her neck or head too much, so I leave it where it is.

"Out of the way," someone yells at me, but it takes every fiber of my being to separate myself from her.

"Val?" I hear Cameron ask as soon as he's out of the car. They've helped him remove his helmet, revealing the panic and tears in his eyes. "Gabriel, tell me she's okay!" he yells as they force him toward the ambulance. I merely shake my head because I have no idea if she'll be okay.

"Can't find a pulse," one of the paramedics says, gently lifting Val's helmet off her head while marshals force James and me to back up.

As soon as it's off, my knees cave in. Valentina is impossibly pale and blood runs from her nose and temple, down her left cheek.

I scream inside of my helmet as I sink to the floor, grief overwhelming me until I can't see straight anymore. Until all the light vanishes from my world as they lift her limp body onto a stretcher and take her away from me.

I didn't even get to give her the perfect ring I found.

CHAPTER 79

Gabriel

Tears are threatening to stream down my face as I sit in front of her grave. Life has thrown many curveballs my way, but losing her was by far the worst I've ever had to endure. Adrian is right beside me, placing a bouquet of flowers in front of the stone. It'll never get fucking easier.

"This weekend is the last race of the season. Abu Dhabi," Adrian says as if I haven't constantly been thinking about it for the past few weeks.

We're head-to-head in the championship. There is only a one-point difference between us, me ahead of him. It's the fight of a decade, but Adrian and I couldn't be closer. After everything we've been through, we need each other, and a competition isn't going to drive a wedge between us now.

The sport of Formula One has gone through a lot of pain these last few weeks.

After checking the security footage of the Velocità Rossa garage, it was found out that Eduardo snuck in at night to fuck with the engine. He sabotaged Adrian's car, causing it to blow in the second lap of the Singapore Grand Prix. Cameron came away unscathed while Eduardo died of his injuries two days later in the hospital. Sebastian was more than happy to inform them of everything. Eduardo wanted Valentina gone because she got the contract for the one seat he was in talks with for next year. He started with messages, then tried to make her perform poorly, until ultimately trying to injure her to the point where she couldn't race anymore.

Everything about what happened is fucked up. In the end, Eduardo underestimated how dangerous the sport truly is, and it cost him his life.

And Valentina... I can't even think about what happened to her, not yet. Not without crying and falling apart all over again.

"I know," is all I reply, cleaning the dirt off the top of the gravestone.

"I hate this place," Adrian says after a few moments of silence.

I give an agreeing nod because this is my least favorite place on Earth. Unfortunately, it's also where I feel closest to the people I've lost.

"Me, too." He's going to go crazy if I keep this up, only speaking very little. But I don't have it in me today to be more talkative.

The darkness inside of my chest is trying to claw its way to the surface and take over. It's trying to destroy the light Valentina worked so hard to transfer into me, and I can't let that happen. I can't let all of her hard work and the happiness she brought me be destroyed because I'm grieving.

"It's getting late. Aren't you meeting Val soon?" he asks, and I get up, still staring at my mom's grave.

"Yeah. I should go," I say and let warmth spread through my chest at the thought of seeing my future wife. It might be the anniversary of my mom's death, but happiness manages to creep in as I imagine seeing Valentina.

She'll make everything better again.

CHAPTER 80

Valentina

GABRIEL HOLDS ONTO MY hand as we stroll down the beach. We have made a habit out of coming to the water every night before we fly to one of the races. It's gotten a little colder now since it's December, but neither of us minds. He and I simply walk more closely together to try and keep each other warm. A strong wind breeze blows through my hair, and I giggle as I stop to readjust it. Gabriel helps me before pressing a sweet kiss to my lips.

I just keep falling more in love with him every day we spend together.

It's been a month since everything happened, and apart from my occasional nightmares, I have been feeling more like myself again. I've been feeling well. Going to therapy twice a week has been helping me work through my trauma. Not to mention, Gabriel's and my daily conversations on how I'm doing make me feel heard. For the past few conversations, I didn't even cry anymore.

It's been getting easier to describe all of the horrible details about the crash. It hurts me to see Gabriel's pain-filled expression as I describe how it felt, but we both have to work through it, and we have been. The only thing both of us struggle with is my nightmares. On the nights they happen, neither of us can get much sleep. I wake up drenched in my own sweat, screaming at the top of my lungs. I don't dream of what happened, I dream of the things that could have happened. Time will help me heal, but for now, it's something Gabriel and I will have to live with.

Eduardo paid with his life, but I would have rather let him see what the world has diminished him to. He's a criminal in everyone's eyes.

At first, no one wanted to accept it, but when the security footage got leaked, people believed what he did. I wish he could feel the hate he deserves to get for attempting to ruin my life, as vengeful as it may be.

Part of me can't believe how wrong I was about Harlow. She had nothing to do with any of this. It was all Eduardo...

I push the thought out of my head, trying to ignore the wave of nausea that fights its way up my throat every single time I think about what he did.

Right now, however, all I want to do is focus on the present, being here with Gabriel and Chase, walking down the beach with smiles on our faces.

I stare down at my left wrist, which is still in a brace because of how hard I hit it against the car. It hasn't been healing as quickly as I would like it to, but I'm almost back to a hundred percent. My stitches, the ones I had to have near the beginning of my hairline, were taken out two weeks ago. My bruises are mostly gone now.

I was upset about how destroyed I looked when I first saw myself, but Gabriel has done everything in his power to make me feel beautiful again. He takes me out for random dates and tells me to dress up to feel confident again. On the days I don't feel attractive, he calls me every type of stunning in the English, French, and Italian languages. It pays off that he speaks all three fluently. He won't ever let me feel bad about myself. Gabriel doesn't even mind that I need more attention now, he actually seems to enjoy spoiling me in every way he can.

"Chase, sit," Gabriel commands in French, and our son does exactly as he's told.

He's grown a lot over the past couple of months, but he's also been learning. Chase is really smart, and a very good boy. He listens to everything we tell him, he loves to play and cuddle, and he doesn't seem to mind spending time with Evangelin when I'm working.

"Ready?" Gabriel asks a patient Chase who is sitting in front of him, wagging his tail. My fiancé throws the toy, and Chase runs after it, quicker than I've ever seen him run.

Gabriel and I both agreed we're not ready to get married any time soon, especially with everything going on right now. Leonard's and my racing school is planned to open in February next year, and we already have a lot of kids applying for the classes. I get excited just thinking about the school's potential to be successful. Then my mind drifts to racing for my own team next year, and I smile at the ground. I've got everything. My dream career. My friends are all well and healthy. The man of my dreams, who I'm going to marry one day, the one I'm going to spend the rest of my life with. I smile even brighter at the thought.

"What's going through your lovely mind?" he asks after throwing the ball for Chase once more, and I bring a small smile to my lips. I stare into his green-brown eyes, which are always wonderfully complemented by his thick and long lashes.

"There is something I've been meaning to ask you," I say and grab his hand in mine.

"Ask? Oh God, am I in trouble?" he replies, but I'm already getting on one knee for him, looking up at him like he's the best thing to have ever happened to me. Because he is.

"Gabriel Matteo Biancheri, I am not as good at cheesy words as you, so I will keep this short. I love you. I've been enchanted by you from the first day I set my eyes on you, and you will enchant me for the rest of my life. Marry me and complete my life in every way a person can complete another's," I say in French, and Gabriel digs around in his back pocket for something.

"Hold on," he replies, and I let out a surprised laugh.

"Hold on? That's your response to me asking you for once?" I ask, but he merely chuckles at that.

"Yeah." I cock an eyebrow at his grin.

He's still digging around in his pocket, but I finally know what he's searching for. Gabriel sinks to his knees next to me, holding up a bright red velvet box. The same one I saw the day I almost died. My heart starts racing and my breathing hitches as he opens it to reveal a silver ring with a yellow sapphire in the middle surrounded by flower petals with little diamonds on them. It's a sunflower. He got me an engagement ring in the shape of a sunflower.

"You're everything to me, Valentina Esmèe Cèlia Romana," he starts and slips the ring on my finger. A perfect fit. "So, yes. Yes, I will marry you. Yes, I want to spend the rest of forever with you." I throw my arms around his neck, pressing my mouth to his.

We may have been hurt more in our lives than we should have had to endure, but we also found each other. We found peace in our worlds of grief, and I will never let go of the man who allows me to breathe.

My pitstop.

CHAPTER 81
Valentina

ADRIAN IS RIGHT BEHIND Gabriel. There are two laps remaining and less than a car length between them.

I can't breathe.

I'm sitting in my brother's box, waiting for the longest two laps of my life to finally be over.

I know who's going to win. It's clear as day to me, but I'm still nervous as I watch my fiancé in first place with tires so old, they look like they're about to pop. Scarlette points at the percentage of Gabriel's tire performance, sending panic through me.

How the fuck can those percentages get so low?

I grip the desk in front of me while Scarlette rubs my shoulder to comfort me. I give her a small, thankful smile, and then decide to focus on James. He's currently in third, sealing his third place in the championship as well.

Being proud of my best friend is overshadowed by the way my brother slips next to Gabriel, my fiancé barely staying ahead as they reach the main straight again. My heart vibrates in my chest, as if I'd just downed four espresso shots.

"One lap," Tomasso says, and I hold my breath.

One lap.

Gabriel is still ahead, but barely. Adrian goes wheel to wheel with him in the next corner but backs off when Gabriel brakes later and slips ahead. My sun defends his place in every straight and corner, but I see my brother gaining on him again and again. He overtakes him briefly in the fifth corner, but Gabriel is too good. He takes back his place and then pushes harder than ever before on tires that look ready to fly off the car to escape the brutal force of this race.

Holding my breath is making my head dizzy, but how could I breathe when the two people I love the most are fighting for the one title every Formula One driver craves to have? It's impossible.

Gabriel fights for first place until he crosses the finish line with Adrian's front tire lined up with his rear.

He won his first Formula One Driver's Championship.

"Oh my God!" I say and run outside with the rest of the Velocità Rossa team.

It takes a while for my guys to drive up to their first, second, and third place signs, but I'm too busy watching the fireworks go off to mind. Abu Dhabi is usually the last race of the year for a reason. They make an incomparable show out of this event, and it's beautiful. Everything is lit up by the lights around the track since this is a night race, but it lets me see all the colors in the night sky as they explode. My heart is racing as adrenalin pumps through my veins.

Gabriel is the first to drive up to his sign, and he doesn't waste a second. He jumps out of the car, rips his helmet off, and runs toward me. His hands move under my armpits as he lifts me over the barricades that usually divide the team from the drivers, and I wrap my legs around his torso as his lips crash against mine.

"I'm an F1 World Champion!" he says against my mouth, and I grin more brightly than ever before.

"I'm so proud of you," I say as I stare into his green-brown eyes, tracing his dimples with my thumbs.

"It's a good thing too because starting next year, I won't be able to win anymore. Not with you on the grid," he says and I let out a small laugh as he drops me onto my feet and kisses me again.

I won't be in a competitive enough car next year, but one day.

One day I'm going to beat my husband in the driver's championship and become the first female Formula One champion.

Valentina and Gabriel
(along with all of the characters in the Pitstop Series)
will return in future Pitstop Series novels.

Epilogue

Gabriel

Fifteen Years Later

"Daddy! Uncle Adrian called you a bumhole," my son says as he runs up to me in the kitchen. I let out a low laugh and pick the three-year-old up to place him on my hip.

"Where is he? I'll go kick his bum," I reply, making Théo laugh in my arms.

We named our son Théodore Maxime Romana-Biancheri three years ago when he was born. One of the best days of my life. I've been trying to rank all the beautiful moments that have happened over the last decade but I always come up short. How am I supposed to rank marrying Valentina, winning my first and second world championships, finding out we're pregnant, watching Val win her first championship, watching Théo be born, and then finding out we're pregnant again? It's impossible. They're all moments in my life I would never want to give up.

"Daddy, when will Mommy be home?" Théo asks, and I lower him back onto the ground when we reach Adrian. He's lying on the beach, tanning his chest.

"Soon. Your mom and aunt are just picking up a few things from the grocery store." Because his mother is so goddamn stubborn sometimes, she insisted on going at nine months pregnant.

"Okay," my son replies and flops down on top of his uncle, making him suck in a sharp breath and let out a strangled noise. I look off into the distance to see my nephews and godson building a sand castle.

"I heard you called me a bumhole," I tell my former teammate and now brother-in-law. He merely smiles and holds up a pinky, a secret he shared with me so our kids don't learn anything they're not supposed to around us. Like bad words. It's been especially hard for Adrian to keep his mouth clean since he's a professional at using curse words.

Adrian retired a year before I did. At thirty-seven, I'm still young enough to keep racing, but I simply don't want to anymore. Valentina decided to retire after she found out she was pregnant with Théo at thirty-two, but it was a decision she made with a light heart. Twelve years of racing in Formula One were enough for her. She achieved everything she ever dreamed of in her career, and now, she's planning on becoming a team principal for Velocità Rossa one day. New dreams, same sport. She's tied to it as much as I am, which is why I have decided to become an instructor at her and Leonard's successful racing school here in Italy where we settled down. Our house on the beach is only half an hour away from the school's building.

"I wonder when they'll be back," I mumble to myself as I sit down beside Adrian. He cocks an eyebrow and smiles.

"You miss Val, don't you?" he asks, and I scoff.

"Are you trying to tell me you don't miss your wife?" I challenge, and he grins at me because I clearly got him there.

"Of course I do. Any second apart from her is a second wasted," he says, and I almost snort at his cheesy words. I always knew he'd fall in love harder than anyone except me, and I was so right.

Instead of replying, I shift my gaze back to our kids. Théo is now standing with his cousins while the big protector Damian watches over what they're doing.

"Where did James, Leonard, and Cameron go?" I ask after a while, and Adrian shrugs again. I feel the urge to punch him. "Do you even know anything?" I ask, but his smirk is set in place as he stares up at the sky.

"Nope. I'm in vacation mode. I don't even know what day it is," he replies.

Fair enough. I often forget what day or date it is too, especially with one toddler and another baby growing inside of Val. She has painful pregnancies, unbearably so sometimes. She will wake up at night with pains in her lower abdomen, back, or legs so bad, she's unable to sleep. It's why we've agreed this would be the last baby she will carry. If we want more in the future, there are always millions of children in the world looking for a better home.

"Mon soleil," I hear her voice call from the top of the stairs leading from our house down to the beach. *Finally.*

I jump up and walk toward her, grinning at her round belly and nodding once at my sister-in-law, Chiara, Cameron's husband, and James' wife. My hands move to cup Val's face as soon as I'm in front of her, my lips meeting hers with a passion so strong, it knocks the air out of my own chest for a moment. There has never been a better feeling than kissing Valentina, even if holding our son comes pretty close. There is something so complete about being with this woman, I can't put it into words. All I know is, Valentina has always been my future and now that we're living out my dream version of it, I will never let it go.

We've spent years traveling and working together, sightseeing all of the beautiful and unique places in the world. We admired art, went skydiving, rode horses, and so many more things I plan on keeping close to my heart for the rest of our lives. When we were both ready, we tried having a baby, and it was one of the best decisions we've ever made. We had our alone time together for years, focused on one another only, and then we were ready for more. For a new chapter.

"I'm finally home," she says to me when I step out of the kiss. I press one more to her lips before I respond.

"So am I, ma chérie."

SPIRIT OF EBULLIENCE
G. BIANCHERI
V. ROMANA
7
@SPIRITOFEBULLIENCE

Sneak Peak

Silver Creek Ranch – Book One

Title TBA

PEOPLE DON'T TALK ABOUT the type of grief one experiences when the person you love most isn't dead but gone. When their minds fail them, making it impossible for them to remember who you are. No one talks about the limbo between grieving their loss and at the same time not comprehending they're gone because *they're still here.* Their bodies remain while their hearts and souls drift more and more to the afterlife with each passing day.

This shit isn't talked about enough.

So, when my grandmother was first diagnosed with Alzheimer's, I had no idea how painful it would be. Lorena Blaze raised me, made me the man I am today, and now she doesn't recognize me whenever I visit her at the Alzheimer's home. Despite my wishes, it was her demand to be put here before her condition worsened. She didn't want to be a burden while I worked to provide for us. I tried to convince her she wasn't a burden, that I wanted—*want*—to take care of her, but she's always been as stubborn as I am. Once the woman put her mind to something, there was no stopping her.

It pains me whenever I visit her. Watching those bright blue eyes of hers shimmer with confusion when she looks at me is like a bullet wound to the chest. I was her pride and joy once, the grandchild she always wanted but never thought she'd have. It's still remarkable to me how one illness could take away a person's entire existence. Everything that made her the Lorena everyone knew is gone, vanished as if it never meant anything more than a blade of grass getting squashed under a heavy boot.

People still remember her. They remember her kindness, her selflessness. They remember her volunteering from sunrise to sunset at the homeless shelter in town. They remember her saying hello and asking everyone how they were doing without ever expecting to be asked the same questions.

They remember Lorena.

I remember my grandmum.

I remember the woman who woke up every Sunday morning at six to drive me three hours to my horse shows. I remember her holding me in the hospital after I busted my knee and couldn't pursue my dream anymore. I remember her cooking for me every single day, especially when I started working at Silver Creek Ranch. No one knew this version of her. No one but me.

"Mr. Blaze? Mrs. Blaze is in the garden. You may see her now," the man at the reception of the home says, and I take off my cowboy hat before nodding my head at him in gratitude.

Every cell in my body fills with dread because I'm fucking scared. Just like I always am.

Will she recognize me today?

Will she look at me and see the boy who's loved her like he's loved no one else?

Will she give me the same confused look I've seen on her face the last three times I was here?

Pain lances my chest. As I said, nothing could have prepared me for losing my grandmum this way. All the research I did in preparation didn't tell me about the nausea I'd feel at the sight of her once familiar eyes now turned foreign. She might still be in there, at least that's what the doctors keep telling me, but hope left me long ago. There is no cure for this disease. There is no antidote. There is nothing left to do but swallow down the tears when I see her and...

Confusion crosses her face at the sight of me.

Fuck.

Chapter One

Tatum

Well, fuck.

The sign of Silver Creek Ranch blurs past me as I drive my newly purchased, bright-red Chevrolet Silverado down the rocky roads toward my father's house. This is the last place I ever thought I'd end up at twenty-seven. My law degree diploma burns a hole through my backpack, reminding me of what I've given up. It was the right choice, I know it was, but it's still a pain in the ass to think about all the hard work I put into becoming a lawyer being flushed down the drain. All because my stupid chronic illness flares up under stress. *That bitch.*

I was diagnosed with epilepsy when I was five years old. The doctors diagnosed me with generalized tonic-clonic seizures. That means, when a seizure occurs, it originates from both sides of my brain.

My life is as normal as anyone else's. Except when there is a burst of electrical activity inside my brain, causing my entire body to seize and shut down. In other words, my brain overloads, signals are sent to the wrong parts of it, and I have to endure thirty seconds of complete loss of motor functions. The postictal period, the time after a seizure, is when I'm usually the most tired. My body aches and my head hurts, so, to regenerate, I often have to lie down for a while.

My former boss didn't like that at all.

It's one of the reasons I quit my job. Another was my doctor's warning. Being a lawyer is stressful, so stressful I had two seizures within forty-eight hours. For someone who gets seizures only because of specific triggers, that's a lot. So, I got a warning, telling me if I didn't find a way to reduce my stress, I'd cut my life a lot shorter than others' with the same chronic illness. I have no desire to die. It's always a possibility for people with epilepsy to die prematurely. It's nothing new to me, but if there is a route to spare myself more seizures, I'll change course.

My father almost demanded I move in with him. He said I could work around the ranch, get paid, and take things as slow as I needed to. I only accepted because I don't have another option. I love my dad more than anything, but there is a reason I didn't move to Silver Creek Ranch with him when he bought it ten years ago. I stayed in the city with my mom, finishing school, and following in her footsteps when I chose my career path.

Staying in Billings also made it easier to see my doctor whenever I needed to. Eight years ago, we finally found the right combination of AEDs that helped with my seizures. It allowed me to live a normal life, the only thing causing my seizures being my triggers—whenever I feel claustrophobic, bright lights flashing in my eyes, or any type of alcohol consumption. I guess stress is now part of my list too, but it's something I'll be able to monitor here. In the middle of fucking nowhere. Living with my dad at twenty-seven. Hours from a big city.

Somebody wake me from this nightmare.

Loki, my golden retriever service dog, lets out a small yawn in the back seat. I turn to look at him, seeing his chocolate brown eyes only half-opened. His gold-colored fur looks shiny as the sun filters in through the backseat window, and I can't help but smile at him. Loki is the best part of my life. Two years ago, my stepdad, multi-billion-dollar company owner Jordan Slate, offered to pay for Loki's training. My puppy's been a great help to me since. Usually, before my tonic-clonic seizures, I will get something called a focal aware seizure. My doctor calls them auras. They're a warning system for people like me, letting me know a much bigger seizure is on the horizon. Loki is able to warn me before my FAS even has a chance to.

However, my focal aware seizures are still useful. They're the reason I was allowed to get my driver's license. Since they warn me about ten minutes before my big seizure occurs, giving me enough time to pull over, the state of Montana allowed me to get my license. With Loki always by my side, it's even safer.

My dog lets out a low humming sound as if he could look inside my head and agree with my thoughts. I almost laugh in response.

"What the fuck?" I blurt out, my foot hitting the brakes when a herd of cows appears on the path in front of me.

I spot a man on a horse at the back of the herd, his head hung low and his cowboy hat covering his face. His broad chest, on the other hand, is on full display for me. All rugged muscles a man only gets through working with his hands outside every day cover his entire upper body. My eyes trail over the dark line of hair trailing from his naval down to the waistband of his pants, and I can't help the way my mouth waters a little at the sight. At the way his arms look so strong, all coiled with muscles and veins. I watch him bounce forward and backward on the horse, the image doing ridiculous things to my body.

I shake my head to regain focus.

"Hey, cowboy, do you mind hurrying this along? I've got places to be," I call out after rolling my window down. His head lifts and... fuck.

His face is even sexier than his body. The cut of his jawline is sharp, his cheekbones high, and his eyes a bright blue. So fucking blue, I see them from all the way in my car. His plump lips curl into a devastating smirk as he faces me, one dimple appearing on his right cheek despite the stubble trying to cover it.

"I'm afraid you'll have to wait a little longer, sweetheart. These cows move at their own pace," he calls back, and I find his voice just as hoarse and gravelly as I expected it to be. The only thing surprising about it is the strong Australian accent.

"Don't call me 'sweetheart', cowboy, unless you'd like me to come over there and show you just how bitter I can be." This gets me a full-faced smile from him. It's breathtaking, almost so gorgeous it hurts.

"Careful, *sweetheart*, I might actually enjoy that," he replies, all smug and smiling.

I only glare at him in response before settling back into my seat and waiting for the herd to move across the road. My eyes keep drifting to the cowboy, no matter how much I scold myself and force my attention away. His hard body demands attention, to study the way his muscles flex with every movement he makes. My heart is hammering in my chest, and I want to squeeze it in my hand for being MIA for the last five years and showing up for someone as infuriating as the man with the blue eyes.

He catches me staring more than once. By the third time, I forcefully drag my gaze away, fumbling with something inside of my bag. It's almost time for me to take my AEDs—anti-epileptic drugs—which means I have to find something to eat soon because my doctor told me taking my medication on an empty stomach can lead to cramps and nausea.

"If you want, I can give you a ride on my horse," a deep voice offers, startling me. I jump in my seat, dropping my medication all over the passenger seat floorboard.

"Great. Thanks very much," I say, not even looking at the sexy stranger who has now made his way next to my truck. "Has no one ever told you sneaking up on people is a dick thing to do?" I ask while already leaning over the middle console to retrieve my scattered pills. Loki is growling in the back, clearly unhappy about the cowboy's sudden appearance at my car.

"Has no one ever told *you* a man should buy you dinner before you show him what kind of panties you wear?" the rude man challenges, and I reach backward to feel how high my skirt has risen. Embarrassment instantly heats my cheeks when I feel my thong-covered ass almost entirely on display for him. I slowly sink back into my seat, wiping the hair out of my face, and taking a deep breath to keep from putting my car in reverse and escaping this horrible moment.

"That's very old-school thinking, don't you agree?" I ask because it's a lot easier to turn this back on him than linger on the fact that he just saw my pretty-much bare ass. The cowboy lets out a low laugh, one I feel traveling through me and settling deep in my bones.

"I guess you're right. I'm Aaron, by the way," he says, extending one of his rough, calloused hands. I stare at it, then at him before cocking an eyebrow.

"And I'm not interested in men who startle me and then ogle my ass." A smirk tugs up the right side of his mouth. It's sexy as hell, something I'm trying desperately to ignore.

"My sincerest apologies for startling you," he replies, retracting his hand and running it down his hard chest. His abs move with the motion, and I swear my mouth salivates again. *What is it about this goddamn cowboy?* "The ogling I'm not sorry about. You've been doing the same to me since you first saw me," he adds, sending more embarrassment to my cheeks.

"Don't you have cows to herd?" I ask, doing my best not to glance his way again. Instead, I study the forty cows still crossing the road in front of me. I can't help but feel my heart warm at the sight of a mama cow and her calf walking together. It's the reason I'm one of the very few vegetarians in Montana. I love animals too much to be the reason they die.

"Yes, but I also have a gorgeous woman to impress, and right now, I'd rather do the latter." *God, this guy.*

"Not interested. Now, can you hurry this along? My dad's expecting me," I say, finally giving in to the urge to look at him again.

And what a mistake it is because *fuck*.

Aaron is breathtaking. He's a rugged kind of beautiful, but beautiful nonetheless. The dimple on his right cheek is in full bloom as he grins at me, his perfect set of teeth on display. His full lips are pulled wide, giving me a hard time not imagining tracing them with mine. His bright blue eyes have specks of silver in them, and they sparkle in the sun as if the damn star wants me to see them perfectly. He's taken off his cowboy hat, allowing me a clear vision of his raven-black, curly hair. The stubble covering the hard lines of his face has me picturing ungodly things, but I can't help it. It's been years since a man has flirted as openly with me as Aaron is, and never one as attractive as him.

"Shit, Old Man Briggs is your dad?" he asks, lifting one of his hands to run it through his sweaty hair.

"Yup, and he hates it when I'm late, screams at me for it," I inform the infuriatingly stunning man who's currently grinning at me.

"Nah, he's an easy-going bloke. Not even you can convince me otherwise," Aaron says and, damn him, he's right. My dad is the most stress-free, hakuna matata person I've ever met. Nothing bothers him, except when something happens to my sister or me. Frustrated, I roll my eyes and turn to look at Loki in the backseat again.

"Can you leave? I need to pick up what you made me drop and have no desire to flash you my ass again," I explain, looking out my rolled-down window to see him pouting. It shouldn't look this fucking good on a man. *You're just distracted by all those muscles*, I tell myself. Yes. That's much better than finding him charming.

"That's too bad. It's a hell of a sight," he replies, the right side of his mouth curling upward once more. Heat immediately rushes to my cheeks.

"Bye, cowboy," I say, willing him away to give my body a chance to untense from the way he looks at me. Like I fascinate him. Like I am a puzzle. Like he wants to take his sweet time undressing me to find all the ways I quiver for someone.

"See you at dinner, Tatum," he calls out as he trots away on his horse. I'm about to call him back and make him explain how he knows my name and why the hell he's having dinner at my dad's house when I notice the cows are no longer blocking the road.

Putting the car into drive, I roll past Aaron on his white horse with brown spots, trying my absolute best not to ogle his back and admire the muscles lining it. It should be illegal to look this good without a shirt. Usually, I hate seeing men in public without them. I think it's unfair that they can show their nipples and bare chest, but when a woman even considers walking around without a bra under her shirt, it's scandalous. Fucking absurd. So, I'm not quite sure why I don't feel the usual irritation with Aaron. It's as if my mind is too busy drinking in every little detail about him to mind, like the way his tan, sweaty skin glistens in the setting sun. Or the way the freckles on his back look like a map of stars drawn by a very talented artist. Or... well, the list goes on.

And ends with seven simple words I need to remember:

You can't have him or anyone else.

Acknowledgements

To all of my readers who have read Rush: Part One & Two and now Chase, thank you. I know Valentina and Gabriel's story was a whirlwind of emotions, drama, and chaos, but I have yet to write a stronger bond of love between characters than theirs. So, thank you. Thank you for sticking with them, even if sometimes you wanted to slap them. I get it because me, too. I'm so grateful for all of your support, for the hours you spent falling in love with them, their story, and their journeys.

To my sister. I love you. Thank you for everything. Thank you for making an incredible cover, formatting this book to perfection, and being the best business partner anyone could ever ask for. I wouldn't be where I am without you.

To Chloe, Sophie, Emma, and Esha, thank you for your never-ending support, for giggling with me over my fictional characters, for cursing me out because of the end, and for always cheering me on, especially when I need it the most. Thank you for everything.

This book was the most difficult book I've ever written because I wanted to make it something worthy of Val and Gabriel's story. I wanted this book to be the perfect ending to their story, and I hope I've achieved that. I hope all of you are as happy with the ending as I am with it now.

About the Author

Bridget L. Rose is a half-German, half-Italian author, who was born and raised in Germany until the age of thirteen. She fell in love with books from a young age, and soon discovered her passion for writing as well. She likes to spend her free time with her family, reading a book, or writing one herself. She also adores the sport Formula One, which led her to write her Pitstop Series.

Books by Bridget L. Rose

The Pitstop Series

Jump-Start

The Inside of a Rainbow

Rush: Part One & Two

Chase: Part One & Two

From Angels to Devils Series

From Devils to Angels

9 781738 978380